SOON

By the same author

SOON

CHARLOTTE GRIMSHAW

Jonathan Cape
London

Published by Jonathan Cape 2013

2 4 6 8 10 9 7 5 3 1

First published in New Zealand in 2012 by Random House New Zealand

First published in Great Britain in 2013 by
Jonathan Cape
Random House, 20 Vauxhall Bridge Road,
London SW1V 2SA

www.vintage-books.co.uk

Addresses for companies within The Random House Group Limited can be found at:
www.randomhouse.co.uk/offices.htm

The Random House Group Limited Reg. No. 954009

A CIP catalogue record for this book is available from the British Library

ISBN 9780224097642

The Random House Group Limited supports The Forest Stewardship
Council (FSC®), the leading international forest certification organisation.
Our books carrying the FSC label are printed on FSC® certified paper.
FSC is the only forest certification scheme endorsed by the leading
environmental organisations, including Greenpeace.
Our paper procurement policy can be found at:
www.randomhouse.co.uk/environment

MIX

— For my children —
This novel especially for Leo

SOON

Roza and Johnnie

The mother and son were upstairs, preparing. He was to go to afternoon kindergarten and she was to spend two and a half hours at home, working. They had passed a leisurely morning together, and now both were looking forward to the moment when he would sidestep her kiss and dodge off into the kindergarten yard that was reminiscent of a sympathetic habitat at the zoo, with its coloured climbing frames, its ropes and swings, its tender attendants.

She would look back twice to make sure he was playing, not rushing after her to stand with whitened fingers gripping the wire. He had done this when he'd first started, before he had understood that she would come back.

'When are we going? When?' he said. He was standing at the basin.

'Soon. Wash your hands. They're black.'

'When?'

'We're going to have to cut your nails.'

He looked up at her: wide-spaced grey eyes, freckles on his nose. Now his eyes narrowed, calculating.

'How much?' he said.

'I don't *still* have to pay you?'

'Five dollars,' he said.

'Five? For nails? It's daylight robbery.'

'Five.'

'OK. OK. Five.'

They went into the bedroom and he sat on the edge of the bed, hunching his shoulders and squeezing his eyes shut, so tight his whole body quivered. He'd always been this way; the cutting of his nails horrified him.

She fetched the tiny scissors and picked up his balled fist. He made himself small, moaning as she gently straightened out his fingers and clipped off a tiny black strip.

'What melodrama. You'd think I was sawing your hand off.'

He snatched his hand away.

'Come on. Full access. Or no money.'

He extended his fingers. There was a silence as she worked. He winced, frowned. A tiny bead of sweat rolled down his temple.

'There. Done.' She took out her purse and solemnly paid him. He inspected the note, folded it and took it to his bedroom. Johnnie Hallwright was very interested in money. For his next birthday, he had requested a safe.

The housekeeper, Jung Ha, came upstairs and handed over his small bag, packed with hat, sweatshirt, afternoon tea.

They waited for the car to be brought around. He fidgeted. 'When are we going? When?'

'Soon.'

'What's soon?'

Roza yawned, looking out at the rooftops that sloped away across the suburb. Far away, the sea was a metallic blue strip. She said in an idle, distant voice, 'Soon is a fierce dwarf who lives under the house.'

He raised his eyes.

It was a year since Roza had made the throwaway remark. *Soon is a fierce dwarf who lives under the house.* Johnnie Hallwright was now four. Roza was thirty-five. And Soon had been living with them ever since.

The Wedding Cake

For three days a tropical cyclone had kept people away from the beach. The wind sent waves sluicing so far up the shore that Simon Lampton, walking on the dunes in the dawn, turned and looked into the belly of an obese green wave, the water spreading out and swamping him, rising to his knees, his thighs, pushing him up the sand. He knelt down, and the warm sea rose to his shoulders. His shorts and T-shirt ballooned around him. Cool spikes of rain fell on his face. He let his head sink back into the water, and listened to the roar and shush of the agitated sea.

He plodded over the dunes, the marram grass whipping against his bare legs. The squalls crossed the dunes, combing the marram into silver waves. The sky was grey, smeared with black. It wasn't fully light.

In the last week he had begun to wake early, at five or six, and had crept from the bedroom, leaving Karen to sleep. Sometimes he would greet a policeman as he passed the pool in the grey light, on his way to the path that led to the beach. He liked to walk all the way to the rocks at the northern end and watch the sun appear, a bronze haze amid all that churning black, later a white coin, riding behind the storm.

Ahead of him was the compound, which occupied a sizable stretch of beachfront. Years before, Simon had come on a trip to this place with friends; the bus had dropped them at the side of the road and they'd looked across the dunes to the extraordinary beauty of the empty beach, with its pohutukawa and bright white sand. The road was narrow then and pitted with holes, and the land on the edge of the dunes dotted with small fibrolite baches. Old people lived there, and alternative lifestylers. There was one shop, a converted garage with a corrugated iron roof. One shop and one bus stop, its sign swinging in the wind.

It was all changed. The road had been widened and upgraded, and a new marina built on the estuary. The beach had become fashionable, then seriously upmarket. There were a few hold-outs, elderly people stubbornly hanging on to a shack on a plot surrounded by mansions, but most of the old baches were gone. Now, monstrosities of glass and steel lined the shore. There were driveways, swimming pools, landscaped gardens and lawns. Only the beach was untouched by the development. It was the same long stretch of white sand coast, with a tidal estuary at one end and a steep, bush-clad hill at the other. Nothing had been built on it; it was clean and wild, still beautiful.

Where Simon stood at the southern end the land had been converted to a single large section. Inside the compound the main house faced the sea, its glassed-in living areas opening onto wooden decks, manicured lawns and flower beds, its grand verandas buttressed with white columns. There was even a flagpole, rising out of a rockery and cactus garden. The walled grounds were bordered on one side by the road; on the sea side they stretched to the dunes. A path ran from the security gate through grassy banks and dunes to the beach. The three-storey house, which was painted white, was affectionately known hereabouts, in the exclusive beach community of Rotokauri, as the Wedding Cake.

Grouped around the main house, also within the surrounding walls, was a series of smaller dwellings: the guesthouse, apartments for staff, garages and outbuildings. One sizable bunker stored equipment for adventurous guests: jet skis, surfboards, kayaks. There were even two

Laser yachts. On the first day of their holiday a young man in a polo shirt had led Simon and Karen to this hoard. They were to use anything they liked. If they wanted they could even attach themselves to a parachute and have the staff tow them at great height behind a boat.

Simon couldn't see the point. Nor could he imagine himself on anything so loud, so frankly moronic as a jet ski. He preferred to lie on the sand with a book. In some moods their host, David, liked to mount his jet ski and drive straight out to sea. As he roared away, the high, thin plume of water spraying out behind him seemed somehow comically insolent. It was a sight that caused his security men to gather anxiously near the boat, ready to go out after him.

Karen had waded out and messed around on a sailboard for a couple of mornings before settling on daily tennis lessons with David's wife Roza and her friends: four burnished ladies and their coach, the muscular Garth.

The security gate opened. Watched by cameras, Simon passed through and walked slowly up the path. It was still so early he thought he might continue his walk, along the coast road, turning inland, past the Kauri Lake and into the valley. He had jogged out that way on a recent hot, blue afternoon, before the arrival of the storm. In the valley the sound of the sea receded and the wind died away and the lake was a shallow expanse of silver fringed by waving raupo stalks. That day he'd jogged past a house that lay in a fat ray of sun angling down from the top of the valley. The grass was so green it looked unnatural. A gaunt white pony, all angles, ambled towards the house, a window opened, and a hand reached out with an offering. The pony stretched out its neck and nibbled with its square teeth, and Simon had stopped on the road, watching. The white pony, the green grass. Silence in the valley. It had all seemed slightly unreal. It was a beautiful place and he wanted to go back there.

Now, at the roadside gate, the guard was waiting out the last of his shift. The chime at the pool house sounded its melancholy tinkle as Simon walked towards the guesthouse (known as the Little House) where he was staying with Karen and their two younger children, Elke and Marcus.

Others came and went from the compound during this summer break: friends, grown-up children of friends, a steady procession of David's staff. There was tight security — cameras, a watch house at the front gate, a team of patrolling guards. David Hallwright was very rich. He was also the Prime Minister.

Simon was not the only one up. David was pacing behind the glass at the back of the main house. He beckoned.

Simon came slowly up the wooden steps and stood in the doorway. 'I've been swimming, sort of. There was a huge wave.'

His phone to his ear, David said, 'I wouldn't recommend that, no.'

He reached out and touched Simon's T-shirt. Bunching the wet material in his fist, he pulled him over the threshold.

'You will not do that,' he said. 'Call Ed. Now.'

Simon, feeling an odd pleasure at being touched, stifled a grin. David put a hand on his shoulder and pushed him across the room to a wood-panelled bathroom (blonde pine, Nordic scents, gigantic jacuzzi).

'Get yourself dry.'

Simon took a towel and caught sight of his expression in the mirror; he looked dreamy, foolish. He dried his hair, rubbed his cheeks until they stung, and stepped out.

David had put away the phone. He was leaning his forehead against the glass. Beyond, the sea endlessly rearranged itself. Zigzag currents crossed the waves; sudden drifts of foam broke from the grey crests and rose into the air.

'Graeme's dead,' he said.

'Oh, mate,' Simon said.

He crossed the room. A gust of wind rippled its way across the grass and smacked against the window. Silence. The white sky. Seagulls out there, riding and riding against the air.

'Old Graeme.'

David smiled. He drew in a long breath. 'Old Graeme.' For a moment he seemed stricken. Then he gave such a look of complicity that Simon went still.

'It's good you're here,' David said. 'Before the others come.'

Instil and Imbue

The Lamptons were the Hallwrights' summer guests, and they were more than that. They were, in one sense, part of the Prime Minister's family. You could read about this. A small amount of media research would tell you that the Lamptons and the Hallwrights 'shared a bond'. That they were 'bound together by circumstance'. That they had 'grown close in recent years'.

Their story had been carefully disseminated by David Hallwright's people. Although, behind the scenes, the connotations were almost impossibly complex, the basic facts were straightforward. When he'd married her, David's second wife Roza had been keeping a secret. It was not a sensational one, as secrets go: aged sixteen, she had given birth to a baby and adopted her out. Eight years later, after the adoption and a number of foster placings had failed, the girl, Elke, had been adopted by Dr Simon Lampton and his wife Karen.

In the following years, the Lamptons had come to love Elke as their own. But just before David Hallwright had been elected Prime Minister, Roza had located the child, and had introduced herself to the Lamptons (and revealed herself to David) as the birth mother.

Very few people thought Roza's secret was in any way shameful. It needn't have been a secret at all, but it was understood that for Roza (the only daughter of cold, rich, fanatically strict Catholic parents), things had been emotionally complicated.

Elke had gone on living with the Lamptons, but she began to spend time with Roza and David. She said very little about this; she remained, in many respects, unknowable. It was Elke's arcane quality, Simon thought, that kept the families together. Both families loved and wanted her, both feared losing her, so they hung together, watching her covertly. Each feared she would disappear into the other family, and never return.

She showed no sign of favour. Deeply attached to her, alert to her moods, Simon took note of changes, developments. This for example: in addition to David's two children from a previous marriage, he and Roza now had a son together, the remarkable Johnnie. As Johnnie had grown from a baby to a toddler he had begun to resemble Elke, unsurprisingly, since they shared the same mother. Prompted by her resemblance to his own child, David had begun to treat Elke as his own.

Simon was disturbed by this. But there were other minefields. Roza and Karen, the birth mother and the adoptive mother, were now officially best friends. They played tennis and took holidays together. They lunched, swapped gossip, attended charity dinners. They were the best of friends . . .

From the top of the Harbour Bridge, Simon looked out and saw white caps on sun-struck green water. A wash of foam, driven by the storm, was churning in towards the docks. It was hot, the light was painfully bright, but the sky at the horizon was dark with raincloud.

The convoy began to descend the curve of the bridge. The sun turned the interior of the car photographic, furred with golden light. Karen snapped open a compact and lined her lips. Simon could see Roza in the car ahead, brushing her hair with quick shakes of the head. There were five cars, with police in front and behind.

He frowned. 'I don't see why so much security.'

Karen slid on a pair of sunglasses. She was dressed entirely in black, which seemed like overkill to Simon. She looked like a Mafia widow.

She said, husky, 'Perhaps they've had threats. We're at war in Afghanistan.'

'Yeah. A Taliban ambush, on the Harbour Bridge. After they've flown down here with their rocket launchers. On Air New Zealand.'

'You're naïve.'

'It's like he thinks he's the US President. Next he'll be wanting a food taster.'

'Roza says he started taking it seriously when Johnnie was born. He's worried he'll be kidnapped.'

'Right. By the Taliban.'

'Well, I'm glad he and Roza are properly looked after. For Elke's sake.'

Simon looked away. Lately, he'd had the faint sense that Karen wasn't real. She was a vamp in an airport thriller. She seemed to be getting sexier. There was a lot of cleavage and make-up and a new way of talking. She was always glancing at the help and whispering. *These walls have ears.* This was what it was doing to her, hanging out with the Hallwrights, travelling in convoys with the Hallwrights.

The driver touched his ear and talked into his sleeve.

'They've got us coming in from St Stephens Ave,' Karen said.

Simon shrugged, irritable. 'Where else would we "come in" from?'

He wondered whether he should go in to work after the funeral. He had his medical practice covered and they were due to return to the beach, but there would be files waiting. He was a doctor; his files were actually patients, with their myriad human concerns, but there was a part of him that was all technocrat. In some moods he wished human complexities away.

David and Roza's driver had gone a different way and would

contrive, as usual, to deliver them to the cathedral last. Karen was sitting forward, her hand on the back of the driver's seat. Simon looked narrowly at her; she would be calculating whether they could delay long enough to walk in with the Hallwrights. It was one of her favourite things: to feel the stilled conversations, the hundreds of eyes.

The driver moved the car into the cordoned park and Karen pretended to consult her watch. 'Go around the block,' she said.

The driver screwed around his head, looking affronted. 'I can't do that.'

'It's too early. Circle round.'

Simon said, 'Let's go, Karen.' He reached across her and pulled the door handle.

The driver jumped out and went around. Karen gave her husband the sweet, mildly astonished smile that said, *You'll pay*. With ironic courtliness he escorted her to the entrance, where the dean of the cathedral was waiting, robed, primped and wearing his most ingratiating smile.

Simon daydreamed his way through the service, hearing very little of what was said. He'd wandered into the garden the previous evening and found Ed Miles at the outdoor table, typing Graeme's eulogy on a laptop while David bounced Johnnie on his knee.

David had told Ed, 'It'll be televised. Make it useful, mate.'

Ed, sitting back, stretching, cracking his knuckles: 'OK, King's, blah blah, rowing. Graeme Ellison instilled his values etcetera in his children, and the scholarships he founded will ensure that young people absorb the principles he cherished. The principles he held dear. Cherished. Before he died I discussed Graeme's work with him. And my pledge to him and to the country is that none of his work will be in vain.'

'You're my prince,' said David, tickling the little boy. And Johnnie, who had his mother's potent eyes, laughed and twisted away.

When Ed had gone, Simon had said slowly, 'There are words that get thrashed in eulogies and death notices. Instil. *He instilled values in his children.* And imbue. People always bandy that one around. They're terrible clichés.'

David was expressionless. He said, 'In politics . . .'

'I thought it was a eulogy.'

'You know what Graeme'd say. It's never just a eulogy.'

During the funeral service he thought of the valley at Rotokauri. The little house, the white pony. The green field . . . The order of service lay on his lap, on its front cover a black-framed photograph of Graeme Ellison — old Graeme, with his avid, gap-toothed smile. Simon now entertained a mental picture of Graeme as Toad of Toad Hall (jacket, bow tie, skinny green legs) giving a last mad *parp* of his horn before motoring off the page into oblivion.

Graeme's wife Trish, wearing a giant black hat, sat between Karen and Roza, clasping their hands. Then there were pews-full of Ellisons: the beefy blond sons and their pale wives; the daughters who all resembled Graeme (dark, portly, solid); a trio of young pinstriped husbands; rows of fidgeting children and a thinly wailing baby in a pram.

David had come in last with his two bodyguards, had spoken to Trish and then slid along the pew next to Simon, who was now registering, at close quarters, the Prime Minister's inability to keep still. David's right leg pumped up and down, he folded and unfolded the printed photo of Graeme until the image was streaked with lines. His phone vibrated in his pocket; he stealthily checked it and never stopped looking about.

Long shafts of light slanted in through the windows. Simon suppressed yawns, his eyes watering. The dean lowered his voice. It was an honour to speak of Graeme Ellison. One of the richest men in Australasia, he lived his life for others. His record of service was second to none: to his many charities, to the National Party, to the Business

Roundtable, to his alma mater King's School (all Ellisons attended King's School). To the sport of rowing, to rugby. Tireless champion. Life member. Founder. Campaigner.

Schemer, Simon thought. Dark master. Perpetrator of subtle frauds. Sly joker. Happy cynic, cigar-smoking boozer. Gap-toothed gasper, sharp-eyed shyster. Old fraud, ogler. He'd been the National Party grandee who'd brought Hallwright into the fold: young Hallwright who was all talent and no privilege, who had 'grown up poor'.

The Ellisons, Simon remembered, used to make their protégé nervous. How things had changed.

Now David walked to the pulpit.

'Graeme Ellison made a difference in this country. And he made a difference to me. He changed my life. He let me see what can be achieved. If we can open up this whole nation to opportunity, *that* will be Graeme's legacy . . .'

Simon's attention wandered. He saw Roza turn and reach for Johnnie, who was suddenly standing up on the pew. A policeman passed the window, talking into his phone, and pigeons swirled up from the square.

David paused and lowered his head. He cleared his throat and gripped the lectern. A ripple went through the crowd. There was a sob, Trish's hat bobbed and the ladies leaned towards her. Men bowed their heads.

Ed Miles looked at his watch.

Now, in the hushed cathedral, David rested his palms on the lectern. 'And I ask you to join me in a prayer.'

Simon was an atheist, so he didn't kneel. He didn't bow his head. All along his pew they went down on creaking knees. He looked straight into David eyes, and David read the prayer to him.

All This

It was early evening in the garden at Rotokauri. Troy hovered diligently over the drinks table, with his ice tongs, his lemon slices.

Simon was listening to an exchange between Karen and Juliet Miles.

'Trish is coping amazingly well.'

'Isn't she amazing.'

'It was an amazing service.'

'Look, I was amazed by it, to be honest.'

David leaned close to Simon. He was on his second gin and tonic. He was sunburnt, and his eyes had a varnish of weariness. 'Instil and imbue,' he said.

Simon smiled and looked down.

David gestured at Ed, who was now pretending to read Karen's palm. 'Ed's speech for the funeral. I don't usually get my Police Minister to write my speeches, obviously. But Ed and I and Graeme have been together from the beginning. Before we had writers, Ed used to do the speeches for both of us. He knows what works.'

'I'm sure he does.'

'He knows when to use instil and imbue *to the nth degree*.'

Simon hesitated. 'Yes. I understand. You don't mind clichés. You have no need for verbal snobbery.'

David laughed. 'What I like about you . . .'

'Roza!' said the ladies, and moved their chairs to make room.

Roza had wet hair, and was carrying Johnnie on her hip. The small boy, freshly bathed, presented his shining cheeks to be kissed by Karen, by Juliet.

Watching his wife, David said, 'What I like about you is that you're not political. You're like Roza, hopelessly apolitical. Your mind's on other things. That's so refreshing for me.'

Simon said, 'Whereas you have to consider the politics in every-thing.' He broke off, suddenly bored and trapped. It was strange; in David's presence he sometimes found himself floundering. One of these days he would hear himself say, 'You're amazing, David. You're just amazing.'

He wanted an excuse to get away for an hour. The evenings had settled into a pattern: drinks on the lawn followed by an elaborate dinner at the long table in the main house and afterwards, now the weather had settled, coffee and more drinks on the deck. David liked to stay up late, and none of them felt quite comfortable going to bed before him. Simon had begun to crave a quick, alcohol-free dinner, a book and an early night. He was short of exercise, too. David didn't seem much interested in physical activity. He worked all day in his office at the main house, and after that he lay on the beach, or took one of his abrupt drives out to sea on the throbbing jet ski. He did have a treadmill in his office and sometimes stood on it when he was on the phone, but Simon had never seen it switched on.

It would be nice to go down to the beach. It was a beautiful evening, the sky clear and faintly greenish over the calm sea. He wanted to swim a long way out and look back at the shore, the lights coming on in the houses and the stars appearing.

He started to get up. But David leaned close and said, 'Ed makes choices for me, and they work. Ed would know what you mean about instil and imbue. I don't, necessarily. Not instinctively.'

15

Sudden laughter from the ladies, who had drawn their chairs around Ed. 'Ed. You're terrible!'

'I need Ed. Maybe I need you too.'

They were looking at each other and Simon held his gaze; for a moment they were competing and then David dropped his eyes.

David said, 'Let me get you another drink. And I'll have one too.'

Simon leaned back in his chair. He was strangely thrilled.

A nanny arrived to take Johnnie to bed. They were summoned for dinner but David and Ed were called away to a phone conference. Now they dawdled through the garden paths towards the house, Simon and the women: Karen and Juliet and Roza.

Simon was thinking about his staring competition with David. He had won it; he kept coming back to that. David made him feel he mattered. All his life he'd run from his shaming childhood and his father's rejection; he had succeeded and yet . . . always the sense of impermanence, unease.

He'd been wary of David at first, unlike Karen, who was embarrassingly thrilled by the association, but he'd been drawn into the Hallwright circle to the point where he and David were regarded as close friends. Simon was acknowledged to have David's ear even though he had nothing to do with politics. He thought of it as a weird twist of fate, a curiosity, but (admit it) he'd come to value the position, to flatter himself he'd earned it. The thing was . . . The thing was, he was straight with David, never asked for anything, had never pursued him. Which contrasted with the sycophantic treatment the PM received elsewhere.

It would hurt if he lost Hallwright's favour. David could withdraw and become inexplicably cold, but Simon had discovered that if he politely ignored the coldness, David would come back all smiles, almost as if he'd been teasing. If David played games, Simon was a match for him, although it cost him effort. He puzzled over conversations, trying to understand nuances, and there were still the bad dreams: his father Aaron checking in to remind him he was worthless.

Juliet was saying, 'It was when I injured my hand. I was pregnant, and had the two other children, so we got her in. She came from ACC, a sort of nurse aide. Anyway, as soon as she arrived she said she was used to caring for people in not-so-nice suburbs, and she was thrilled to be in such a lovely big house. She was an amazing housekeeper. So after my hand was out of the cast and the baby was born we kept her on. And now, it's just getting weird.'

'Does she steal things?'

'Go through your drawers?'

'Try on your clothes?'

'She's just sort of *turned*. She's quite sharp with the cleaner and the gardener's scared of her, and she completely freaks out the au pair. The other day she locked me out of the house. I had the baby and all his things and I was calling through the letterbox. I was furious, I remonstrated with her and she opened the door and gave me this look, I can't describe it. And now she's . . . changed. She looks at me strangely. And there's a tattooed man, some sort of friend of hers, who waits for her outside the house in the afternoons. Peering in. Sort of *glaring* in at the gate.'

'Ed'll find you gone and her dressed as you.'

'She was telling me she'd lost weight and that she felt really "light" and she lifted her foot and stuck it right near the baby's face.'

'That's symbolic. A foot in the face.'

'Ed's never home. And he doesn't listen. It's all, *Don't be so imaginative*, and, *She seems perfectly normal to me.*'

Roza said intently, 'They work for you and you think you get on. But you can't tell. Sometimes you find out that they hate you. They *really* hate you.'

They reached a wooden gate. Simon held it open as they passed through. Roza and Karen were minimally dressed in the hot weather;

Juliet, who had ginger hair and freckles and pale blue eyes, was swathed as usual, in a kaftan, floaty scarf and a hat. The sun was Juliet's enemy. It pursued her, tricked her, never left her alone. She would take shelter in the shade only to find that reflected glare had got in under the canvas and left her pink and peeling, like a cooked prawn.

Roza never burned but only got browner. Like all the men in the compound, Simon spent a lot of time either trying not to stare at her, or placing himself where he could look without being noticed. And now Garth the personal trainer had arrived, with his weights and diets and workout programmes, and she'd been playing all that tennis . . .

Since she'd had Johnnie, Roza seemed stronger and less fragile, Simon thought, and yet somehow just as frightening. She was still ungovernable, but her power was turned outwards, and he no longer worried she might damage herself, as he'd feared during their negotiations over Elke.

Karen had initially tried to keep Roza at bay. It was Roza, he thought, who'd recovered herself first. He had watched her taking Karen in hand — that was the only way to describe it. Roza had seen to it that Karen wouldn't stand in her way.

Karen loved Elke even more than she loved her own — her biological — daughter, Claire. She wasn't giving Elke up. In order to gain access to the girl, Roza had turned herself into Karen's best friend. And so a new world had opened up to Karen; she was photographed, noticed, mentioned in social diaries. She rode in convoys with the Hallwrights. Simon knew that if Roza had not had a great deal to trade, Karen would have kept her away. She would have been implacable.

They didn't talk about it. Karen would only say, 'It's lucky we get on so well.' He didn't discuss it with Roza, either, but his conversations with her were always charged with covert understanding. *I know that you know that I know.*

He latched the gate and came towards her, saying, 'I've got to pick up Marcus after dinner.'

'Oh yes?'

'I dropped him this afternoon at a house on the other side.' He meant the other side of the peninsula, where there was a settlement as ostentatious as Rotokauri, but bigger and less exclusive. 'This huge house on the marina, with a pool party going on.'

Marcus had been invited by a school friend. When they'd got there a woman in a silver bikini had ushered them in, grinned and vanished. Marcus had gone ahead to the pool, where a group of teenagers was lounging by the thumping stereo, and Simon had wandered alone through rooms like glasshouses, full of refracted light.

'It was one of the new houses at the marina — enormous, all glass and granite and steel. White leather sofas. And a gigantic gin palace parked outside.'

He'd found a group of middle-aged people drinking and sunbathing on an upper veranda. The host, Marcus's friend's father, offered him a cocktail.

'They were all completely drunk. The father's got a new girlfriend, Marcus says, who likes to have sex in the spa pool on the deck. Doesn't care who happens to stroll past. And he says she flirts with the sons. The father did have his hand clamped on a woman's arse the whole time I was talking to him.'

He thought of the grey-haired, handsome man with his boiled face and blue eyes and the woman in a leopard-print bikini and, behind them, over the steel rail, the gigantic boat.

Roza said, 'Ugh. Drinking in the day. Was it Gibson, the booze tycoon? He's got the biggest house on the other side. He's a good friend of the Cahanes. He comes over here and we have to be nice to him.'

'That's it. Peter Gibson. His son's called Harry.'

'He's got some terrible new slag. She's all Botox and mini-dresses and "signature handbags". Unbelievably tacky.'

'Roza!'

She grinned, showing her pretty teeth.

Simon said, 'Anyway, Marcus is fifteen. I suppose he'll be fine.'

'Gibson's house, the local den of vice — he'll have the time of his life,' Roza said.

The path wound through lavender and rosemary bushes and led to the main house, where David and Ed were talking on the veranda. Across the lawn some young people were good-humouredly disputing over a tennis match, and others were splashing in the pool.

Juliet picked a piece of lavender and held it to her nose. She said, 'I mean, Karen, what can you actually *do* if you start being stalked by the help?'

They were joined at the house by Claire and Elke. The small Miles children had been rounded up by a nanny and carried off to bed in the apartment next to the Little House.

With kisses and in her usual manner (affectionate, sweet, vague), Elke greeted her two mothers, her two fathers. Claire, who was nineteen now, a university student and only here for two nights, kept back. She disliked physical contact. She seemed to Simon, who was vague about clothes, to be dressed as a soldier, in a grimy khaki shirt, jeans and boots. Her face was set in an expression that Simon recognised; anticipated hurt and defensiveness made her look myopic, as if the mere act of seeing were effortful. Karen always expected trouble from Claire and tried to patronise her, which made Claire boil with fury. Simon took his daughter's arm, feeling how tense she was. He made sure she was seated next to him.

Claire was training to be a doctor. She wanted to work as a paediatrician and had once, to Karen's horror, bailed up David and asked him why children in South Auckland were so poor and neglected they suffered from diseases eliminated from most first-world countries. David had smiled tenderly and thanked her for the question; he'd told her how much his government was doing in this important area, 'although the recession ties our hands, of course'. After that he'd not only avoided her but no longer enquired after her, never mentioned her at all.

They gathered around the table. Roza laughed lightly and said,'No, hang on. Karen, you sit over there next to Ed. Then we've got the mix right.'

Karen had been about to sit down between David and his chief of staff, Rick Short. A mottled blush rose to her cheeks as she moved down to the end of the table and took her place between Ed and someone's teenage son.

Roza said, 'Ed, you can read Karen's palm.' Then she leaned across to Elke and put her hand on the girl's wrist. She said, 'I've just remembered. I've got something to show you. After dinner.'

David's gaze slid across Claire to linger on Elke. And Simon felt a sudden compression in his chest. One Lampton daughter had ceased to exist for David, but the other had come sharply into focus, and Simon had brooded over the new phenomenon: David being aware of Elke. There was a series of photos in the office at the main house: Elke and little Johnnie, hand in hand on the beach, building sand castles, jumping through waves. Roza's children. They both had freckly noses and deep, watchful eyes.

Elke was beautiful like her mother, although shorter and slighter, and her face was round where Roza's was angular. But her mannerisms and expressions were Roza's, exactly. Nature had trumped nurture. The laugh, the smile, the graceful hands. The abrupt changes of mood. She wasn't as volatile as Roza, but they both specialised in non-verbal communication; they were geniuses of the unsaid — so unlike poor, clever Claire, who could never shut up.

Simon thought, what was wrong . . . Lately, he'd sometimes had the primitive urge to grab his adopted daughter and shoo her out of the room. Sometimes he could understand the point (just not the justice) of a burqa.

What was wrong was that the compound was full of men. They looked at Elke's mother as much as they dared, which wasn't much. And then their gaze turned.

She was eighteen and the compound was full of men. And none of them was her real father.

Coffee and dessert wine were served on the deck. David took Roza's arm and said something quiet in her ear and she laughed and turned to Elke.

'Come up to our room for a minute,' she said to the girl. 'I want to give you something.'

They went inside.

'Look,' Karen said, and they admired the moon, round and silver, coming up behind the rocky island out by the point. And soon there was a waving pathway of light across the water and the sky above it was studded with pinpricks of light. Out here on a clear night you could see the satellites, just like stars except they moved briskly across the sky.

Simon watched a security guard pacing slowly around the swimming pool. Juliet was saying, 'But Ed. I wore the zinc and the hat. I stayed under the trees. And look, I'm peeling everywhere.'

It was time to pick up Marcus. He crossed the grounds, heading for the Little House. Looking back he saw Roza and Elke sitting on an upstairs deck, talking.

He drove along the coast before taking the road that turned inland, winding uphill through dense bush, towards the other side of the peninsula. Possums appeared on the road, their round eyes fixed on the lights, and he slowed and tooted, waiting for them to veer away into the dark.

On the other side of the hill the bush cleared and he could look down on the lights of the settlement below. He drove down onto the coast and headed for the marina. As soon as he turned into the road he could hear music. Gibson's house was lit up, its glass panels glowing like a jukebox and vibrating with crazy sound.

Simon stopped to look at Gibson's boat. He leaned over the rail, drew back then looked again. It was a novel sight, down there on the lower deck — sex from above. A man's bare back and arse, a woman's bare knees and thighs, and one of her feet raised in the air, a white jandal dangling from the toes.

The music was so loud he could feel the bass vibrating in his throat. From somewhere above him there was a scream, a shriek of harsh laughter, the sound of breaking glass. Then a cheer. Then more glass breaking, and a bottle spinning in the air before it exploded on the road.

The door was open. He walked through the foyer and paused at the edge of the open-plan space. At one end of the room middle-aged people were sitting around a coffee table, drinking. On the other side, five teenage boys had stripped to their underpants and were gyrating to the music. Two had climbed onto the kitchen bench. The room was harshly lit and in disarray, with chairs tipped over, food on the floor, a vase broken. On a wall-mounted TV black American rappers mouthed and posed, showing off their guns and their bling.

He asked the teenage boys, where was Marcus Lampton? But they shook their heads and went on dancing. He asked the adults around the coffee table, and they too shook their heads, glazed.

Out by the pool he found only a man and woman kissing exhaustedly in the spa. He passed through a room full of gym machines, a sauna and a home theatre with widescreen and rows of seats. As he climbed the stairs a group of teenagers came thumping down and a girl told him, 'Marcus is gone. Maybe to Jason's?'

'Jason who?' But she was sliding past him, her palms upturned.

He looked into an empty room, a television showing a news channel: floods in Queensland, evacuations, snakes and crocodiles in the floodwater. Five people arrested in Copenhagen on suspicion of planning a 'Mumbai-style' terrorist attack. A magnitude-seven earthquake in Chile. He watched it for a minute or two.

There was a light on at the end of the dark hall. Simon called out, then put his head around the door. On the bed Gibson and a woman were asleep, tangled in a satin cover, their mouths open, breathing harshly. A TV above the bed showed a blank blue screen. Porn DVDs were piled on the bedside table and more strewn on the floor. Beyond, a door was open to an en suite bathroom, its tiles puddled with vomit.

A Burmese cat leapt up onto the bed, twitching its tail. It sniffed and jumped emphatically off again. The smell in the room was foul. The curtains were open; the moon shone on the water and in the distance lights were moving over the dunes.

Simon stood by the bed. The woman groaned and turned, her hair trailing across her face. The rank smell reminded him of his father, Aaron Harris. Aaron had got drunk out of bitterness, because of all he wanted and didn't have. Gibson had *all this*. But here he was, smashed, in ruins.

The woman opened her eyes and stared straight at him. He stepped back, but her eyes were glazed and blank, and she turned and buried her face in the pillow.

He went downstairs, followed by the cat. The couple on the boat were now clothed and sharing a cigarette on a sofa on the upper deck. He called out to them.

'There's a whole lot of kids on the beach,' the woman said, indifferent and surprisingly sober.

He hurried to the car, imagining bottles spinning in the air above his head. Down at the beach he saw lights moving across the dunes and after a while he could make out a line of kids down at the water's edge, walking through the shallows. He flashed his headlights on and off, and soon Marcus detached himself from the group and jogged up the beach towards him.

Strategy

Simon arrived at the pool with his book and his towel. He had been for a strenuous early morning run to the Kauri Lake, and so it was with a sense of earned luxury that he arranged his gear on the table beside the deck chair and lowered himself down. It was a clear, still, blue day. There was a sheen over the garden and the water made loops of dancing light on the wall of the pool house. Nearby, one of the staff, Trent, had stretched himself out on the hot concrete to reach into a drain while another polo-shirted young man, Shane, stood over him, twirling a net on a long stick.

He applied suntan lotion and put on sunglasses. He couldn't be bothered with his book but lay toasting his aching legs and watching Trent and Shane, intent over their plumbing. A pair of grey herons flapped over the garden, slow and jerkily uneven on their string-puppet wings.

Roza said to Juliet, 'Maybe some men are attractive *because* they're thick. A big guy with a nice personality and lots of muscles. The sexy thing is that he's not complicated. He's sort of generic. Some men prefer women to be a bit simple. It's a sex thing. It's easier to have sex with someone who doesn't see you too clearly.'

'Mmm. I suppose.'

They both looked thoughtfully at Trent and Shane.

Her face coated with white zinc, in hat, sunglasses and loose Lycra rash shirt, Juliet left the safe shade of her umbrella and stood at the pool steps, dipping a toe in the water.

Roza touched Simon's shoulder. 'Good run?'

'I went to the Kauri Lake. It's beautiful in the valley.'

'It *is* beautiful. It's eerie too, by the water. The wind makes that sound in the reeds. Almost a moaning. And there are those funny little houses.'

'We could walk there some time, if you wanted exercise.'

'I'd like that.'

'If you got sick of lying here, ogling the help.'

'Mmm. There's only so much ogling you can do.'

'Before what?'

'Before you have to go and work it off, I suppose.'

'Roza!'

'What are you two laughing about?' Karen called from the pool. She'd been swimming lengths, and her eyes were underscored with red loops from her goggles. She launched herself backwards without waiting for an answer, floating on her back while Juliet breaststroked gingerly past her, her shirt billowing with trapped air.

'It's quite nice,' Juliet said doubtfully, adjusting the cap on her orange hair.

Roza tried and failed to get up. 'Oh, Simon, I'm trapped. Can you . . .' She was lying on her back. 'Look, my necklace, it's got caught on the fabric. I'm pinned. I'll suffocate.'

She laughed up at him. 'You'll have to reach behind my neck. Oh, ow!'

He couldn't get at the necklace from behind, because the deck chair had its own little awning over her head. And so he found himself straddling her, a leg on each side of her chair and his hands on her neck, feeling amid the strands of soft hair for the clasp of the necklace while she laughed into his face and his hair. And when he'd finally freed her from the webbed fabric of the deck chair and clambered off her as she sat up smiling and flushed, he turned to face four pairs of steady eyes: Juliet and Karen treading water in the pool, and beyond them Trent and Shane.

'It was chaos,' he said half an hour later. 'Huge house, total debauchery. It seemed so nihilistic, I was really struck by it.' He corrected himself, 'Or, I would have been if I wasn't worried about Marcus.'

'Nihilistic,' Karen said.

'He's off.'

'One of his tangents. Pass the zinc, darling. Look, now my palms are peeling.'

'It can't have been that bad,' Karen said. 'He always exaggerates. Harry Gibson's a lovely boy. Peter says his new partner Janine's been amazing with him. She's really brought him on.'

'Well, his father's a lovely drunk,' Simon said.

'They'd probably just had a few. Holidays, people want to relax.'

'He was so relaxed I nearly called an ambulance.' Simon shifted in his deck chair. He was actually very distracted. It was now safe, he felt, to take the towel off his lap. Climbing all over Roza had had a pronounced effect. He'd been obliged to throw himself down on his deck chair, covering his groin.

Roza said, 'Let's walk to the Kauri Lake.'

'Oh, that's miles,' Juliet said.

'It's not that far,' Simon said to Roza.

Juliet sat up. 'Well, I suppose . . . Do you want to, Karen?'

Simon said, 'Well, actually, it's *quite* far. And there's not much shade. I did get quite burnt running out there, even in a hat — the glare comes up off the road.'

Karen looked at him.

He said, 'I think David'll be down soon. He wanted a swim before the Cock turns up.'

'Haven't you just *run* out to the lake?'

'Yeah, but you know it's the only thing that keeps me happy, loads of PE. And anyway, we haven't had much exercise for days.'

'I'd better not,' Juliet decided, arranging her scarves.

'I'll come,' Karen said.

'That's the spirit.' Simon was expressionless.

Troy appeared in the gateway between the hedges. A tiny cloud of flies flew up from the grass and glittered in the air above the pool. Roza was gathering her things and shuffling into her pink jandals. She slid on her dark glasses.

'Here he is.'

David limped around the side of the pool house, wearing baggy board shorts decorated with hibiscus flowers.

'Hello all. Roza, are you going? Who's going to keep me company? You'll stay here, won't you, Karen?'

Karen said of course she'd stay. She took David's towel and lotion from Troy and arranged them on the table beside his deck chair.

David tossed his shirt to Troy and dived into the pool. They watched the wavering form under the water, frog-kicking through the loops of light. He surfaced with a snort of bubbles, fair hair streaming.

And now Elke came through the gate and stood at the edge of the pool in her striped bikini, one hand on her hip and shading her eyes. She was wearing a necklace Roza had given her the night before. Vague, tentative, she walked to the side and lowered herself to sit with her legs in the water.

Simon remembered when she was eight, back when they'd brought her home for the first time. She had long, slender fingers, thin arms and legs, soft hair. She was always shying away. She still had that elusive quality. But when Roza passed behind her and touched her shoulder

Elke leaned her head back and looked at her mother upside down and actually grinned.

Karen called out. 'Elke. Put on some lotion.'

'God, Mum, you're obsessed with the sun.' She slid into the pool and sank to the bottom to sit cross-legged on the tiles, her hair waving above her head.

Roza and Simon walked up to the main house. She said, 'Can you wait while I get changed?'

He sat out on the deck, looking at the sea, with its million points of light. David's elder son Michael was lying on a towel nearby texting, and his sister Izzy walked past, carrying her giant white cat, Suzie. Izzy paused and frowned at her brother.

'Tulei says you fed Suzie,' she said.

He said, looking at his phone, 'So what?'

'But you don't care about Suzie. You've never fed him. He's mine.'

The boy lowered the phone. He smiled. 'You think Suzie's yours. You think he "loves" you. But it's all just about food. If I fed him all the time, he'd love *me*.'

Izzy stared. Then she walked down the steps and away across the lawn, lugging the cat.

Roza appeared in the doorway. 'Why did you say that, Michael? She loves that cat.'

The boy rolled over. 'I just *fed* it.'

'But why? You don't care about the cat. That's so gratuitous. Telling her it doesn't love her.'

'I fed it,' he said. 'Why shouldn't I? Maybe I just felt like being nice to it.'

'Oh, rubbish.' Roza turned away angrily. 'Come on, Simon.'

At the gate she was peremptory, refusing when Ray, one of David's staff, said he would go with them.

'Let's get out of here,' she said, setting off at a furious pace. 'That Michael. Why think up something like that, just to upset Izzy?'

Simon's legs were aching. He said, 'You mean he's trying to demonstrate that it only cares about food? He's trying to take over the cat? To show her?'

'It's so bloody gratuitous. Why shouldn't she believe the cat loves her?'

'Even though he's right.'

'Yes, he's right, but why — oh, I don't know, strip her of her illusions? It's nasty.'

He hurried to keep up. 'What if he really just wanted to feed it? What if he's got fond of it? It's not necessarily a *strategy*.'

She gave him an amused, bitter look. 'In our household, everything is a strategy.'

They went to the shop to buy drinks. A blonde woman in a tight white dress was bending over a toddler, unwrapping an ice cream.

'Roza, hi!'

Roza didn't smile. 'Janine . . . Simon Lampton,' she said, waving her fingers and looking away.

He shook her hand, 'Hello, we've met. I brought my son to your party.'

She was all smiles, licking ice cream off her thumb, shaking hands. She seemed to have no memory of him standing over her bed.

'Oh yes, the party.' Roza turned back, with a lilt in her voice. 'How did that go? It was a wild success, I hear.'

Janine gave the child a complacent pat on the bum. 'Look, it was just a few quiet drinks. With some really good friends of Peter and I. But the boys get on amazingly well. They had an amazing time, just really chilled out, relaxing by the pool.'

Roza was already moving away.

'Awesome,' the woman said, and a breeze came up the pavement and lifted her short skirt, and the ice cream paper flew out of her hand. The child ran after it; she shouted, 'Harrison! Don't go on the road!' and a tall, muscular man stepped forward, catching the ice cream wrapper and putting out an arm to stop the child.

'Ray,' Roza said. 'What a surprise. When are you going to stop stalking me? No one's going to bother us here.'

Ray was all amiable forbearance, allowing himself to be waved off, dismissed, charmingly cursed, Roza flapping her hands at him, pretending to hit him with her hat.

They walked on.

'You like that Ray,' he said after they'd walked for a while.

'He's all right.' She looked at him, deadpan. They turned inland towards the valley. The wind died away and the bush was still in the heat. The track leading to the Kauri Lake started at a bend in the road and wound away through stands of toetoe, its white plumes waving against the blue sky. As they got further in the path was walled on both sides by ti tree. The only sound was the sawing of the cicadas, but Simon supposed Ray was behind them somewhere.

'They were completely out of it, in bed,' he was saying. 'And she opened her eyes and looked straight at me. She obviously doesn't remember.'

'God. Disgusting,' Roza said.

He ventured, 'Are there AA meetings around here?'

'Mm, there's a local group. They meet above the PostShop. I've been going along.' She sighed. 'It's nice to get away, just by ourselves. The Cock's coming this evening, and I'll have to spend hours with his wife.'

'What's she like, the Cock's wife?'

'Not bad, as wives go. I do get sick of them.' She hesitated. 'Except Karen, of course.'

'You and Karen have got so close.'

Roza's smile was wide, bland. 'It's wonderfully lucky we get on so well.'

'I suppose you talk about Elke a lot.'

'Not *all* the time. Actually, Karen quite likes talking about David.'

'Ah.'

They reached the edge of the lake. The water was smooth and glassy, fringed with raupo stalks. Roza ventured along the edge and got into a bog. He gripped her wrist, and her foot came out of the mud with a wet sucking sound. They rinsed off in the lake water and took another branch of the track that led away from the lake and rejoined the road into the valley, passing the row of small houses, where he showed her the skinny white pony. At the far end of the valley, where the hills cast a shadow and the road began to wind upwards, they turned and made their way back.

Roza said, 'What you said about Peter Gibson's party — I was thinking. There's a mood . . . I suppose it's exhilaration or defiance, what you might feel driving a fast car listening to loud music. That sort of fuck-the-world feeling.'

'Yes . . . ?'

'A lot of people don't seem to get into that kind of mood, ever. Even when they're young. Mild little women, say. Or mild little men, for that matter. Maybe it's to do with testosterone. Do some women have more testosterone than others?'

'Possibly.'

'Well, that kind of emotion is what got me into trouble in the past. Wanting extremes, wanting to smash myself against the world.'

He considered this. 'It *is* possible to be a quiet, retiring, mild addict.'

'I know. I'm just saying *I* got into trouble at first, became an alcoholic, because of that kind of sensation-seeking.'

He said, cautious, 'I thought you were numbing your . . . distress, over Elke.'

'Later, maybe. But at first I was just wild. I was an addict before I had Elke; I was born an addict. See, I know how people can change, because when I was young I was a very bad person.'

'I'm sure you weren't.'

'I was dishonest. My mother was a bad role model. She was completely cold towards me — hated me. I had to work out for myself how to behave.'

Simon hesitated. 'You mention testosterone. My colleague Peter Brown thinks genius is related to testosterone. He says very accomplished women have more masculine traits. He told me that over a beer. Privately.'

'Mm. Best not to bandy that notion about. Brilliant women are butch.'

'He just thinks they have more masculine personalities. As in, they don't love shopping, and they don't stab each other in the back all the time, and they don't endlessly discuss shoes.'

'Do you think he's right?'

'I think he's just an old-fashioned sexist, probably.'

'Probably?' Roza laughed.

'Look,' Simon said. He parted the leaves and showed her what had caught his eye — a vivid green gecko sunning itself in the ti tree.

'It's beautiful! Catch it.'

But the lizard ran down the trunk and disappeared.

They walked on. Roza said, 'Is it possible that relationships, marriages, are better if the couple don't completely understand each other? Is it off-putting, knowing someone too well?'

He wanted to say, fervently, no. To the contrary. But he only answered, 'That's another way of saying opposites attract.'

Roza went on, 'People say they just want someone who understands them. But I think, be careful with that. You might be better off with someone who doesn't.'

He was silent.

She said, 'Don't look so serious!'

His smile was pained. 'You're a brilliant woman, Mrs Hallwright.'

'But I have hundreds of pairs of shoes, and I love to shop.'

'Only proving our Peter wrong.'

'Although, I'm no back-stabber.'

'No. You simply mow people down from the front.'

They carried on walking and talking, although Simon suddenly felt he had rather a lot on his mind.

At the crossroads, Ray stood scuffing his feet on the grass verge and talking on his phone.

Simon lowered his voice, 'I suppose you feel you're never alone.'

She sighed, 'It's possible to feel one's *always* alone. Even in a crowd. Don't you think?' She added, 'Although it never seems like that when I'm with you.'

He had an immediate sense of happiness. His legs ached pleasantly, the colours were beautiful, the light was intense, and he was walking along the sunny road with Roza.

Make Soon Talk

Karen said, 'How was the lake?'

'It was nice. Hot.'

His cell phone rang. It was a young man's voice, polite, well-spoken.

'Hello, Dr Lampton, my name's Arthur Weeks. I was hoping I could speak to you — it's about a friend of mine I think you might know: Mereana Kostas?'

Simon looked at a patch of light on the wall above Karen's head.

'Hello? Dr Lampton?'

'You must have the wrong number.'

'You're Simon Lampton? I'm just looking for some information—'

'Sorry. Don't know the name. Can't help you. Thanks.' He hung up.

Karen looked up. 'Where are you going *now*?'

He paused at the door. 'Swim.'

'God you're hyperactive. Don't you want a rest?'

'I'm hot. I'll just fall in and get wet.'

He pretended to dawdle off down the path, although he felt like breaking into a run. It was years since he'd last seen Mereana. He didn't know where she was, but he was sure she was gone for good, and as far as he knew no one could link his name with hers. Who was this Arthur Weeks? Who?

Heading for the beach, he met Roza coming down from the main house. She said, 'I'm going to take Johnnie for a swim. Want to come?'

They found the boy in the upper garden, being pushed on a swing. Roza took charge of him. 'Look at your hair, all on end. And your nose is sunburnt. Pool or beach?'

He ducked away. 'Pool.'

The nanny, Tuleimoka, went to the house and came back with a bag containing towels, sun lotion and goggles. She said, in her ceremonious way, 'Mrs Hallwright, here is his gear.' She pronounced it 'kea'. Tuleimoka Faleuka was a tall, stately Niuean. Simon liked her beautiful voice and her accent: 'fitteo' for 'video', 'tala' for 'dollar', 'Cray Lynn' for 'Grey Lynn'. She'd decided Johnnie was running wild and needed to be taken in hand; consequently Roza, who was inclined to be permissive, spent a lot of time trying to get rid of her.

'Thank you, Tulei. You can go and . . . see what Jung Ha's doing for his dinner. And after that, we might be back, or we might go for a last walk on the beach or . . .'

'Mrs Hallwright?'

'Oh, I don't know where we'll really. We'll come and find you.'

Johnnie took his mother's hand and they walked through the grounds.

'Make Soon talk,' he said.

'No, Simon's here, we have to talk to him.'

'Make Soon talk!'

'Don't mind me,' Simon said.

'Oh, all right. Let's see, then. Phew, it's still hot.'

Roza put on a pair of oversized, movie-star sunglasses, and they walked slowly along the path. She cleared her throat.

One morning Soon and the Village Idiot were on their way to the Idiots' Village, where a ceremony was being held in honour of the Village Idiots' God, the Great Wedgie. But they hadn't got far when Starfish came panting up behind them.

"Come quickly," Starfish said. "Everyone's assembling in the castle. The Green Lady has arrived with news."

"Go away, Starfish," said Soon. "You're a poof." Studious Starfish was carrying two of his textbooks and Soon knocked one out of his hand into the mud and laughed, but Starfish ignored him and they went on.

Roza stopped to cram on Johnnie's hat. They took the path through the flower beds.

Starfish said, "Soon, you're monstrous, but it's because you're deranged from a bad upbringing. Your mother, Mrs Soon, was a monster too."

In the clearing they found a crowd assembled: the Green Lady and her soldiers; the Weta; the Praying Mantis; the two wise men, Tiny Ancient Yellow Cousin So-on and the Red Herring; and, from over the treetops, came the Bachelor flying in his bed, with his girlfriends the Cassowaries on board, ruffling their feathers and hissing angrily.

The Bachelor landed his bed and said suavely to the Green Lady, "Dear Lady, you look ravishing. Come and sit on my bed." The Cassowaries nearly hissed themselves to death with jealousy but the Green Lady, who always resisted the Bachelor's charms and often had to call her men to shoot at him when he hovered in his bed outside her castle, thanked him coolly and said she would remain on her horse. At which point the Red Herring was heard to observe, "It is always darkest before the dawn", and his colleague, Tiny Ancient Yellow Cousin So-on, sagely agreed . . .

'. . . Johnnie, don't pull the heads off the flowers.' Roza looked at Simon. 'Sorry.'

'No problem,' he said, his mind on the stranger who'd called. Week? Weeks? How had he . . .?

"I have received a message from the Universe," the Green Lady said. "We are to expect a visit from the Ort Cloud, who has been having fresh trouble with his Wife." The Ort Cloud's Wife was said to be in league with the evil Barbie Yah herself. She was, like the Ort Cloud, vast and purple, with luminous eyes, but where his eyes were wise and steady, hers were boiling and ferocious. When the Ort Cloud and his wife fought, the turmoil in the Universe was truly terrible . . .

Simon undid the pool gate and stepped back to let them through.

'Keep going,' Johnnie said.

'Right. In you get.'

''S cold.'

'Only at first.'

Johnnie launched himself off the concrete edge and into the deep water.

Roza arranged her towel. 'God, Soon. I have to make him talk morning, noon and night. I say, "Can't we just be Mummy and Johnnie for a while?" But no, he wants Soon.'

Simon was reluctantly familiar with Soon. Soon behaved appallingly towards his adoptive brother Starfish (who was a starfish); Soon was rude, foul-mouthed, unwashed, sly, wicked and a liar, while Starfish was studious, well-behaved, kind and endlessly shocked by Soon's behaviour. Soon never missed a chance to have Starfish blamed for his crimes. Soon wore armour, was always bristling with weaponry and dreamed of being a warrior, but was thwarted by the fact that he was only three inches tall. The story was being told by 'Mrs Hallwright', who produced the story in her Boardroom. Sometimes, in a postmodern interlude, Mrs Hallwright and Johnnie had disputes in the Boardroom over plot developments, and Mrs Hallwright would become menacing if Johnnie argued too strongly, and would mutter, 'The boy grows cocky.' There was a ban on technology in the plot, and if Johnnie wanted to insert a computer or other modern device he would be pursued by the Technology Police, who would arrive in the story to arrest him. Whenever Soon banged his head, he would turn into the hippy Dandelions, and preach peace and love until his head cleared and he became bloodthirsty Soon again; but in a recent episode, when Tuleimoka was at the dentist and Roza had made Soon talk for three hours, there had been a rent in the Universe and Soon had been trapped between selves: half Soon, half Dandelions. And so on.

Roza didn't make Soon talk in front of David; she said it would drive him insane. Simon tried to feel flattered, but he sometimes wished Soon would shut up. He had to content himself with the sound of Roza's voice, and Soon's, and Starfish's, and the rest of 'the friends'. Roza had recently added another group, the Guatemalans, tiny people who lived in Soon and Starfish's room and were violently excitable, discharging their shotguns at the slightest provocation. Recently Simon had endured an episode in which the Bachelor had taken up poetry and had held a reading, at which his girlfriends the Cassowaries had adoringly applauded, the Green Lady had laughed (many of the poems were dedicated to her) and the Guatemalans had become outraged and shot down the poems with their guns.

Johnnie was a subtle and verbally acute child. He had every plot detail in his head and exhausted Roza with his appetite, but she hated to disappoint him, and the boy knew exactly how to goad her with a mixture of charm, persistence and nagging, so she wore herself out giving voice to a three-inch, comically violent, obnoxious dwarf.

Johnnie climbed the ladder, trotted along the concrete and threw himself into the water again. The sun had moved across the sky; the flower beds beyond the pool were drained of colour in the powerful light and the gardener, moving slowly along the top of the hedge with his clippers, sent flashes off the metal of his blades.

'It's as if you've given him siblings,' Simon said. 'When he takes Soon and Starfish in hand and orders them around, it's like he's learning how to deal with younger brothers.'

Roza said, 'I suppose I should have another child. David'd like to.' She got up and paced along the edge of the pool. Johnnie called out but she ignored him and said, 'Do you ever have the feeling you're trying to work out *how* to live?'

He thought about it. 'Do you mean, working out a way to live that's bearable?'

'That's exactly what I mean. I suppose it's to do with having been a disgraceful addict. Now I'm sober and go to my meetings, the question is how to live. Before, I was trying *not* to live.'

'Do you still feel like that? It's been a long time.'

She stopped and looked intently at him. 'They say I'll always feel like that.'

'Oh yes, I suppose so. Once an addict . . . etcetera.'

'There's so much to drive you crazy in life — I mean, having to spend time with Juliet. I want to tie her to a pole under the noonday sun and leave her to cook.'

'Goodness.'

'Stake her out on the beach and leave her to fry.'

'Roza!'

'Mum, watch!' Johnnie shouted.

'Well done darling, good dive. And then there's Ed Miles — I feel him sidling around me. That's what he does, he comes up beside you and never looks at you directly, but he says something that gives you a chill, because it tells you he's watching. Ed can sniff out anything. He was the perfect choice for Minister of Police.' She crossed her fingers. 'He and David have been *like that* from the beginning; he was the one who encouraged David to go into politics, before Graeme Ellison did. He just lives for David. It's almost creepy. He doesn't care about anyone else. Especially not Juliet,' she added. 'He's appalling to her.'

'He does have rather X-ray eyes.'

'It used to make me so anxious, that I'd ended up married to this huge entity, the party. I felt they were all spying on me. I stopped trusting David. I thought if I threatened his chances he'd be ruthless. But he was tied to me; he couldn't get rid of me. And when I'd realised he needed me, we reached a balance.'

She was in an unusually frank mood. Simon didn't want to put her off, and only nodded. Johnnie shouted again, but she went on.

'Have you noticed the way David shows disfavour? He doesn't say anything direct; it's always something subtle, like suddenly using someone's proper name instead of the usual nickname, or leaving them out of a meeting, or seating them a long way away. He gives them the frost, and then some sanction or demotion — or it just turns out to have been a warning. When the signals are subtle like that it keeps people on edge. They watch him; they're straining all the time to read him.'

Simon hesitated. He was David's guest, and he sensed Roza wouldn't welcome criticism, no matter how freely she talked.

He said, 'He's not like that with me.'

'No, because you're not part of the team. You're family. No need for terror tactics with you. Besides, have you noticed how much he likes you?'

Simon hid his pleasure. 'I hope he does.'

'There's one particular thing about you. You're so articulate, you sound terribly educated. David loves that. He wishes he could sound like you.'

'Really?'

'Mm. Mind you, I love the way he talks. It's the only thing about him that's innocent.' She frowned, considering. 'He's really taken to Elke.'

'Oh. Yes. That's nice.' He looked away.

'He's quite delighted that Elke and Johnnie are so alike. It makes him feel as if she's related to him, because she's related to his son. Blended families are complicated, aren't they? It's strange to think someone can be related to your son but not to *you*. It's sort of counter-intuitive. So he feels a bit like her father now.'

'She's quite spoiled for fathers.'

'He could never replace you,' she said quickly. 'He just feels warm towards her. You know, protective, like he feels about Johnnie. And the other kids.'

Simon said, 'Blended families, yes, they're complicated. When I met you I had a strange feeling I loved you, because I already loved Elke. You reminded me of her, before I knew you were her mother.'

'So you felt like I was family.'

In a way, he thought. I felt like you were the mother of my child. And there were some specific rights I was missing out on . . .

'That's a funny face you're making.'

But she was talking to the boy, who'd tired of her ignoring him, and had a mouth full of water ready to squirt her.

'Don't you dare . . . oh, you horrible brat. Monstrous child. Mummy will have to *beat* and *slap* you.'

Simon thought, Everything she says to the child is satirical. She is endlessly playing a game. Does she play like that with me?

He sat in the afternoon sun watching her, the mother of the child that was his, the mother of the child that was not.

The Cock

Tuleimoka met them at the gate. 'Pathtime,' she said to Johnnie.

'I don't want a bath. I just had a swim.'

'You need a path to get the chlorine off.'

'Don't want the chlorine noff. Make Soon talk!'

'Just a minute, Tulei,' Roza said, waving the nanny away and walking ahead with the boy. 'Right, let's finish off quick . . .'

At the castle, preparations were made for battle, supplies were laid in and weapons were polished, and then the friends waited. They would have no idea where their next battle was to take place until the Ort Cloud had arrived from the Universe.

After three days of waiting Soon got bored and challenged Starfish to a duel, to which Starfish said with dignity, "Don't be silly, Soon."

The Green Lady's man, Crackers, got into the Bachelor's bedside drinks cabinet when the Cassowaries weren't looking and stole a powerful liqueur that made him so drunk he had to be locked in the castle dungeon. The Bachelor, who had been following the Green Lady about as usual, was outraged to find he couldn't offer her a cocktail, and demanded that Crackers be banished. Soon said that if Starfish wouldn't fight a duel he was a poof, and then there was a crack of purple lightning and the Ort Cloud appeared in the sky to tell the friends that his Wife had met with BarbieYah, and had been plotting to take over his realm. He would need help in battling his greatest adversary, the poisonous, violent purple cloud he had once called My Jewel and Most Beloved Wife . . .

'OK. Tulei?'

The child was led away, Tulei saying musically, 'Don't you be naughty poy.'

Roza frowned after them. 'The woman has a mania for cleanliness. Isn't that out of fashion now? Aren't we supposed to let children be dirty?'

'Mm. Germs are good,' Simon said.

'Tell her that. She wants to *disinfect* him.'

Simon was glad to have a break from 'the friends' (he was starting to think of Soon as quite a nuisance), and was hoping Roza would go on talking to him in the frank way she had before, down at the pool. But they found the full company assembled at the tables under the pohutukawa tree. Troy and Shane were tending to the snacks and drinks, Karen and Juliet had returned from a trip to town, Ed was holding a drink and a phone and was texting while he talked to the ladies, and David was standing off to the side conferring with the Cock. The Cock's wife now appeared on the deck, in conversation with Trent.

David and the Cock settled their private discussion and sat down.

'It's a matter of managing the optics,' the Cock said.

'Set up your working group,' David said. 'Get the people you want on it, maybe Dame Maud Spalding, then when they bring out their dire report, move in and fix up the disaster. But less radically than they recommend, right?'

'Dame Maud's already on two working groups. She's booked solid. Legal aid, welfare reform. Prisons.'

'Well, who else is as useful as her? You can find someone.'

The Cock said, 'We need to discuss the other thing. The emergency recovery legislation. The latitude that allows us. If we're really bold.'

David nodded. They started talking about the floods in Queensland.

The Cock's wife came across the lawn to kiss Roza. 'I've been talking to your Trent. Where do you get such sexy help? Is there a Sexy Help Shop?'

Simon thought of the thing he'd heard Claire say about men: sometimes it just takes *one thing*. They say *one thing* and you know you'd never go out with them.

Karen said, 'They're pretty gorgeous, Roza's polo-shirt brigade.'

Ed Miles leaned over to her and whispered, 'I don't think they're interested in women of *your* age.'

Karen gave him a startled look and turned away.

The Cock's wife was celebrated for being the mother of twins, a patron of the arts and a beauty. The other big thing about Sharon Cahane was that she 'didn't take herself too seriously'. She sat down, accepted a drink from Troy, and beamed at the Cock, who looked back steadily.

'We got stuck in a traffic jam. What a fuss *he* made. He sat in the back making threats at the driver. I've never known anyone as impatient as my husband. He nearly blew a valve.'

The Cock was expressionless. 'I was perfectly calm,' he said.

'There must have been an accident, but he's saying he wants the roads cleared, he wants heads to roll.'

'I have no idea what my wife is talking about,' said the Cock.

'Mate, you could have choppered up here,' David said.

'What would have been the optics of *that*?' Roza said.

The Cock smiled. 'Indeed.'

Sharon said, 'Roza, Juliet, Karen, I've been meaning to say I want you to come to my book group. We're going to have it at Trish's as soon as she's ready — something to cheer her up. Trish doesn't actually read the books, she just likes a laugh. Poor Trish.'

There was a respectful silence.

Juliet said, 'It was an amazing funeral.'

'Wasn't it amazing?'

'And Trish is being amazingly brave.'

'She's an amazing woman.'

'My wife spends her life in a state of astonishment,' said the Cock. 'If she's not amazed, she's stunned. If something isn't unbelievable, it's incredible. If my life were full of such extremes I might die of shock.'

Sharon tapped her long nails on her glass.

'Listen to him.'

'He's off.'

'*Anyway . . .*'

The Cock turned to David. 'On a lighter note, Vince Buckley wants us to talk about suicides.'

'Why?'

'The Chief Coroner wants suicides to be publicised, and Buckley's taken up the cry. More people kill themselves each year than die on the roads. He wants us to discuss it.'

'Wants who to discuss it?'

'The community. The punters. He wants prevention campaigns. Like for the road toll.'

David finished his drink and rattled his glass at Troy. 'Doesn't that mean everyone gets obsessed with it and more and more people do it?'

'Like lemmings,' Karen said.

'Thanks, Troy, another please. I suppose like lemmings. Sort of. Anyway, car crashes are accidents. Why should we stand in the way if someone actually *wants* to die?'

The Cock laughed. His eyes were intelligent, his expression was alert, and when his eye fell on people they tended to squirm. The big thing about the Cock was that he was the brains. (David was the brains but also the charm.) The Cock was tall and solid, with symmetrical features, narrow eyes and a thin, hoarse voice. It was said that he wanted David's job, but didn't have the support, since voters and many in the party found him frightening. He had wide and intimidating interests, including a fondness for Norse mythology. He had a degree from Harvard as well as from Auckland University; he was supposed to have extraordinary financial prescience; and was more right wing than it was advisable for the party to reveal. His preferred tone, when selling unpopular policies, was one of hypnotic blandness. He specialised in creating what they called 'a mood for change' — this involved manipulating the public into demanding the very measures he and David had planned to foist on them all along.

Simon always felt wary, as if he had something to hide, when the Cock was around. Karen was repelled by his smoothness and quite frightened of him.

'Suicides. Vince Buckley is a complete arsehole,' David said.

'But he's *our* arsehole,' the Cock replied.

'He's *your* arsehole.'

'He's an arsehole we're all saddled with.'

'Oh please,' Sharon called out. 'Do you mind?'

'Who is that lovely creature?' the Cock said.

'Isn't she,' David said with pride. They watched as Elke crossed the lawn on her way to the beach.

The Cock said, 'My, how she's grown. She doesn't look like you, Roza, but she's very like you. It's the way she moves.'

'How observant,' Roza said.

'She's conscious of being looked at but she's not going to show it,' the Cock added with a little flourish, as Elke disappeared down the path between the hedges. Simon took note: the Cock had uncharacteristically shown his hand. He wanted to impress Roza.

Roza gave him a gracious smile.

David said, 'Bravo, Cahane.' The Cock registered the mocking tone. He caught Simon's eye and stared for a moment, as though coldly weighing up whether he mattered.

The group broke up before dinner. Karen disappeared, and Juliet and Sharon went off with the young Miles children. David took the Cock and Ed Miles into his office, and Simon and Roza were left alone.

He said, 'The Cock's wife's very animated.'

Roza paced nervously. 'Good God, I can hardly stand it. Let's walk somewhere. The High Priestess has got Johnnie; she'll be fumigating and delousing him, so I've got nothing to do until dinner. Let's walk along the beach.'

'We haven't got much time.'

'I can't stand the insipid talk; I feel caged.'

Simon said, 'Cahane's always interesting.'

'He's too interesting.'

'He likes you.'

Roza paused. 'He does. I suddenly thought that, just now.'

'And David noticed, and then Cahane was irritated. No, disconcerted.'

'Yes! I thought all that too. The Cock's wife is so vacuous. Thank God you're here. You're not vacuous.' She added, 'You and Karen, I mean.'

'It's lucky you and Karen get on so well.'

She stopped pacing. 'What do you actually mean by that?'

'Nothing. Just what I said. It's great that you're friends.'

'You were being sarcastic.'

He tried to fend her off. 'I'm just tired, that's all, and then I had this great whack of gin on an empty stomach. Trent makes it like rocket fuel. Sorry.'

'I rely on you to be honest,' she said.

He reacted to her imperious tone. 'Really. Are *you* completely honest?'

'Of course.'

'Well, that's all right then.'

She planted her hands on her hips. 'Are you saying I'm not?'

'No, I'm not saying that.'

She said, 'Karen and I get on extremely well, which is lovely for Elke's sake.'

'Yes.'

'It's Elke who matters. And Johnnie, who now has a big sister.'

'Yes. Roza, don't be so intense; I just made a throwaway remark. It's nothing.'

'And you and I matter. If I didn't have you to talk to I'd go insane. Sometimes I think if I have to hear about another book group or charity lunch or fundraising dinner I'll start screaming.'

'You need to work out how to live.'

She laughed, to his relief. 'I do. What do you recommend?'

'Work. Hard exercise. Reading. Plenty of sunlight. A good diet.'

'Oh, if it were that simple.'

'It *is* that simple. Or rather, that's all there is. That's it, that's life. And sometimes you find, to your surprise, that you're happy. But don't expect to be happy all the time.'

'*I live in a world I didn't make.*'

'Exactly. You're not the only one who's had to work out how to live. Y'know when you were having your crisis over Elke, I had a few problems too.' The gin was hot in his stomach and he felt tipsy. 'If I tell you something, will you promise not to tell Karen, or anyone? It's important.'

Roza clasped her hands satirically. 'I swear.'

He hesitated, looked around. 'Back then I was depressed — I now think I was clinically depressed — and I did something crazy. I had an affair.'

'Simon! How intriguing.'

'But it wasn't just any old affair — it was with someone so unsuitable I can hardly believe it.'

'Unsuitable?'

'She was . . . not only an ex-patient, although from a long time before, but she was really, um . . .'

'What?'

'She was . . . young and impecunious.'

'You mean she had no money?'

'Yes. Poor, no education, no prospects.'

'Was she attractive?'

'Extremely. But she lived in a sort of chaos . . . in a ramshackle house and . . .' He broke off with an embarrassed laugh. 'It was in South Auckland.'

'South Auckland!'

'I met her at the airport. She worked in a café there. I recognised her because she'd been a patient years before.'

Roza laughed. 'It sounds like Forster, *Howard's End* — where the respectable Miss Schlegel has an affair with the lower-class Mr Bast. Everyone said to Forster, "You'll have to change the plot. A person of Miss Schlegel's class would *never* have an affair with a lower-class man." But Forster refused to change it. Because it was the whole point.'

'He probably knew it *could* happen. God,' Simon looked around uneasily, 'I can't believe we're having this conversation. You'll keep it secret, won't you? I can trust you?'

'Of course you can.'

He said, tense: 'In *Howard's End*, do they live happily ever after?'

'No. It's complicated. Actually Mr Bast gets crushed by a falling bookcase.'

'Right. Because I'll tell you something else. Now I'm past it, I wish I hadn't done it. I sometimes think if there was a button I could push that would eliminate her, I'd push it.'

'That's horrible.'

'There's nothing as horrible as wanting to escape from yourself. From the things you've done. I only had the affair because I was in a low state. I wasn't myself.'

'But it's brutal, to want to "push a button and eliminate her".'

'Yes. It's cruel. But you want me to be honest, remember? I feel revulsion for the whole thing. I'd sunk. I was drowning.'

'But she wouldn't see it that way.'

'No. She probably thought she was raising herself up.'

She stared at him. 'It *is* cruel.'

'That's what happens when the haves get with the have-nots. The centre cannot hold.'

Roza frowned. 'You could have stayed together, out of, you know, love.'

'Love? She was completely uneducated. But there's more. When I first met her, all that time before, she was brought into the hospital, in labour, with an escort. A prison guard. She'd been arrested for a drug offence. We had the affair years later, after she got out of jail.'

'I don't believe this.' Roza wasn't laughing now. 'Jail. And she has a child?'

'It had died by the time I met her again.'

'Died! God, Simon. Is there anything else?'

'No, that's it. The child died naturally, according to her — of meningitis.'

Roza said, 'Why are you telling me this now? She's not around, is she? Not a nuisance?'

'No . . . but she exists. She's out there.'

'Does she make contact?'

He held back from mentioning the stranger's phone call. 'I haven't talked to her for years. I shouldn't have told you all this. You'll keep it a secret, won't you? It would be a disaster if anyone found out. We have to think of Elke.'

'Elke?'

'I mean, the children, the family, Karen. And I don't want David hearing about something like this.'

'Oh yes, we all need to stick together,' she said in a distant voice. She bit her thumbnail, thinking.

'Roza, you won't tell him?'

'Of course not. Think of all my secrets. I know about shame. I was a disgraceful addict, remember? I know how it is. Your whole self recoils at the thought of going back. You hate the thing that brought you low, and the people you met while you were down there. Don't worry, I'm your friend; I'm your fan; I love you. And you're right — we have to think of the children.'

'Do you really love me?'

She squeezed his arm. 'Poor Simon, you've gone all bleak and crushed. Of course I do.'

Talking about Mereana had increased his anxiety, but Roza had switched abruptly to her old playful tone. Every answer she gave would be joking and ironic, and it would be impossible to know what she really thought.

She went off to rescue Johnnie from the nanny. Simon walked over to the Little House to shower and change. He found clothes strewn over the floor and Karen lying on the bed, staring at the ceiling and looking inexplicably bleak.

Revulsion

'What is it, my jewel?'

But Simon realised he'd just imitated Roza as 'the Bachelor' in her endless Soon stories. He cleared his throat. 'I mean, what's wrong?'

Karen turned on her side. 'I hate, I *loathe* Ed Miles.'

'I thought all you ladies found him amusing and nice-looking and stylish.'

'He's horrible.'

'Well, I've always wondered what you saw in him.'

'He insulted me. It was so unexpected. He made a comment about my age, which was rather bitchy, now I think back. But then, as we were all getting up he leaned over to me and whispered, so no one else would hear . . .'

'What?'

'First he looked sort of pointedly between me and Roza and Sharon, to show he was comparing us, I suppose because they're both so tall and thin and stylish. And then he whispered, "Of course, Karen, that shirt is the most unflattering thing you could possibly wear, with your curves."'

Simon sat down on the bed. 'Christ.'

'He'd know I'd never repeat it to Roza, because you don't want to repeat an insult, do you? And you don't want to make trouble. It was so sneaky. I thought, boy, you really don't like me.'

She blew her nose. Her face was flushed and her hair was all on end. He thought of the care she'd taken that morning getting dressed. He'd been bored by her going on about some new outfit; now she seemed only innocent and harmless, and humiliated. The new shirt was crumpled on the floor.

He lay down beside her. 'Don't even think about it, darling. You're right; he wouldn't dare let Roza hear that. She'd despise him. Whispering and bitchiness, and about *clothes* of all things; it's so petty, it's beneath contempt.'

He stroked her shoulder. 'I suppose he's got some idea of divide and rule, among the ladies. Just ignore him. He's tried to hurt you, so don't let him see he's succeeded.'

'But I was so disconcerted, I rushed off. I think the others wondered why I'd gone and were a bit disapproving, as if I'd been rude to Sharon.'

'They wouldn't have even noticed.'

'It's weird to be insulted out of the blue by someone who's supposed to be a friend . . . by a man . . . and so personally insulted. I know I'm not beautiful and slim and fashionable like Sharon and Roza but I try . . . And I'd been enjoying myself. And I'd thought my clothes looked all right and then I felt like a fool . . .'

He lay beside her and said soothing things. He supposed the Police Minister played dirty in every sphere, out of habit, but still, it was a warning not to be too relaxed at Rotokauri. He thought how frank he'd just been with Roza.

The TV at the end of the bed was on without sound, a shot of Julian Assange in front of a crowd, reading a statement about WikiLeaks. The ticker at the bottom of the screen announced record low temperatures and blizzards in the United States, travellers stranded, six thousand flights cancelled. A snow scene. Above it, the window was a rectangle of cloudless blue summer sky.

Karen sat up, clenching her fists. 'So now I know he doesn't like me. What if he tries to damage my friendship with Roza?'

'He can't.'

'I have to be friends with Roza. If we fell out, she might take Elke away.'

He said, 'But I thought—' He stopped himself and didn't say what he'd always assumed: that Roza had cynically befriended innocent Karen in order to keep Elke close.

'You thought what?'

'Nothing. Just that Elke's pretty much grown up these days, and she adores you. No one can take her away from you.'

Karen lay back down.

'Everything's all right,' he said. 'Roza and Juliet love you. Roza would have no idea you worry about Elke; she's just pleased we're all friends. Enjoy the rest of the holiday. We'll be back in town soon, and then you won't see Ed.'

She sighed. 'I do love you.'

'I love you too.' He put his arms around her. 'Now, I'm feeling very knackered, and pissed from Trent's gins, and we'll have to sit across the table from Ed and act nice.'

'Oh God. What am I going to wear?'

'Wear the shirt! You look lovely in it.'

'Shall I? Do you know, I think I will. I mean, he's no oil painting himself, is he?'

'That's the spirit.'

She said, 'Claire's gone back to the city — she's got a party to go to. She managed not to offend anyone, thank God.'

'Ah, they can stand a bit of offending.'

'I dread the thought of her having a go at David. He hasn't forgiven her for that spiel about "third-world diseases". Although I don't think she got far; he just fixed her with his death stare. Anyway, she left this.

We've been trying it out.' She showed him a sheet of paper.

'A Kessler score. Why'd she give you that?'

'I suppose they're looking at them at med school. I think she wanted to prove I'm insane. She's always telling me I am. Anyway, I did the questionnaire and guess what? Not a hint of mental illness. Not a speck of anxiety. Totally normal.'

'I'm not really surprised, darling.'

'Aren't you?'

'No. You're as solid as a rock.'

'Claire was disappointed. Anyway, let's try it on you.'

'No, let's not.'

But she insisted, following him around with the questionnaire while he showered and got changed and he answered the questions, too tired and distracted to be untruthful.

She added up his score.

'Ah,' she said with delight, 'you're mentally ill!'

'I am not. Give me that.'

'Look, count it up: "indicates mild mental illness". It's the bits about lying awake at night that put you over the limit. And being often restless and unable to rest or keep still. And the one about sometimes feeling nervous.'

'It's too extreme. This would make everyone mildly mentally ill.'

'Not me. Nor Elke. She's completely sane too. And Juliet, would you believe. Claire says it's a reliable clinical tool.'

'Claire. What does she know.'

Karen laughed. 'So, mentally ill, eh. My mentally unwell husband.'

'Oh, bollocks.'

They got dressed and went to dinner. On the way through the garden Simon urged her, without much hope, not to sulk or show hurt with Ed. Any black looks or pouting or attempts to hit back would be a mistake.

He would have liked to snub Ed, but he concealed his distaste. Karen made sure she sat next to Elke, and he heard her suggest a trip into town the next day, to which Elke agreed. Simon could tell Ed was watching them. Sly, predatory operator that he was, he must have noticed Karen was slightly embattled. He was programmed to home in on weakness and exploit it. Simon was bothered by the suggestion he'd initially dismissed, that Ed might do her some damage with Roza.

But Karen was rising to the challenge. She talked about the Kessler test and how she and Elke had proven to be completely sane. She didn't mention Simon's score, only looked across at him and grinned.

The young people finished their dinner and went off, led by Marcus, to watch a movie, and Karen managed to draw David and Roza into a conversation that left Ed out. Then she and Roza and Sharon disappeared upstairs, leaving Juliet with the men. Juliet was disconcerted at being excluded from the party upstairs, and said she was going to her room to read.

Karen had given no hint she was offended. It was smoothly done and left Simon wondering when his open, straightforward wife had learned to be so guarded.

Ed wandered over to Simon. David and the Cock had gone onto the lawn to smoke cigars. They were pacing slowly towards the pool, smoke billowing over their shoulders.

'They're plotting,' Simon said.

'No doubt,' said Ed.

'You're not invited to join in?'

Ed smiled. 'My work is done today.'

'Oh, right. The world of policing's all in order.'

'They could be discussing any number of things. Personally, I've knocked off for the day. We were discussing social housing all afternoon.'

Simon said spiritlessly, 'How to have less of it.'

Ed said, 'How to harness aspiration.'

'Harness aspiration. You mean making people fend for themselves.'

Ed smiled. '*Helping* people fend for themselves.'

'Helping them? Don't you just mean telling them to get on with it, and letting them rot if they can't manage?'

'Exactly. Harnessing aspiration.'

They both laughed.

'David grew up poor . . .' Simon said.

'But he harnessed his aspiration.'

Simon thought of Roza. He quoted, 'You hate the thing that brought you low, and the people you met while you were down there.'

Ed said, 'What's that mean?'

'Do you think David has a revulsion to the poor?'

Ed held up his glass. 'David has a revulsion to *failure*.'

'Not a revulsion to *failures*? With an s? You know what they say: he's one of those people who's used the social ladder then kicked it away from the ones behind.'

'Certainly not. We are not the party that kicks away the ladder. We supply the ladder of aspiration. What we say to people is: You make life happen. Don't wait for life to happen to you.'

'That's excellent, that is.'

'Thank you.'

'I propose a toast,' Simon said, 'to the Ladder of Aspiration.' They raised their glasses and clinked them together. They were both quite drunk.

He climbed the stairs. He didn't usually venture into this upper part of the main house, where the Hallwrights lived. But David had asked him to find Roza. David and the Cock were now quite drunk too, and Ed had taken over from Troy and was mixing them a round of his special cocktails. Sharon and Karen had gone to bed, and David said he and the Cock couldn't settle the dispute they were having unless they consulted Roza.

He followed the sound of her voice. She was in Johnnie's room and the little boy was sitting up in bed. His night light was a glowing planet Earth, casting blue shadows on the walls.

Simon suppressed an impatient sigh, listened.

The Bachelor brewed one of his most complex nightcaps and, not wishing to be disturbed by his jealous Cassowaries, gave them each a sip of his potion, sending them into a deep sleep. Then he set off to find the Green Lady. But when he got to her jewelled tent, intending to ply her with strong drink while reading her his finest poems, he was disappointed; the object of his greatest hopes was inside the castle with the Ort Cloud, where an important conference was taking place. A spy had reported that the Ort Cloud's Wife and Barbie Yah were amassing their own forces, and were planning a devastating attack. The battle would take place on the western plain, possibly as soon as the following morning, and the Ort Cloud's Wife had made a vow: this time she would finish off her husband, kill his friends, and take any survivors to be her slaves.

The Bachelor, followed by Soon and Starfish, suavely entered the conference room.

"Dear Lady," he said, brandishing his bottle, "I will fight alongside you. To the death if necessary. Perhaps a light snifter before we prepare?"

The Green Lady rolled her eyes.

Soon and Starfish had sneaked in and were now hiding behind the curtains. They'd been missing since the afternoon, when their tutor, the High Priestess Germphobia, had announced they needed a bath, and had come after them armed with soap and scrubbing brushes. They'd been forced to take refuge in the Idiots' Village, and then in the forest . . .

Simon said, 'David wants you.'

Johnnie glared. 'Make Soon talk.'

'Bed. Tomorrow a terrible battle will ensue.'

'Make Soon talk.'

Roza ignored him and came out onto the landing.

'The Cock's drinking cocktails,' Simon said.

'I don't see why I should go down.' She went to the window. 'Look at the moon.'

He followed her onto the balcony. She said, 'I was thinking. You didn't tell me *why* you had an affair with someone so unlike you, so unsuitable. You could have had an affair in your own circle.'

Because I was in love with you. Because you can only do so much looking before you have to go and burn it off.

'I don't know,' he said.

'Oh go on, I want to know.'

He said, reluctant, 'I was depressed, and she offered me comfort, and we became friends. I wanted some uncomplicated love and warmth. And then after I'd recovered myself, I didn't need her any more.'

'You used her and threw her aside.'

He said steadily, 'Yeah. I took the comfort she offered me. I recovered myself. And after that the mere thought of her became repugnant and shameful.'

Roza raised her chin. 'Are you showing me how cold and hard you are, or are you flagellating yourself?'

'I'm just answering your questions.'

'I think you feel guilty.'

He shrugged. 'She was twenty-eight and quite tough. She could look after herself.'

'Didn't you get uncomplicated love and warmth from Karen?'

He said sharply, 'Am I allowed to ask about you and David?'

She smiled. 'You could try.'

'Karen and I were going through a bad patch. I was head of obstetrics at the hospital, under pressure, a heavy workload, constant night shifts. I was in a state of depression and . . . you know, she said to me, "We're friends." She was a good friend; she was very direct, straightforward, kind. I was touched. Grateful.'

'You *do* feel guilty.'

'No. It was grotesque. You know what you said, you hate the thing that brought you low and the people you met while you were down there.'

'What if she turned up now?'

'I don't know where she is or what her circumstances are, which means I have no idea whether to expect to see her or not.'

Roza yawned. 'Ah, you'll never see her again.'

'I didn't tell you . . .' He paused, debating whether to go on. 'When I said she disappeared, I meant she *actually* disappeared, from her work, her house, everything. I got the idea something bad might have happened to her.'

'Why?'

'Because she vanished suddenly, after I'd told her I couldn't see her any more. No one at her work knew where she'd gone. Her house was just empty one day, with stuff left behind. I was glad she was gone. But at the same time I thought, if something bad's happened, then people might start looking for her.'

'And then they might find you.'

'Exactly.'

'But you've done nothing wrong.'

'Nothing wrong! What about cheating on my wife?'

'Oh well, there's that.' She was thoughtful now, studying his expression. 'You must have looked for her, to know she was gone.'

'I went back one more time.'

'Why?'

'I felt sorry for her.'

'You could try to find out where she is.'

'The last thing I want to do is find her.'

'But do you think it might be a good idea to try? So you're sort of forewarned?'

'No. I don't think so.'

He still couldn't bring himself to mention the phone call from the stranger.

Roza said, 'There are some things in my past — I suppose this might be so with lots of people — where I don't know what really happened. I was in such a hurry to move on and change my life that there are quite a few lost threads. Not knowing and not finding out is part of moving on. But still, you think about it sometimes; there are these narratives that were cut off, questions you'll never answer.'

'Best to keep going forward.'

'Just so long as nothing happens to drag you back.'

He said, 'Are you trying to torture me?'

'What do you mean?'

'Nothing.' *Weeks. Arthur Weeks . . .*

She went on, 'Still, some people would say *I* disappeared. And I didn't want to be found. Your friend might be the same.'

'Maybe. We'd better go down. They'll wonder what we're doing.'

'One more thing. You say you were depressed.'

'I was working too hard. Arguments at home. Nothing interesting.'

'Is that the only reason?'

'Well, I'd met you, and I couldn't work out what it was about you that I recognised. It was because you resembled Elke, but I didn't think of that at first. You must admit, it was a weird situation.'

'You used to sort of stare at me,' she said.

'I was trying to work it out.'

'You used to stare as if you had a crush. David noticed.'

He said coldly, 'Sorry about that. But like I said, it was a strange situation.'

'You used to stare at Elke, too.'

Her eyes were very bright.

'Is that right? And now *David* stares at her.'

She blinked. 'Only because she looks like Johnnie.'

'But he looks right through Claire.'

There was a hard silence between them. Then she smiled, 'We're friends because we can talk about things like this. We shouldn't have any secrets between us. Promise?' She leaned forward and kissed him on the cheek.

He closed his eyes. 'Yes, sure.'

But what was he promising?

Weeks

Simon made a resolution: he would work on his mental health. He went for a long run out to the Kauri Lake, lay by the pool with his novel, and made sure he didn't drink too much in the evening. He played some strenuous games of tennis with Marcus, which knackered him more than he admitted to the boy, although they were fairly evenly matched. Like Roza, he would try to find a way to live. To look after the body was the plan — look after the body and the mind will improve.

Instead of getting out of bed at dawn he tried to sleep in, and his tossing and turning woke Karen and led to a satisfactory encounter there in the tousled bed, with the early light shining through the slatted blinds of the Little House and the tuis warbling in the trees outside.

Afterwards they lay in the striped light. Karen said, 'David's got himself a personal trainer.'

'What about Garth?'

'Garth's Roza's. You've got to have your own, or it's not personal. David's hired one called Dean. He came yesterday.'

'What, in a crate I suppose.'

'He took David for a full session. Weights. Running.'

Simon yawned and stretched. 'He'll have to go easy. David never does any exercise at all.'

Karen said, 'He's written David a programme, and told him what they need to work on. And he said David specially needs . . .' She pressed her lips together.

'What?'

'He said he needs a bigger bum.'

'A bigger bum?'

'Bigger muscles there, I suppose. Anyway, he has plans to enlarge it somehow.'

'Are there special exercises?'

Karen snorted, 'Garth, on the other hand, is working on making Roza's bum smaller.'

'Mm. Meanwhile, does David actually *want* a bigger bum?'

They lazed about until it got too hot, and then wandered down to the beach. Simon thought, It's good to slow down. To live in the moment . . .

It was a fine, hot day, with no wind and the waves breaking evenly along the shore. They swam out and looked back at the Wedding Cake, its glass windows reflecting the sea. The flag hung limp on its pole. A convoy of cars was making its way along the coast road.

After the swim, Karen went off with Roza, Juliet, Sharon and Ray to a café in the town centre and he wandered up to change. At the Little House his cell phone was signalling a missed call. There was no message. He checked; it was the number of the stranger who'd asked about Mereana.

If he ignored the calls, the man might give up. But would he start asking questions elsewhere?

He retrieved the number from his call log and rang it.

'It's Simon Lampton,' he said. 'You rang me?'

'Dr Lampton. Thanks for calling back,' Arthur Weeks said. 'I wanted to ask you about Mereana Kostas.'

'I'm sorry, I'm not in my office at the moment. What was the name?'

'Mereana Kostas. I think you know her.'

'I don't. What's this about?'

'I thought you knew her.'

'No, I don't know anyone of that name, unless she's a patient, but I have hundreds and of course I'd need to know what you . . . ?'

'She's not a patient.'

'I don't know her.'

'Can I meet you?'

'What for?'

'Your number's in her cell phone, listed under "Simon".'

Simon ducked, involuntarily. He waited, then said, 'Well, she might have been a patient at some stage, but I can't discuss patients obviously.'

'I'm trying to find her address.'

'Can't help, sorry.'

'There's a photo of you in her phone.'

Silence.

'A photo . . . How do you know what I look like?'

'Google Images. In the picture you're laughing and reaching towards the camera. You look happy.'

Simon closed his eyes. 'How do you come to have this person's cell phone?'

'She left it behind. Can I meet you?'

'But why? What's your interest? Who are you?'

'I'm a journalist, and I guess a film-maker.'

'Christ,' Simon said.

'I could give you the phone.'

'Why would I want it? I don't . . . I don't . . . Oh . . . I suppose . . .' Another silence. 'You could give me the phone? But I have no interest . . . I'll be at my rooms later today, I have a clinic. But there's no point, since I don't know anything.'

Weeks said, 'Great. I'll see you then.' He hung up.

Simon washed his face. He raised his head and looked in the mirror. Every year that had passed since he'd last seen Mereana had made him feel safer, more sure that he would never hear from her again. But this didn't need to be complicated. All he had to do was deny knowing her, get the guy to give him the phone and then throw it away.

On his way to the car he met Roza dressed for the pool in a towel and flip-flops, with a pair of sporty goggles on her head. Behind her came Tuleimoka and Johnnie, hand in hand.

'Hello,' she said. 'Karen tells me you're mentally ill.'

'She's spreading it around, is she?'

'And that *she's* completely sane.'

'She's thrilled to imagine that I'm nuts.'

'Well, take care of yourself. You're on a knife edge.'

'Thanks, darling.'

'Hurry back!' She kissed his cheek. 'Take your medication.' She turned to frown at Tuleimoka, who was now instructing Johnnie on the importance of wearing shoes.

'We didn't get up early enough,' she whispered. 'Now we've got the Priestess in tow.'

'Pecause in the ground, in the tirt, there are tirty things,' Tuleimoka was saying.

'Oh, for God's sake.' Roza rolled her eyes. 'Is it only for the day? Do hurry back.'

He drove south until the city appeared ahead of him, its blocks and spikes ranged against the cloudless blue. Crossing the bridge he looked down at the marina, at the hundreds of white-rigged masts jinking and clinking in the breeze. He liked the alien quality of the city during the few weeks of summer holiday, when the streets and buildings became a hot, empty, concrete landscape — a different place.

The radio played him the news, a string of curiosities from far away:

extreme cold weather had damaged pipes in Ireland, leaving thousands of people without running water; Israeli rabbis' wives had issued a public letter warning Israeli women not to form relationships with Arab men — such marriages would lead to beatings and humiliation, they advised . . .

He headed straight for the surgery, stopping to talk to his receptionist Clarice before shutting himself in his office, turning on the computer and looking out at the park, its grass all brown and withered after the long, hot summer.

Having got the idea from the stranger himself, he Googled 'Arthur Weeks' and found Weeks was a freelance writer and film-maker who'd made a trio of short films called *The Present*. He ran through a review of the films, and a posting by a blogger called Stars-In-Her-Eyes, who said they'd 'done nothing for her'. Weeks had also written a comic play about Captain Cook, it seemed, and some episodes for a local television drama. He consulted Google Images and found Arthur Weeks to be young and handsome, with dark, wavy hair, a wide mouth, an angular face and small, keen eyes. None of this helped. He tidied his desk. So much for improving his mental health — he had a stress headache.

His clinic was soon behind schedule. A young woman sat in his room with her six-week-old baby in a car seat at her feet. Her clothes were expensive and immaculate but her face was expressionless, dark circles like bruises under her eyes. He vaguely remembered the baby's birth; checked his notes for its sex, which wasn't obvious.

'How's it going?' he asked, jovial. 'He letting you get any sleep?'

'No.' She didn't look at the baby. 'He cries and whines all night.'

'They settle down after a while. Have you got yourself some advice?'

'They all tell me different things. Nothing works.'

'So . . . you might be feeling a little bit tired, a bit down?'

'No.'

'Oh good. That's the spirit.'

'Mostly I feel nothing.'

'Ah.'

'Do you remember my husband, from the birth?' She gestured at the baby, angry. 'He looks just like him. Same hair. See those black tufts, how thick they are already? They're not soft like baby hair.' Her face wrinkled with disgust.

'Right. I see . . .' *Shall we say moderately mentally ill?* He made a series of notes, glancing down at the baby, which balled its tiny hands and began to wail. The woman looked out the window and he went about making notes for a referral while the poor, unwanted kid screamed itself hoarse and the mother sat barely moving, with her numb, glassy stare.

He said gently, 'Try picking him up.'

'It won't do anything.'

He touched her sleeve. Her eyes were dark, strange, empty.

'Just try,' he said again. He smiled, tried to will life into her eyes.

Lunchtime, he went out for a sandwich at the café down the road. A young man came in after him, called out his name, offered his hand.

'Arthur Weeks. Hi,' he said. 'Buy you a coffee?'

Simon nodded and sat down. The young man ordered coffees, came back, stumbled against a chair, seemed at a loss for a moment. He sat down, coughed. 'So. It's about Mereana.'

'I don't know anything.'

The man looked sharp. 'You don't know anything, but do you know *her*?'

Simon leaned back, touching his fingertips together. 'No. Why don't you tell me about this person.'

'I've known her since I was a kid.'

Simon straightened up. 'Really?'

'You're surprised!'

'Not at all.' It was too hot in the café. 'Could we get to the point, please? I have a lot of work on today.'

'My parents had a holiday bach next to her father's land up north. We used to go every summer, and she'd be there, and we'd play on the beach, swim, go fishing. Her father was Greek; he came from Australia and married into a Maori family. They own a lot of land, including beaches, and we all used to mix every year, the Pakeha families like ours, and theirs.'

'I see.'

'So I was there this summer, and they asked me to look up Mereana when I went back to Auckland. Her parents are dead, but the rest of the family, especially these old women, these matriarch types, have wondered where she is. They never go to Auckland, so they see me as a connection. They invited me in for a cup of tea and talked about it. They suggested I drop in on an old friend of hers, a guy called Lydon, who lives in Whangarei, to see if he knew her address.

'I went to his place on my way back to Auckland. He said she'd disappeared, but that she'd left one of her phones, and he still had it. We looked through it and he knew most of the numbers, but there was yours. I rang it and got a phone message — it said the number had changed, but it gave a new number, which was the one I called you on.'

Simon cleared his throat. 'The message probably listed my number by mistake.'

'But there's the photo of you.'

'As I said, she may have been a patient, but if she was, I can't discuss her. I do make my cell phone number available to some patients, given the nature of my work.'

'Can you check if she was a patient?'

'No. And even if I did, which I won't and can't, it wouldn't locate her, would it?'

'You're an obstetrician. Was she pregnant?'

'Oh, come on.'

'Sorry — no, don't get up; I know I can't ask that. But you must admit it's strange she had a photo of you.'

'Perhaps she got it off the internet. Sometimes patients form attachments . . .' Simon felt heat rising to his face. He looked away, ashamed.

'Like a stalker? Like she was fixated on you?'

He stood up. 'This is not appropriate. I don't know this person, couldn't discuss her if I did, and I can't see what's to be gained by this.'

'But the photo's not like a press picture off the internet; it's intimate, taken by a friend. The expression, the laugh.'

Simon said, without knowing whether this was possible, 'Perhaps she got it off someone's Facebook page.'

'The picture must have been taken by the camera in the phone.'

Simon's anger was increasing. 'Let's have a look at it then,' he said.

Weeks hesitated, then took a Nokia out of his pocket. He brought up the number in the contacts, listed under Simon, and then he held up the picture of Simon laughing and reaching towards the camera, wearing a business shirt and no tie. Behind him was a wall with the weatherboards partly exposed and a blind with sunlight shafting through it, and below it on a windowsill a cigarette packet and a beer can.

She must have held up the phone and pointed at him and he'd reached for it and pulled it off her, not realising she'd taken a shot.

He looked; he was silenced. It was impossible to explain away that background — the beer can and the cigarette packet and the weatherboards and the shabby blind. Anyone who knew him would see it was not his house, and not the kind of house his friends owned. He was back in the room with the afternoon sun and Mereana lying on the couch with her feet propped up, swigging on her beer, teasing him.

'Her friend Lydon told me that's her house in the picture.'

Simon reached, but Weeks pulled away.

'You said you'd give it to me.'

Weeks put the phone in his pocket. He held up his hands. 'Show it. I said I'd show it to you.'

'You said you'd *give* it. That's why I agreed to meet you.'

There was a silence. Simon considered wrenching open the jacket and grabbing the phone, but it was impossible, the café was full of people.

Weeks said, 'So why do you want it? If you don't know her?'

'You've got me curious about it myself. There's no photo of *you* in there, is there? Maybe I've got more right to it than you have. Why shouldn't I try to find out why she had my photo? And you don't know it was this Mereana person who took the picture — anyone could have taken it.'

Weeks said, 'I'll help you find out. I like mysteries. And if you truly don't know her it, *is* a mystery, isn't it.'

'It's her phone, her business.'

'I like other people's business. I'm a journalist. I'm always looking for material. Anyway, Mereana's an old friend.' His tone softened. 'You know, she's got the most amazing dark skin and green eyes — because her mother was Maori and her father was Greek. She's really striking. I was in love with her from when I was about twelve. I was always trying to get her to kiss me. She's clever . . .'

Simon thought of her, on a beach, aged twelve. Something bad went through him, the thought of Weeks trying to kiss her. He said, cold, 'Where is this bach, your parents' bach near her land?'

'In the Far North, beyond Kaitaia.'

'Do your parents still go there?'

'Yeah, sure, about four times a year.'

Simon was silent. Mereana had told him about her father hitting golf balls into the sand dunes, about a little house so close to the beach they could fish from the front veranda.

Weeks went on, 'I write for *Metro, North and South*. I've written a couple of things for TV. And I've made some short films. One I made last year's going to Sundance.'

'Give me the phone,' Simon said.

Weeks looked up quickly. 'You *do* know her.'

'What if I do? Why is it your business?'

'Because she's disappeared. People are looking for her.'

'Not very seriously, by the sound of it.'

'So, should they file a missing person's report?'

Simon said, 'Most people are just living their own lives. They don't want to be disturbed. You say she was always escaping from you. Maybe you should leave her alone. Maybe you're stalking her. Is that why she's disappeared?'

'I'm not stalking her.'

'Are you stalking *me*?'

'No. Honestly, they asked me to find her address. I'm just doing what they asked.'

'Well, I've got work to do.'

Weeks said, 'I'll write down my details, in case you think of anything. Give me a call, any time.'

He wrote numbers on a scrap of paper. 'Sorry to have bothered you.' He took a DVD out of his pocket. 'Can I give you this too? Three of my short films. I made these a while ago now, four, five years. I based one of the characters on Mereana.'

'Sure.' Simon took it and tried to smile.

'By the way,' Weeks said, 'I've read about your adopted girl, how she's the daughter of Roza Hallwright. So you're quite closely connected to the PM.'

Simon looked at him.

'That's so interesting.' Weeks's grin was eager, slightly buck-toothed.

'Is it.' Simon turned away.

Back in his office, there was no chance of concentrating now. He did what work he could, mechanically, before driving home to check on the house, which he found all in order, and Claire diligently studying in an upstairs room. He talked to her for a while to satisfy himself she was all right — he worried about her — and then set off to drive back to Rotokauri.

He frowned ahead at the road — and his frown felt impossibly weighty. He was oppressed by a feeling of confusion. He thought of Weeks's description of Mereana as 'clever' and 'beautiful', the wistful mention of her on the beach aged twelve. He recalled the photo of himself, laughing and reaching towards the camera. 'You look happy,' Weeks had said. But he knew nothing, the presumptuous little bastard. Simon hadn't been 'happy' back then, he'd been desperate. The very details of the picture showed the wrongness and squalor of the affair — the shabby backdrop, the beer can and fag packet.

He had recovered himself; he was back in the real world, and that was where he would stay. This sentimental busybody, this Weeks, would have to be kept at bay.

Training

Roza said, 'I've got to do my session with Garth.'

'I don't like Darth.'

'Garth. What's wrong with him?'

'He's got a big chest.'

'That's because he lifts weights.'

'He's got big tits.'

'Don't say "big tits", it's rude. He has big muscles.'

'Make Soon talk.'

'God! Can't we just be Mummy and Johnnie for a while?'

'Make Soon talk!'

Roza lay on her back on the sand, with Johnnie sprawled next to her.

Soon and Starfish, who along with the Village Idiot had avoided the High Priestess Germphobia by taking refuge in the forest, now came out of hiding and joined the Green Lady in front of the castle. All the friends were assembled; the Weta and the Praying Mantis struck up a battle tune; Crackers had sobered up; the Bachelor and his Cassowaries were mounted on his bed and hovering above the trees, the Cassowaries gaudily decorated in battle feathers and hissing threateningly; and the Red Herring and his colleague, Tiny Ancient Yellow Cousin So-on, had climbed onto a tree stump to address the troops with some wise words. There was a blast of shotguns as the Guatemalans arrived late in the clearing and then the Red Herring held up his hand. An expectant silence fell.

"A bird in the hand is worth two in the bush," he gravely began. A cheer went up. He went on, "A stitch in time saves nine." Another cheer. "But most of all, my friends, a cat may look at a king, and . . ." He paused and looked around the clearing, "A leopard may change its spots!" Everyone cheered, much heartened and refreshed by the Red Herring's pearls. Beside him Tiny Ancient Yellow Cousin So-on had lit some mysterious incense and an eerie, smoky scent wafted through the crowd, sending the friends into dreams of jewelled gardens. Now they would be calm and strong for battle.

Roza shaded her eyes. 'Here he comes.'

Simon looked at the cords and ropes of muscle in the trainer's neck. Garth wore a T-shirt so tight you could see his pectoral muscles twitching as he came stumping through the dunes.

Johnnie drummed his legs on the sand. 'Make Soon talk!'

'I'm going for my torture session, darling. Garth bends me into all these interesting shapes.'

'And how's it going,' Simon asked politely, 'with David's bum?'

'Mm, good, I think. Dean's got special exercises for him and a potion to drink — some kind of protein. It's probably steroids.'

'Is the bum getting any bigger?'

'Well, it's early days. Dean's very optimistic.'

Simon flopped on his back with a mirthful sigh.

'You could use Garth if you wanted, Simon. He does Karen and Juliet.'

He knew this, for that very morning he and David, eating scrambled eggs together on the veranda, had watched Karen, Juliet and Sharon Cahane lying on mats on the lawn and scissoring their legs in the air. Garth had them on a light programme: a round of exercises followed by a brisk walk to the gate, and then a warm-down, which took just as long and involved Garth lying with them on the mat and manipulating their muscles. The ladies seemed especially keen on this part. David had watched Juliet, who was wearing baggy khaki shorts and bright pink sneakers, having her plump, freckly leg stretched and pummelled by Garth, and said, 'What's he supposed to be doing to her? It's just sort of foreplay, isn't it? He's a sex tool.'

Simon had said, 'Is that what it's like with you and Dean?'

'Well, no, we don't get that close. Not yet, anyway. He stands with his hands on his hips and looks at my arse from all angles. Sort of making plans . . .'

Now, on the hot beach, Simon rolled over close to Roza and whispered, 'All that massaging and muscle-flexing — it's just sex.'

'Garth's totally professional. He has ethics. And a degree in PE. So has Dean.'

'Oh, bollocks.'

'He's doing great things for me. I'm going to have a body to die for.'

'You've got that already. Don't let him turn you into him.' He smoothed the sand with the flat of his hand. 'Anyway, what was the character's name in *Howard's End*? The lower-class one.'

'Mr Bast.'

'So the higher-born Miss Whatever falls in love with him?'

'Miss Schlegel. She has his child. She has an affair with him, because she's impulsive and a romantic and she has a sense of justice — she looks beyond class. The Miss Schlegels are a bit like Eleanor and Marianne Dashwood.'

'Oh?'

'*Sense and Sensibility.* Have you read it? No? Well, never mind. Mr Bast is rather superior, but thwarted by class.'

'Oh.'

'Why do you ask?'

Simon said, 'It's not that she just fancies the oik in him?'

'Er, no. Shall I lend you a copy?'

'Thanks, I've got a book to be going on with,' he said.

Garth reached the top of the neighbouring dune and started down the other side. His head was too small for his powerful body. There was a scalloped crease in the centre of his chest and his muscles — chest, arms, barrel-shaped thighs — were so prominent that he had a permanent air of strain, as though he might explode. He was a warning against overdoing it, Simon thought. But then, you could only look like Garth or Dean if you were twenty-four, and exercising all day long.

'Gidday, buddy,' Garth said to Johnnie.

Johnnie scowled and looked down. 'Hello.'

'Can I borrow your mum?' Winking at Roza.

'No,' Johnnie said.

'Sorry, champ. Mum's got to do her workout!'

Garth had a very small chin, Simon noted. And a big bum. He was faintly camp — with his twinkly 'buddy' and 'champ' — and amiable, and he had tight blond curls and pale, prominent blue eyes. His big arse projected his torso slightly forward. He had a habit of clenching his fists, and looked as though he should have little horns and cloven hooves. Simon reminded himself to suggest to Roza that Dean and Garth were secretly a married couple.

She was gathering towels and gear.

He said, 'My brother's coming.'

'Oh, good. Ford. I really want him to.'

'He said he'd come for a day, but I've told him he can stay in the Little House.'

'Did you tell him it's my idea? He can stay as long as he likes.'

'Yeah, I did. It's kind of you. When you've got all these extra people. Ford's . . . well, he's lonely, since Emily left him. He's a bit spiky and fierce; I hope he doesn't annoy David. He tends to be quite, you know, left wing.'

'Don't worry about that. Now Johnnie, we'll go and find Elke. She and Ray and Shaun are going to take you for an ice cream. Would that be nice?'

Johnnie brightened. 'I saw Ray's gun.'

'His gun? He didn't show it to you?'

'Yeah.'

'Oh. He shouldn't do that, should he, Simon?'

'I don't know,' Simon said, lazily watching the waves breaking into lines of pure white foam. 'What's the etiquette with guns?'

'Well, you're not supposed to wave them about. You're not supposed to brandish them. At the *children*. Um, would you mind taking this? And this? And this? ' She loaded Garth with towels, togs and a bucket and spade. 'Bye Simon. See you for lunch.'

'He lifted up his shirt,' Johnnie said.

'What about his trouser leg?' Roza said. 'I've always imagined he'd have a gun strapped to his leg, just above his boot. Shall we ask him? Are you all right, Garth? Could you just take this little one as well? And if I just pop that on the top . . .'

They went off across the dunes, Roza and Johnnie hand in hand and Garth balancing his teetering load, following a short distance behind. She would be making Soon talk.

Simon spotted Sharon and the Cock down at the water's edge, carrying swimming gear and a beach umbrella. He lay low in the dunes, watching through the marram grass as they passed by. A minute later a couple of David's bodyguards ambled past.

There was no shade. The sun was directly overhead and the hollow in the dunes grew hotter until he started to feel light-headed. He dumped his bag down on the shore and waded in, swam out beyond the waves, floating over the swells and watching the gannets diving. Sharon and the Cock were two wavering shapes in the distance; they'd gone all the way to the estuary. He swam further out, until the gannets flying overhead made him nervous and he turned back, imagining a missile of beak and talons plunging towards his scalp. When he reached the shallows he found the water had swept him some way south and he had to walk back for his bag.

He crossed the lawns. Voices drifted from the pool. Marcus and the Gibson boy had managed to import a trio of girls into the compound, and were engaged in strenuous and loud attempts to impress; there was much splashing and shouting, shrieks from the girls. The Little House was empty. He stood in the warm, sunlit room, listening to the creak of the wooden walls and birds squabbling over the roof tiles. The light was green, shining in through the grapevine that grew across the veranda trellis. In the bedroom he took the DVD of Weeks's films out of its hiding place and put it in the machine.

The first film opened with a rural scene, in summer. A man and woman were living in a small wooden house by a beach. They were poor, their lives were basic and their relationship was troubled. Simon watched, bored. He wanted to find something significant, a clue to Weeks.

He paused the DVD and sat dreaming in the warmth. Beyond the open door the tuis squabbled in the bushes and rosellas flew between the trees, bright flashes of colour. He thought about his daughters: conscientious Claire, alone at home with her books, and Elke, who had, that morning, signed up for tennis lessons with Garth. Simon was now grateful for Garth's campness; it was a relief, what with all the male virility hereabouts. Elke wandered though the compound in her minuscule, loose bikini, her shirt slipping off one brown shoulder, and with her sweet manner and her vague, distracted air she seemed unaware of the eyes that followed her. Could she really be so artless?

Simon had watched the Cock ogling her by the pool, and David watching the Cock, and the Cock noticing David watching — and that minor tension seemed part of a deeper unease between David and his deputy. As lazily apolitical as he was these days, Simon had noticed a personal chill between the two, and he supposed the Cock was straining to rein in his ambition.

But David had it over the Cock. The PM was not only popular; he was the most psychologically acute and manipulative person Simon had ever met. After an evening with him, Simon sometimes felt exhausted and drained. David expected certain responses and this required an adjustment in Simon's conduct — only a minor deviation from his natural manner, but maintaining it made him tired and hollow. And yet he went on conforming; they all did, as if mesmerised. Only Claire hadn't responded to the demands of David's court; she had rebelled, and been excommunicated.

The Cock was subtly challenging, but the Cock wasn't quite sure of himself and he was distracted — he couldn't keep his eyes off David's women.

Simon frowned. 'David's women.' But Elke wasn't David's.

He tried to look at it in a detached way. These days he grappled with the private sense that since Elke was his daughter and Roza was her mother, he and Roza belonged together. But then there was David: Roza was his wife and the mother of his son, and his wife's daughter resembled his son. Ergo, David felt that Roza was his, and Elke was his . . .

Did he hate David?

The idea gave him a jolt. Everyone remarked on how attached David had got to him, how David always wanted Simon around, insisting he be present on expeditions and at functions, how he reserved a seat for Simon next to him, had a trick of drawing him aside for private conversations, leaving others awkwardly looking on. The court was jealous and suspicious, but Simon was spared its worst machinations by the fact that he wasn't a politician. With the exception of the Cock, who kept a cool distance, David's staff and friends made sure to ingratiate themselves with the Lamptons. Until recently Simon had been 'family', but now they'd started calling him David's best friend.

Admit it, he did enjoy the obsequiousness of the staff and the way David's circle deferred to him. He and David (like Roza's Mr Bast!) had both grown up poor. David had been an orphan, farmed out to relatives in Tokoroa. Simon and his brother Ford were the sons of crazy, drunk taxi-driver Aaron Harris, from whose South Auckland house the family had fled in terror. Their mother had struck it lucky in the end, marrying Warren Lampton, their stepfather, a good man. But the rented house where Simon had visited Mereana had been no shabbier than the dump they'd lived in with Aaron.

He and David and Ford had dragged themselves into the middle class, although David still sounded like a yob, always getting his words wrong. The Cock was a mandarin, with his private-school education and his university degrees; he was smoothly fluent. But David's inarticulacy made him popular.

Simon watched the birds dancing this way and that around the bird table, like bossy women with large, fanned skirts — women at a Trish Ellison fundraiser. In what spirit did David stare at Elke? Was his attention 'fatherly'? You could never tell what was in David's mind. But Simon kept part of himself hidden too. One necessary precaution: making sure David never suspected how deeply he felt about Roza . . .

After dozing he woke feeling sharper.

He pushed play and watched episode two of *The Present*, set on a beach (pohutukawa, white sand, heat haze over dunes). The story, about people living in the Far North, starred a young woman with long hair and green eyes. She was lively, slim and dark-skinned, and had a way of looking at you sideways which gave her a sly, ironic air. Simon sat very still. It was a portrait of Mereana.

For years he had wished her dead. 'Why do you look at the funeral notices?' Karen would say. And there he'd be at the breakfast table, casting his eye expectantly down the columns. He had buried her, and the details of the affair: the row of tiny houses where she lived near the airport, the squalid pub they'd once visited, the quirky interior of her house, the smoky smell of her hair and skin, her primitive way of talking, her rough hands and feet. Her memory was tainted by the depression that had made him crave her kindness and her love. And here, controlled by Weeks, she was lithe and beautiful and wandered across the sand and tossed her hair and swam in the sparkling water, spoke corny dialogue and made a joke, while a young man ('Hamish') trailed after her, yearning . . .

Weeks had called her Anahera, which means angel.

Taking the DVD out of the machine, he hid it. Sleep came again, an escape.

He woke with a crick in his neck and a dry mouth, thought his phone had rung and that Karen had called out, but there was no missed call and no one in the Little House.

Everything lay still in the heat. The tuis and thrushes had stopped squabbling at the bird table and there was a hush in the green shade under the trees, only the sound of the sea coming across the dunes and the faint drone of a car on the coast road. The teenagers were no longer shouting and splashing over at the pool. His sweaty legs peeled off the canvas of the chair and he was dizzy when he got up, lurching into the bathroom to wash his face.

He tidied himself and walked across the compound to find David holding court under the trees and Troy and Trent hovering with trays and glasses; it was a Saturday which meant, according to David's regime, they were allowed wine with lunch, although Simon hated to drink during the day, the afternoon narrowing into a tunnel of lethargy, headaches.

The Cock was holding a spray can which he squirted fitfully around his feet every few moments, complaining of mosquitoes.

Johnnie arrived with Tuleimoka. He had something to show everyone: a jar with holes punched in the lid.

'It's a poisonous spider.' His small face was solemn, thrilled.

They all peered at the dark shape in the jar.

'It's deadly,' the boy said, shaking the jar. 'I caught it.' He brushed past the Cock, tipping over his glass. The Cock, mopping the table, visibly irritated, said, 'I'm starting to feel sorry for that spider. Why don't you let it go?'

'It's a specimen.'

'Surely it would be more humane if you tipped it into the bushes.' A bitter, hectoring note entered the Cock's voice. He stood over the boy. 'It's not going to be a pet. It's going to die in there.'

David watched the Cock without expression.

Roza said, 'I think in this case my sympathies are with the human creature, rather than the animal.'

The Cock, incredulous: 'The human?'

'The child,' Roza said.

'The human's not in a jar.'

'It's Johnnie's find. His prize.'

The Cock shrugged, picked up his can of insect spray and squirted along the edge of the table.

Ed Miles said to Sharon, 'Can you tell your husband to stop squirting me?'

'But he seems to be enjoying it,' she said.

Ed lifted his feet out of the way. 'He's not so high-minded about flies and mosquitoes, is he. Not all David Attenborough about *them*.'

David went back to sorting through photographs. 'Here's a good one of you and me,' he said, beckoning to Simon. 'Put these aside, Roza, I'm going to frame them — the one of me and Simon, this one of us and Karen, and this one of Elke and Johnnie.'

Roza, Karen and Juliet crowded around. Roza snatched one up. 'That's going in the bin.'

There was a chorus. 'Give us a look, no, you look gorgeous Roza, what a waste, don't throw it away.'

Ed held out his hand. 'Can I see?'

'No you can't,' Roza said. 'It's terrible.' She folded it and put it in her pocket.

David said, 'What about this one of all the four ladies together? You like that one, Ed?' He handed it over.

'Nice,' Ed said. He looked at Karen. 'Lovely trio.'

Karen was expressionless.

The four women looked and regretted their own hideousness and praised each other's beauty, and put the picture aside.

David said to the Cock, 'Cahane, here are the ones Roza took yesterday — you and Sharon on the boat, you two on the beach, you and Sharon looking lovely by the pool.'

The Cock fished reading glasses from his shirt pocket and dutifully took up each print before Sharon passed them around.

'Great,' the Cock said, bored.

David collected them and patted them into a pile. He handed them to the Cock. 'These are all the pictures with you and Sharon in. Take them.'

There was a silence.

'Oh, you keep them,' Sharon said. 'Honestly, we . . .'

'Go on. Take them. Summer memories.' He started gathering up the rest of the photos. 'Where's the box, Troy? Let's put the rest away and have lunch.'

Trent came around with more wine, and they rearranged the chairs so lunch could be served.

Sharon and the Cock looked at each other, a flicker of anger in his face. She took out her sunglasses and started polishing them, her pale eyes vulnerable.

David said, 'Troy, take the Cahanes' photos to their room, and can you put the ones we're *keeping* in the box — only keep these four out, because I'm going to get them framed.'

Roza said to Ed, 'A trio is three. Not four.' She smiled at him, not nicely, and sat next to Simon. Ed pressed his thin lips together, amused.

'Shall we have a quick lunch,' Roza said to Simon, 'and then we could walk out to the Kauri Lake.'

'I'd like that,' he said. Glancing at Ed, he felt guilty. 'We should ask Karen if she wants to come.'

'Of course. But she and Juliet are going to town, to buy sports bras.'

'OK,' Simon said. Happiness. Simple treats: lunch, exercise in the burning sun, Roza's company. To live in the moment, to look after the body; it was very good.

'I had a look at *Howard's End*,' Roza went on. 'I've found a copy if you want to read it. There's a bit in the introduction about the affair between poor little Bast and Miss Schlegel. It says critics of it as a plot element — who included Forster's mother; she was *shocked* by its impropriety — have "perhaps forgotten how sympathy given and received can take an erotic turn".'

Simon vacantly rattled the ice in his water glass. He cleared his throat.

'Possibly true,' he said.

Ford

On their way to the gate they met Ford, who was carrying a sports bag with a broken handle. He looked shy shaking Roza's hand. He was tall, rangy and pale; his big blue eyes and bony face raised a memory of Simon and Ford's father, Aaron. His outfit — khaki shorts and running shoes — made Simon feel prissy and twee. He eyed him, irritated; couldn't the stupid bugger have made an effort? He loved him and wanted to protect him, but Ford was always big brother: tough, inscrutable, spiky, mocking.

'Will you come?' Roza was saying. 'We'll show you the Kauri Lake. It's beautiful.'

'Sounds good,' he said. 'Just need to dump my bag.'

In the shade of the veranda, Tuleimoka and Johnnie were lying on grass mats, playing ludo. Tuleimoka was singing hymns. She was teaching Johnnie to sing. She also told him about Jesus and read him Bible stories, to make up for his parents' ungodliness.

They stowed Ford's bag and Roza tried to persuade him to stop at the kitchen and get some lunch from Jung Ha.

'Had a pie on the road,' he said.

Playing the rough diamond, Simon thought. It was the way Ford acted when he felt at a loss. He could come across as a complete yob;

you'd never know he was a university academic.

They passed Marcus and the Gibson boy sunbathing on the grass with the three girls. Simon noticed his son's hand resting on the nearest girl's brown thigh.

Beyond the gate the road was sheltered from the sea breeze and the heat was intense. Roza walked between the two brothers. 'Johnnie thinks God's a big Niuean,' she said.

'He might as well be,' Ford said.

'Well, I don't think God's anything. Which shocks Tuleimoka. Islanders are so churchy.'

Ford said, 'She's got a beautiful voice. Out where I live there's a Pasifika church — all the women in their white Sunday dresses, big hats. You can't believe the singing.'

'I like her speaking voice too,' Simon said.

'But you don't run into many Islanders where you live,' Ford said.

Simon smiled. 'They do the cleaning, the ironing.'

Silence. Simon added, winding him up, 'The driving, the gardening.' He thought, This is like lancing a boil.

Ford said, 'They're struggling out where I live. Thanks to your friend's fuck-the-poor agenda.'

Simon said, 'Here he goes.'

'Tuleimoka's so annoying,' Roza said. 'She thinks I'm a bad mother.'

'Roza's ignoring me,' Ford said.

She touched his arm. 'No I'm not.'

Simon returned his brother's stare. The burning eyes, the thin face — Aaron Harris. He thought he was calm but suddenly his throat closed over.

'OK?' Roza said. 'Are we done?'

Ford kept staring for a moment. 'Yeah,' he said.

At the lake Ford walked along the edge, pushing the long raupo stalks out of the way. 'Beautiful place,' he said.

Roza sat down on a log and took off her sandals to soak her feet in the water.

'You going in?' Ford called.

'No.' She said to Simon, 'When I was about ten I was swimming in a lake and a big eel got hold of my ankle. I screamed.'

Ford had taken off his shirt and shoes and was wading in.

Simon sat next to Roza and slipped off his shoes, watching his brother. 'Jesus. What a nature boy.' Ford had changed since Emily had left him. He used to have a sweet tooth and a big heavy frame; now his body was hard and muscular.

They watched him launch into the water and swim towards the middle of the lake with smooth, even strokes. The summer light shone, hurtingly bright. Simon said, 'What you said about sympathy given and received . . .'

'Taking an erotic turn. Respectable Miss Schlegel and lowly Mr Bast.'

'Yeah. Them.'

'Is this about your affair?'

Simon held up his hands, nervous. 'Not so loud.'

Ford was swimming backstroke. Roza said, quiet, 'So he lives alone, does he?'

'He's been unlucky. After his wife died he lived with Emily. She had a daughter, but he's got no kids, which is sad; he should have some, he'd be a good father.'

'Big eel out here,' Ford called.

'I knew it. I hate them!'

He came wading in, water streaming off his strong thighs. The shorts sagged on his arse; he hitched them up. Simon looked at his own brand-new shoes placed carefully on the bank, clean, just the odd fleck of mud. Ford's aggravating grin and sagging pants got to him.

There'd always been a provocative side to their father. His alcoholism grew out of defiance and rebellion: he lived in a world he didn't make. Ford's hair was slicked down wet and Simon saw Aaron's ugly head; the big, intelligent, vulnerable forehead; the burning pale eyes. Aaron had been musical and mathematical, intelligent and thwarted, all his life a taxi-driver, his talents wasted, stewing in failure and rage and booze. Simon couldn't remember how old he was when he first perceived the blackness in Aaron. He had loved Aaron and nothing had come back.

When he looked at his brother, something savage opened in him. But, he thought, I was protected by being younger, and by Ford. I should be grateful for that. Simon knew there'd been something in their father so hurt and bewildered that all he could do was defy the world, stick up two fingers. It had made Aaron low, ungenerous, a liar; it made him turn away rather than help anyone; it made him grandiose, and finally degenerate. Ford wasn't like that. He was solid; he didn't turn away from the world. He only looked like Aaron; you could say that was his cross. Did he shrink from the mirror some tired, hungover mornings, see a ghost in his own eyes?

'I like this place,' Ford said. He sounded happy.

Simon slipped on his shoes. Ford dragged his T-shirt over his head. Big wet patches formed on his back and shoulders. He roamed ahead through the reeds, slashing at them with a stick, his shoelaces untied.

'Herons,' he said, pointing at a graceful pair, motionless against the green bank.

Ford crashed his way through the reeds, and they followed him. All his young life Simon had followed Ford, before he'd got himself set up, married Karen, gone his own way. Ford had told him to try for medical school. He'd told him to wash his hands, not steal things, be kind to animals, don't let anyone make you do things you don't want to do.

'Are we lost?' Roza said after a while. They were in a green world, waving stalks, the burning blue sky. The reeds had given way to high grass and scrub. It was hot, there was a sharp, peaty smell and the ground squelched underfoot. They slapped flies away from their faces.

'We'll join up with the track,' Ford said, whacking with the stick.

Simon stopped. 'We're going the wrong way.'

'No we're not. Look at the sun.'

'Fuck the sun — the track's back there.'

'We need Ray,' Roza said. 'Ray and his GPS.'

'We don't need anyone — look.' Ford pointed with his stick. 'See those cabbage trees? They're growing along the fence we climbed over that runs north–south — we cross it, and that'll take us to the track.'

Simon's shirt was sticking to him. 'I don't think so.'

Roza wiped her forehead. 'Aren't we going away from it?'

'Trust me,' Ford said.

They wallowed on. Simon stuck his foot in a bog, and his new shoe came up soaked and brown.

At the cabbage trees they allowed Ford his moment; the track was exactly where he'd said it would be. Simon said, 'I've wrecked my shoe.'

They followed the track to the road and then walked into the valley, past the little wooden houses. Roza picked handfuls of long grass and fed the thin white pony. Simon and Ford sat on the side of the road, watching.

Simon said, 'You've got to be polite to Hallwright.'

Ford looked sideways. 'What are you these days? His right-hand man?'

'We're friends. Good friends. It just happened.'

'Did you vote for him?'

'What if I did?'

'He takes from the poor and gives to the rich. He's anti the welfare state that nurtured him. He's the soft face of a very right-wing agenda. You've seen the way he goes all dreamy when he talks about money? It's his god.'

Simon sighed. He scraped at his muddy shoe.

'When did you start hanging around with the fascists?'

Simon took off his shoe and wiped it on the grass. He said, 'Presumably you're going to partake of the fascist barbecue and the fascist wines, and the luxurious fascist bed they've made up for you?'

'I had to come. Voice of reason. Persuade you to defect.'

Simon lay back on the grass. 'I didn't vote for him.'

'That's no excuse. Karen thinks you did. They all think you did. So you might as well have.'

They watched Roza leaning close to the pony, whispering to it.

'You should go out to South Auckland,' Ford said, relentless. 'Then you'd see.'

'What do you know about South Auckland?'

'At least I think about it.'

'Great. You think about it. I've done more than that.'

Ford looked sharp. 'What do you mean?'

'Nothing. Forget it.'

Ford let out an amused grunt. 'What is it you're not telling me?' he said.

Simon hesitated. 'Only that a few years ago I was depressed.'

'Weren't we all.'

'No. Clinically.'

'Clinically. What happened?'

'I nearly went off the rails.'

Ford looked him over, his eyes lit. 'So?'

'That's it.'

'But now you're all right. Fit and healthy. Worrying about your thousand-dollar shoes.'

'Yes. I'm all right now.'

Ford looked serious. 'But you've lost something.'

Simon groaned. 'Ah, give me a break.'

Silence. Roza farewelling the pony with a pat on its flank, its slanting shadow black on the field. She closed and latched the gate.

Ford said, 'When we were kids they used to leave you with me. Hours and hours following you around. Steering you away from things.'

They watched a dog crossing the paddock towards Roza.

'It was such a drag.'

Simon laughed.

Ford said, 'I could do with a fascist beer. Swim in the fascist pool.'

'Come on then.' Simon shaded his eyes. 'That dog.'

'Yes,' Ford said, and they both started running.

It was coming at Roza, its body low, growling. Standing still, she looked at them, her mouth turned down. It was a male, a bad breed, massive head and jaw, long-legged, heavy, huge balls, a bald scar patch on the side of its head. It was crouching, coming forward as Roza backed away.

'Distract it?' Simon spoke low.

'OK. Same time.'

Ford shouted. 'Hey! Hey!' The dog turned to them, then back to Roza. It advanced on her, snarling.

'Shit. It wants her.'

The dog started barking, strings of saliva coming off its teeth and jowls. They ran, shouting, Ford waving the stick, slashing with it, and the dog veered sideways, trying to plant itself to face them, confused, Ford brought the stick down on its head, it let out a high-pitched bark and Simon saw Roza skimming up the bank, holding her skirt around her thighs. The dog got hold of Ford's stick and wrenched it, Simon whacked its head with his shoe and overbalanced, falling on the grass, the stick broke and Ford jabbed the dog on the nose with the broken end. It yelped and ran away, disappearing into the scrub.

Roza was standing at the top of the bank, her hands over her mouth, laughing.

'Very funny,' Ford said. He reached to give Simon a hand. 'Got your shoe, mate?'

They walked out of the valley. Roza said, 'Here comes Ray, caught up at last. Don't tell him about the dog. We'll never get rid of him.'

'He could have shot it for us.'

'Bodyguard, is it?' Ford said, looking Ray up and down.

Simon laughed.

'What?' Ford said, a half smile.

They joined Ray on a path that ran through the beachside properties, down to the dunes. The beach was dotted with small groups of swimmers and sunbathers, the air rippling above the hot sand. Roza shaded her eyes. 'Who's along there, Ray?'

'Kids. Marcus. Girls. Mrs Cahane, Mrs Miles, Mrs Lampton; the others I'm not sure.'

On the beach directly below the Wedding Cake, women were sitting under striped umbrellas, kids were ranging about, Troy was coming out of the dunes carrying a chilly bin. There were a couple of vans parked above the dunes, big men pacing, watching.

Simon recognised Peter Gibson from the marina and his girlfriend Janine sprawled on the sand next to Sharon Cahane. A man walked out of the sea and stood on the wet sand, energetically towelling his hair.

'Here come Tulei and Johnnie,' Roza said. But Simon was looking at the man drying his hair. A young man, thin and dark. They got closer. It was Arthur Weeks.

Roza introduced Ford. Sharon Cahane gave him a long, considering look. 'You're a lot like Simon. Only taller.'

Simon let out a breath. The young man wasn't Arthur Weeks.

The women were inspecting Ford. 'He's bigger,' Juliet said. Little simper, soft look.

Karen rolled her eyes.

'Older,' Ford said.

Juliet shook Ford's hand; the bracelets on her freckly arm jingled, she tossed her hair, turned her head on one side. Simon was surprised. He saw Ford as a stranger might. Slimmed down, he was impressive — tall, muscular and broad-shouldered, with those penetrating blue-grey eyes.

Ford stooped to kiss Karen, who said, cold, 'Hi Ford, how are you?' and looked away. She'd argued against this: how could they have him here, even for a day, it would be unfair to the Hallwrights, Ford was eccentric, rude, hopelessly left-wing. But the visit was actually Roza's doing. One night, sentimental after a few wines, Simon had expanded on Ford's misfortunes, the death of his wife May, his new partner Emily's abrupt departure. Roza and David had immediately said, 'Invite him to Rotokauri.' Simon would have forgotten about him, but Roza kept bringing it up: 'When are we going to have your poor brother to stay?'

Now Roza told a story: Ford swimming in the eel-filled lake, Ford finding the lost track, Ford driving away a savage dog. The women listened, smiled, brushed hot sand from their legs and thighs. They shivered over wild dogs, cold water, walking in the bush; they professed a loathing for eels. Endorsed, certified, eyed from all sides, Ford was urged into a space on the crowded beach mat. He looked bemused, not displeased, and not yet restless. But Ford wasn't inclined to cooperate with anything for long.

Simon sat down on the sand. Peter Gibson was planning an outing on his boat. 'So yeah, probably go out tomorrow, depending on the marine forecast, put out the lines, few beers, make a day of it.'

'Hi,' Simon said to Gibson. 'We met at your house. The party. I brought my son.'

'Mate, everyone knows who you are,' Gibson said, so hammily obsequious it was obvious he was drunk. 'The Doctor. Best friend of the PM.'

Janine said over her shoulder, 'Peter. If you think you're going to drive back, stop drinking.'

Gibson went over and lay down beside her, rubbing her back. She slapped his hand away.

Simon's phone rang in his pocket. He didn't answer it. Later, when he checked he found another message from Arthur Weeks, suggesting a meeting: he had something else to say.

That night, in the hot silence of the Little House, Simon turned and dreamed. He was in the operating theatre at Ascot Hospital, intent under the white lights. On the table a woman lay prepped for a caesarean. He opened her up, but when he looked for the baby it wasn't there. He made another incision, and another, but found nothing. Around the table, faces watched behind masks. He stood back. The anaesthetist pulled down her mask. It was Ford's wife, May.

She looked down at the mess he'd made. She said, *The words of his mouth were smoother than butter but war was in his heart; his words were softer than oil, yet they were drawn swords.*

Karen

Ford said, 'You all right?'

They'd got out of the hot cars and were waiting for Roza and David, who were delayed by a phone call. David had declared his Sunday free and they were to walk part of Crosby's Trail, a track that led around the coast, across bush reserves and beaches to a secluded and beautiful bay.

'Fine,' Simon said, looking at a long thread dangling from the frayed hem of Ford's shorts. Ford's sartorial standards were actually dropping; there were white stains on the underarms of his T-shirt, he hadn't shaved, and he was wearing yesterday's baggy army shorts. Yet the women, Juliet, Sharon, Roza, favoured him with soft looks, small kindnesses. They liked a bit of rough, Simon supposed. Ford playing the silent manly role. With tragedy thrown in, his beloved wife May having died in a car accident, and now his girlfriend walking out on him with her little daughter. David, forewarned that Ford was 'eccentric', hadn't paid much attention to him, and Ford hadn't said anything controversial, hadn't said much at all.

'Quite a party,' Ford said. 'Here comes Papa Doc.'

They watched the Cock rocking himself out of the car wearing beige trousers, sturdy boots, a khaki shirt with faux epaulettes, and big opaque sunglasses, like welding goggles. The driver held the door, still and narrow as a chess piece in his dark clothes.

'Mama Doc . . .'

'Not so loud,' Simon said.

Sharon Cahane emerged, lithe, tanned, long-legged in white Bermuda shorts and a floppy hat. She put her hand on the Cock's shoulder and turned up her foot, inspecting her shoe.

'And here's Baby,' Ford, amused without smiling, talking too loud, winding Simon up.

Ed Miles idled by the fence at the cliff-top, dressed in neat casual trousers and a linen shirt. He was watching the women, as usual: Juliet, swathed in protective veils like a beekeeper, Karen vaguely rummaging in her bag, Sharon losing and regaining her balance with grace as the Cock answered his phone and reflexively moved away, drawing in the dust with his shoe. Below the cliff the sea stretched to an indistinct horizon; the islands were shrouded and the sea was patterned with the wash of moving currents. It was going to be very hot, perhaps the hottest day yet of the summer. The roadside grass was parched brown, the trees were dull with dust, and the cicadas, grown to corpulent full size, filled the air with their crackling.

Simon looked at the rock formations below, oddly shaped outcrops rising sheer from the sea, iced with bird shit. The sea swirling around a red-and-white beacon, white flashes of foam, dark shadows of the reef under the swells. The cicadas and the dazzling light stunned his senses; he closed his eyes, soaking in the heat.

'Here they come.'

Crunch of gravel as the Hallwrights' car pulled in.

Sharon's voice: 'The Gibsons are taking the boat around.'

That morning, Simon had made sure to hide the DVD of Arthur Weeks's *The Present* in a zipped compartment in his suitcase, between a stack of medical journals. He'd actually thrown it away first, then after a moment's reflection retrieved it from the bin out the back of the Little

House, standing against the hot wall brushing dirt off the plastic cover, eyed by the bossy tuis. He wanted to get rid of it, but he also wanted to watch it again. In Weeks's third short film, Anahera and Hamish had met in the city years after they'd got to know each other on the Far North beach. She was busy, purposeful; he was wondering which way to go career-wise. She'd joined an up-and-coming social class — chic urban Maori woman — and worked in the Newmarket studios of Maori Television.

Simon thought about it, a brief daydream: Mereana redux. Mereana taking courses, earning a diploma or degree. Pacing the floor of Maori TV with her earpiece, her clipboard. The inner-city flat, the careful budget: rent, food, the stylish clothes she saves for. And one day outside the studios, young Hamish returns . . . But it was idealised, sentimental. Life wasn't like that, and neither was she. Was she?

He thought, Stick to facts. Don't let Weeks mess with your mind. Simon preferred facts to fiction, avoided novels, liked the odd thriller — book or movie — quite liked biographies, but stuck mostly to the vast and evolving narrative of his own sphere: obstetrics and gynaecology. He gave women information about their bodies that surprised them, supplied explanations they couldn't have arrived at themselves. He knew their bodies, knew only just enough about their minds . . .

Now David was taking charge at the cliff-top, issuing orders, hurrying the group along. They assembled at the beginning of the track. Roza went back to the car for something and Johnnie, following her, strayed too close to the road and was shooed back by Tuleimoka. Trent and Troy wore black shorts and T-shirts and carried backpacks, crew-cut twins. Lunch was to arrive by boat with the Gibsons, and those too tired could be ferried back around the coast on the boat. Marcus and the Gibson boy had declined to come, preferring to toast themselves on the beach with a group of girls that seemed to be getting bigger each day. The young Miles children and their nanny had stayed behind at the pool. The party was preceded and followed by a select group of muscle in short sleeves, caps and earpieces: Ray, Ron, Mike, Shaun, Jon, Rick . . .

Simon and Ford walked together, near the back. The track led them along the cliffs, under stands of brightly flowering pohutukawa, over rough paddocks full of waving grass and wildflowers, then into a puriri glade, thick tree roots growing across the path, sunlight shining through the trees in stripes. They crossed a cold little stream, the path wound through dense bush then came out in a paddock fringed with cabbage trees where they jumped over a stile and Juliet tore her skirt on the wire fence.

They began descending gradually, the track leaving the paddocks and narrowing to a rough dusty path over rocks and tree roots. Soon they were skirting along the cliff, the sea below them, light glancing off waves, white foam around rocks, gannets diving, and the hiss and sigh as the water rushed in and retreated, sucking and gulping in cracks and crevices. Close to the reef it was hot, the air trapped and still against the cliff, and the back of Ford's neck turned red under the merciless sun, big dark loops of sweat spreading over his T-shirt. Sunburn made his eyes burn blue, sweat rolled down his face.

He was walking just ahead of Simon on the narrow path. 'I was talking to Karen,' he said.

'You were?'

'She told me something funny.'

'You and Karen talked. To each other.'

'I know. Anyway, she told me you'd done a shrink's test for madness, and that you were mildly mentally ill.'

'The Kessler score. It doesn't mean anything. But she thinks it's really funny.'

'She said she'd done the test herself — she told me it's oversensitive, it makes out everyone's a bit crazy — but when she did it, her score was "moderately" mentally ill. That's more than "mildly".'

It was a surprise. He slowed. 'That's not what she told me. She said she was a zero. Not a flicker, not a hint of anything.'

'Not so.'

'But Karen doesn't tell lies. She's too straightforward.'

'Mm.'

'Why did she tell you?'

'I don't know. We were drinking wine after dinner. She was laughing.'

'The other women fancy you. It's made her come round to your charms.'

'She never liked me. But she's changed.'

'Has she.' Simon thought about this. To him, she was a fixed reality, a constant. He'd married her because she was uncomplicated, open, happy; he'd always thought of her as 'golden'. She was blonde, beautiful; he wouldn't have said it to anyone, but she was a symbol of success. She was the antidote to everything he hated about his childhood and Aaron Harris.

He said, 'Why would Karen be depressed, unhappy, whatever? She's got everything she wants.'

'Don't know. I didn't ask her. My guess would be it's about Elke.'

Simon now thought about his daughters. Elke, who was so like Roza. And Claire, who had a look of Aaron, and Ford. (Worse luck, Claire.) Straightforward Karen had given birth to angry, complex, clever Claire, the girl she'd never been able to handle or love. From the age of about eight, Claire had been irritated by Karen, questioned her authority, found her explanations of the world wanting, sided with Simon over everything, adopted a manner that insulted and infuriated her mother, resisted and despised Karen's attempts to guide and instruct. It was a vicious circle: sensing Karen's growing coldness, Claire hated her for it. Karen would not touch Claire, ever. She only reluctantly pecked her on the cheek, for form's sake.

When they'd adopted Elke, Karen had found a girl she could love.

She would hug Elke, rub her back at night, take pride in her appearance and modest achievements, all her sense of failure with Claire soothed by the lovely little stranger. Elke was dreamy, affectionate, sweet; she was infinitely touching. With Marcus and Elke, Karen had found unconditional love.

'What do you mean it's about Elke?'

Ford said, 'Karen and Roza are competing. Karen'll be thinking Roza's going to take Elke away.'

Simon checked Ray wasn't too close. He said, 'Is it about winning, or actually being worried she'll lose Elke?'

'Love or power,' Ford said. 'They're not mutually exclusive.'

'Elke's eighteen. She'll be making her own way.'

'Women want their daughters for life. They want to be out shopping with them when they're ninety-five. Not losing them soon as they get old enough to vote.'

'They seem to be sharing her all right.'

'But Roza, I don't know. She's a little bit threatening, isn't she. And Elke is actually hers. Why would she want another woman in the picture?'

'For Elke's sake,' Simon said.

'Maybe.' Ford tipped up a water bottle. 'But does she think Elke needs another mum? What mum thinks that?'

Simon took the bottle. 'You think Karen's worrying about all this.'

'Maybe. Because there's another complication for Karen. She doesn't want to give up the Hallwrights. She's got a crush on your mate David — the man with the power — and she likes the life.'

Simon threw the bottle back at him, hard. 'A crush. You can be a cold, clinical prick. You should have some children. Realise how painful all this is.'

Ford tipped water on his hand, wet his forehead. 'Need to find someone first. And I'm bringing all this up, I've been thinking about it, so why am I cold? Maybe I'm sensitive.'

Simon sighed. 'It does my head in.'

'I can see the point of not having kids. Travelling light. The amount of grief Emily used to get from her daughter Caro. She could be a right little shit.'

'It's worth all that. Don't ever think it's not. You should have some kids — I mean it. It's the best thing. You'd be good.'

Ford gave him a brief, sour smile. 'Find me a woman who's willing.'

'Look, I'm sorry Ford. Sorry about Emily.'

Ford said nothing, strode ahead over rocks and tree roots, nimble for a big man.

Simon, catching up: 'Is there no way you and Emily can get back together?'

'Wouldn't want to.'

'What went wrong?'

'She said she got sick of me looking at her and thinking she wasn't May. I told her I never thought that.'

'Was she right?'

'Course. Every day I thought: well, no choice. She's not May. She'll have to do.'

Simon laughed. 'Christ, Ford.'

'I was on the rebound. Now it's time for something meaningful.'

'God, you're a cynical bastard.'

'I'm writing a book, the sequel to my PhD.'

'That'll fill the long winter evenings.' Simon paused. He kept blundering, touching a nerve, but he was tired of not talking. 'Was Emily upset about leaving?'

'Yeah she was. Unhappy I didn't try hard enough to get her back.'

'You didn't?'

'Well, she wasn't May.'

'Yes, but life must go on. After May. May would want you to be happy.'

'Indeed she would.' Ford's tone altered. Silence. He said, 'Losing May . . . If Karen died, that's the only way you'd understand.'

Simon nearly said it. *But you loved May.*

After a pause he said, 'You were lucky.' He was thinking of himself. The secret he lived with, was comfortable with, had never regretted: Karen was a cover, she was a symbol of success, she was necessary and dear and he'd be lost without her, but he'd never been in love with her. Shamed by his childhood, he'd done everything to remake himself: he'd accumulated career, kids, house, cars, trappings, trappings. Karen.

Ford had waited until he found someone he really loved. Ford was free, always had been.

Karen believed Simon had fallen in love with her. It might as well be true, except in his private core, where a sting of regret now touched him. He thought of Roza. Elke. Roza.

'Yeah, I was lucky,' Ford said. 'Then very unlucky.'

The track took them through a gap between two sheer sides of rock, the walls jagged and raw, as though a seismic jolt had split one enormous boulder in two. The path led down to a short white-sand beach, pohutukawa growing off the cliffs, the branches hanging low over the dunes, their red flowers carpeting the sand around them. The others had crossed to the other side and were on the rocks. They were looking at the water, pointing.

Simon took off his sunglasses. The sea was painfully bright. The sand was so deep and soft it was hard to walk, his legs ached from all the jogging he'd been doing. They laboured and wallowed across and heard Johnnie shouting.

It was a pod of orca, playing around a rock out from the reef, surfacing, diving, turning, putting on bursts of speed and then lolling, one weird glistening eye staring, their skins streaming and shiny. Simon had seen plenty of dolphins but not orca this close, the weight of them, the gloss of the black-and-white patterned bodies.

'Killer whales,' Johnnie said.

'Aren't they big?' said Tuleimoka.

'So shiny. You could see your face in them.'

'Stand there, Sharon,' commanded the Cock, looking down at the screen of his camera. 'Roza, you too.' He angled, peered, shading the camera screen with his hand.

'How about one of you and Roza and Sharon?' the Cock said to David.

David ignored him, turned away.

An orca leapt right out of the water. There was a collective gasp.

'They revel,' said Ford.

'They revel and frolic,' Roza said.

'Can you frolic in water?'

'Yes, but not gambol.'

'That's lambs. You need legs to gambol.'

'What about frisk?'

'Do they really kill you?'

Ford said, 'Yeah, ones in marinelands. The captured ones. They do the tricks with the balls and hoops and then one day they turn. The keeper gets his head wrenched off.'

Roza said, 'You can see why. How could you keep an animal like that in a tank? They play, they love the sea. I bet they feel misery too.'

'And rage,' Ford said.

'Exactly. The keepers deserve what they get.'

'Roza!' Karen said.

'Well, I'm just saying. Look, the Gibsons. In their freighter. Their ocean liner.'

The bright white boat, tall, polished wood decking, flag on the stern, heading briskly for the beach at the end of the point.

'That's lunch. Lead on.'

The orca swam along the coast for a while and then, perhaps

following a school of fish, turned and veered out to sea, no longer leaping but only surfacing occasionally.

They crossed the rocks to a beach covered in grey stones. A stream ran down a cleft in the rock face, crossing the beach to the sea. A reef jutted a long way out from the shore, and Gibson had steered a wide arc to avoid the rocks, the boat plunging through a patch of chop, gulls whirling around the stern.

'Windy out there.'

But here you could feel the heat from the grey stones through the soles of your shoes. The size of the stones made walking difficult; they slowed, teetering, overbalancing. The heat came up into their faces and the stones moved underfoot with a hollow, clopping sound. There were brackish pools full of tea-coloured water and dead leaves, insects skating across the surface. When Simon and Ford climbed onto the rocks Tuleimoka was dragging Johnnie away from the corpse of a puffer fish, its spines dull yellow, its mouth open in a frozen O.

Roza said, 'He can poke it, surely. The germs won't come swarming up the stick.'

Karen said to Simon, 'What?'

'Nothing.' He smiled, limply.

'You were staring.'

'You look so suntanned. So fit.'

She sighed and reached for his hand, and he pulled her up onto the rocks. They stepped across sharp beds of broken oysters and skirted around hot rock pools, the surfaces shimmering as sea water washed in, creatures retreating as their giant shadows passed, crabs sidling, tiny fish veering. Simon looked down into the glassy worlds. When he was a boy he would touch the fronds of a sea anemone to feel them close around his finger, the strands sticking as he pulled gently away. He would pick up a crab by its back and watch the frantically waving legs, lower the creature down into its pool, watch it bury itself in sand. He would do no harm, not like the boys down their street who killed the small animals they came across, beheaded eels, smashed crabs, ripped off their shells and watched them curl up. Down at the hot mudflats in summer, the stink of blood, salt, cruelty. Ford had once punched a boy for torturing a gull he'd found tangled in a fishing line. Ford had pushed the boy away and finished off the bird with a rock. Simon had cried, angry about the rock, but Ford had said the bird had no chance, was in agony. Simon wanted to shout, who are you to decide how something dies? It was wrong, self-righteous. He ran at Ford; Ford fended him off with a few perfunctory blows and kicks, unbothered.

He remembered the bird's pierced eye, the red centre of the black hole.

Simon lay in the shade watching the swimmers. Even the Cock had waded in up to his waist, his hands hovering over the surface of the water, his large, pale body mottled pink with sunburn. Karen was swimming strongly. Near her David floated on his back, watching. He turned and swam after her.

Roza patted the top of a sand castle with a plastic spade. Johnnie silently placed a shell and looked at his mother, eyes narrowed.

'Make Soon talk.'

Simon dozed. Words, the sea, the crunch of feet on shells, the crackle of cicadas, sounds carrying him out of consciousness and back again, in and out, words, his own breathing, the waves.

They assembled in front of the castle, and though the battle had been long and hard and men had been lost, the mood was triumphant. The enemy had been driven a long way to the south and even if they and their henchmen regrouped and rearmed, they wouldn't be able to attack again for some time.

The Ort Cloud made a speech thanking all who had had the

courage to fight his terrifying wife, and the Village Idiots sang a
song of praise to their God, the Great Wedgie. Crackers got into
the Bachelor's drinks cabinet again and had to be imprisoned
for drunkenness after shouting from the tower, "Green Lady, I
love you!" The Bachelor proposed a toast to the Green Lady that
went on for so long the Cassowaries nearly hissed themselves to
madness, and the Red Herring made the following observation:
"A house divided against itself cannot stand." His colleague, Tiny
Ancient Yellow Cousin So-on, added, "A drowning man will
clutch at a straw." After that there was feasting and merriment.

The Bachelor recited poems, got drunk and drove his bed wildly
over the treetops in an attempt to impress the Green Lady. His
Cassowaries clung on, their feathers flying. The Guatemalans let
off their shotguns, the Village Idiots danced. They all farewelled
the Ort Cloud, who went whirling off into the Universe.

Then the Green Lady called for quiet. "I have grave news." She
looked around the group. "There is a traitor in our midst. One of
our number is in the pay of Barbie Yah."

For a time in the slow, drugged afternoon the sun rode like a white-hot
coin behind a bank of thin cloud, but an hour later it had burned away
the haze and directed its full glare on the cliffs. The trees made patterns
of light and shade on the sand. Gulls picked their way along the shore,
pecking among the seaweed.

David held a briefing paper in front of him but his sunglasses had
slipped down his nose and he was looking over the top of them at the
sand dune, where Elke lay on her back having her legs buried by Johnnie.
Out in the water, between the Gibsons' boat and the shore, were the
small dark heads of swimmers: Karen, Juliet breaststroking after them
in a hat and shades. Ford was swimming to the boat and back, part
of his new fitness regime. He had a powerful stroke, overarm, no sign

of slowing. The Cock, disturbed to find there was limited reception for his phone, fussed and fiddled with it before wandering off to try high points along the beach.

Sharon Cahane's harsh voice: 'Honestly. The way he goes on.'

The Cock had now climbed up a bank at the end of the beach and was hanging onto a branch for balance.

Roza said something. Sharon Cahane cackled. The Cock slipped, clutched at the foliage, righted himself. From across the water came the sound of a door slamming on the boat; a figure appeared and emptied a bucket of liquid over the side. Ray and Jon were walking slowly towards the Cock, who was bending to look at something on the sand.

Simon slept, then surfaced; some remnant of his dream had returned, May pulling down her mask, the bloodied figure on the table. He looked up and saw dazzling light between branches, a kaleidoscope of flowers and trees and sky. There was something missing.

He raised his hand to his eyes, felt the thump of displaced sand as someone flopped down beside him. The lost fact came to him: May was dead.

The walk back, for those who hadn't opted to go in the boat, was rugged and exhausting. Simon slogged behind Ford, enjoying the heat and the tired ache in his legs, Ford setting the pace, not slowed by all his swimming. A stingray as big as a door had swum under him, he said; it had followed him, like it was using him for a sun shade.

'Could have Steve Irwinned you,' Simon said. He imagined Arthur Weeks: dragged ashore, blue-faced and rigid, a long barb in his heart. Suddenly he wanted to tell Ford about Weeks and Mereana, ask for his help, unburden himself. But silence was wiser, if you talked about things you gave them life, better to stifle the whole problem with denial. He fixed his eyes on the back of Ford's shirt as he used to when they were boys, walking home from the mudflats, Ford leading, Simon silent, daydreaming. Ford taking charge, out the front of the house hosing the mud off their legs, ordering him to go and wash his stinking hands, spraying Simon's sandals, laying them out to dry.

'It's good you came,' Simon said.

Ford didn't slow down. 'Nothing else to do,' he said.

Karen had opted to go in the Gibsons' boat. When he got back she was lying on the bed in the Little House, a flannel over her eyes. 'I got windburnt,' she said. 'Janine was flirting with Ray. Outrageously. Johnnie's been stung by a jellyfish.'

Ford went for a shower and Simon joined her on the bed. He said, 'You look so smooth and brown.'

She threw the cover over them and he pushed up against her. Her body was hot, she smelled of suntan lotion. He peeled off her shirt, pushed at her shorts, felt her hands moving down over his stomach. After a moment she said, 'Quick. Someone. Ow. Fuck.' He kissed her, held her hard, she said, 'No, there, yes.' She pressed her forehead against his, they were trying not to make any sound, she suppressed a giggle and said, 'no, what if the kids . . .?', she went silent, clutched his arms, they moved together, he came and lay still. They could hear birds squabbling on the roof, Ford humming in the shower. He rolled on his back, his hand across her stomach. They lay in silence for a while; she stretched out her arm and examined her hands, the manicured nails.

'We'll have to go to dinner,' she sighed.

After they'd showered and dressed and were walking with Ford through the grounds he thought, Sun, exercise, sex — I'll be serene now, nothing will bother me. He had armed himself.

They joined the group. But after the first glass of rocket fuel he was irritated rather than soothed by the booze. Sharon Cahane's laugh was too loud; he hated the way Ed's eyes slid around the company; and Ford's pent-up silence made him worry there was some embarrassing argument on the way. Karen was flushed, voluble and clearly under surveillance by Ed, who gave Simon a deadpan look, lips parted, eyes deliberately void. Ford noticed, and looked curiously at Simon.

Roza said, 'Simon, Karen, it's so sweet — Johnnie's been waking up in the night and asking for Elke. He wants her to come and stay with us in the big house.'

Karen frowned. 'But Elke needs her sleep too.'

'I told Johnnie he's not to wake her up. She can stay in the bedroom next to his.'

'We'll send her up to say goodnight. She's happy where she is.'

Roza said, 'It's all arranged. I've already asked her, she's keen to change. It's so nice she and Johnnie have got close.'

Karen looked down.

Simon felt Ed's eyes on them. He smiled blandly. 'That Johnnie. He's a great little kid,' he said.

It would have been wise to stop drinking. He accepted another of Troy's cocktails, and drank wine through the meal. Karen was strained, brittle and drinking a lot too. Her laughter was forced.

Afterwards he stood out on the veranda and looked at the first stars and the sky streaked with skeins of black cloud near the moon. The sea was unusually still and full, a brimming high tide, and there was a glimmer over the sand, shapes moving down there, couples walking along the water's edge, a lone jogger, and a swimmer splashing out with strong strokes, riding over the gentle swell. Across the dunes he could see the glow of a floodlit tennis court, figures moving silently in the unnatural green light behind the wire. Closer, the Hallwrights' pool was lit up chemical blue by lights hidden in the surrounding ferns, and Marcus and Elke and other teenagers were messing around in the pool house, banging doors, talking loudly, a splash, a shriek. Boats were making their way out of the estuary for night fishing, testing their floodlights.

Smelling smoke, he went silently to the side of the deck. Below, Karen and David were sitting on the wooden seat where David liked to smoke his cigars. He could hear the booze blur in her voice as she said, 'One puff, that's all I can stand. I don't know how you do it.'

'You gotta be tough,' he said, passing her the cigar.

She puffed, coughed. 'No. It's too strong.'

Simon was going to move away, but David said, 'Like me.'

'Yes, like you. Dear Leader.' She giggled.

Simon hesitated. It wasn't her flirting that bothered him, it was David's tone. He sounded stone cold sober.

'You like strong men?' Teasing, ironic.

'Oh, of course.'

'I like strong women.'

Simon was caught between needing to hear and wanting to break it up. Karen said something he didn't catch.

'That sounds very naughty,' David said.

'It's a double entendre,' Karen said.

'Is that right.'

After a silence Karen said, 'Roza's a strong woman.'

'Yes. She's the boss.' David's tone altered.

She tilted her head, 'There's one thing I've never been able to get my head around.'

'What's that, darling?'

Her voice turned coy, sugary. 'There's one thing that would take incredible strength. I've never been able to understand how you, how you . . . could give up a baby for adoption. Once you'd given birth to it, surely it would be—'

Simon coughed and jogged down the steps onto the lawn. 'There you are.'

David looked up at him, calm, his cigar clamped between two fingers.

'You as knackered as I am?' Simon said. 'I know Karen's shattered — it's the sun partly, and the big walk. It's good, but it's lethal to drink afterwards.'

'Fatal,' David said.

'Shall we go to bed?' Simon said.

Karen hadn't noticed David's stillness, his lack of expression. She was annoyed. 'I'm not tired, Simon. Actually. *You* go to bed.'

David stood up and stretched. 'Well. It's late.'

He stubbed out his cigar and shook Simon's hand, gripping his shoulder and looking into his eyes in the way that moved Simon. He was understood. David cared about him, they shared something.

'Goodnight Karen,' David said, and moved neatly away as she positioned herself for a kiss on the cheek. He glanced at Simon again, the look of charged complicity.

The Lamptons stood alone together on the lawn. Above them the rotund moon, like a button made of bone.

He wanted to say, *you stupid, stupid woman.* To think she could gain something with David by criticising Roza. But she was massaging her temples, looked exhausted and crumpled, and vaguely troubled, as if she sensed she'd misjudged something, and he felt sorry for her; she wasn't equipped to deal with these complicated people, his poor, straightforward, innocent Karen.

These people. He stood looking out at the sea, the moonlight on the vast, moving stretch of water. She'd tried to ingratiate herself, she'd wanted to flirt; as Ford had said, she had a crush on him with the power, but there was something else — in her dim-witted way she'd been trying to make a point about herself and Elke. She was saying, 'I love my children and I love Elke. *I* would never give her up.' But it was a point made at Roza's expense and David wouldn't tolerate it.

'Come on, let's go down the beach. Look how beautiful it is.'

She consented, still grumpy, and they walked slowly through the grounds, out the gate and along the path through the dunes, taking off their shoes to feel the cool, sliding sand, down to the water's edge.

They didn't talk. She was thawing out, put her hand on his arm, but he was thinking about David. Karen had been shut out just then, but the channel between David and Simon had lit up. He felt a thrill from it, as if he'd been blessed, and it made him feel merciful. He put his arm around her.

The entire court, including the Cock, was nervous around David. Even Ford's silence was a kind of wariness. The only people who behaved like David's equals were Simon and Roza. It was a fact Simon secretly contemplated, hoarded to himself like money in the bank: that he'd been singled out as the friend of the country's most powerful man. He had achieved the position by straightness. He'd never ingratiated himself or played power games. He was the only one who argued with or contradicted David, who treated him without reverence. He felt he'd been tested by the friendship, he'd held his nerve and been rewarded, and he was thrilled.

And he knew what David had just signalled to him. No matter what blunders Karen made, Simon's place was safe.

They went back up to the Little House. He steered her through the gate. Ford was sitting on the veranda.

'Let's go to bed,' Simon said.

'Would you mind,' Karen said, 'not putting on that tone. Like you've just been given a prize by the headmaster.'

He was suddenly angry too. 'Don't blame me if your little chat didn't go the way you wanted.'

'What d'you mean by that?'

'Trying to ingratiate yourself. I heard you. David didn't like it, and now you're taking that out on me. Because you're pissed off with yourself, and you've had a few drinks.'

'You patronising shit.'

Simon stumbled on the uneven path and lurched sideways. Pain stabbed through his knee.

'You all right?'

The pain made him angrier. 'See, I treat David like an equal. You're all either flirting or grovelling. I have his respect.'

Ford's deep voice came out of the dark. 'You sure you're not bending yourself into whatever shape he wants?'

It wasn't worth answering. Disgusted with them both, Simon left them on the veranda and limped off to bed.

Rage

At six in the morning he put his feet on the floor and winced. He tried again after an hour; the pain was sharp. Karen was restless and sighing, looking for the cool side of the pillow; she would be hungover, she couldn't drink much without suffering the next day.

In the hot bathroom, sun already shining through the blind onto the wood panelling, little thumps and scrapes of birds squabbling on the roof, he hitched his heel on the edge of the bidet. The knee was swollen but not too dramatic and he decided to ignore it, taking his towel and limping out into the bright morning. The air was still and pure, and the pine-covered hill at the end of the beach stood in sharp outline against the perfectly clear sky.

Dwayne came around the corner of the pool house carrying a clipboard and a coffee mug. Trent and Shane were conferring at the door of one of the equipment sheds; Troy had set a portable stereo on the concrete and was listening to rap music while stacking a pile of orange life jackets. From across the grounds came the sound of an early morning tennis match.

It was already warm in the dunes, and it felt good wading into the sea, the water soothing his aches, lifting his spirits. He swam beyond the breakers, looking along the sweep of coast. The sand was damp after the high tide, a crowd of oystercatchers browsed along the water's edge and a fishing boat headed into the estuary, sending up spray as it chugged against the outgoing current.

He sank under the water, a million bubbles rising around him; he listened to the sea. He thought about Ford and Karen. His anger had subsided, he was magnanimous. Karen, ridiculously, tried to patronise him, and Ford couldn't stop treating Simon as his inept, dreamy little brother. But they were both naïve, and neither was equipped to handle Rotokauri. He would forgive them, protect them.

Roza emerged from the dunes with Garth. They talked on the beach, the trainer giving a long-winded exposition, then set off towards the northern end, slowly jogging.

And now he saw Elke, in white bikini, a white towel turbaned on her head and sunglasses with white rims. Shading her eyes with a languid hand, little movie star . . .

'Like them? Mum says they're too short but Roza says they're cool.' Elke clicked the seatbelt, leaned back and hiked her feet up on the dashboard.

'Yeah, nice,' he said, glancing at her incredibly brief shorts. 'Get your feet off.'

He'd tried to be positive about the knee but it was bothering him now, not just the ache but the frustration that he hadn't been able to go for a run. He'd got addicted to exercise. A run out to the Kauri Lake in the heat left him spent, satisfied, fulfilled. Jogging was good drugs. It was also a preventative measure: against anger.

Now he thought, Why the anger? He dealt with it every day. Jogging, sex, work, drinking/not drinking — all were strategies for controlling his anger. He hadn't seen it clearly before.

'Feet,' he said.

'Yeah, yeah.' She searched in her bag. 'Want some gum?'

He took a piece. Father and daughter chewed silently as he drove towards the gate. She blew a bubble, popped it with a cracking sound, waved at Ray, who raised his forefinger, butch, expressionless. Simon had noticed this about Elke: she made men snap to attention. Their eyes followed her. She seemed unaware of this. She had Roza's unaffected presence; it was one kind of charisma.

'What you got planned?' he asked her.

'Shopping!'

His girls and their differences. Claire: acutely sensitive to every nuance. Her quickness and blushes and sudden rushes of mirth, her infinite capacity for taking offence. She was too sensitive to act natural, she was so busy reacting. She noticed everything, could be shrewd, was intolerant of human failings, had a strong sense of justice. Was scathing about her mother and yet wanted to be loved. Hard for Karen to love a daughter whose capacity for contempt was limitless. During a recent row Claire had looked thoughtfully at Karen and said, 'The Hallwrights. They couldn't care less about you. You know who they care about? Each other.'

'Oh fuck off,' Elke now said to her phone, genially chewing, texting. She was regularly stalked by suitors.

'Some boy?'

'Hm. How shall I play this?' She was able to text without looking.

He said, 'Marcus seems to be acquiring quite a collection of girls.'

She rolled her eyes. 'I know! God.'

After a moment she said, 'I talked to Mr Cahane.'

'Did you.'

'He watched me have my tennis lesson with Garth.'

Simon frowned. He would have enjoyed that, the bastard. Elke bouncing around in her little white skirt. He'd seen her going off with Garth that morning. Escorting his pupil across the grounds the trainer had looked censorious, as if he wasn't going to be distracted by all this feminine glamour, and Simon had thought, Good. Garth's gay. Garth and Dean: it's David's arse they're after.

He shifted in his seat, his knee burned.

'We went for a swim. I needed to cool off, it was boiling.'

'You went for a *swim* with Cahane.'

'What's wrong with that?'

How to explain the wrongness. 'He's a . . . strange person.'

'Whatever. He's really nice. Actually.'

'What did you talk about?'

'He asked about the family, about me and Mum and Roza and David and you.' She sent another text.

Simon swore, braked, swerved.

'Dad. Slow down.'

He eased his foot off the accelerator. 'You should be careful what you say to people about private stuff. I've told you that.'

'Whatever.'

'I don't mean Cahane, but other people, strangers. People make things up. They get some real details for authenticity and then twist them. *Will you make up your mind.*' He tooted his horn at the car ahead. An arm emerged from the driver's window, an emphatic finger.

'God, Dad. Relax.'

Elke had taken her feet off the dashboard and was sitting up straight.

Simon glanced at her. 'Sorry.'

'What's that noise?'

He listened. 'What noise?'

'That kind of thumping. Like there's something banging in the engine.'

'I can't hear anything.'

After a while he said, 'I tripped last night, did something to my knee. I wanted to go for a run this morning, it was no good.'

'Mm.'

'I might have to get it X-rayed.' He flexed his hands on the wheel. 'So. You're moving into the big house.'

'Johnnie wants me to. Roza says all he wants is me and Soon and Starfish. It was her idea. She said she was sick of him asking for me.' She looked pleased, hiked her feet up on the dashboard again. 'Hey, you know what old Cahane asked me? What I'm going to vote.'

'What did you say?'

'I said, God, I don't know. I probably won't bother.'

'You have to. It's important.'

'But I don't care.'

'It affects everything, who's in government.'

'Well, I'll vote for David then, but honestly, I don't care.' She added, amused, 'Anyway, Cahane went on like you, saying it's important to vote and I said OK, you've convinced me, I'll vote for *you*. He liked that.'

'I bet he did. Sounds like you were flirting.'

'With that old man? Anyway. You know what Claire says? You vote for the one you'd go out with.'

He thought about it. 'That's only a political test if you're political. If you're like Claire or Ford and you'd be turned off by someone who doesn't have the same opinions. Whereas Roza says she's not political, so . . .'

'*Whatever.*'

He waited, then said, 'We'll be hoping you come back.'

'From the big house? Why does it matter where I sleep?'

'It doesn't. Course.'

'Johnnie is actually my brother. My *real* brother.' Her tone was wronged, self-righteous — unusual for her.

'He is indeed. Good. It's important.' It cost him something to add, 'You and Johnnie look alike.'

She was texting again and Simon, speeding up the passing lane, took advantage of the space to get ahead of four cars. Gaining his place in the queue just as the lane narrowed, he powered over the ridge and coasted down the long straight. When he was young, he and his friends, coming back from trips up north, had used this hill to compete for speed records; surprising they survived in the old cars they used to drive, rusty bombs that overheated and broke down, the old Ford Cortina so dilapidated the bottom was falling out of it, he'd ended up selling it for scrap.

They were on the motorway, the city ahead of them. They crossed the Harbour Bridge to the jittery flashes of light from the hundreds of white masts in the marina, rigging and flags and cables blowing in the breeze, sun moving on white hulls, the wake of a ferry a pure white V in the blue. Cars moving on the marina road, cars heading up onto Shelly Beach Road, up onto the Southern, movement but no sound except the roar of the air conditioning.

He said, 'I've just remembered a dream. I was trapped in a train station, there was a terrorist attack. A guy stood in a doorway and killed a woman. He stood there with her dead at his feet, then he slammed the door. The funny thing is, him slamming the door was more scary than the killing.'

'Weird,' Elke said.

'Why was that, you think?'

He remembered the violence, the speed, the finality of the slam. The closed door. He'd woken in a sweat.

'Maybe you had one of your headaches.' She received a text. 'Can you drop me in Newmarket?'

'Going to be a big shopping session, is it?'

'Yes — pooh, can you smell that?'

'I can actually. Burning rubber.' He peered at the dials on the dashboard.

'I hope you're not about to blow up, Daddy dearest.'

They drove the rest of the way in silence. He dropped her off, watched her sauntering away, still texting. She was beautiful and droll and unknowable and he felt the weight of loving her.

As he pulled away there was a pinging from the dash and a red light came on. He caught the faint smell of burning rubber again.

It was still early so he drove home to check on Claire. She was out on the deck, the table covered with notes, a laptop, empty cups. Before heading to his surgery he sat down with her and had a coffee, asked how the studies were going. He told her about his dream. He was still wondering why all the fear was in the slamming of the door.

She said, 'Maybe because it seemed arbitrary, irrational. Harder to make sense of. It meant he could attack again without warning. You wouldn't see him coming and you wouldn't be able to reason with him. Lack of communication is scarier than violence. Or makes violence scarier.'

He gave her an affectionate little punch on the arm. 'The strange thing is, the brain constructs the story — creates the fright with one part of itself in order to scare the other part.'

She tilted back her chair, yawned. 'And then spends a whole lot of conscious energy working out what its own story actually means.'

He thought about this, looked at the crooked parting in her fair hair, her freckly, pleasant face. Her nose and jaw were shaped like Ford's and she'd inherited Simon's ungainly figure, worse luck, his shapeless legs, big bum and heavy bones. No, she wasn't beautiful like Elke, but her eyes were lovely: striking and full of clear intelligence. She could stare you down. He thought: eyes like a physicist. You see a physicist interviewed on some TV documentary, he'll have those searchlight eyes, those lamps.

He said, 'Who are you going to vote for next election?'

Amused curl of her lip. 'Not the rich prick.'

'What's his being rich got to do with it?'

She hesitated. 'I talked to David about politics.'

'I know, you asked him about "third-world diseases".'

'There was that, but there was another time, when you and Mum weren't there.'

'Oh God. How did that go?'

'It's strange. He's not political. It's like, with him it's personal. Don't you find it weird that they don't talk about politics at Rotokauri? There's just a stream of inanity about movies and tennis and workouts. They talk about what's happened on *CSI New York*. They're totally anti-intellectual. Don't you die of boredom?'

Simon sighed. 'They don't conduct business at the dinner table, no. They run the country, then they go and have dinner and unwind.'

'But it's so unsatisfying — it's all wrong. There's no ethics, the only thing they worship is money. They're not Conservative or conservative or anything. And with David, there's all this stuff going on underneath. He . . . hates something. He wants to kill something in himself.'

'He probably wants to kill you.'

She ignored this. 'There's a reason why you and he fit so well together.'

'What's that then?'

'For one thing, he's in love with you. Or he loves the idea of you. Wants to be like you, maybe. But Dad,' she turned serious. 'I worry.'

'Oh, do you now.'

'Roza. She and Mum are best friends, right. They do everything together. But Roza . . . she hates Mum. *Hates* her.'

'Oh come on.' He thought, *You* hate her. Don't project your own feelings on others.

She said, 'I worry. Because—'

'You're imagining it. Roza's good friends with Karen.'

'No. You're wrong.'

He sighed. 'Why would Roza hate Karen?'

'Elke.'

He thought of Ford, and Aaron. Aaron's genetic legacy: suspicion, paranoia. The old man was so minutely attuned to undercurrents that it killed off all his spontaneity and generosity. Simon thought, Maybe the less sensitive you are to signals from the animal kingdom, the easier it is to love and be loved.

He said, 'You worry too much. Everything's fine.'

'If Roza could hurt Mum, she would.'

'Ah, that's crap, Claire.' He thought, Why would *you* care? You've been hurting your mother all your life.

'I know what you're thinking. Just because I don't get on with Mum, you think I'm not telling it like it is. But I've *seen*—'

He cut her off. 'OK, I get the picture. Thanks for the warning.'

Irritated, he gave her a quick kiss on the cheek. She shied away. Outside, he got a cold feeling, didn't want to leave her like that. He went back in.

'Claire.' He put his arms around her. 'Don't worry. I understand.'

'Do you?'

'Count on it. I understand what you're saying. Never think I don't. And you're the cleverest person I know.'

He held her tight. 'Just don't be so . . . imaginative.'

'Watch this space,' she said.

'Darling, you're just ridiculous.' He kissed her cheek. 'See you later. Drama queen.'

He took Karen's little Honda, thinking he would call an AA mechanic later to check his own car. He cleared off a pile of ChapSticks and lipsticks and worked himself gingerly into the driver's seat, amused at the tininess of his wife — how did she fit? His knee throbbed as he made room for himself, pushing the seat back, rearranging the mirrors. On the passenger seat she'd left a stack of brochures and magazines and tubes of hand cream and a tangle of netball bibs and a pair of running shoes and two Nike caps.

The car was an automatic, the only kind Karen would drive, its tinny engine whining and lurching its way between gears. After driving his big smooth beast it was like being crammed into a pedal car. He much preferred manual gears and took a moment to adjust, hitting the brake once, thinking it was a clutch. What a risible vehicle; he should buy Karen something better. He drove leaning down to massage his painful knee.

He was driving along the street towards his office building when he saw Arthur Weeks. Swearing softly he pulled over, lowering the window. His phone started to ring.

Weeks leaned down. 'I knew you were in town today. I called your receptionist.'

Simon looked at his phone. Clarice calling. He let it go to messaging. 'What can I do for you?'

The young man hovered with an anxious, twitching smile. 'Come for a coffee.'

Silence.

Weeks raised his voice, eager, urgent. 'Quick coffee at my flat, it's not far away. I want to tell you a couple of things. And I'll give you Mereana's phone.'

Simon shook his head. But he thought of what Claire had just said. Lack of communication had its own risks. Perhaps it was better to know what Weeks was up to.

'Come on, what've you got to lose?' Weeks said.

Simon's phone started ringing again; he looked at it, distracted.

'It's literally two minutes' drive away,' the young man urged, repeating the address, the phone shrilling again. Simon said, 'Yes, OK, I've got it. Just go away, will you? Let me deal with this and I'll come.'

'OK. See you in two.'

Simon watched him walk to his car and drive off. He checked his messages. There was nothing urgent, just Clarice making work for herself.

He started driving then stopped the car, trying to decide what to do. Was it a mistake to follow Weeks? The phone rang again. Clarice.

He had an irrational sense that the phone *was* Clarice, a little nagging, spying outpost of her that he had to lug around. Would she be able to tell if he turned it/her off? Irritated, he put the thing on silent, and when it went on vibrating and flashing he got out of the car, walked along the street and slipped it into his office mailbox in the gatepost. He glanced around. From a window opposite two small white dogs stared down at him. They had patches of black around their eyes, two little ghosts, their ears twitching.

The flat really was only two minutes' drive away, at the very top of a small, quiet street running up the side of Mt Eden. The young man was waiting, and he led Simon up a flight of concrete stairs to his flat. The rear windows looked onto the grassy slope of the hill; from the front there was a view of the suburbs stretching away across the isthmus.

Weeks showed him to a concrete deck out the back and bustled inside, saying he would make coffee. Simon sat on a canvas chair. Across a wire fence the paddock rose sharply towards the summit. It was a dazzling morning, bright sunshine, and there was a rich, hot smell of grass and manure. The traffic sounded distant below.

Weeks came out with two coffee cups. He said, 'Strong brew. I need it. I don't sleep, insomnia. It's got so bad I've started taking sleeping pills. Then in the morning I need coffee to clear my head.'

Simon didn't look at him. 'That's called a vicious circle,' he said.

'I know. Anyway. How's your holiday going? You've been staying at Rotokauri with the Hallwrights. And the Cahanes. Ed Miles, our charming Minister of Police. I read it in the paper. Must be interesting. That Cahane — knows everything, finger in every pie. Apparently he's interested in Norse mythology? I was thinking about him — he's quiet, but there's that intensity, what is it, patrician anger? A vast sense of entitlement? Ambitious, incredibly right wing, fanatical; you can imagine him being a kind of hysteric.'

But what did he know about Cahane, or any of them? Anger rose in Simon like gas. One spark and he'd go off.

Weeks went on, 'I'd like to meet them. Hallwright. Cahane. Ed Miles. The beautiful Roza Hallwright. And your Elke Lampton, Mrs Hallwright's daughter.'

Neither spoke for a moment. A butterfly fluttered lopsidedly over the long grass, the cicadas clicked and crackled. Avoiding Weeks's sharp little black eyes, Simon fixed his gaze on the paddock, the bees climbing and toppling in the grass stalks, the drunken flight of the butterfly. He heard the coy voice lingering on the loved names: Roza, Elke.

Weeks said, 'Speaking of the beautiful Roza Hallwright, are the rumours true?'

Silence.

'Mrs Hallwright and an extremely wild youth? Possible recent relapse? Suggestion of drugs? I met a glamorous woman at a party, her name was Tamara Goldwater. She was drunk, she said she had a tale to tell about Roza Hallwright. She mentioned the Hallwrights' main housekeeper. Mrs Lin Jung Ha . . .'

Simon controlled his anger. 'So you want to meet them. But you're not just some hack, you're a "movie director". Only a failed one. With your "short films" and your "Sundance". Just an ageing kid hanging around the real people. Making up ugly gossip. Trying to find some life. Because you don't have one of your own.'

'Whoa.' Weeks put up his hands.

Simon looked at him, sensing the young man's ego properly flicked.

'When did you last see Mereana?' Weeks asked. His voice turned hurt and hard now.

'I don't know her.'

The young man was pale, his face pinched, untouched by the summer sun. His eyes were like wet stones. 'So you won't mind me mentioning to people that I've got her phone with your picture in it.'

'Yes, I will.'

'Why?'

'Because it's none of your business where my picture is. It's none of your business.'

'OK . . .'

'When did you last see . . . this woman?'

Weeks said, 'You mean which one of us was last to see her. Let me guess. That's important to you, because you want to know when she disappeared. You want to know, did she disappear because of you.'

'I don't know what you're talking about.'

'I know you had a relationship with her,' Weeks said.

'Well, you know wrong.'

'She told me.' Weeks smiled recklessly. Triumph, anticipation in his eyes.

'You're lying. When did she tell you?'

'Wanting to know when — that's what gives you away. You're trying to figure out what happened to her. If you didn't know her you wouldn't care about *when*.'

'Why don't you leave it alone?'

'I want to know what happened to Mereana.'

'I don't know what happened to her.'

A pause. Weeks looking at him.

'OK? I don't know.'

'So you know *her*. Come on, did you like my films? The woman who plays Anahera, you know what we did? We gave her green contact lenses. Remember Mereana's eyes?'

Simon stared, hating him. He said, 'Did the woman, the real Mereana, get a job at Maori TV?'

'No. It was Mereana's ambition, that's why I put it in the film. She — the real Mereana — finished school, she was going to go to Auckland University, do a media course. But as soon as she got to Auckland she wasted all that; she went off with an idiot — a rich boy who'd been to King's. He was bright, good family, been a genius at school and then dropped out. She was stupidly in love with him and careless, which meant she got pregnant. Then she got busted, because her boyfriend decided to pull off a series of enormous drug deals with some ancient dinosaur bikers, Hell's Angels, and she was surprised one day coming back from the supermarket by the Armed Offenders Squad. A house full of fat bikers and ninjas and the boyfriend covered in blood because he'd run into a glass door trying to get away. The cops found wads of cash and drugs. She said it was nothing to do with her but they charged her as well.

'He got a big sentence and she went to jail and they took her baby away for the last bit of her stretch. Her boyfriend's family banned her. She had to fight to get the kid when she got out, and then it died of meningitis, and the family blamed her for that. After that she was just lost, she didn't care about anything. She had a job managing a café out at the airport.'

'Nice story,' Simon said.

'She told me about you.'

'Oh really.'

'She came to see me here. It was summer, we climbed the mountain and sat up there. She described you. A doctor. Obstetrician. Married. Rich. Willing to go and fuck her in the really bad house she was living in, because it was close to the airport, which fitted with his business trips. She said there was something wrong with this doctor; he was unhappy, there was something bad going on in his life, and since there was something wrong with her too, they got on well.

'She said he reminded her of her loser boyfriend who'd gone to King's, the jailbird, he looked similar, curly hair and broad shoulders, only the doctor hadn't gone to King's, she said he'd grown up poor. She said she loved him but he was married and had kids and he was really old.'

'What did you say?'

'I said, the doctor's no good, that's a hiding to nothing, married guy, old guy. Get rid of him and move in with me. She didn't want to. I wasn't her type.'

'Your love was unrequited. The doctor was her type.'

'It was. He was. I said to her it's doomed with the doctor, which she knew, but she let it happen because she was lonely.'

It was new detail: Mereana's arrest, the fact that the father of her dead child was a middle-class ex-King's boy. He'd never asked, only listened to her stories about living in the Far North as a child. For a moment he thought about her: face, body, eyes, voice, without revulsion and disgust. But he didn't want her memory, he pushed it away.

Weeks said, soft, 'Do you think about her? Worry about her? I remember, she had a theory about why the doctor liked her. It was to do with his childhood. He thought there was something bad about himself and he was taking it out on her. Using it up on her.'

'You've got the wrong doctor.'

'I've got the one who's in her phone.'

'Means nothing.'

'Do you miss her? Feel guilty?'

The anger broke through. 'I've got nothing to feel guilty about. But listen, Weeks, that time up here with her, did your friend *tell* you you weren't her type? That could've made you angry. Maybe you fought, you were drunk, you smacked her head into a rock. Maybe you dragged her down the hillside, put her in the boot and drove her out to the Woodhill Forest. Now all you've got left is your insomnia and your pills and your corny film. Close-ups of sparkling green eyes, shots of tossing hair, all that shit, and meanwhile you're trying not to think about the muddy hole you rammed her in when you'd finished with her.'

Weeks stared, blinked.

'Nice story,' he said.

Silence between them. Words carried across the paddock from a conversation between two people on a walking track: 'Summit.' 'Perfect.' 'South.' 'No.'

'Did you love her?' Weeks's voice had gone dogged, hurt, like a youth confronting his father. Simon felt something through his anger. He thought of his boy, Marcus.

He said less roughly, 'You make things up. I'm a doctor so I like facts. She's your creation. Make up whatever you like.' He added, 'You're the one on the guilt trip.'

'Why guilt?'

'You've used details about her, put them in your film.'

'No. She's my friend. I want to find her.'

'What a hero. Nothing to do with your career.'

A reckless smile broke out on Weeks's pinched face; he quelled it like a boy nursing a pleasingly evil secret.

He said, 'I *have* had a new idea recently.' He lowered his eyes modestly. 'I've written a screenplay about a National Party Prime Minister.'

There was a steel water bowl on the concrete, set there for a cat or dog perhaps, and the sun caught the water and made a dazzling white glare. Simon kept his eyes on it, and when he looked at Weeks there was a black hole in his vision, an absence of light surrounded by a burning border.

From behind the blackness Weeks said, 'What I'd like is for you to let me in.'

He was dizzy. 'Let you in?'

The young man's voice seemed to come from far away behind the shimmer, the crackle of the cicadas. 'Into your circle, or, OK, even if it's just a few times, let me meet these people, the Hallwrights, the Cahanes, all of them.'

'So you can spy on them.'

'I'm not a gossip columnist. This connection between us is a gift.

I want to make a good film, a work of art. Come on, why not?'

'A gift.'

Weeks's voice went on: 'It's not political. I'm an artist. I need to do a bit of research on that world. Check my facts. Let's face it, I don't have any money, I don't mix with that kind of people. I want to make portraits of contemporary society. I want to do the rich and powerful as well as the poor. I've got the idea for a kind of modern-day Victorian melodrama. I've been reading a lot of Dickens . . .'

Dickens. Simon thought about how much Dickens he'd personally read: zero. He said, 'The Hallwrights? Look at them on YouTube, like a normal stalker. I'm not letting you in anywhere. It's not going to happen.'

Weeks lowered his voice. 'What about Mereana? Do any of your friends know about her?'

He was dazzled again. The black hole in its circle of light. 'No. Why would they?'

'So you wouldn't want me to ask them?'

Simon sat forward. 'That's a threat. I let you in and you don't spread rumours about me.'

'I just think we could help each other.'

'I don't want your help.'

'I'll just have to go on looking for Mereana by myself.'

Simon stood up. 'Weeks, I'm not going to do anything for you. Whatever you threaten me with. I will not be talking to you again. Do you understand?'

He limped down the steps. A cat prowled along a fence, somewhere in the distance a siren started up. The car was parked next to a rickety fence, on the other side of which, about ten metres down, was the concrete yard of the house below. All was quiet; there were gardens behind concrete walls, high hedges, a ramshackle garage sagging under the weight of a milkweed vine. He stood listening to the emptiness, the hum of traffic below.

The car had turned into an oven. He started the engine and cranked up the air conditioning. Sweat rolled down his face, his hands were wet. He tried to remember the exact words Weeks had used. The threat in them.

There was a bang, so sudden everything flew out of his mind. Weeks was at the passenger window, he'd banged hard on the glass. Simon writhed. In his fright he'd wrenched himself sideways, and something had popped in his knee.

Weeks was coming around the front of the car.

The pain in the knee was huge; it filled Simon's whole body. Anger flooded him. He stamped the accelerator to pull away. But his sweating hands slipped on the steering wheel, he didn't turn hard enough left and the front right bumper hit Weeks's hip, sending him backwards against the low fence. The fence gave way, his arms flew up in the air and he went over the top of the wall.

Simon braked and got out. He stood waiting for a furious Weeks to scrabble up over the edge, come at him. He was ready.

Silence. Only the cicadas sawing away. He edged forward, looked over, clapped his hand to his mouth. He hobbled along the road, found steps, limped down into the yard. Weeks had fallen ten metres and landed on his head on the concrete.

He looked at the angle of the head and body. Weeks's eyes were open, blood and fluid trickled from his ear and nose. His skull was fractured; he could possibly have survived that. But his neck was broken too.

A phone lay in bits near his hand. Simon put the pieces in his pocket and backed away, looking around at the yard bordered by the windowless back of a house and the high retaining wall Weeks had fallen down. Struggling up the steps he passed an empty garden, a washing line with sheets, a closed back door. A vast stillness seemed to have descended, as if the oxygen had been sucked out of the world. His eyes blurred, he floundered, realised he was holding his breath, sucked in air and heard himself let out a moan.

On the street he toiled back to the car, looking at the house above; one side of it was Weeks's, there was no sign of life in the other; the front window had its blinds lowered.

One more look down at Weeks, the grotesque angle of the body, the head squashed sideways. His shoe had come off, exposing a sock and a thin ankle.

He forced himself to climb the steps to Weeks's back deck. It was a peaceful scene: the warm air trapped in the shelter of the house, the summer paddock, the bees climbing and toppling in the dry stalks. Across the hillside, the walking track was deserted. He picked up the two coffee cups. Every step down to the car the pain slowed him but also carried him, forcing him forward when all he wanted was to sink down.

Putting the cups on the passenger seat he drove slowly down the empty street, crossed the main road and entered the grid of the suburbs. He stuck to residential areas, winding his way west as far as he could, avoiding main roads, shopping centres, bus routes. The rows of houses had taken on a toy appearance; the colours looked unreal in the morning glare and he was distracted by the illusion that Karen's car had been at once shortened and heightened, transformed into a Lego-mobile in which he trundled, trundled, with mad toy-town slowness.

Eventually he parked under trees on a road on the edge of an estuary. He pulled himself out of the car, sat on a bench, his sore leg stuck out awkward and stiff, and found himself taking an interest in the speed of the tide creeping in over the mudflats, as if he'd entered a new world in which things taken for granted had assumed powerful significance: speed, colour, sound. There was a noise in his head, the sound the world made as it turned. The mangroves and flax bushes gave off a bright sheen, a heron stood motionless at the water's edge.

There was a hard object in his hip pocket. He pulled out the pieces of phone that had been scattered near Weeks's hand. He slotted in the battery and fitted the back, and when the cracked screen came to life he saw it wasn't Weeks's phone, it was Mereana's.

Banging on the window, the young man had said something. It could have been, 'Here. Here it is.'

He must have decided to give up Mereana's phone.

Had he fetched it, hurried down the steps after Simon, banged on the window, come around the bonnet towards the driver's side, and offered to hand over the one thing he could hold over Simon as proof?

Simon looked at the gold sheen on the mangroves, the dark purple-brown of the estuarine mud, the pinks, greens and yellows in an oil slick on the slow water. It seemed to him that something was coming writhing up out of the colour, that it was alive.

The Green Lady

Soon, Starfish and the Village Idiot were crossing the forest on their way back to the castle. They were carrying fishing rods.

"Starfish, you poof," Soon said complacently, "you're a failure at most things, and fishing is one of them."

Little Starfish ignored him and went back to help the Idiot, who'd got tangled in a creeper. Then they heard hoof-beats, and the Green Lady and her men rode past them, armed and on their way to the castle.

Keeping a wary eye out for the High Priestess Germphobia, they followed her to the castle to see what was going on. But the Green Lady entered into a secret conference and they were told nothing.

Later that evening they heard a rumour from the Bachelor, who was parked in his bed in the courtyard and drinking cocktails with his girlfriends the Cassowaries.

"It has come to me through the grapevine," the Bachelor said in a languid voice, "that the secret conference concerns your sister, Soon."

"Her!" Soon said in a scornful voice. He preferred to ignore his sister, the mysterious and beautiful Soonica.

"It seems," the Bachelor went on, "that Barbie Yah herself has hatched a diabolical plot, and that your sister is involved."

"Involved? Then let's have her arrested!" Soon cried. "Detained. Thrown in jail. Or perhaps tortured. What do you think, Vill?"

"Ha ha," said the Village Idiot.

"That's monstrous," Starfish said. "Your own sister!"

"You're right. Forget torture. Let's have her executed," said bloodthirsty Soon.

Starfish said, "What else have you heard, Bachelor?"

The Bachelor lay back on his pillows, drew his satin robe around himself and narrowed his eyes. The menacing Cassowaries hissed softly. Coloured steam rose from the Bachelor's potent cocktail. "The witch Barbie Yah, in cahoots with her henchwoman, the Ort Cloud's Wife, has tried to cast a spell on your sister, to draw her away from us forever. She has had their paid spy put a spell on Soonica, in order to create a door into her dreams. Soonica received a message in a dream to enter the Dark Forest. The Green Lady rode after her and brought her back, but Barbie Yah told Soonica in another dream how to escape. Soonica woke in time and returned to the castle, but she is in danger every time she sleeps. She must not sleep unless she is under lock and key!"

The Bachelor turned to Soon. "The Green Lady will save your sister; I have no doubt of it. But the battle may be difficult. And it will be fought in the world of dreams."

Johnnie was silent. In the trees, a tui ran through its repertoire of squeaks and trills.

Finally the boy asked, 'Does the Bachelor have a name?'

Roza considered. 'He does actually. Now you ask. The Bachelor's full name is Schlong Lovewand. He's the son of another great bachelor, Cock Lovewand.'

'What's his mum's name?'

'She's . . . let's see. Mountain Titswoman.'

Simon looked up from his book. Roza went on pushing Johnnie on his swing. Mother and son faced him, with their potent eyes, their identical smiles. The sound of their laughter filled his ears.

From his station, propped and braced with cushions on a chaise longue, he watched the mother and the little boy, now on their knees in the grass hunting for specimens. His leg was tightly bandaged. He'd had an appointment with an orthopaedic surgeon who had told him the damage wasn't severe enough to require surgery, at least not at this stage, and had recommended physiotherapy and special exercises, a period of rehabilitation that should improve it.

He hadn't had to invent anything about the injury: he'd described getting out of the car in a hurry, wrenching the knee sideways, the terrible click or pop, the pain. He'd been given strong painkillers; they were effective but at night they made the edges of reality blur; he saw images melting, like photographs set on fire and curling as they burned. Somewhere inside him there was a vibration like the crackle of cicadas, a wall of noise.

Karen was sitting up in bed, hunched over. It was morning, hot sun coming in through the blinds. He put his hand on her warm back.

'What's wrong?'

She clenched her fists under her chin. 'Roza's asked Elke to go on their trip to America.'

'That's nice. She'll love it. If she can fit it in with her studies.'

Recently Elke had, without much enthusiasm or purpose, enrolled for a BA at Auckland University. He wasn't convinced she'd see it through but they'd encouraged her.

'You'll need a career,' he'd told her. 'What are you interested in?'

Her vague smiles, her shrugs. 'Dunno. Like, journalism? The media? Something with animals?'

Karen said, tense, 'There's more. Roza wants Elke to move in with them. In Auckland.'

He stroked her back automatically; he was partly trying to soothe himself. 'She's old enough to move away from all of us. We can't control where she goes.'

'I've devoted myself to Elke. Slaved for her. All that time we spent getting her right when she was little, the sleepless nights, the worry, year after year, while Roza was swanning around being the grand lady, having *abandoned* her. How can she get rid of her own child and then just suddenly decide, OK, I want her back, now it suits me. She'll take her up and then get sick of her, like she's a toy or a puppy. She'll hurt her.'

'Karen—'

'How dare she? She sees what a beautiful success I've made of Elke and she thinks, I'll have that. Just decides to take her away.'

'Elke's grown up; she has to make up her own mind.'

'Roza's manipulating her, trying to turn her against me.'

'That's not true. I know it's hard, but they *are* going to have a bond; they're mother and daughter.'

Karen let out a harsh, doomed laugh.

'Come on. When she adopted Elke out she was so young, she was in confusion, she had the Catholic-zealot depressive mother. Then she had her alcohol problem, and she didn't know where Elke was for years. It's natural she wants to make up for it now.'

'I could never adopt out my own child. It's sick. Unnatural.'

'Ah, you don't know what you'd do.'

'You think I'm competitive. You think I want to "own" Elke. But I can tell that woman will hurt her. What hurts her hurts *me*.'

He pulled her down to the bed, hugged her, stroked her hair. 'There comes a point where you have to let go, let nature take its course.' She didn't answer, only looked bitter. 'Anyway, look at the way Roza is with Johnnie. She wouldn't hurt *him*.'

Karen waved her hand, dismissive. 'That little boy is exactly like David. Nothing could hurt him.'

'Really?' Simon was distracted by this.

'And no, Roza wouldn't hurt Johnnie, he's completely her creature. He's like her creation. The way they talk and talk together, always the secrets and private jokes; the kid is unnatural. What is he, four? The *vocabulary* he has already, like an adult. They're like a witch and her familiar.'

'A witch.'

'But Elke's been mine, so Roza thinks she's *tainted*. She thinks she's got to get her back and purify her, make her into her own again, like Johnnie.'

'Tainted? This is starting to sound quite mad, Karen.'

She pushed him away. 'You don't know because you're a man and a doctor, you're utterly unimaginative. You don't see anything. You've got your secure world, everything up front and straightforward, nothing below the surface. All your medicine and your reason, and half the time you're blind. I sense things. The world is more animal than you think.'

He felt the noise in his head rising. 'We need to be rational. And if we can't, we should invent an excuse and go home.'

'No.'

'But if Roza knows you're thinking all this it's hopeless, we can't stay here.'

Karen smiled. 'Roza? She doesn't know what I think. Roza loves me. She thinks I'm simple and easygoing and we're best friends.'

Simon stared. 'I see. And . . . David?'

'David and I have a bond. We understand each other.'

'So, the other night . . .'

'When he and I were talking and you came barging down? It was so obvious you were jealous.'

Simon thought for a moment. He put his arm around her shoulder and drew her close. 'Darling, I understand what you're saying. But these are complicated people we're dealing with. Do you think you can keep your thoughts to yourself while we're here? There's just a faint possibility that you — or I, of course — might get some signals wrong. Misjudge things. And we have to think of Elke. We wouldn't want to ruin what we've got with the Hallwrights just because we've misunderstood.'

She groaned. 'Don't patronise me. I can't stand it. You have no idea about people. You're all science. With human beings, two plus two does not always equal four.' She lay back, inspected her nails. 'Poor David.'

'David can look after himself.'

'Oh sure, in politics. But dealing with Roza.'

Simon thought, David is the only person around whom Roza is just slightly uncertain.

'I'm sure David'll be fine. Meanwhile, there's Ed Miles to watch out for. And I wouldn't confide in Juliet. Since she's an open book and Ed reads minds.'

She sighed. 'I told Elke I didn't want her to move out.'

'What did she say?'

'She just hugged me, very sweet, very dreamy. She never says anything.'

Simon fixed his eyes on her. 'David's got attached to Elke too, because she looks like Johnnie.'

'Oh.'

'Not that you'd be jealous of David.'

She looked up quickly. 'David's influence is good for Elke.'

Their eyes locked. It felt like something was twisting in his chest. He squeezed her shoulder, got dressed and went out before he could say anything he would regret.

He walked slowly under the pohutukawa trees, across the lawns where Trent and Shane were browsing over the hedges with clippers.

141

He skirted past the dancing lawn-sprinklers and took the broad shell path to the seaward side of the Wedding Cake where David, wearing a tight Lycra shirt and a towel around his neck, sipped from a glass of dark green fluid. Below the deck Dwayne and the new guy Chad stood hands on hips, silently contemplating a flower bed.

David raised his glass. 'You're late.'

Simon sat down with the usual pleasure that he'd been expected and waited for. He hadn't got over the thrill that he was the only one at Rotokauri who was invited to join David for breakfast. Roza and Johnnie slept late and Simon and David met early each morning like a couple of lovers, with their shower-wet hair and their yawns and their occasional sleepy exchanges about what was in the newspaper — they were provided with one each — or the weather, or what had been said by whom at dinner the night before. Simon felt chosen. It was partly excited vanity — he, the son of loser Aaron, picked out to be friend of the country's top man — and partly affection for David, who could be charming and confiding in the mornings, bleary-eyed, relaxed, talking blokeishly or even crudely about women, asking Simon's opinion of politicians and staffers, sometimes describing a recent altercation, grabbing Simon's arm, working himself up: 'You wait. I'll get him. I'll fuck him up.'

Now he said, 'Try this shit Dean's got me on. It's seaweed. Fucking disgusting but makes you live forever. And I'm supposed to have lean protein and no butter or cheese. And guess what. We've just been for a run. Right to the end of the beach.'

Simon nodded, sliding into his seat.

David signalled to Troy. 'Bring Simon some of this green stuff. And what else? Your usual?'

Troy received his instructions and glided away.

'It's going well with the training then?' Simon spoke politely, with correctness; he was naturally reticent, careful.

'I'll have a body like iron.'

Simon's eye fell on the vivid blur of colours in the flower bed. Still hazy from last night's pain pills he murmured, 'It's already bothering me that I can't run. With the knee.'

'It'll get better. Try this.' Solicitous, David handed him a glass of liquid seaweed.

He sipped. 'Mm. Yuk. Vile.'

'Swill it down.' David rustled the newspaper, raised it, and the headline appeared in front of Simon: *Mt Eden Death Investigated*.

Whipping the paper away, David said, 'Vince Buckley's got his publicity about suicides. What an arsehole. I'll laugh if the suicide rate goes up. Sudden waves of jumpers and wrist-slashers.'

Simon smiled thinly. David shook the paper up again. 'Cahane's tax working group's about to report. They'll recommend something radical and we'll act moderate, go for the middle ground. It's Cahane's method, sort of like good cop–bad cop, isn't it. Drink your seaweed.'

The article bobbed in front of Simon: *The man found dead in a suburban back yard on Wednesday was local journalist and film-maker Arthur Weeks.*

They would see that Weeks had fallen over the retaining wall, but would they realise he'd been pushed by a car? There'd surely be a bruise on his leg or hip. Maybe there were tyre marks on the road, maybe someone had seen the whole thing: an old lady high in the house next to Weeks's, hiding behind her curtains, telling her story when the police came knocking.

Simon drained his glass. His stomach was full of ice. Troy arrived with plates, scrambled eggs for Simon, poached for David. Below, Dwayne worked his way round the edge of the flower bed. Chad followed, intent, a plastic pack strapped to his back, a thin hose spiralling out of it. He stooped and sprayed, little rainbows dancing in the drops of liquid.

David had got rid of the sports towel and was busy with his eggs. His cheeks and neck were flushed from the morning workout, his blond hair damp. He glanced up and Simon met the hard grey eyes, took in David's pink-and-gold charm, the solidity of his body in the sports clothes. Claire had said David was in love with him; she was all hot air and fiendishness but he did himself sometimes feel love for David.

As a boy he'd hung around in loose gangs with Ford; later he'd been so driven and uptight he hadn't been good at making male friends. He was better with women; the barrier of difference allowed him to relax. No surprise he'd chosen to practise O and G. He'd married Karen in order to belong, in order not to be alone, and yet in some ways he'd remained alone. There was Claire, his own girl, the best girl in the world, and Elke and Marcus; all three of his children were a joy, but still there was something he yearned for and had never achieved; it was what Ford had had with May.

He'd been singled out by David, and it had turned his head. The people surrounding David were politicians and staffers; you could tell he didn't trust any of them. David's only close friend had been old Graeme Ellison; now Graeme was dead, David seemed to be drawing Simon closer. It occurred to Simon that David, for all his power and popularity, was oddly solitary. He had Roza and Johnnie; he had his two older children, Izzy and Mike; but no extended family, no large circle, at least not one that was close. He had Simon and Karen. He wanted Elke . . .

Simon caught sight of the newspaper headline again. He felt nausea at what he was hiding and what damage he could inflict. There was no way to come clean, nothing to do but wait. If they came for him, he could bring everyone down.

That hot, stunned morning, driving slowly down the mountain and entering the plain of the suburb, he had crossed his Rubicon. His mind clear, he'd envisaged the alternative: frantic and pointless CPR on Weeks while on the phone to the ambulance, full explanation, submission of his knee, car and statement for inspection. Handwringing: so dreadfully sorry, the poor young man, a tragic accident, I did everything I could. He'd briefly considered this course and rejected it, because it was impossible.

The mistake had been agreeing to go to Weeks's flat. If he'd rung an ambulance as soon as Weeks had gone over the wall, he would have had to explain too much. Why, the police would ask him, had he gone up that street instead of driving into work? To look at the view? If he denied knowing Weeks and they discovered Weeks had rung his cell phone, they would want to know why he'd lied. They would conclude the pair must have met, and for a reason. Simon Lampton — David Hallwright's friend — and an unknown young man. What had they been up to? Some gay thing, a lovers' fight? Once a police inquiry was under way the media interest would be unstoppable. It would not stop until everything was tainted and everyone he loved was damaged.

So he'd checked the neighbouring windows for signs of life, and when he'd satisfied himself there were no witnesses he'd retrieved the two coffee cups, got in Karen's car and driven away. Crossed his rust-red river, driven slowly west, carrying in his head the shimmering wall of noise. The sound hadn't left him. Late that night as he drifted between dreams, he'd imagined it was the sound of Weeks's soul shrieking out into oblivion.

He'd pulled himself together reasonably quickly, driven back home and put Karen's car back in the garage without going inside or seeing Claire. There were no marks on the front bonnet; he'd only nudged Weeks, after all. He got into his own car and drove into the car park at work with the dashboard warning light pinging and the faint smell of burning rubber. After he'd finished his paperwork and seen his patients he drove all the way back to Rotokauri without breaking down, and left the car at the local garage.

During the day he could think rationally in his own defence. The death had been an accident. Weeks had threatened him; his nerves had been on edge; the bang on the window had startled him; the pain in the knee had been extreme. He'd tried to drive away and his hot, sweaty hands had slipped on the wheel. The young man, when he'd got to him, had had a fractured neck and had died instantly, and as a doctor he was qualified to judge. There was absolutely nothing he could have done to save him. More damage, infinite damage, would be done by owning up and trying to explain.

But if the police caught up with him now, it would be harder to convince them the death had been accidental. He could plead panic, but it wouldn't go down well. The scandal would be greater; he could even be charged with manslaughter. Or murder. There would be questions about the time of death. Had he driven away while Weeks was still alive? He knew that wasn't the case, but the evidence would have to be analysed, discussed, picked over. It would be the end.

The night before, loosened by the evening pill (his knee hurt more at the end of the day), his mind had ranged free. He remembered his anger, heightened by his fright at the bang on the window, then the wrenching pain in his knee. Had he driven at Weeks in rage? Would the young man have gone over the flimsy fence if Simon hadn't jammed his foot hard on the pedal? In his agitation, driving Karen's automatic rather than his own manual car, had he pushed the accelerator thinking it was a clutch? He couldn't recall.

In a dream he saw Mereana. It horrified him that she was smiling. She said, 'Did you wish you could push a button, make him disappear?'

He woke with a dry mouth, compulsively smoothing the top sheet with his hand. He thought: but what was my crime? I had an affair with Mereana Kostas. I got involved with her because I was at a low point. That's all. He lay listening to the rustling, moving black night. He slept and dreamed again: Roza walking in a green forest with Johnnie, shapes in the trees behind her, the light unreal, theatrical clouds writhing in the sky.

He heard Roza's voice. She said: 'I am the Green Lady. I am the Voice. I made this happen to you.'

Roza and Johnnie laughing and the sound again. He saw a dark cloud; it was a whirling cone of insects, coloured shapes shimmering inside the darkness. They were dragonflies.

There will be no mercy, he thought.

He was walking towards the dunes. It was hot and still and the track stretched ahead, broad and overgrown and pitted here and there with the tracks of mountain bikes. He stopped to rest, adjusting the tight bandage on his knee. Now when he walked across the lawns with David, people joked about it: 'They even walk the same.'

David's limp was permanent, the result of a car accident in his youth. Simon's was less pronounced already and would eventually disappear, he hoped, although the improvement that morning was partly due to the double dose of painkillers he'd popped before leaving the Little House. In his bag he was carrying towel, suntan lotion, book, two phones and two blue coffee cups.

He'd tried to think it through. Weeks had called Simon's cell phone and those calls must be logged, most obviously in Weeks's phone. Those who got away with crimes were *forensically aware* (it was so easy to slip into the jargon). He decided to get rid of his own phone, as well as the cups and Mereana's phone. But he would still have to think up a reason why Weeks had called him.

There was so much he couldn't control. Had Weeks told anyone about meeting him? In a city full of eyes, it seemed impossible that he hadn't been seen on Weeks's street.

Someone calling. He turned, shielding his face, saw a dark shape against the blaze of early sun. Karen.

'Marcus wants to go over to the Gibsons. Can you give him a ride?'

'Off for a swim,' he said, shouldering the bag.

'I'd drive him but Juliet and I've got Garth for the hour, they're waiting for me.'

He sighed, trudged after her.

'They've invited him out on the boat.'

'You think it's safe?' He pictured Gibson drunk out of his mind, exuberantly ramming the wharf.

'Of course it's safe. It's not like they're going out in a dinghy. They've got *crew*.'

They reached the gate, passing Ray, whose eyes seemed to follow them unpleasantly. Karen went to get Marcus, Simon fetched his keys and waited in the car. He didn't want to see his son. He didn't want to talk to him or look at his hands or his messy hair or his young, volatile skin, the quick changes of expression: bravado, secretiveness, baffled innocence.

There was a voice in his head, very light, tired, washed out. He blocked it. A seagull swooped down and landed on the fence, and he looked into its pitiless black eye, like a tiny peephole into the universe. The bird stood ruffling its pure white feathers against a blue sky that was bright, hard, clean.

A memory came to him: a couple whose baby he'd delivered, the husband a gushing TV personality, Scott Roysmith. All psyched up to act in a drama called the wonder of birth, he'd told Simon about a night-time storm during which the lightning had lit up clear sky, great patches of bright blue in the dark.

'I realised that if only you could see it, the sky at night is blue,' Roysmith had said, while Simon tended to the writhing wife and the nurses popped in and out, checking on the celebrity patient. The wife shrieking at her husband to stick his blue sky up his arse . . . The baby was a girl, he remembered.

He had seen so many babies, handled them, looked into the empty blue of their eyes. Their eyes are always blue and cloudless, before they've lived. Because they haven't lived.

I've helped people to be born. Does that even the score?

I can't think of what I have done.

Marcus opened the car door.

'Hi Dad . . . What's wrong?'

'Nothing. Just thinking.' He coughed. 'Seatbelt.'

His bag was on the back seat. As they drove over the hills he could hear Weeks's coffee cups clinking.

At the Gibsons' there was no answer to their knock, but from inside came the sound of raised female voices, shrieks of raucous laughter.

Simon shouted out hello. Another collective shriek, then Janine called out, 'Come in.' The room was full of women and the floor was covered with balloons and feathers.

Janine, hectically rigged out in leather miniskirt, teetering golden sandals and a see-through top, came wading through the detritus. 'Excuse us, we had a hen party last night. My Chloe's getting married. We haven't been to bed yet, we're all a bit spacey. Have a coffee, Simon. Marcus, the boys are all on the boat, they're waiting for you.'

Sharon Cahane was reclining on a white sofa, a gaudy pink boa draped along her elegant frame. With manicured fingers, she wafted an artificial feather over her nose.

Janine said, 'We had a burlesque dancer come; she showed us how to strut our stuff.'

Sharon looked at Simon and minutely rolled her eyes.

'Then we hired a bus and went back to town, to a strip club.'

'It was hilarious.'

The way they all shrieked in unison. *Native birds,* he thought.

He said, polite, 'I didn't realise people still did these things. Hen nights.'

'Course they do. The men had a stag party. They even got Colin Cahane on a jet ski.'

Peter Gibson put his head around the door. He winked, his face boiled. 'All right, ladies? We're off now, leave you to it. Gidday Simon, I'll bring your boy back around eight. Colin's coming; he can run Marcus over the hill.'

He disappeared, and the native birds shrieked again, as if the mere sight of a man was exquisitely funny. The feathers kicked up, drifted down.

Outside, the water glittering with points of light, the flags snapping. Gibson's boat was heading out of the marina, churning through the green water. Simon felt he wasn't quite present in the hot room; he had a sense of floating amid the brightness, the rustle and stir of balloons and feathers, the yellow rectangle of light sliding across the ceiling and down the wall as the boat glided past, its hull reflecting the sun. A hen party. Were these people stuck in a time warp?

His grip on things had loosened, leaving him uncertain. He seemed to be groping for explanations. While the world spun, while the world raced on (flood fire tempest famine) these women floated in their provincial, feather-headed bubble. He thought . . . He thought, Don't tell Claire. And then, yes, tell her. Describe every detail. Strip clubs, balloons, feathers. Claire would be merciless.

But the women were not oblivious to the world. The coffee and cake roused them from their hungover torpor, and they started to talk. They frowned, serious. The faux accents, that had slipped a bit, returned.

'They have another baby so they can get more benefit . . .'

'They're draining the country *dray* . . .'

'. . . lazing around . . .'

'. . . on taxpayers' money.'

'The country's drowning under the . . .'

'Welfare dependency . . .'

There was a short silence.

Another yacht went by the window. Janine yawned, covering her mouth. Her gold bracelets pinged.

'Colin wants to buy shares in a vineyard . . .'

'Oooh, lovely.'

'Don't *talk* to me about waine. My poor *head* . . .'

The shriek of mirth was more subdued, they were yawning, glazed. Sparkling dust floated in the shafts of sunlight.

Simon got up, made his excuses, left them among the drifting feathers, slumped in their pile of boas.

How Could You Have Got This So Wrong?

He turned onto the Rotokauri road, winding up into the hills. Near the summit, where the land fell away from the highway in steep slopes, he pulled over, walked up and down the edge of the road, looking into the dark bush, listening. He saw his reflection in the side of the car, tall and thin and curved. The wind sighed in the tops, a native pigeon landed on a branch and looked pompously down at him.

Taking Mereana's phone, he threw it so hard he hurt himself. Instead of soaring away into the valley it hit a tree, rebounded and disappeared, too close to the road. He couldn't even get a simple thing like that right. The pigeon cocked its head, watching him as he stooped on the roadside, straightening his elbow with elaborate care. Crime was a young man's game. It was killing him.

He leaned against the car, feeling the warmth of the metal against his sore leg and his strained elbow. He heard Weeks's voice. *Do you miss her? Feel guilty?* He raised his eyes and there was the pigeon, stupid, astonished, preening its white bib.

Should he throw his phone and Weeks's coffee cups down there too, or find another spot? Was it better to spread the evidence, or would that make it easier to find? A little stab of self pity: he was so beleaguered and alone, so *inexperienced*. He needed support, information, peer review (the little gnome in his head, blackly laughing). He needed the hushed silence of his office and a textbook that would tell him: *Disposal of incriminating evidence: international best practice.*

Pressing his fingers to his eyes he saw red sunrise against his lids. Then he straightened, fighting the urge to turn, run.

'Hi,' he said.

The man coming towards him was big and broad, with a satanic little goatee beard.

'All right, mate?'

'Yes. Fine, thanks.'

'Not broken down?'

How had he arrived without any noise? It was unbelievable. Simon looked for the milk float or silent Prius, but saw only an ordinary red Holden Omega, its driver's door open and the still shape of a woman, vigilant in the passenger seat. But the athletic build, the Holden, the official tone, that Westie brute's goatee: a cop, he thought. He twitched the bag on his shoulder.

'Just on the phone. Getting bit fresh air.' His tongue was frozen; it was like talking through a mouthful of porridge.

The man was already turning away, making a signal to his passenger.

'But thanks for asking,' Simon called after him.

The man turned, actually looked at him, considered, seemed about to ask another question but only said, 'No worries.'

The red Omega pulled away, Simon raising his hand.

Leaning back against the car, his arm to his face, he had a moment of bitter incredulity. A cop. Possible cop. Even if not a cop, a witness, in fact two witnesses, who had seen him in this spot, who would remember later if questions were asked. They would search the bush beneath the road, find the phone.

·

He was already plunging down the slope, his feet sinking into the soft piles of rotting vegetation, looking for the tree the phone had hit. Everything looked different below the bush canopy and he was soon disorientated. The bush smelled of tea and spices, a rich brown reek. The air was cool near the ground; he skidded, landing on his rump in a pile of rotting nikau fronds, their fibrous dust rising around him. He lay on his back for a moment, gazing at the sky. Against the blue the manuka trunks were black, covered in a furry fungus. A weta, its feelers waving, scrambled over the top of a dislodged palm frond, so close he could see its shiny black eyes. He flinched away. A car droned by on the road above.

After an age of searching he slumped down on the soft ground and his eye fell on something metallic inside a pile of manuka twigs. The phone had landed in the centre of a network of spider webs strung among dead leaves and fallen branches. He stuck his hand into the sticky membrane and extracted the phone, tearing the webs away with it.

It was a long way back up to the road. He fought through a patch of toetoe and cutty grass that he hadn't passed on the way down, and tore his shirt on a tree branch. When he reached the road his mouth dropped open, he could have sunk to his knees. The car was gone.

He set off walking one way, changed direction, dithered, rounded the next bend and found it parked exactly where he'd left it. He should have realised: in the bush, sense of direction is the first thing to go.

At Rotokauri he bumped the car over the rough grass drive and through the gate, remembering a wave for the watchful sentries, Jon, Shaun, Ray. With a sense of futility — the farce he'd made of things — he left the car and shouldered his bag of contraband, heading for the Little House.

All was silent and the sun's blaze was pitiless, the trees still in the heat. Even the birds were subdued, their squawks drowsy. On the other side of the lawn Trent or Troy crossed the shell path, plugged into an iPod and actually dancing, clicking fingers, swinging elbows. Simon watched him shimmy past in the silence. He disappeared behind a tall hedge and reappeared on the slope of a further lawn, a figure cut out of light, graceful and mad. He turned and seemed to beckon, as though drawing Simon into the strange, dark core of the world. The garden was a mesh of bright colour, the light so merciless it seemed it could fray the very substance of matter, revealing what pulsed behind.

The image suddenly reared up before him of Weeks's grotesquely distorted body, his splayed limbs and vulnerable, bare, boyish ankle.

He closed his eyes, listening. Yes, it was there, the shimmering wall of sound.

In the hot utility area behind the Little House, among the rubbish bins, piles of recycling and reeking containers of rotting garden clippings, he loosened a brick from the wall and set to work smashing the coffee cups into dust. It was harder than he'd expected; the pieces kept shooting about and getting lost in the grass and he had to stop every few minutes to make sure he was still alone. In his agitation he hit his own thumb with the brick, raising a dark crimson half-moon of blood in the nail.

He had seen plenty of death, had handled bodies, babies who died being born or were born dead — you filled out the form *Status: Not Born Alive*. Sometimes, rarely, women died in childbirth or afterwards from complications, and he and the team would pull off their masks and step back and listen, as if they could hear the grief building behind the swing-doors, in the waiting rooms and corridors.

I have prevented deaths. I've brought babies back to life when they were floppy and blue. I have *held back* death. Does this count in the score?

In the stillness the tuis let out little exhausted warbles and clicks, pure drops of sound. A rosella flashed between the trees. After their pounding, Weeks's coffee cups lay in blue and white shards on the concrete slab beneath the bins. Simon scuffed them about with his foot, replaced the brick and limped inside.

In the bathroom he washed his hands and rinsed his face, dabbing gingerly at his sunburnt cheeks. He wondered how to dispose of the phones; he had yet to construct a plausible lie if he were asked about Weeks's having called him. Brooding on this he shambled out of the bathroom and smashed his knee into a table leg. He hopped back into the bathroom, scrabbling for the pain pills. All that bending over the coffee cups hadn't helped the injury; the skin below the bandage looked red and tight. He pushed his finger doubtfully into the strange-looking flesh.

It was good to take the weight off and sink down on the soft bed. He plunged into a queasy, uncomfortable sleep; he seemed somehow to be hanging on, as if the bed were tilting, and at one point had the sensation of being awake but paralysed and unable to rouse himself, his breath growing shallower and his limbs inert until, with a massive effort, he wrenched himself towards consciousness. He sank into sleep again and saw Ford's wife May, her shiny dark eyes fixed alertly on him, one hand to her glossy hair, bracelets jingling as she flicked a strand from her face.

He woke, dozed, woke again, thinking about May. She was beautiful, but what had always struck him was her intelligence. She gave the impression she could see into his soul; worse, she was greatly inclined to laugh. It was her ridicule he had feared. Once, lulled by an implausible rumour that the old man had dried out, Ford had unwisely taken her to meet Aaron. May was Sri Lankan and Aaron, after downing about a barrel of whisky, had unleashed a tirade of racist abuse. Ford had feared he'd lost her but she'd come back. After the old man had gleefully called her, among other appalling things, a 'curry bitch', May had shrugged it off. All she asked was that they never see Aaron again and Ford had been happy to oblige her on that.

His thoughts blurred. That May. In the dreamlight, her gaze held him. And she began to dance, very slowly at first, without taking her eyes off his face, and then she began to spin, until her body blurred and the air around her began to whirl so fast that light was gathered in and he was looking at a cone of spinning air, points of light glittering inside it.

'Make it stop,' he said.

May said, 'But this is not my dream.'

He coughed, rose on his elbows and nearly cracked his head on Karen's forehead. She was leaning over him, her ruby pendant dangling on its chain and coldly touching his nose.

'Sorry. You looked so peaceful,' she said.

She stood at the window, arms crossed, one hand cupping an elbow. The pose was theatrical. She turned, swung her arms, went to speak and then gazed away out the window, her eyes on a distant point.

Christ, out with it. Spare me the pantomime. She had presented him with a glass of iced water. He sipped it irritably.

'We need to talk.'

'Ah yes?' He raised his eyes, a sudden ache in his teeth from the cold water.

'Your behaviour. I can't . . . It's not . . .'

He sighed, waited.

'Even your expression right now, you should *see* yourself. Like a sort of *gargoyle*.'

'Thank you.'

'You look contemptible. I mean contemptuous. There's something

I have to tell you. That silly Kessler test. It didn't tell me I was normal. It said I was stressed.'

'Really.'

'It made me think about why that would be. I'm worried about Elke. But there's also our marriage. Your behaviour . . . When we eat dinner, I look up and you're waiting for me to finish. Just staring at me, waiting. When we go to the beach you wait for me to stop lying in the sun. Anything we do, you stand about waiting for it to end, with that gargoyle look on your face. I don't think you're capable of enjoying anything we do. You terrify me in the car with your speeding. You hardly eat. You're thinner. Sometimes when you look at me all I can see are these huge, cold, pale eyes with tiny little black pupils in them and this square grey face, and it's like being looked at by a *reptile*.'

He cleared his throat. 'Don't hold back.'

'I want to tell you something.'

There was more? He pressed the glass against his eyes.

She sat down next to him on the bed. The springs let out a small affronted squeak.

'Simon, I know you had an affair. OK? There's no point in denying it. Women know. I don't know who it was with or anything about it, but I know it happened, and that it ended a while ago.'

He stared.

She'd never said a word. His Karen, who was so straightforward, an open book, who couldn't control herself and always blurted out whatever was on her mind no matter how tactically foolish, who was . . .

Admit it, who was simple-minded. Beautiful, graceful and simple-minded. The perfect, undemanding presence, radiant with common sense, wonderfully unimaginative and calm, the sexy, dyed-haired goddess whose greatest pleasure was to receive the wealth, to revere him for his manly skill at bringing it home, to spend it on trappings, trappings, oh God.

She fingered the ruby pendant. 'The details aren't important now. I know you, Simon. I know you think I'm a featherbrain. It's my fault in a way.'

'Your fault?'

'How else would I have got you to marry me? It's another thing women know. They can tell what men want. If they want the man, they give him what he wants. Featherbrain, ice queen. Whatever. Get it?'

Silence.

'I know what you wanted. Like I keep telling you, women know. You didn't want to live alone, but deep down you did. You wanted to be with someone who wouldn't really know you. Who wouldn't see you. So that you could be married and have a family but in yourself, you could be alone.'

He looked at her almost with fear.

'But here's the thing. Sometimes you've wished you weren't alone. You've looked out of your little hermit's cave and wondered why you took such a lonely path. Why it was even necessary. And you dreamed of being in love. Requited love.'

His eyes burned, he squeezed them shut. How could she be capable of an insight like that? It was almost supernatural. He had an alarming sensation, something catastrophic happening to his chest. To be understood. Stripped bare. It was pain but the pain was exquisite.

'Get it, Simon? I wasn't "not seeing you" all this time. I was *looking away*. Because that was what you wanted.'

Her tone hardened. 'But my telling you all this is a very bad sign. Why would I let you in on all this if I still wanted to be married? I'm telling you because I don't care. I'm laying down my cards. I'm out of the game. I don't want to play any more . . .'

She tossed back her hair and seemed to lose focus; stuck on the metaphor she ran on, wandering through 'Showing my hand', 'Resigning', 'Leaving the field', 'Heading for the bench'. He was so struck with surprise he simply looked on, his hands placing themselves feebly about him; he tremblingly touched his sore knee, his eyes, his mouth. Good God. Karen. His golden Karen, goddess of furniture and foreign travel, of coffee mornings and fundraising lunches, Karen who said 'Taxpayers' money' and 'Wet bus ticket' and 'To be honest, I need a bit of Me Time after the gym.' Was it any wonder he'd thought her a fool? His beautiful, ferocious, golden fool. All this time she'd understood him. She'd known of his affair but had not said a word . . .

He swallowed, took a breath.

'Karen,' he began, and his voice deepened and steadied as he searched for the right words. 'An "affair"? I thinking you a "feather-brain"? Yearning for "requited love"? What can you possibly mean?'

A sorrowful note crept into his tone. He shook his head and felt control returning, his wild heart slowing down.

'My darling Karen, I can't, I just can't believe it. *How could you have got this so wrong?*'

Later, after she was lying in his arms sighing and laughing lightly at herself and saying, 'Oh who cares' and 'It's just so silly', he turned and whispered, 'Did you really mean it? You'd leave me?'

'No, no.'

He said, 'I can't live without you. You're my world.'

'Yes.'

'You've had some strange notions in your head. Weird ideas. An "affair". Me in a "hermit cave". You made me quite worried.'

'No, no,' she said vaguely again.

'I'm sorry about your Kessler score.' He added, 'There are plenty of ways you can get help for non-specific anxiety.' He paused, not breathing. It was outrageous but she took it, although she stayed silent. Was it his fancy or did her cheek, pressed against his, grow suddenly colder? Oh shameful, reptilian husband.

They dozed in the heat. After a while he gently pulled his arm out from under her sleeping head and went to the bathroom. He looked at his face. Age had softened and loosened his skin, he bore the imprint of the ribbed duvet cover on his right cheek, and there was a small network of broken capillaries under one eye. Experimentally he smiled, then winced — the effect was ghastly. No wonder she'd called him a reptile.

He brooded, looking down at her sleeping form. She was lying on her side, facing away from him, her blonde hair spread on the pillow. He turned to open a window and had the impression he'd caught her watching him in the dressing-table mirror. Was it a trick of the light? She was sleeping, her eyes tight shut, her expression innocent. No. She had been watching him.

A perverse thrill buzzed in his body. He went close to her, looked at her shining blonde hair and smooth tanned skin, he lay alongside her and pressed his face against her body, breathing in her clean scent of soap and suntan lotion.

He found himself considering a startling new idea. Is it possible I could fall in love with my wife?

He left her sleeping, stole away to the beach. Limping over the dunes with his bag of evidence he felt like a mad gnome in a fairy tale, setting out to lift the curse, leaving his princess in her drugged sleep. A fish would grant him three wishes, the skies would writhe, a storm would smite the House of Hallwright. He would look down from his lonely hermit's cave to see the Green Lady's armies massing on the distant beach.

Fool. Bungling idiot. It is criminally negligent to have held onto these phones for so long.

Passing freckly twin girls about nine years old he greeted their mother, a tall fat woman, her large white legs ending in tiny feet encased in yellow swimming shoes. A cartoon woman, shooing along her improbable children. The twins, identical, thin, sidling, sucked ice blocks and fell against each other with sudden mirth at the sight of him. He laboured past, doing his best with the bad knee on the soft sand, shooting the girls a look that made them both freeze then subside into hiccups of needle-sharp laughter. Go on, laugh at the cripple.

The mother's voice rose, scolding. A seagull abruptly bombed into the air in front of him, screaming and flapping. He flinched, floundered on.

He stopped at a place where the beach shaped itself in a long bow. Here the shore rose, causing the beach to shelve away steeply below the waterline. Oystercatchers were running along the water's edge, following some mysterious directive that made them all turn and crowd in the same direction at once, calling to each other like an excitable crowd at a sale.

Leaving his bag up on the dunes he waded in, carrying Mereana's phone. He swam a long way out, paddling over the swells, sculling on his back and watching the gannets as they plummeted into the milky blue sea. How far out was enough? Each time he decided to let go of the phone he changed his mind and swam further, until the land was a grey smear in the hazy light. He wondered how far he'd have to go before the shoreline disappeared behind the great curve of the earth. Out here was where David sometimes came on his thuggish jet ski, sending his minders into a panic.

The swim exhilarated him, he went further still.

At the last minute he wondered whether he should have weighted the phone. Treading water he took it apart, dropping the bits separately, pushing the floating pieces down, swivelling about in the water, eventually losing sight of them as he swam into a patch of seaweed. The surface was scummed with feathery purple fronds, the temperature suddenly warmer. The water gleamed, viscous in the fierce light, bubbles floated on the surface, a stick bobbed, and quite near him a penguin surfaced and looked at him with a round eye. A cloud shadow passed over and the seaweed seemed to be moving, as though he'd swum into a strong current. He thought of orca, sharks, had a sense of his vulnerable legs scissoring away under the surface.

He kicked to get away from the flotsam, reached the edge of it and swam into a mass of tiny jellyfish. He could feel them against his body but could barely see them, little ribbed lemon-shaped blobs with a tiny seed of green-gold matter nestled inside — perhaps they were not jellyfish but the eggs of some large fish. They flickered in the water, slipped and slithered against his chest; he could even feel them between his fingers. It began to seem that the sea was not mere substance but a live thing that would swallow him. Oh, Karen. Have I found you only to be sucked to a watery grave? But some frantic and undignified overarm, his face averted high, as though primly scandalised by the slithering globules of marine jelly or egg or sperm, got him through to clear water.

The sun had moved and now the land was sharply defined, reachable. He took a breath and dived, kicking strongly. Down here the sea moved peacefully, a million million grains of sand were shifted, bubbles rose. He opened his eyes and saw the surface wavering above and shafts of light angling down and there was a dreamlike peace in the vast mass, its moving currents slopping against the edges of the world. He thought of the expression 'buried at sea' and saw his own body gently drifting among brittle fish skeletons, skeins of seaweed, flickering water-light. There was a singing in his ears, he looked down and saw his white waving hands, his bony feet kicking, shafts of light and beyond, darkness, a black curtain drawn over the deeps. He kicked upwards and surfaced in a streaming caul of silver bubbles. Out near the horizon a rain cloud had arrived and a gannet, turning at the point of plummeting, brushed its wing tip against the edge of the darkness. Then it plunged, and there was the small white flare as it broke the surface.

As he swam in, a breeze came down and smacked the surface, breaking it into shards. There was a metallic smell in the air. Fat drops started to plop around him, large and far apart, an invisible and inexpert sniper taking aim at him from the clouds. And then the darkness opened with a single flash of lightning and a lone thunder crack, one of those violent summer outbursts that are over almost as soon as they've begun. Warm rain drummed on his scalp, his eyes were cleansed of salt, his face streamed with it and then it stopped, the sun broke through and he was surfing in on a perfect wave. The rain cloud, having dumped its load, broke up, leaving only a sheen on the beach and a line of oystercatchers fluffing out their wet feathers and stamping their footprints in the sand.

His clothes had stayed dry in the bag. He was chilled, his fingers numb and fumbling. He dried himself and made his way through the dunes to the path.

By the time he got to the pool he was sweating again, his knee aching. Figures lay on loungers, slumped in the heat, a rectangle of dancing white light playing on the side of the pool house. At the edge, Roza stooped to fish something out of the water while Ford stood beside her, watching. She stood, nearly overbalanced and caught Ford's shoulder. His big arm reaching to hold her steady. She laughed and flicked back her hair and looked Ford in the eye, suddenly serious. A wrench in Simon's chest, as if he'd received a sharp punch in the solar plexus, stopped him in the act of opening the child-proof gate.

'Simon. There you are.' She was wearing sunglasses on top of her head like a second pair of eyes, and a white bikini exactly like Elke's with a gold ring in the front clasp.

Johnnie climbed up the ladder and sat on the edge of his mother's deck chair, looking expressionlessly at the two men. 'Make Soon talk,' he said.

'Yes, yes.' She put her hand to her hair, distracted. In the distance someone sneezed three times. Behind the hedge Shane, or was it Troy, drove back and forth on a ride-on lawnmower.

Simon felt the hard shape of his phone in the pocket of his shorts.

'God, it's hot,' he said to the air. Hesitation (could it be stage fright?) made his legs stiff and awkward as he crossed the hot concrete. He dived in and surfaced, snorting. Roza, with Johnnie leaning against her, rested her chin on her hand and regarded him steadily. He shaped his mouth into a smile (his reptilian rictus) and turned his body away, sculling gently with his hands. His throat closed over. Really, it was ridiculous to feel so unnerved. But no, it wasn't. Considering what he was up to, it was surprising he hadn't had a breakdown. What would his Kessler score be now?

For a moment there, amid the dancing blue-and-white light, he examined the idea: Arthur Weeks was dead, and Simon Lampton had killed him.

Had he touched the body?

He willed Roza to look away, but no, she was still gazing at him, a slight smile on her face. To distract himself he began a series of splashy lengths; it was the only way he could get hard exercise after all, with the bad leg. The bad leg sustained while driving Weeks to his death over a concrete wall. He had a sudden urge to laugh, to burst out of the water shouting his secrets. You think you know me. Poor deluded fools!

The stunned unreality of that morning. The heat. The quiet terraces. The sound of traffic below. The way the air had seemed to compress, as though the oxygen had been sucked out of the world. He had stooped and looked. Had he felt for a pulse? No, one look had been enough. The spinal-cord injury had been catastrophic, death immediate, no need of amateurish fumbling for airway or pulse. But if you did touch, there could be DNA. A hair. A piece of skin. And when you backed away, did your clothes catch on the bushes? Did you leave a hair on the deck where the coffees were drunk, did you touch the arms of the chair Weeks gave you? Of course you did. He saw Weeks's back deck silvered with chemical substances, lit with special lights, scrutinised with all the fiendish tricks of the forensic trade. Little flags to mark the places where Simon Lampton had sat and drunk coffee, where his shoes had rested, where his fingers, always restless, always touching, had nervously placed themselves. But they have no record of your DNA. They can only use this evidence if they find you.

But the phone calls. The phone calls.

He stopped swimming and lay on his back. Roza's voice.

"But why," Starfish asked, "does Barbie Yah want to take Soonica away?"

The Red Herring threw some potions into his cauldron and considered long and hard. "Many hands make light work," he finally said.

Starfish sighed. "I see," he said, not really seeing at all.

The Red Herring looked strangely at Starfish.

"But too many cooks spoil the broth," he said.

Soon snorted. "Starfish is a moron," he chanted quietly.

Starfish ignored him and asked, "Red Herring, where is the Green Lady?"

The Red Herring looked into the fire. It was said he could read the future there.

"She is preparing for combat," he said. "And when her armies and the armies of Barbie Yah meet, none who falls in battle shall be spared."

Johnnie singing, tunefully. An Island song. The drone of the ride-on mower as it trundled across the lawns. Simon looked at tiny fat reflections of himself in the chrome as he climbed up the metal ladder. He lowered himself on a deck chair. No sudden movements, careful of the knee.

A moment passed. Ford turned a page. Roza said sleepily, 'Johnnie, don't.'

Simon sat up, stretched and clapped his hand to his thigh.

'Shit,' he said. 'Oh shit.'

They ignored him. Ford turned another page. Roza yawned.

He got up and flapped around the chair. 'I've . . . Oh, damn . . .'

Finally they looked.

'I've jumped in the pool with my phone in my pocket. It'll be ruined. I'll have to throw it away. What a waste . . .' Shut up, he thought. 'It's . . . Only I've . . . I'll have to get a new one straight away. Otherwise work . . .'

'Oh. What a pain,' Roza said.

They watched him holding up the phone, showing them, shaking it, trying to make it work. His clumsy fingers stabbing at the buttons, he had the sudden fear it would survive the drenching and surge busily into life. But the screen stayed blank, thank God. There were little beads of moisture inside it.

'I'll have to drive in and get a new one. Clarice'll have to work it out for me. I have to be available for patients . . .' He was gabbling.

Roza sat with her chin on her hand. Roused from her torpor, she was looking at him with interest.

Ford put his fingertips together, thoughtful.

'Yep. You've killed it,' he said.

Simon looked at his brother silently. That's right, Ford. Good. Testify to that.

Evidence

Karen was standing in the sitting room of the Little House while Elke walked to and fro in the second bedroom. Karen turned, her expression pinched, angry.

He squeezed her shoulder, went to the bedroom door. A twitch of amusement at the sight of Elke's chaotic open suitcase, then sadness; their girl was packing her bags. And with what touching, what characteristic ineptitude.

She tossed a T-shirt onto the pile of crumpled jeans, tiny shorts, shoes, belts, a hairy brush sticking up at an angle, glossy women's magazines: Beat Bad Hair Days, What He Really Wants, Great Sex in Eight Steps. Forcing a tennis racquet into one of the side pockets she crammed the lid over the bulging pile.

He stepped over her white bikini with the gold clasp, dropped in a damp puddle on the floor.

'Nice bikini.'

'Roza bought it.'

Behind them, Karen made a small hissing sound.

Elke raised her eyes. 'What?'

Karen said, 'I don't see why you need to move up to the big house. Johnnie's got sleep problems; why should they make you play the nanny? They've got that Polynesian.'

'You mean Tuleimoka. God, Mum.'

'Surely they pay her to get up.'

'I'm his sister.'

'Well, you need sleep too.'

'He's not going to wake me up. He likes having me there, at bedtime and that. It's cosy. And we're going home soon, what's the big deal?'

Karen squeezed her fists, a spasm of frustration. 'Oh . . . It's Roza, isn't it. It's her idea. She wants you up there so she can—'

Simon said, warning, 'Karen.'

'Why? Why can't I say it? So she can claim you, so she can make out she's the most important person in your life.'

'Karen!'

But something had come loose, she smacked her palm against the door frame, 'We loved and cared for you, brought you up, and where was she then? *Where was Roza?*'

Elke looked at Karen as though focusing on her for the first time.

Simon tried to herd Karen away but she waved him off. Mother and daughter didn't move, eyes locked. Elke slowly extended her hand. Her tone was formal, polite. 'Excuse me while I finish packing, Karen,' she said, and slammed the door in her face.

Elke marched off to the big house and later Simon carried her suitcase up there, handing it over to Chad, who silently vanished with it indoors. Tuleimoka and Johnnie were having their singing time on mats in the cool shade of the veranda. He recognised one of the Maori songs from his own childhood, an action song, to be performed with sticks for beating time. At primary school they'd done their Maori stick songs using rolled-up newspapers.

Sudden memory: the back of Ford's head in assembly, a humid, windless grey morning, steamy Christmas weather, the sky full of hot rain, Ford's voice among the others singing while the rolled-up sticks beat time, and the sudden surreal appearance of their mother up the front, red-faced and distraught as she whispered and gesticulated at the headmaster, her voice cracking and rising, so sorry but she'd come to collect them, they were leaving town, escaping from crazy Aaron for the last time.

They never went back to that school.

Funny how the embarrassment was the worst of it, getting up in front of all the beady eyes, threading through the rows, the teacher's face, half censorious, half thrilled by the interruption. His mother's gestures impossibly exaggerated, the faces she made as she explained in a stage whisper. The memory sent a chill of shame up his spine. He and Ford had got in the car still holding their singing sticks. They threw them out on the highway, watched them bounce away, over and over . . .

All afternoon huge white clouds came together and broke apart, their edges seamed with dazzling silver. He sat on the deck of the Little House, massaging his knee, desultorily going through a few physio exercises. In the last hours the knee had developed an irritating click, the sound made him wince. He brooded. The knee, Karen's look of persecution as she trudged away towards the dunes. Elke's luggage. His mind made the leap: he still had the DVD of the three short films by Arthur Weeks, stuck in the side pocket of his suitcase.

Picture it. The damp room, the bare table and chairs. The thickset interrogator with his eyes of ice. Yes, Dr Lampton. Arthur Weeks. Remember him? The guy you've 'never met'. And what do we find but a DVD of his very own films stuffed in your suitcase.

He went to get up, the knee clicked horribly, he sank down, so exasperated by this new consideration it settled on him almost like boredom. Crime. Who knew it would be so utterly, exhaustingly irksome? If only he could wave a lordly hand and shout from his office,

'Clarice, another piece of incriminating evidence.' And she would bustle in with her fat and her irony and her spinsterly devotion, and clutch it to her massive bosom, and make it go away.

Only she'd be back, wouldn't she, popping her head around the door. 'Just off home, Simon. I've binned the DVD, but what do you want me to do about the *phone records*?'

Crime was a terrible little car chugging along while from its exhaust pipe a cloud of foul black smoke billowed and billowed and eventually obscured the road ahead and behind, no going forward, no way back. That's what crime was. Yeah.

He closed his eyes.

Were criminals ever captured because they just couldn't be bothered any more? Yes, those would be the cases where they said, 'In the end, he wanted to be caught.'

He opened his eyes. A tui let rip with the most elaborate trilling and piping, clicks, whirrs, plonks, drips of sound; it ran through its whole repertoire while he stared at it in disbelief. It got him on his feet at least, the tyrannical soloist, the arsehole. The tui: our woodland Cacofonix. Was it his imagination, or was he laughing more? Perhaps the closer you got to losing everything, the funnier it got. It would be nice to think so.

Unable even to face the problem of the DVD, he limped to the pool. He entered the path between the hedges and saw Roza and Ford at the edge of the pool, steadying a purple blow-up dinosaur while Johnnie launched himself onto it. There was a loud squeak as child and plastic connected. Under the little boy's weight the dinosaur bent fore and aft, as if it was eating its own tail. Roza had her hand on Ford's shoulder.

Something in him assented sadly, without bitterness. He loved Roza, but she would prefer Ford, because Ford was more attractive. It was nature, what could he do? Everyone found Ford more attractive. When the two brothers were together, faces turned from Simon to Ford;

171

he drew people, because he was sure of himself. In the same way, people gazed at Elke a lot more than they were willing to contemplate Claire, something Claire had realised, absorbed into herself, a wound. But these bitter little wounds made you lean and hungry, they sharpened you. If she wanted one, Claire might score herself a better husband than Elke because she knew she was plain. She couldn't afford to be dreamy or lax. Likewise, David craved money because he'd been poor. Ageing men yearned for young women, because of the youth they'd lost. And Simon? He'd done his share of clawing and grabbing. Yes, sure.

He dumped his towel and began swimming lengths, avoiding Johnnie on his slowly revolving plastic barge. He swam until his arms gave out then lay down on a deck chair in the sun.

Johnnie called from the pool. Roza got him out and tucked him in a towel on her deck chair. Simon dozed. The slop of the pool water in the pump. Ford turning the pages of his book. He dreamed he was far out at sea, drifting amid the wrack and rot, the mild blue water stretching far. Roza's voice.

When Soon and Starfish brought news from the battle against Barbie Yah, the Red Herring stared long and hard into the fire. Finally he looked up and gave a rare smile.

"Loose lips sink ships," he said.

Simon sat up. Johnnie was watching him.

Uncanny child. Those startling eyes.

Evening. A full table, at the head of which David, to the delight of the group, was explaining how it was going with Dean, and those exercises for the enhancement of his gluteus maximus.

Simon was hardly eating and was drinking steadily, first two of Troy's powerful gins, now wine. They'd both crossed a line, he and

Karen. He'd done the unthinkable and she'd said the unsayable; he guessed what she'd lost with her outburst. If only she could have kept her cool, let the girl go off and be with her little brother, no big deal, waited until they were back in Auckland and claimed her with kindness and humour and all the natural affection between them. But she'd lost it, set up a barrier; she'd antagonised, forced Elke to make a choice, the fool. Worse, she'd insulted Roza to Elke's face. She'd likely damaged *his* relationship with Elke too, with her raging and jealousy. But we're all fools, and weak, who among us can keep cool when the situation demands tactical shrewdness, iron self-control? He wondered whether Roza had goaded Karen, tweaked her jealousy. It wouldn't have taken much. He remembered Claire's little warning he'd dismissed so easily, 'Roza hates Karen. *Hates her.*'

Karen was flushed, her eyes glittering, she laughed too long and loud at David's jokes; he felt nervous watching her. Poor Karen. After her outburst she'd cried a bit, moped for an hour, eventually trudged off to the beach for a swim, refusing his company, hand to brow; no, no, she wanted to be alone. Left on the deck he reproduced in his mind Elke's face as she slammed the door, she who had been always the dreamy, inept and clumsy one; hilariously so: she couldn't make a sandwich without dropping bits all over the floor, she bumped into doors, she created mess wherever she went, a room as neat as a pin would magically disarrange itself as she entered, books would slide off piles, cushions would fall to the floor. So unlike Claire's athleticism, and manly driving, and spartan room, Claire the brilliant, plain one, all wry humour, freckles, shapeless legs, big bum, the one Karen didn't love but he did; he should have listened to her, his clever girl. What else had Claire said: that he and David were alike, that David was in love with him, or was it that David was in love with the *idea* of him? No, that was going too far. She had a vivid imagination, his Claire, and a tendency to humorous bitterness.

Yes, Elke lived in a dream, but think of her expression, slamming the door in Karen's face. Out of the blurred, childlike beauty something hard and sharp had formed. This was what Karen was up against, why she could never win — if you could call it winning — the thing she wanted, the hold she wanted to have. That expression, or — what could you call it? — that quality, he'd seen forming in his adopted daughter's face, was the very essence of Roza.

At the evening hour, the quiet voices. Burners had been lit to keep the insects away, trailing black lines of smoke in the air. The attendants hovered, David shifted his conversation from workouts to movies, the women argued with him over films and stars. When he laughed they laughed, when he looked serious they lowered their eyes and vaguely smiled.

The sea was calm and gleaming under the moon.

There was an unwritten rule at the table: no political talk. If Simon had said 'Should our soldiers be in Afghanistan?' or 'Has American foreign policy actually changed since Obama?' they would smile, their eyes would slide away. They talked about which schools were good and the best ways to fundraise, the Cock and Ed talked about boutique wines and investing in vineyards, David ranged from movies to restaurants to the merits of foreign resorts. Roza complained privately about inane conversation but she was apolitical and rarely talked about the outside world. She did know a lot about books. She worked for a publisher and they all respected her knowledge. If a book was mentioned, people said, 'Roza will have read it' and often she had, or she knew about it; it was her party trick, she would smile and say, 'Actually, I do know about that one', and tell them a bit, not too much, just enough to show she could tell you more if she chose. David would beam with pride. My beautiful, clever wife. Not just a pretty face.

David didn't read recreationally: novels bored him and he didn't fancy non-fiction. Aside from work, money was his interest; he pursued it single-mindedly, with devotion. Although his personal interests were in blind trusts there were ways around that, trusts set up to mirror the blind trust, other methods only he and Ed discussed. In rare moments of spare time he watched television, sitting hunched forward with his fingers pressed to his temples. *House. Grey's Anatomy. CSI New York.* He called it 'chilling out in front of the box'. This was a phrase associated in Simon's mind with 'Me Time after the gym'. The fatuousness made him wince, although he wouldn't have admitted it to Claire. Or Ford.

Simon had locked away his own political instincts; they'd been swamped by David's friendship. He thought about Ford's take, which Ford had relentlessly hammered out to Simon at pre-dinner drinks. Side by side in wicker chairs holding their tinkling tumblers of gin, far enough from the main group that Ford's quiet tirade couldn't be heard, thank God. The deficit was huge, Ford said, unemployment was climbing, the government was borrowing vast sums every week, they'd cut taxes to the rich (true, Simon's income had increased: good) and they were slashing social programmes to pay for it. The poor were finding it increasingly hard to buy food. They were building extra prisons for the underclass they were creating. And this was a court, Ford whispered relentlessly, that was increasingly cut off from the nation it was supposed to serve. They weren't even worrying, these airheads, they were talking about Brad and Angelina (in the last few minutes a heated debate about the Jolie-Pitt twins) and Jennifer Aniston (was Jen still hot?) and the best method for the maintenance of swimming pools, and whether their expensive private schools were giving value for money.

'I'm grateful for the insight you've given me,' Ford said. 'They're even more frivolous than I'd imagined.'

Simon scowled. Ford had a tiny pearl of spit in the corner of his mouth. Pompous prick. Ford and Claire: the bitter ones. Never impressed, always negative. Always looking for the bad. Ford didn't mind hanging around Roza, though, did he . . .

Now across the table the Cock and Gibson were leaning close together, Gibson writing something on a table napkin, the Cock nodding with a faint curl of the lip. Gibson showed his too-white, too-even teeth, waving the bit of paper, blurred with booze as usual. The Cock sat back.

'Maybe,' he said coldly and stretched out his long arm to receive more wine from the hovering Troy without looking at the young man, who was looking down the front of Sharon Cahane's low top, she clad in a kind of black catsuit that showed off her stunning figure, as tall and shapely as Roza's although she was not quite beautiful, her features skewed at the corner of her mouth by a scar from a car crash. Having exhausted the topic of Brad and Angelina she had now begun to talk about *her* workouts, the thrill she got from being pummelled and told off and manipulated by someone as sexy as Garth.

'Ooh, call me a cougar,' she said, 'an old cougar. Tell me you don't love it, Roza, those long runs along the beach with Garth, the way he orders you about, the warm-downs.'

'Mmm,' Roza said, and Karen laughed like a good sport, and Roza turned to her, benevolently smiling, and signalled to Troy. Her sweet voice, honey-coated, but what did the coating conceal? 'Karen, you look like you need more wine.'

Simon's elbow slid off the table. Steady. Was he overdramatising? Looking around the laden table at the complacent faces, it seemed unbelievable that his secret could damage, even derail, something as solid as the government of a small, peaceful country.

But think. They would call it 'The Weeks Affair'. It would be noted that he'd left the Prime Minister's summer residence, killed Weeks and driven straight back to Rotokauri. 'Taken refuge' there. Lived with the secret there, disposed of evidence there, he who was a member of the Prime Minister's extended family, his close, even his best, friend, and part of a group that included Ed Miles, the Minister of Police. The taint would spread and billow like black ink.

Should he kill himself? But the children.

David lit the Cock's cigar, their faces illuminated red as they leaned together. A look passed between them.

Roza had moved to a soft chair at the edge of the deck. Elke came out of the house and sat down next to her, leaning close, and Roza put her arm around the girl and started pointing out the stars. The pot. The Southern Cross. The Cock watching them, Sharon's harsh voice: 'I said to him, don't fuss. And you know what he does? He bins the whole suit. Because it's got this teensy little mark you can't even see.'

Juliet Miles laughed, glanced nervously at the Cock, red flaming in her cheeks.

The Cock looked levelly at them.

Sharon: 'He's listening. Don't give me the evil eye, darling. You know you're unbelievable.'

'My wife is astonished again. My wife finds the extraordinary in everyday things.'

'And then the other day, he—'

'No, it's not difficult to keep my wife diverted. There's so much for her lively mind to take in.'

Ed said to Karen, 'Enjoying the workouts? Losing weight?'

Karen gave him a wide-eyed look and moved away.

'In fact, if my wife encounters more than one idea at once, she's left reeling.'

Screech of laughter from Sharon Cahane.

Ford had fallen silent. He was staring at everyone grimly, as though making a final tally of the failings of each.

Simon went over. He said, quiet, 'You're looking left-wing.'

'Feeling left-wing.'

They watched Elke and Roza.

Ford said in an undertone, 'How can they not look alike and yet *be* so alike?'

'Body language,' Simon said. Sadness weighed him down. 'We've lost her.'

'No. You don't lose people.'

'But she wasn't ours to begin with. We got her late, eight years old.'

'Karen,' Ford said.

'Yeah, she's . . .' She was standing at the rail now, facing the sea, her arms crossed over her chest. A forlorn pose.

'Life. Nothing's fair.'

'Thanks. That's very comforting.' Simon frowned, trying to hold on to a thought. His poor brain, marinated in Trent's gins. 'So if nothing's fair, Ford, what's the point of your politics? Why not just let nature take its course, let the poor die; that's survival of the fittest.'

'Some of us see human nature for what it is. But we still have a duty to elevate ourselves.'

Simon snorted. 'Self-righteous bastard.'

Ford turned to him. 'What do you actually care about, Simon? No, seriously.'

Care about? Family. David. Yes, he did love David. And Roza. His patients. In a different way.

'I'd do anything to protect them,' he said.

Ford looked at him, curious. 'Protect? Who, Simon?'

Anything.

In the warm dark, fumbling with his suitcase, he pulled out the DVD in its plastic cover. It was turning into a big night over at the main house, they had the stereo cranked up loud. David must have got his second wind and no one would dare to go to bed before him.

The sound of the bass drifted over the compound. At a party he'd once seen Sharon and the Cock, drunk, get up and head for the dance floor. Expecting middle-aged ineptitude they'd all been transfixed by the Cock's dancing. His thin, sinister face expressionless, he'd danced with the smoothness of a pro. He was fit, no move he made was out of rhythm. His wife wasn't bad either. 'White men *can* dance,' some wit had shouted but the Cock and Sharon just danced on, impassive, tranced, in their own world.

Unnatural that an uptight middle-aged man, a government minister, could move like that. Karen said that after she'd seen the Cock dancing she was even more scared of him than ever.

He shivered. Something walking over his grave. What to do with the DVD? Another swim? But the weather had turned in the late afternoon, the wind had got up and the sea was messy, running with currents, uneven waves rolling across the shorebreak and seaweed tossing in the hubble and bubble. White foam flying in the air, the gulls riding the currents. There was another big summer cyclone out in the Pacific Islands; they would be brushed by the edge of it. It had got hotter all evening. A suffocating humidity had crept over the settlement, until you felt you had to suck the air hard to get anything from it. The air was laden with moisture, everyone sweating. One minute Roza was pointing out the stars to Elke, the next they were snuffed out, the whole sky black and pressing down like a blanket.

For a moment he considered putting the DVD in the machine and watching it again. The story of Hamish and Anahera. Instead he went out the back and broke the disk and its cover into pieces. He had a sense of sacrilege, as if he was breaking Mereana's bones, crack crack. There was an outside light faintly pulsing, moths and insects bombing into it. Mosquitoes settled on him, he slapped them away. Somewhere out beyond the light he heard rustling. He stopped and listened to the harsh chatter and purr of a possum, and in the distance a morepork crying. The sea was making a low roar, stirred up by a weather monster far away.

Forward Slash

His consulting rooms. Clarice had an unflattering new haircut, cropped short and dyed. The back of her neck looked sore and chafed. She'd put on even more weight over the summer; loneliness, he thought, nights in front of the TV with the wine and potato chips.

'Nice hairdo.'

Red crept into her jowly cheeks and she looked so brave and *triste* he wanted to make some gesture, squeeze her arm, but that would never do, to show he felt sorry for her.

'The Robinson woman called.' She rolled her eyes. In her role as dragon and gatekeeper she enjoyed dealing with the few patients who were difficult. There was a tone she used with all the patients; it was borderline offensive and often irritated him. Her policy was to treat all as insane until proven rational.

He'd referred the Robinson woman to a colleague, but she kept coming back, kept calling in tears. She believed that he loved her. Previously she'd believed that a local GP loved her, but he'd emigrated to Australia.

'I saw her walk past the building yesterday. Twice. Slowly.' Clarice dumped a pile of files on his desk.

The clinic began. His first patient told him, 'I had a breast cancer scare.'

'Just a scare?'

'I found one lump, the GP found another. I was terrified. They got me an urgent appointment for a mammogram. You know what I found out? That you really do wring your hands. I had to drive across town to have a scan and I was thinking *this is it*. Two lumps, I'm going to die. There was this nurse, she goes, "Do you want to read some literature about cancer?" I said, "No I do not, thank you very much."'

Simon, continuing his examination, said, 'OK, give me a cough.'

'So I go in, and the doctor finds *eight* lumps. Literally. I was having an absolute meltdown. But when they scanned them, they were all cysts.'

'Ah, so no problem. Breathe in.'

'They were fine. The funny thing is, I turned to the nurse, right, and there was something in her face. Disappointment. As if I was a big let-down. After that she was grumpy with me. Isn't that strange?'

Simon thought, There are things I could tell you about nurses. The few who liked to menace and bully. One trick was to tell patients they shouldn't be in pain after an operation, to hint that something must be seriously wrong. You'd come in on your patient in tears because a malevolent nurse had made her beg for pain relief and then said, 'You shouldn't be asking for painkillers. You'd better ask your doctor exactly what he's *done*.'

He sent out for a sandwich, ate lunch in his office. Anxiety made him tired. This humidity. After weeks of cloudless blue, the sky had turned woolly grey. Lightning flared occasionally, thunder cracked far away, the clouds swirled and boiled but there was no rain, not yet, only hot mist. How brown the park had got, the grass positively scorched. It must have been a record summer. Was it global warming? The Hallwright government didn't believe in climate change. They were hoping to boost the economy by mining fossil fuels, by drilling for oil in the Raukumara Basin. Caring about the environment was a luxury;

that was what Ed Miles and the Cock said. Cue Ford and his whispered condemnations about short-sighted fools and locusts squandering all the good we have.

What do you actually care about, Simon?

Oh, fuck Ford. Fuck him.

Across the way, in an upstairs window, the two small dogs, side by side, had their identical hairy white faces pressed up against the glass, moving slightly when something caught their eye, two uncanny masks, watching.

He sat listening to a blonde woman.

'Simon, my allergies also cause me to put on weight. I'm allergic to gluten and dairy, both of which cause me bloating.'

'Ah. Bloating.'

'I'm on the blood-group diet. My naturopath recommended it. She's an amazing woman. Just amazing. I had no idea there was so much wrong with me until I found her. And I see a homeopath and an osteopath, and I've got onto crystal therapy.'

'I see.' He looked at his notes.

'I take a lot of supplements. I have to, Simon. If I don't, my immune system crashes. Even though I flush out my system constantly, I have a lot of toxic build-up. You've got to flush out the toxins, or it's just crazy.'

He said, 'I'll have to do a quick examination.'

She continued, from the bed. 'My daughter's a Taurus, so she's amazingly strong-willed. She's had a lot of problems. What I found really useful was . . .'

'Breathe in,' he said.

'St John's wort, charcoal patches, a list of homeopathic remedies and a strict diet. Dukan. But she relies on the crystals. If she's separated from the crystals it's just crazy.'

'And breathe out.'

'Simon, I've realised that the thing about maintaining my immune system is . . .'

He dipped his head and thought, Her body is a temple. Yeah, a beautiful temple, festooned with tributes to the Great Wedgie.

Smiling, he said, 'You can get up now.'

She came around the curtain, pulling her bright blonde hair back into a ponytail. He said, 'I'm going to recommend some minor surgery,' and then sat there, gently nodding and smiling and repeating himself while she sternly put him through his paces, making sure he was as well qualified as the witch doctors and quacks and bullshit artists who presided over her everyday care.

Two elderly patients followed, one sternly pragmatic, the next horrified by his intimate questions: a small, vulnerable woman, squeezing her hands drily together.

Running late now, he ushered in the next woman, apologising for the wait. They knew each other: over the years he'd delivered her twins and another child. She sat down and said flatly, 'You'll see I got the GP to do all those tests for STDs.'

He sifted through them.

'I found out that my husband was having an affair. I was worried I might have caught something. It's not because *I* was, you know, going round town catching things.'

He said, polite, 'The tests are all negative.'

'Yes. I just had to explain.'

'I understand.'

She smiled and looked away. 'The bastard.'

'Yes. I mean, no. Sorry to hear that.'

A bit later he said, 'Just describe exactly where the pain is?'

'He had an affair at work. I was furious with the woman. I wanted to hunt her down and kill her. But then I was lonely and hurt and stuck with three kids and no husband and what did I do? I fell in love with a married man. And when I thought about how that would hurt *his* wife, I didn't care.'

Simon knew what Ford would say to that: We're all animals.

'Sorry, I don't know why I'm telling you. Well, I had to explain the STD tests.'

'Yes, of course. Now when you say you've had this pain . . .'

'I suppose you hear some weird things in here.'

'Sometimes.' He paused. She was looking upset. He touched her arm very lightly. 'Not weird. Everyone's pretty much the same, really. Everyone wants the same things.'

She looked at him intently.

'The pain?' she said. 'The pain is *everywhere*.'

Afternoon, all patients dispatched, he was turning his mind to the drive back to Rotokauri. Just a few more days of the holiday left.

The phone shrilled. Clarice said, 'Someone to see you.'

He was clearing his desk, gathering up his gear, keen to get off, beat the traffic on the bridge. 'Not the Robinson woman?'

'A detective.'

He sat, winded, the silence a fraction too long. 'A what?'

'Detective.'

He said hectically, 'The Robinson woman's killed someone.'

Clarice let out a dry little chuckle. She'd be enjoying making the guy wait.

'OK. Coming,' he said.

It wasn't a man.

She said, 'Hi Dr Lampton, or should that be Mister, since you're a surgeon? My name's Detective Marie Da Silva.' She offered her hand, he shook.

'And this is my colleague, Detective Philip O'Kelly. Show your ID, Philip.'

O'Kelly was a young man with a long face and keen eyes. He produced his ID and the woman said, 'Can we go in your office?'

He ushered them in, shut the door, pointed to the chair, sat down behind his desk. The man sat down. The woman went to the window and looked out at the park, not obedient like a patient; patients did what you told them; you pointed to a chair, they sat. She was slim, dressed in a short jacket and trousers with a hint of combat about them, as if they'd have tools jinking from them, probably did: handcuffs, pepper spray, telescoped baton.

Holding a big black notebook under one arm, she turned to face him. She had a sharp, pale face, slightly pointy teeth, freckles on the bridge of her nose and thick wiry hair so blonde it was almost white, the hair falling thickly to her shoulders but standing up on her crown in unruly gold-white strands that caught the light, a real mane, and there was something leonine, or at least feline, about the sloping contours of her cheeks and the strong, straight nose. Those wiry strands of hair standing up on her head made him think of a cloud of bright insects around her, a nimbus.

Silence.

'OK,' she said. 'You're looking at my eyes.'

'No. Well, since you mention it. One blue and one brown. That's rare.'

'So I'm told. Frequently. And yes, before you ask, they're real.'

'Heterochromia iridum.'

'Yeah. I've got in the habit of mentioning it first. What happens is, people look at my eyes, and don't actually look at me. They get distracted.'

'Well. What can I do for you?'

She had very small hands. He imagined twining his fingers in that bright hair. If he came near, she would probably punch his lights out.

Cops. Could they tell what you were thinking?

A pause. She had a little frown mark between her pale eyebrows. How old was she — say, twenty-eight? The same age Mereana was when she . . .

'We're investigating the death of Arthur Weeks.'

'Who?'

'Arthur Weeks. Do you know him? He's fallen, he's also possibly been hit by something, maybe a car.'

'Hit and run?'

'We're not calling it that yet.'

What else would you call it?

She smiled, 'We like to keep an open mind.'

'Always good to have one of those.' *Oh, shut up, fool.*

'Anyway, we've noticed he's called your cell phone a couple of times. We're just wondering why he'd call an obstetrician and gynaecologist.'

She laughed and he joined in. How funny, a man calling him, the women's doctor. Yes, it was inexplicable, wasn't it.

Silence. Why had he not prepared for this?

'He called your cell phone,' she repeated.

'My cell phone. Did he? I've just had to get a new phone actually. I jumped in the pool with the old one.'

The little frown deepened. She leaned forward, her tone sharp. 'You've just got a new phone.'

He suddenly realised: they had the record from Weeks's phone. There'd been no point getting rid of his. It just drew attention, made him look guilty. Destroying evidence.

'I've upgraded to this new thing. An iPhone. The latest model apparently.' He pushed it across the desk. His tongue had stopped working properly.

'Why did Arthur Weeks call you?'

'I'm sorry I don't . . . Who is this Weeks?'

'He's a sort of journalist, film, arts person. Done a bit of work for TV, comedy shows. Young man, aged in his twenties, found dead outside his flat.'

Simon paused, pretended to think. No, don't scratch your head, ham actor. 'Never heard of him.'

'He *rang* you.'

'Maybe . . . I had a caller not long ago, probably a journalist, I can't remember his name. He said he wanted to ask some questions, but the questions turned out to be about my family so I cut him off.'

'Your family.'

'I have an association with the Prime Minister. My adopted daughter . . .'

'Yes. I know about that. OK, so assuming that was Weeks, he wanted to know what?'

'I can't remember. The caller asked me about being on holiday at the Hallwrights' summer place and I realised he was just prying and I said, "Can't help you, sorry", and hung up. My wife and I do get questioned; we've learned to be a bit careful. There's interest in our lives, in our younger daughter, because of the Hallwrights. She, our girl Elke, is Roza Hallwright's . . .'

'Weeks rang you *twice*.'

He looked at the fine gold strands of hair at her temples. She shuffled pages in her big black book, checking something. Those eyes. One in a million, genetically. What had she said, that people looked at her eyes instead of looking at her. What did she mean? Surely she *was* her eyes. She must mean they looked without seeing beyond the colour, to what lay behind the blue and the brown.

From the window across the car park the two white dogs were watching. Motionless white dogfaces. The male detective was content to sit in silence; he looked almost sleepy, watching from under half-closed lids.

'Dr Lampton?'

'Sorry. Twice? I can't remember, but I would have done the same, cut him off. Journalists are a hazard, a minor one. When my wife goes out with Roza Hallwright they're followed and photographed sometimes. Every now and then someone rings the house.'

His confidence rose. It sounded convincing, and it was true after all. She'd stopped frowning.

'Weeks wasn't that kind of journalist.'

'What was he then?'

'He had a mix of interests. He did have a preoccupation with politicians.'

'There you go.'

'He rang you twice, and then you rang him.'

'I rang him? That's not possible.'

'You did.'

His stomach let out an embarrassing, audible groan. 'I suppose he left a message, or I saw I'd missed a call. I have to be available for emergencies. I would have assumed it was a patient trying to get hold of me.'

She made a note, left-handed, her wrist awkwardly bent. She would have backwards-slanting handwriting.

'You say you jumped in a pool with your phone?'

'Sadly, yes. It's the kind of thing I do all the time. Just ask my secretary.'

He laughed; she laughed along then her smile dropped and her lip curled. He was taken aback, almost hurt. She didn't believe him. Or were police trained to unnerve you like that, to lull you then suddenly show their teeth?

Clarice might have seen Weeks standing on the road outside the office. There might be CCTV in the surrounding streets. How thorough was the feline Ms Da Silva?

'When did you jump in the pool with the phone?' She had her notebook open, pen poised. She clicked and clicked impatiently. Her biro was much chewed at the end. Claire. She glared, not unlike his elder daughter: aggressive, impatient.

'I don't know. A few days ago. I can't remember.'

She was staring at *his* eyes now.

He pushed his chair back. 'I was contacted by a journalist. I cut him off. It happens every now and then. I go through cell phones like there's no tomorrow. Are we finished? Because I'm about to drive back to Rotokauri, and I want to beat the traffic.'

There was a slight shift in atmosphere. She hesitated. Yes, it was worth a try. Think of Claire; it's possible to put *her* off with a show of male anger. Be authoritative. Mention Rotokauri, the Prime Minister's summer residence. She's all very diverting with her golden mane and her rare eyes, but you're a busy man. Things to do. The PM's waiting. Why, in an hour, in fact, I'll be having drinks with Mr Ed Miles, the Minister of Police. Your *boss*, Detective Da Silva.

She said, 'Do you know a Mereana Kostas?'

He went hot then cold. He felt his smile, the reptilian rictus. His voice, when he got it working, was faintly scandalised, as though she'd made some truly obscene crack. He could feel the male detective watching him. His stillness and silence were unnerving.

'Kostas. Is that another journalist?'

She was deadpan, no light in her eyes, delicate hands flat on the notebook. She had uneven, bitten fingernails. 'You tell me.'

'I have no idea.'

Silence.

He said, 'So . . . ?'

She chewed the nail of her index finger and appeared to consider. 'Well, Weeks had a list in his flat. Like a to-do list, the kind of thing you stick on the fridge. Reminders. At the end it says, 'Simon Lampton-forward-slash-Mereana Kostas.'

'Forward-slash.'

'A forward-slash suggests a link, don't you think?'

He blinked. 'I guess two people he intended to ring. Or whatever.'

'You don't know that name?'

'No.' He added, 'Do you?'

'Maybe.'

Maybe. Had they found Mereana?

He said, 'Why don't you ask this person, Costas did you call him?' (Actually, *no*. Don't find Mereana, don't look for her, don't talk to her.)

No answer. The man coughed and brushed something off his trouser leg. She slapped her hands on her knees and stood up and again Simon heard, or imagined, the jink of concealed weaponry as she rose. Her smile was sardonic. The fine golden hair: it was an eighties' hairstyle, short on top, long at the sides, think Rod Stewart, think Aslan . . . yes, he really was losing his mind, interrogated by a detective and all he could do was silently prattle. *Aslan*, indeed.

They left, he shut the door. He had a vague sense there'd been something positive in the end of the conversation. Was it . . . yes, it could be that she'd told him about the list with his and Mereana's names on it. Wouldn't she have withheld that detail if she thought he was significant? She's used to dealing with criminals; it wouldn't occur to her that a respectable doctor could be involved in a suspicious death. Weeks was interested in the Hallwrights, which perfectly explained the two short calls. She hadn't mentioned anyone seeing him at Weeks's. If someone had seen him there they'd have dragged him off to the police station for a full interrogation. It was a routine inquiry, he'd never hear from her or her colleague again.

But take care. The police assume nothing; they don't care about 'respectability'. They proceed slowly and they trick you. They're in the business of tricking you.

He hurried past Clarice, locked himself in the toilet and sat down, his face in his hands. This will pass. But a list with his and Mereana's names on it, a forward-slash linking them. Mereana with her prison record. It was enough, wasn't it, with the phone calls, to put him in danger of further scrutiny. What else would they find if they went through Weeks's effects: more careful notes-to-self, references to Simon and Mereana, a memo about asking Simon to his flat. How could there not be more for them to find?

Oh Karen, what have I done?

Driving towards the Harbour Bridge he stopped at an intersection and saw a dark-haired woman walking away from him, the light behind her, she stopped on the pavement and shaded her eyes, it was May.

He pulled over, got out and she turned towards him. Her mouth formed the words, 'Tell Ford.'

A cat running low and fast across the road. May walking west, passing through long shadows. The sun sinking in the sky, the earth rolling on its way.

At Rotokauri, he drove alongside Ford, who was wearing a towel wrapped around his waist, an army T-shirt and peaked cap. He was carrying a book under his arm.

Ford drummed on the roof of the car. 'Want to come for a swim?' And then, 'What's wrong?'

'Bad day.'

'What happened?'

'Nothing.'

He went on down the drive to the Little House and found Karen and Elke sitting at the table on the deck looking at photographs. Karen looked up, her eyes soft. He kissed them both, went inside to change, and caught sight of Elke's suitcase on the floor of the second bedroom. He walked out onto the deck.

'What's happening?'

'Looking at pictures,' Karen smiled.

He put his hand on Elke's shoulder and said, 'You've come back.'

Karen gave him a quick look, warning him. There was that familiar sense between them that Elke would shy away if they made any sudden moves. But he was tired and distracted and said, 'You haven't fallen out with Roza?'

Karen glared.

Ignoring him, Elke held up a photo. 'This is the best one, Mum.' It was a picture of Karen and Elke on the deck of the Gibsons' boat, Karen with her arm around Elke's shoulders, the two of them leaning close.

Simon watched them, silent. Well. Wonders never cease. What had Karen done to get Elke to come back? There was something different about the girl, a self-consciousness. She lined the photos along the table, pointing things out, chatting. He remembered her expression when she'd slammed the door in Karen's face — the look he'd thought of as the essence of Roza, a sudden hardness, as if she'd understood the power she had over Karen. But now, when they both looked up, Karen had a little glow of triumph and the girl looked slightly vulnerable and strained.

He said, awkward, 'What you been doing the last few days?'

'Nothing much,' Elke said.

Simon sat down in a deck chair and put his feet up on the veranda rail.

Elke scratched a bite on her tanned arm, frowned. 'There was one little drama.'

'Mm?'

'You know they've got that big white cat, Suzie?'

'Suzie? Oh yeah. Izzy's always carrying it about.'

'Well, Suzie's had cancer, and he got so sick he wouldn't eat. So we went with Roza to the vet on the other side to have him put down.'

'Suzie's a boy?' He added, 'Sorry to hear that.' He rubbed his weary eyes.

'We like said farewell to him and they took him away and we waited in this room and then they brought him out dead in a cardboard box that looked like a pizza box. Izzy was crying and Roza . . .'

'Poor old Izzy.'

'And Roza laughed. She laughed but she hid it. When she lifted the lid of the box and saw Suzie in there.'

'Oh . . . Awkward moment, I suppose. Sometimes people . . .'

'I don't know if Izzy saw her laugh.'

'People laugh nervously, some situations.'

'No. She thought it was funny. I could tell she was thinking, like, Dead Cat Pizza.'

'Well. Anyway.' Simon glanced at Karen.

Elke went on, 'You know how she tells Johnnie stories about a dwarf called Soon. Well she's put Suzie in the story. Suzie dead. Soon's got a new friend called the Dead White Cat.'

'Like a ghost,' Simon said, uncertain, looking over at Karen again.

'Charming,' Karen said. 'Let me guess. Johnnie thinks it's hilarious.'

'He just accepts there's a new character, a dead one. All he wants is Soon stories. Him and Roza, it's like they've got their own language. She's controlling the story but he makes it up too. They have arguments about the plot.'

Karen said, 'A dead cat. How lovely for Izzy. Making fun of her grief.'

'They don't do the Dead White Cat when she's around.'

'Thank goodness for that. I probably shouldn't say this . . .'

Simon caught her eye, frowned. *Then don't.*

She ignored him, 'I probably shouldn't say this but it does sound a bit weird, this Soon thing. It sounds a bit intense. If it replaces normal . . . interaction between parent and child. I've never heard it, of course,' she added, censorious.

'Dad's heard it. He hears it all the time,' Elke said.

Karen turned. She said, sweetly, ominously, 'Really. Does he now.'

He said, 'Only every now and then. It's harmless. Vaguely annoying.'

She folded her arms. 'Well. Aren't you lucky. Hearing about the secret dwarf.'

'It's just kids' stuff, it's background noise. Drives you mad after a while.'

'Really.'

Elke giggled. 'Maybe she's put us all in the story.'

'I wouldn't know,' Karen said. 'Are we all in it, Simon?'

'I have no idea.'

'You'd *like* to be in it, Dad,' Elke said.

There was a silence. Karen looked from the girl to Simon.

He said roughly, 'I don't know what you mean, Elke.'

Karen had moved close to Elke and was smoothing her hair. Their expressions were odd, and he had a sudden understanding of what it would be like to lose them.

'I'm going to find Ford.' Making a big effort, giving Elke a friendly pat on the arm, he added, 'And we'll be going home soon and you've got university to look forward to.'

He persisted. 'Anyone coming for a swim?'

They shook their heads. He was irritated by the loaded silence and wished Karen would stop stroking Elke's hair. She had such a crude, corny way of claiming the girl, as if only she could protect her from the world. He saw how it would anger Roza, how she might feel she was being obliquely insulted. As for the dead cat, all that nonsense, it wasn't his fault Roza and Johnnie had a secret language. Nice if Roza was relaxed enough to tell Soon stories in front of him, but he'd be just as happy if she didn't, since it meant he couldn't get a bloody word in; he was continually talked over by a dwarf and a starfish. And a village idiot. And if Karen knew the trouble he was in she'd stop looking at him in that self-righteous, damp-eyed way, the fucking stupid *bitch*.

Clarice. Can you help me with this terrible file, this dog's breakfast? The days and days. There are things I have done. There are things . . .

The Ghost of May

Ford was down at the shoreline, hands on his hips, inspecting something on the sand. Simon watched his brother: the way Ford absorbed himself in things. When they were boys Ford could lie for hours on his bed reading, whereas Simon found it hard to focus, especially when their father was working up to one of his rages and the air was loud with tension.

Simon thought about this: he was hypersensitive to noise. He winced at high-pitched sounds, knives on plates and fingers down the blackboard, but he especially hated repetitive sounds.

Cold-blooded old times: when Aaron was drunk, and sometimes when he was sober, he would tease Simon by singing fragments of songs over and over. His voice was a perfectly tuned instrument of torture. It was during those times when Aaron was tormenting him for his own amusement that Simon had perceived the blackness in his father, expressed in distorted nursery rhymes and advertising jingles and silly songs that had him clamping his hands over his ears in helpless misery and rage. If you begged him to stop, if you shouted and threw things, he'd just get louder. Aaron had turned his voice into a weapon, maybe expressing his frustration that he'd never done anything with his musical talent, a fact he blamed on his family, the loser. Teasing Simon, he'd always made out he was joking, just singing. He hid his hostility in fooling. The evil clown. Ford developed the ability not to hear and Simon got in the habit of avoiding: closeness, people, repetitive noise. When his own kids had been young and had got some innocently repetitive chant going he would feel himself tipping into fury, would have to restrain himself.

He thought of Arthur Weeks banging on the glass.

The large woman with twin daughters came stumping through the soft sand, the girls following in their matching T-shirts and caps. A boat headed out through the estuary, its bow hitting the waves with a hollow, smacking sound. Ford stooped, picked something up then skimmed it away into the waves. He came jogging up the beach and stood towelling his hair.

'I keep thinking I've seen May,' Simon said.

Ford tilted his head, shaking water out of his ear. 'I see her all the time. In crowds, on the street. She turns up in dreams.'

'The ghost of May.'

Ford dried his hair. 'If you see her ghost, does it exist?'

'If no one hears the tree fall, does it make a sound?'

'If you hear the sound it exists. So if you see the ghost it exists.'

'Or you're hallucinating.'

'Speaking of hallucinating, are you still mentally ill?'

Simon sighed. 'I'm not only certifiably mad, I've done my knee in and I can't go for a run, which was my best defence against madness. But Ford, I need to tell you something.'

Ford narrowed his eyes and said tonelessly, 'You want to get out of the clutches of these shallow, materialistic right-wing shits and rejoin decent society.'

'Ah, fuck off.'

'But Karen won't let you. And you've got used to the help. And the celebrity lifestyle, and the *New Idea* photographers hiding in the bushes.

All the fabulousness of hanging around with the tin-pot ruling elite of our tiny, tin-pot nation.'

'Yeah, yeah. Fuck off.'

Ford went on, 'You know what our great Prime Minister Norman Kirk died of? He took ill one morning after struggling to open his garage door. On his way to work. As the Prime Minister. Can you imagine Barack Obama struggling to open the garage door? Can you imagine him struggling to open anything? That's how ridiculously tin-pot this country is.'

'But Norman Kirk, that was a long time ago. Why is it relevant?'

'Because Karen thinks David's grand. Whereas he's just . . . shallow. And tin-pot. Even though he's got a biggish house and a whole lot of gay servants called Thor and Schlong and Zeus, he's still ridiculously small beer.'

'Right. So we're all second rate. I hope you've enjoyed your holiday. In these second-rate surroundings.'

Ford rubbed his face hard with the towel. 'No, I've had a good time. It's a beautiful place. Thanks.'

'You're welcome.'

'Despite the tin-pot company.' Ford gave his annoying, sideways grin.

'I assume you don't include Roza in that.'

'Well, I'm not quite sure why she married *him.*'

'Why? Because he's the only one who can deal with her.'

'You think?'

Simon leaned forward; the exchange was making him even more tense. 'Everyone else is scared of her.'

'Maybe.'

'You think she's superior to David because you're in love with her. But he's cleverer.'

Ford said, teasing, 'I'm in love with her, am I? And you're in love with *him.*'

'According to Claire he's in love with *me*.'

Ford was amused. 'That Claire.'

'You like that idea, don't you?'

'I like all Claire's ideas.'

'Well, she's so like you she could be your daughter.'

Silence. They looked at each other then they both laughed and shook their heads. Ford punched Simon on the arm.

Simon frowned at the horizon, the sea with its swimming sheen of evening light. He said, 'If David was Labour he'd still be small time. We're a small country.'

'But if he was Labour he'd have a social conscience. He wouldn't be venal, money-obsessed, vulgarly commercial, inane, shallow, blind to the suffering of the poor, a beneficiary-basher. Chattering about Angelina Jolie while Rome burns . . .'

'All right. Jesus, Ford.'

'That's the National Party. In my humble opinion.'

'Oh yeah, you're incredibly humble.'

'As for you, it's *not good enough* to be apolitical. It's not intellectually good enough.'

'That's right, Ford. Some of us are not good enough.'

'Ah, you were always a lazy little shit.'

'Lazy! This is my first holiday in a year.'

'But politically, intellectually, you're the lazy little shit you always were.'

Simon thought about the frantic effort of his life, how hard he'd worked, for how long. What he'd worked *at* was getting away, from his father, from the miserable little house they'd grown up in, from shame. He'd achieved and succeeded; he had money, respectability, status; and here was Ford pulling on his ripped old T-shirt and his dingy denim shorts and telling him it wasn't good enough. Calling David Hallwright not good enough. What a laugh.

Ford said, in his clairvoyant way, 'It's not enough just to "succeed". You've got to succeed in the right way. I mean, Hitler was a raging success, in his heyday.'

'Hitler, now. Hitler, no less.'

'All Hallwright's crap about "aspiration", standing in for real politics. It's rubbish. What's the point of becoming the Prime Minister if the whole purpose was just to get to the top? With no thought for the society you're supposed to be leading?'

Simon picked up a stick and stabbed it into the sand. 'I do good. I work hard for my patients. I've adopted a child. I pay taxes. Karen fundraises for charity.'

'Not good enough.'

'Fuck off, Ford,' he said distractedly. The pale fronds of marram grass, blowing like hair, had reminded him of the young policewoman, Ms Da Silva. If Ford knew the half of it. Simon had achieved and succeeded and yet a counter-impulse had risen in him, one that threatened to sabotage everything.

He'd fallen in love with Roza and, in the confusion of that, in seeking to sublimate so many forbidden emotions, he had gravitated to the tiny, shabby South Auckland house, so similar to the one in which he and Ford had grown up, and begun an affair with Mereana, a woman who couldn't possibly fit into his successful life. And that had meant Arthur Weeks had come searching . . . It was an irony; after all Simon's striving after respectability it was Ford, who didn't care about it, who'd achieved it. Ford had married the woman he loved, had never cheated on his wife, had never killed anyone. *Killed anyone.* Simon hunched his shoulders. It was grimly funny.

He thought of the photo in Mereana's phone. The sunlight on the bare wooden wall, his blissed-out expression. He remembered how it had been, those visits to her house. He'd had the sensation of everything slipping away, a sensual feeling of letting go, of giving up the clawing and striving.

How did the line go? *I have been half in love with easeful Death* . . .

And then, when he'd recovered himself, he'd had such a revulsion to Mereana and to the surrender she represented that he'd redoubled his clawing and striving, had turned away, had actually wished for proof that she was dead. He had, it was odd to think, taken out his love on her. And had he (face it now), had he taken out his frustrations on poor, lonely Mereana because she'd seemed expendable?

He traced the horizon line with his stick. 'I suppose you'd like me to bring Hallwright down.'

'Bring him down? I'd like the people to bring him down.'

Had he killed Mereana, as well as Arthur Weeks? No, that was too much. He had loved, not her exactly, but her kindness and warmth. But could you separate her from her kindness? It was part of her, just as Ms Da Silva's eyes *were* her soul, and not some curiosity distinct from . . .

Ford was speaking. '. . . like you've got something on your mind. And you look a bit thin, mate.'

'I do have a lot on my mind.' He wanted to tell Ford everything, to appeal to him for help. But what could Ford do? He had no power to change anything. Others had the power.

'What do you mean bring Hallwright down?' Ford was looking at him closely. 'You said you had something to tell me. You wanted advice. Do you know something?'

'No. Let's go back.'

The impulse to confess had passed. They walked slowly back over the cooling sand. The marram grass rippled in silvery waves, oystercatchers ran back and forth. Down at the shorebreak the sea churned itself into pure white foam, the waves spreading up the beach slick as mercury, pushed by the incoming tide. They walked along the top of the dunes, Simon following Ford, his eyes on his brother's broad back.

Ford went off for a shower and Simon walked alone through the lavender bushes towards the pool. It was sheltered here, the evening air warm and still. He could hear Roza's voice. She and Johnnie were sitting on a wooden bench under the pohutukawa, a pack of cards arranged between them, although they weren't playing. Johnnie was kneeling on the seat and Roza was shuffling cards and staring intently ahead, concentrating on something unseen. Her low voice:

The messenger gave the Green Lady the grave news: Barbie Yah had called on the evil power of the Ort Cloud's Wife, and despite all the efforts of the friends, she had succeeded in luring Soonica away. The Green Lady summoned her men. Soon and Starfish, along with the Village Idiot, abandoned their plans to go hunting and went to the clearing.

The Green Lady was in conference with the Red Herring, and did not speak. The Bachelor's bed appeared, the Bachelor himself magnificent in a turquoise robe, and the Cassowaries gaudy, cold-eyed and ferocious, shedding feathers and squawking as the bed swooped over the trees and landed in the clearing. The Bachelor, holding a cocktail, stepped off the bed and approached the Green Lady.

"At your service, Madam," he announced, but she only glanced at him, nodded impatiently, and went on talking to the Red Herring. The Bachelor stalked back to his bed, waved the Cassowaries off it and arranged himself in a louche pose to wait for his beloved. Time passed. The Green Lady summoned Tiny Ancient Yellow Cousin So-on. Crackers stole close to the Bachelor's drinks cabinet but was driven away by the shrieks and pecks of the Cassowaries.

Soon, who didn't really mind at all that Soonica had been kidnapped, and looked on it as a good excuse for a bloodthirsty battle, got bored and began playing with matches, but after he'd set fire to a bush and then to the Village Idiot's hat, the High

Priestess Germphobia got hold of him and smacked him with her scrubbing brush, at which pandemonium broke out. Soon yelled, the Cassowaries hissed and flapped, the Guatemalans fired off blasts from their shotguns and Starfish uncharacteristically laughed.

"Starfish, you're a traitor," Soon shouted, and Starfish guiltily apologised.

"Ha ha," said the Village Idiot, waving her blackened and smouldering hat.

Now the Green Lady made her way towards the crowd. The Bachelor stood up, straightening his turquoise robe.

"Dear Lady," he began, "your flashing eyes, your splendid complexion . . ." But the Bachelor was the only one who dared speak, and even he fell silent. For when the Green Lady turned to face them, all who had waited for news of Soonica drew back in fear at the expression in her eyes. It was like looking into the blackest and most distant part of the Universe, a place where no mortal pity could survive.

Johnnie was kneeling up on the seat and running his hand over the rough bark of the pohutukawa. He turned and regarded Simon expressionlessly.

How alike they were, mother and son. They had the same stillness and watchfulness. But it was when they laughed that the resemblance was plainest, something mocking and anarchic in the way they confronted the world.

A voice called across the warm dark garden: 'Johnnie, path time.'

Tuleimoka appeared in the space between the hedges, wearing a white flower behind her ear. Her hair smelled of coconut oil, reminding Simon of school. Sudden nostalgia. All the Island kids had greased their long black hair with coconut; the classrooms used to reek with the heavy, pungent scent. It was sad there were almost no Pacific Islanders at his own children's expensive schools. Only one or two brown faces among the Pakehas and Asians.

'Oh, Tulei.' Roza looked away, cold. She said to Johnnie, 'You'd better go darling, and be fumigated.'

The boy looked like arguing but she hustled him off the seat, her eyes on Simon. 'Go on, get on with it,' she said. It wasn't clear whether she was talking to the child or the nanny; both looked sharply at her, Johnnie with his hot, alert eyes, the nanny with a stubborn set to her mouth.

As they walked between the hedges Tulei raised her arm in mock threat at the boy, as if about to give him a backhanded slap, and he laughed, and she in turn allowed her face to relax and gave him a beaming smile. Roza didn't notice this; she was staring fixedly away. Simon remembered that the last time he'd seen Tulei and Johnnie singing hymns together, Johnnie had had his arm thrown around the nanny's shoulders. The boy was so close to his mother, he'd probably always have an easy way with women.

'Off she goes, the Bible-banger,' Roza said.

She chafed her hands uneasily and looked about with an expression of disgust. 'I hate Christians. You have to be a liar to be a Christian, and a hypocrite.'

'She seems like quite a nice nanny.' Simon sat down next to her, cautiously.

'Tulei thinks she's "saved" and I'm not. I mean, really. Saved. How *primitive*.' She gave a high, scornful laugh.

Simon waited. She gathered up the deck of cards and shuffled them, her hands moving rapidly. A cloud of midges hovered near, making a dark smudge in the air, abruptly zooming away as Ed Miles came up the path from the pool, his head down, a towel around his neck and his cell phone clamped to his ear. He saw them, said something quiet and folded the phone shut. He was wearing swimming trunks and plastic flip-flops; his feet were narrow and pale, almost dainty. He stood dabbing his hair with the towel and looking them over, various calculations and impressions registering in his pale grey eyes. Out of his clothes the Police Minister looked colourless and oddly sexless, even feminine, as though a lifetime of sedentary plotting had turned him into a hothouse plant.

'Hello Ed,' Roza said, not nicely.

Ed acknowledged her acid tone, glanced at Simon.

'Good swim?' Simon asked.

'Wonderful,' Ed said, and gave a sardonic salute and walked on.

'Creep,' Roza said under her breath.

Simon stood up. 'Should I leave you alone?'

'Why?' She looked furious.

'You seem in a bad . . .'

'Oh rubbish.' She pulled him down beside her. 'Tell me about your affair. It was like Miss Schlegel and Mr Bast. Only you were middle-class Miss Schlegel and she was low born . . .'

'No.'

'Tell me more about it. Give me details. What she was like, where did you meet?'

'No, I don't want to go into it. I feel bad about it.'

'You can't start a story and then not finish.'

'I shouldn't have mentioned it.'

She put her hand on his arm. 'I've been thinking about it. You having an affair. It made me feel . . .'

He stared. His arm burned where she was touching it.

'. . . a little thrill. Almost jealous.'

They were sitting very close. She leaned forward and kissed him on the lips. Adrenalin shot through his body. He pressed against her but she drew back and he looked into her eyes. Her teeth were slightly bared and her breath was on his cheek. He glanced towards the hedges — what if

Ed Miles were lurking there? — then took hold of her arms and kissed her. He said her name; it sounded almost like a gasp. She put her hand against his chest, pushed him back and said in a high, breathless voice, 'Let's go out to the Kauri Lake tomorrow, just the two of us.'

'Yes.' He had a moment of pure happiness.

She got up and walked towards the hedges. The kiss had surely broken the prohibition against touching; he followed her and when they were on the narrow path between the overgrown bushes he put his hand on the small of her back, but she turned and put up her arm, forbidding. They were standing in the shadows under a big spreading pohutukawa. The ground was raised and they could see there was no one on the path in either direction. She came close and breathed in his ear; he put his arms around her.

'Funny. We have a daughter together,' she said.

He drew back and looked at her. She smiled strangely.

'You love our daughter.' She pressed herself against him. 'You really love her.'

'What do you mean? Yes, I love Elke.'

'I *know* you do.'

A prickling started up in his body; little stabs of alarm.

'What are you saying, Roza?'

Her eyes opened. 'Does Karen know you had an affair?'

'No. Well. She might have had a suspicion.'

'Does she know you were out in South Auckland, consorting with the low born?'

He said sharply, 'I'm pretty low born myself, if you want to use that term.'

'Is that why you did it? Were you returning to your roots?'

He was stung by her tone.

'Or, was the poor little South Aucklander a substitute for what you really wanted?'

They stared at each other.

He said, icy, 'No, Roza. She was *exactly* what I wanted.'

She blinked, then gave a merrily spiteful laugh. 'Goodness, Simon. You surprise me.'

He was silent. Her mood changes were so abrupt. Was there a threat in what she was saying? What *was* she saying?

With an impatient little shrug she took his arm. 'Let's go, it's time for happy hour with the Cock.'

Walking beside her he regretted his lost happiness — she had actually kissed him! — and wondered whether, despite her now unfriendly tone, he might after all expect a blissful rendezvous out at the Kauri Lake. Brief daydream: lying with Roza in the long grass, the hot wilderness, the feathery toetoe plumes waving against the blue sky in celebration . . .

But she was so unpredictable, she would probably come on like a nymphomaniac and then scream and knee him in the balls. And then the bodyguards would arrive, Ray, Jon, Mick, Shaun, and drag him before David Hallwright in handcuffs.

'What's funny?' she said.

The absurdity of it. Everything threatened by his situation with Weeks and here he was dreaming about sex with the Prime Minister's wife. And then he thought, But I'm always dreaming about sex with the Prime Minister's wife. I've imagined having sex with her every day since I met her. He sighed, and gloomed after her through the soft dusk to the tables under the trees, where Trent and Troy had lit scented coils and candles to keep mosquitoes away, and the Cock was sitting next to boozy Peter Gibson, and Ed Miles, who had put his clothes on, had drawn his chair close to Karen's and was looking at her intently while she talked. Karen's nervous laugh rose above the murmur of voices. Ed was wearing linen trousers and effete loafers with no socks, and his expression was sinisterly respectful. God knew what indiscretions he had been drawing out of poor Karen, who looked up at them now with a troubled expression, as though she thought she might already have let something slip.

Sharon Cahane's buzz-saw voice: 'He talks in his sleep! He wakes me up in the night droning about his portfolio. The budget. The deficit.'

The Cock held his glass between finger and thumb and gazed into the clear liquid. 'My wife is an inventive woman. My wife loves to make things up.'

'Honestly, it's unbearable. He runs the place even while we're in bed. He wakes up shouting about the nation's credit rating. I've started wearing ear plugs.'

'If my wife only possessed the necessary cognitive powers, she would be able to write fiction.'

'Stop glaring, darling. Look at that face. The wind'll change.'

The Cock smiled. He had placed a circle of burning mosquito coils around his chair; at intervals he reached down to check and rearrange them. He said, 'The wind'll change. My wife's famous wit. Sometimes I think I might expire with mirth . . .'

Roza said with quiet amusement, 'You'll set your trousers on fire with those things.'

The Cock stopped tending his smoking coils, turned his head to one side, and gave Roza a charged glance. He would have been handsome if there weren't such an air of thin-lipped, sinister restraint about him.

It now occurred to Simon that Roza liked the Cock very much. She was a junkie for power, and the Cock radiated ambition, competitiveness, ferocious cleverness. Something else was suddenly clear to Simon: at the centre of Roza's personality was a craving for things stronger and more potent than herself. Only the most powerful mixes would do.

Now she and the Cock looked at each other through the lines of drifting smoke, each with a hint of secret laughter, and Simon felt a weight settle on his shoulders: he would never be able to supply the mysterious thing Roza wanted. She would always look beyond him. Tormented by her own restlessness she wanted to meet her match, to be arrested, contained, held.

Sharon carried on, 'One mosquito bite and it's a catastrophe. We practically have to go to hospital . . .' Her voice trailed off and she sat biting her thumb and looking from Roza to the Cock.

Juliet Miles let out a theatrical sigh and clapped her hand over her mouth. Ed had turned his attention away from Karen; his gaze travelled from Roza and the Cock to David.

David caught Simon's eye and gestured to the chair next to him.

Simon accepted a drink from Trent. He wondered what Roza had meant before, about Elke. Her manner had frightened him — and now he had so much to fear. He sensed she was angry about Elke's return to the Little House, which she would see as a wounding defection by her daughter and a victory for Karen, and the idea of making Roza angry was unnerving in any circumstances, let alone now.

David said, 'It's never going to be popular.'

Ed leaned forward, running his finger around the rim of his glass. 'That's precisely why you need to inoculate. You say, "We won't do it in this term but we won't rule it out. We'll consider it if we're re-elected."You need to bring it up, deal with it, show you're not avoiding the issue, admit a certain amount but by no means all, and then move the debate on.'

'Yes, yes, I know all this.' David nodded, impatient, eyeing the Cock.

'We need to run through two inoculation speeches before the conference; you've got asset sales and tax. You've also got an opportunity, re, um, boat people. It would be helpful if the punters thought there were hordes of them on the way, and that you were the man to keep them out.'

'A tried and true strategy,' the Cock said sarcastically.

Ed smiled. 'It never gets old. What we need is a boatload, foundering and disintegrating somewhere off Australia, and to put it about that they are heading here. Preferably about four hundred of them, looking sick and obviously ethnic and, you know, hungry for the nation's benefits and jobs.'

The Cock said, irritated, 'Don't forget to throw in that they're terrorists.'

'Yes, terrorists and Muslims and riddled with disease, all that.'

'Gosh, I suppose we're lucky we're so far away,' Juliet said, 'or else they would be arriving all the time.'

'It wouldn't hurt if people thought they were.'

The Cock said, 'Well, Ed, why don't you hire some actors to bob about in the ocean starving and dying and waving pitchforks, and holding signs saying "We want to come to New Zealand and blow you up and steal your jobs".'

'Yes, why don't I?' Ed said with a bland smile.

The Cock scoffed and glanced at Roza.

A red spot appeared on Ed's cheek. He pressed his glass against it. 'You're such an intellectual, Colin. You shouldn't concern yourself with spin this crude. It's beneath you.'

'I suppose it is,' said the Cock.

'It's also not your forte,' Ed said.

The Cock turned from Roza to Ed with a cold, steady look.

Ed leaned hastily towards David, 'As I was saying, David, there are the two inoc speeches and also—'

'You told me,' David said, dismissing him.

Karen laughed. Ed sat back in his chair, pressing the glass against his cheek and darting a bad look at Karen.

Roza, who had been watching the exchange with keen enjoyment, laid her hand on the Cock's arm. 'Brrr. Has it got a bit chilly?' She grinned and shivered. The Cock's expression seemed to blur, as though he was suddenly, drunkenly lost in contemplation of her wicked smile and her beautiful hot eyes, and Simon felt the tension in the air rise another notch. Trent crossed the grass with his tray and the wind blew a piece of paper up and over the hedge, sending it whirling in the air. Karen lifted her empty glass and waggled it at Trent, who came obediently forward, and Roza said something quiet in the Cock's ear. Simon could feel David beside him, watching Roza leaning close to the Cock, playing with her hair, laughing, crossing and uncrossing her legs.

'Let's take a turn around the garden,' David said. 'I want to smoke.'

They got up and everyone stopped talking, uncertain. Roza took her hand off the Cock's arm and frowned.

'Where are you going?' she said.

David only looked at her and smiled. He signalled to Simon and walked away with no explanation, leading him across the lawn towards the lower garden.

They went down the path to the beach, where Ray was standing guard at the gate. The wind was blowing hard, making the dry bushes rattle. David took out a packet of cigarettes and lit one.

Simon said, 'I didn't know you smoked those. I thought it was only cigars.'

'Secret vice.' David blew out a long stream of smoke. 'I get them from Tuleimoka, the nanny. That's why I won't let Roza fire her. She's just fired Jung Ha, but I told her we're keeping Tulei.'

'Jung Ha?'

'Lin Jung Ha, our old housekeeper. Roza's sacked her.'

'Actually, I think Johnnie really likes the nanny.'

'He does. Roza says she hates Tulei because she's religious. But it's really because Johnnie loves her.'

'Oh?' Simon kept his tone cautious, polite.

David drew in a deep breath of smoke. 'Roza wants to be loved.'

'She *is* loved.'

David looked sideways at him, amused. 'Of course she is. But she doesn't know it. She wasn't loved by her mother, maybe she doesn't know what it feels like.'

'That's too complicated for me.'

'Roza's not complicated. Roza is a simple organism.'

Simon smiled. 'Jesus.'

'What?'

'You're the only person who could say such a thing. Roza seems *unbelievably* complicated to me.'

'Roza is very easy to understand.'

'For you.'

'For me, yes.'

'You're obviously a genius,' Simon said.

'Well, yes, that's true.' He grinned.

'She's in a . . . good mood tonight,' Simon said.

David seemed to read his mind. 'Cahane's a sharp bastard but he doesn't understand her at all. He can't read why she does what she does. He's just glazed and charmed and pussy-whipped, the poor prick. What he doesn't realise is that everything Roza does is directed at me.'

Simon scuffed the sand with his shoe.

David smiled. 'I know what you're thinking. What confidence.'

'I suppose you're right,' Simon said. He looked up. 'No, I think that might be right.'

'Tonight she's feeling uncertain.'

'What about?'

'Me.'

'Oh. Really?'

'There's no harm if Roza sometimes feels uncertain.'

'I see. I wonder if she's also . . .' He hesitated again.

David drew on his cigarette. 'Preoccupied about Elke? Roza wants to be loved. Roza wants to be *sure* she's loved.'

They walked a short way along the dunes while David smoked another cigarette. Ray and Shaun followed. The beach was deserted apart from a couple of joggers down at the shoreline and nobody came their way. The sand was soft and squeaked underfoot and the tide was high, breaking far up the beach in long sweeps of foamy water, receding with a hiss over the shells. Simon wondered whether there was a brutal simplicity about David that allowed him to deal with a person as complicated as Roza. Could he manage her because he just didn't see the complexities? Or was it that he was equally subtle, and a match for her? Simon couldn't fathom the Hallwrights' relationship; he wasn't, after all, very good at understanding relationships, he was a technocrat, better at solving physical problems than intangible ones. David had changed. He used to be wary around some people; the Ellisons used to make him nervous, and Roza did too. Not any more.

On a rocky bit of the path through the dunes David slipped and caught hold of Simon's arm. Simon steadied him. He said, 'I don't really understand what you meant about Roza.'

David paused, turning the cigarette packet in his fingers. 'Well, here's a theory. Roza's mother didn't love her. Roza loves people fiercely, but if you tell her she's loved back, she doesn't necessarily believe it, because she doesn't know what it feels like. So she goes looking for, I don't know what, an approximation of love. Something to overwhelm her, quell her.'

'I see,' Simon said, uncertain.

David looked intently at him. 'I grew up without parents.'

'Yes.'

'But have you seen the polls? The *people* love me.'

Simon thought for a moment. He said, cautious, 'I didn't know Roza actually wanted to fire Tulei?'

'Oh yes, because Johnnie loves her, you see. I stand between the nanny and the firing squad. Roza hates Tulei. *Hates* her.'

Cold Blood

There was a burst of laughter from the group downstairs. Simon dipped his head and waited.

At dawn the Green Lady rode out of the forest on her black horse and climbed to the roof of the castle. Smoke rose from the Idiots' Village, and across the forest came the drone of the Idiots' early morning prayer to the Great Wedgie. Soon and Starfish and the Dead White Cat had a secret; they had managed to lock the High Priestess Germphobia into the pantry, where at least, Soon pointed out to Starfish, who was racked with guilt, their fat tormentor wouldn't go hungry or thirsty until she was discovered. "What about her . . . ablutions?" Starfish whispered, at which Soon sniggered, the Village Idiot said, "Ha ha", and even Starfish looked guiltily amused.

The Green Lady turned to look at them. Her eye fell on Suzie, the Dead White Cat. "Are you dead?" she asked him.

"Yes," the Dead White Cat replied.

"Yet you live."

"I am rare," said the Cat with dignity. "I move between worlds."

"How useful," the Green Lady said, and the Cat bowed.

"Have faith, Green Lady," the Dead White Cat said. "Soonica will return." And the Red Herring added: "He who laughs last laughs longest."

Somewhere in a room below, the Weta and the Praying Mantis began playing an eerie tune. Over the forest the clouds were black and full of rain.

The Green Lady took off her veil and spoke. There was rustling in the air, and the clouds formed a swirling black cone above the forest. There was colour glittering in the cloud, and Soon saw that it was made of dragonflies. The Green Lady's cape had a sheen like dragonflies' wings. Her voice was as smooth as oil, but men shuddered at her words . . .

'There. End of the chapter. Sleep tight.'

'Make Soon talk.'

'No, no more.'

The boy sat up. 'I want Elke.'

'She's with Karen. Now stop talking or I'll have to beat you.'

In the hall, Simon said, 'You still want to go out to the lake?'

Johnnie shouted, 'Make Soon talk!'

'Shut up!' Roza shouted back.

Tuleimoka opened her door, frowning. She said, 'I'll look after him.' Behind her, a hushed television voice said, 'Wanda. You're such a beautiful person. But we need you to let that beauty *show*.'

Roza didn't look at her.

'Tulei!' Johnnie wailed from his room. Roza clicked her tongue and walked off.

Simon followed. In the hallway she stopped and put her hand on his chest, was about to speak but turned away. His heart sped up; he hurried after her.

She turned again, 'I'm not quite sure how Karen could object to

Elke spending time up here. With her brother.'

Simon protested, 'Karen doesn't object. Far from it. She's delighted. It's Elke who changes her mind all the time. We never know where we are with her.'

'Really.'

'We're always struggling to keep up.'

'It must be hard work.' Her eyes were fixed on him. 'I'm grateful for what you've done for my daughter.'

'No. It's been great. We love her.' He felt trapped. Every answer he gave implied possessiveness when he wanted to convey the opposite.

Roza said, 'You must feel you love her most.'

'Me?'

Her tone was odd. 'An adopted daughter must be different from a real daughter. For a man. It must be . . . unsettling.'

'I don't know what you mean. There's no difference.'

Her expression hardened. 'If Johnnie wanted his sister around, it would be wrong for anyone to stand in the way. Wouldn't it.'

'I said to Karen, it's up to Elke. She's eighteen.'

'So you've discussed it.'

'We have various ongoing discussions, as parents.'

'As parents. Of course.' Her smile was unnerving.

'Adoptive parents,' he added awkwardly.

They rejoined the company. Karen was telling Marcus to put his phone away and stop texting. Simon sat next to her and said, quiet, 'Why did Elke haul all her gear back to the Little House?'

Karen was irritated. 'I don't know. She wanted to.'

'You didn't put pressure on her?'

'How could I do that?'

'You don't think it might be good for everyone if she goes back for the last few nights?'

'Why does it matter where she sleeps?'

'Well, you were completely preoccupied with the question until you got your own way.'

'Oh what rubbish. It's so petty, such a non-issue. And it's up to Elke.'

He pressed a cold glass against his sunburnt cheek and muttered, 'You don't think you're cutting off your nose to spite your face?'

'Eh? What? Speak up.'

'If you try to win every battle you might lose the bigger one.'

'Battle? What battle?'

Near them, Ed Miles said, 'Calls were flying back and forth. They're lucky they pulled it off; the thing was a shambles. We'll get Vince on a conference call tomorrow. If he denies it, tell him we'll get hold of his phone records.'

Karen said to Juliet, 'I spoke to Trish today. She's doing amazingly well.'

'She has incredible strength.'

'Absolutely.'

'Look, she's amazing. Isn't she, Simon?'

But Simon was looking at Ed.

What had he been doing? In his panic over Weeks he'd been caught up in a kind of magical thinking; getting rid of phones when call records must exist independently of the phones themselves. Like a simpleton, he'd believed that if he threw a phone in the sea, the records would simply disappear. What else had he got wrong?

He had a bleak sense of his own isolation, as if he'd been pushed into a parallel universe, forever separated from the group.

Beside him, David said, 'Dean had me doing squats and lunges on the beach. I looked like the Minister of Silly Walks. I was thinking, I hope no one's in the bushes with a camera.' He nudged Simon, who said mechanically, 'I suppose the soft sand . . .'

How incriminating could the phone records be? All they showed was brief communication: Weeks wanting information. There'd been no texts between them, and there couldn't be a record of the content of conversations, unless one of them had been under surveillance.

'What do you think?' David asked.

Roza and David had both turned to him.

'Sorry, I was miles away.'

He excused himself early and went to bed. That night he dreamed he was on the beach in the early morning, before it was properly light. It was stormy. He stood on the sand in the warm, black, howling dawn and saw two figures walking at the water's edge. He pushed towards them against the wind, trying to make out who they were. He was filled with terrible anxiety; he yearned to speak to someone, to relieve his loneliness and ask for help. They stopped and turned and he saw it was Roza and Elke. He wanted to reach them but he heard Karen's voice and woke. It was hot, the sun was already shining through the wooden blinds and he would only just have time to drive into the city.

Looking down at his notes, he waited for the moment to break in. His patient continued, 'We've been married twenty years. Suddenly he's going, "Leave the boy outside on the pavement." That was so he didn't have to see me when he came to pick up our son. He's getting a flat. He's got this twenty-three-year-old. I mean, he's forty-six, and he's got this twenty-three-year-old — and what's she, by the way, some kind of incest victim, some creepy daddy's girl? — and he's telling me everything by text. We were married twenty years and my husband dumped me *by text*.'

'I'm sorry.'

'How about that, Simon?'

'Yes.'

Silence.

He pressed a thumb to his temple. 'On a brighter note . . . your results are good. The symptoms are calming down. No more pain?'

'Sorry. This isn't relevant.'

'No, not at all. I mean, yes . . . I hope things are getting a bit brighter for you.'

'He came back, right. It was over, he said. It was all a mistake. He was sorry. He wanted to carry on like it never happened.'

'Well, that's great. Now, I'm going to give you a prescription . . .'

'And then he decided we should go on holiday, and about one day into the week he said he'd changed his mind. I don't know how I got through the week. Our son said, "He's treating you like shit. This has to stop." When we got back to the city I snapped. I laid into him, tore strips off him, insulted him to the core. I told him he was worthless, that I'd married beneath me, that he should go. So he disappeared again.'

Simon looked at his watch.

'I left the kids with my parents and went to Sydney. I said to my father, "It's over. I'll just have to write him off." Then, when we'd all resolved to carry on without him, he came back again, apologising and swearing he'd made a terrible mistake and that he would stop behaving badly. And he has. He even wrote letters apologising to me, to my family. He's been a model husband.'

'Great. Excellent.'

'But what I wonder, Simon, is this: how do you take up again with someone when you know they're capable of that? I mean, he didn't just get caught having an affair and go, oh I'm sorry, I won't do it again. He decided he was going to eliminate me from his life. It's like he was going to have me killed. And then he couldn't go through with it. But he *wanted* to.'

'I see what you mean.' Another pause, the distant roar of a plane, Clarice walking heavy-footed past the door. Simon thought about it. He'd had an affair, but leaving Karen? Telling her (by text!) he was going off with a twenty-three-year-old? He'd met his patient's husband, when he'd been engaged as their private obstetrician. Loud, muscular, a bit of a swagger. A tough guy, cold-blooded . . .

'Issues of trust, I imagine,' he said. 'Now I want you to make an appointment with the physiotherapist.'

'One funny thing, Simon. Houses.'

'Houses?' He laid down his pen.

'At every stage of this crisis, I dreamed about houses. When he was leaving, I dreamed about broken-down, ruined houses. When he'd gone I dreamed the children and I were trying to find our way into a lovely house, but we were locked out. And when he came back and said he was sorry and grovelled and started to behave like he really meant it I dreamed about the most incredible, vast, beautiful mansion, a paradise . . .'

'I'm sorry, Simon, are you all right?'

'Just popping out for a sandwich.'

He swivelled in his chair, nodded at Clarice: yes, whatever. A line of birds sat on the power line outside his window, black musical notes against the white sky. In the park a woman ran to catch a small child as it toddled towards the road.

He'd seen off the last patient. She was reluctant, standing at his door, folding the prescription into tiny pieces. Breaking the rule (keep it impersonal or you'll be here all day), he said, 'I heard a bit of advice. It was for disaster victims, after an earthquake.'

'Oh yes. What was that then?'

'Increase your tolerance to uncertainty.'

She went on folding and folding the piece of paper. 'That's not bad,' she said finally, rolled her eyes, gave him a smile and went away.

He was due at a seminar being held for a visiting Swedish professor of physiotherapy. Running late, he cabbed across town, scrambled out and dropped a folder of notes on the pavement, slinging money at the driver while a doorman gathered up a slew of brightly coloured diagrams of the female pelvic floor.

The visiting professor was on a stage flanked by pot plants, finishing the first half of her presentation. Glamorous, thin to the point of emaciation, severe, she was the mentor for physiotherapists in the field, a visiting star (you could download her books and exercise videos from the internet) and there was an earnest and reverent atmosphere as she wound up her spiel and started to take questions.

Her microphone squawked. A break was announced. Simon headed for coffee and was joined by Pete Brown from the hospital who said, 'Did you read what Silvio Berlusconi called Angela Merkel?'

'No.'

'An unfuckable lardarse.'

Simon pressed a hand to his temple. 'God. With his orgies and that. He's like a Roman emperor.'

'And then there's Sarkozy, married to a supermodel. The unfuckable lardarse must have a terrible time dealing with those guys.'

Simon, checking his cell phone for messages, signalled for him to shut up. Pete was always too loud.

Pete leaned near. 'Physios. They're like nurses and midwives. They carry on like we don't know anything, and they think you can achieve anything with muscles. They're like a cult. What do you think of the Professor of Pelvic Floor? She's going to levitate after this. She could probably kill you with her . . .'

'Hello, how are you? Can I introduce you to Professor Kaisla Jansson.'

They turned and shook her small, cool hand. Her glance lingered on Brown, who'd slicked back his hair and was looking handsome and louche, if slightly raddled. He had his stock of personal charms: the novel he'd been writing for a decade, his 'troubled' marriage, his fondness for poetry and cannabis. The Professor of Pelvic Floor inspected him and coolly smiled.

'You were speaking of the EU?'

'We were!'

Simon's phone started shrilling. Distracted, he apologised and moved away, answered without checking the caller. A mistake.

'Dr Lampton, it's Marie Da Silva.'

Anxiety came down on him like a grille. He looked for a place away from the crowd. 'Ms Da Silva. What can I do for you?'

'We're outside, need to pop up for a minute.'

'I'm in a seminar.'

'We'll be up in two minutes.'

'How did you know I was here?'

'Two minutes.'

They were harassing him. He couldn't be seen talking to them here, in front of everybody. He could refuse, but she would barge in.

Pete Brown was looking over. He said, 'I'll meet you in the lobby.'

Riding down in the lift, anxiety flared in his body like a bad cramp. They were putting pressure on him; they must think he had something to hide. It was brutal having hope squeezed out of you like this; it must be how cancer patients felt when you told them, I'm sorry, the news is not good.

Here she came, marching through the lobby holding her notebook in the crook of her arm, her silent partner O'Kelly in tow. She was wearing cargo pants and boots and a short leather jacket, she was frowning, and the frown and the odd-coloured eyes made her face slightly crooked. Her hair was messy, the blonde strands standing out from her head and catching the light. He thought she looked like his own Claire when she was tired, dark shadows under the eyes, narrow cheeks and that pained look of concentration, and suddenly he saw Weeks's body sprawled on the concrete, thin shoulders, bony ankle, the fingers of one hand gently curled, a defenceless boy's hand.

The three of them sat down in the big squashy seats by the plate-glass window. Pedestrians walked past noiselessly outside. Simon's phone rang, he checked the screen, let it go to messages. Da Silva was looking closely at him. O'Kelly opened his notebook, clicked a ballpoint pen.

Simon said to the young woman, 'Been working hard?'

'I'm sorry?'

'You look tired.'

'Thanks.'

'I suppose shift work's tough.'

'I don't mind it at all. Now, can we just go over something again — what did you say you and Arthur Weeks talked about when he rang?'

Simon pretended to consider. 'I told you. He wanted information about the Hallwrights.'

'Did he tell you about his project?'

'Project?'

She said, 'He wanted to make a feature film about a National Party Prime Minister. A tall PM with blond hair and a limp, would you believe. Who mispronounces his words.'

'That'll be why he wanted to know about the Hallwrights. That explains why he rang me.'

'The screenplay's in his flat.'

'You read it?'

'No. Not personally.'

So, were others poring over it? Her silent colleague, O'Kelly? Simon looked away from them, out at the moving crowds. 'How did this person die again?'

'He fell, broke his neck.'

'Why are you spending so much time on him?'

'We'd like to know how he came to fall.'

'You mean, was he pushed? Can you tell?'

'Maybe.'

Simon said, 'I suppose you must have plenty of physical evidence.'

She said, unsmiling. 'You tell me, doctor.'

He looked at her eyes, the dark and the light. Her expression was definitely antagonistic now.

'Why are you asking me?'

'Why shouldn't we?'

Should he try anger on her, or should he tone it down? A little rush of panic, he couldn't think how to pretend to behave. The male detective's silent stare was distracting, as was the repetitive clicking of his pen.

She said, 'Can you think of anyone who would want to harm Arthur Weeks?'

'I told you. I. Don't. Know. Him.'

Weeks's 'screenplay'. What detail had he worked into it? How about: a married doctor who visits a young woman in South Auckland on his way to and from the airport. A little wooden house on the edge of a South Auckland field, where he goes to escape from his life. He saw Mereana walking away across the grass, the metal roofs of the warehouses across the field reflecting the evening sun.

Da Silva looked at her notebook. 'If you think of anything else about Mr Weeks or the night book, ring me.'

'The what book?'

'That's the name of his film script.'

'Knight, like knighthoods?'

'As in opposite of day.'

'Oh.'

'Dr Lampton, do you think anyone would want to harm him because of what he was writing?'

'No.'

Her eyes were fixed on him. He hesitated.

'Well . . . actually, I don't know what he was writing, but the idea of someone harming him because of material he was inventing; that sounds like fantasy, like a conspiracy theory.'

She didn't say anything.

'Anyway, who do you mean? David Hallwright? Because Weeks was writing about a Prime Minister? That's pretty far-fetched. Not to mention outrageous.' His voice had risen, he felt the heat in his cheeks. Careful. But he pushed on, 'I mean, what are you trying to insinuate? Someone pushed him off a wall because of a film script? We're not living in a dictatorship, some . . . *banana republic.'*

Her mouth was turning up. She glanced at her partner; his eyes crinkled. They were laughing at him.

He wanted to grab her shoulders and shake her. 'You're supposed to be investigating a death. You think it's a laugh?'

She looked very young suddenly, under her mop of hair, the odd eyes lit with savage enjoyment, as if his indignation was the funniest thing she'd seen all day.

Then she dropped the smile. 'Thanks for your help,' she said.

He took a breath. 'All this bothers me. This man rang me. I don't like the idea he was some kind of stalker, trying to get to the Hallwrights through me.' He avoided her eye. 'But I also don't like the idea of a young man dying. You said he was young? It . . . bothers me.'

He was sweating, rambling. He'd lost it. It wouldn't be surprising if they handcuffed him straight away.

But she only said, 'I don't find it amusing, no.'

He was too far gone to gauge her tone. Her phone rang, she answered it, said yes a couple of times, sounded flustered. She ended the call and said, 'I take it you have no idea how Mr Weeks came by the contact numbers?'

'Numbers?'

Her phone rang again.

'Just a minute.' She answered, listened, said yes another couple of times, hung up.

Simon looked from one cop to the other, 'You said numbers?'

She sent a quick text, looked up. 'I asked how Weeks managed to get hold of private cell phone numbers.'

The male detective coughed, frowned.

She glanced at her partner and changed tack. 'It must be interesting spending time with the Prime Minister.'

Simon leaned forward. 'You're interested in him? That makes me wonder . . .'

They waited. He swallowed and went on reedily, 'That makes me *wonder* whether you're spending all this time, wasting my time, interrupting me at work, because you have some voyeuristic interest in . . . in . . .'

The man had stopped clicking his pen. Da Silva put her head on one side.

'. . . Some *recreational* interest in the Prime Minister. His fame, his private life. Just as your dead writer apparently did. And if that were the case, it would be highly unprofessional, I would have thought. Worthy of a complaint to . . . to . . .'

'He wants to complain,' Da Silva said. She turned her mouth down on one side, a cartoon grimace.

A long silence.

The male detective got up and put a hand on Simon's shoulder. 'Put it in writing, mate. Don't hold back. Make sure you mention we shouldn't talk to you because you're the Prime Minister's friend.'

Sunk in the big soft chair he watched them go, imagining he could hear the tiny clinking of metal as they tramped through the hushed lobby. *Jink jink.* The exchange had been so disastrous he was actually surprised to see them leave. Did they not realise how close they'd come, how weary crime had made him? He didn't have the strength for it; a soupçon more of their youthful aggro, a few more sarcastic cracks from blonde Marie and he would have broken down, perhaps with a burst of hysterical laughter. But they'd walked away, and now emerged on the street in deep discussion; the man leaning one elbow on a car roof and making a forceful point before they got in and pulled away. Last glimpse of Marie Da Silva's face through the driver's window: a flash of laughter.

Pedestrians streamed past the window. It was hot in the still air of the lobby. She was actually *laughing* as they pulled away. Had she no sense of . . . What? Decorum? Decency? No, of course not, none of that. She would be hard as nails and enjoying every gritty moment. Even *I* am a step away from hysterical mirth, the hilarity of despair. How close were Da Silva and Detective O'Kelly? Did they go for beers after work, fall into bed together, exorcise the day's crime scene horrors with strenuous lovemaking? Brief daydream: Da Silva pouring herself a restorative chardonnay, rustling up a stir-fry in her rented apartment, O'Kelly lounging with a glass of red wine. Fractured thoughts. Yes indeed, he was close to . . .

The phone broke in, roused him: it was Clarice with a complaint, something about one of the other receptionists on their floor. Nag nag. He listened but didn't hear, made soothing noises. The exchange distracted him, gave him strength to take the lift up to the conference room, where the Professor of Pelvic Floor was demonstrating exercises with the aid of a giant silver Swiss ball. A detail bothered him. Da Silva had referred to cell phone numbers, plural.

Could Weeks have called others?

Weeks had asked about Roza, implying she had things to hide. Was it possible he'd phoned her, that she and Simon had been secretly worrying about the same thing?

Increase your tolerance to uncertainty.

Sudden memory: sitting on the deck at home, holding the newspaper and running his eye down the column of Death Notices, hoping he would see a name: Mereana Kostas. Losing himself, he'd clung to Mereana; when he'd recovered, he'd turned away. Now, through Weeks, Mereana could take everything from him — as if the universe had observed his behaviour, had judged it unfair and bustled in with its hands on its hips and given her the comeback she deserved . . .

But there is no God, he thought. There is no divine justice, no higher power. Which was why it was still possible for him to hope.

He was driving up the Harbour Bridge after the conference when another memory rose: Elke in the kitchen aged eight; he'd come in out of the rainy night and she was awake as she often was, the child who couldn't sleep, who greeted him when he walked in at five in the morning, exhausted but still buzzing after a chaotic shift.

'Dad. You see people die. Is death different for you?'

'Most of my patients stay alive, actually! And I don't know what you mean, different.'

She took hold of his hand, plaiting his fingers. 'If you can cut people's bodies without freaking out, would it be easier for you to kill them?'

'Easier?'

'Easier for you than for other people.'

'No.'

She was trying to find her way to a question that eluded her. 'Everyone else sees dead and not dead. Do you see something different?'

'No.'

Sudden, huge rain on the corrugated iron roof. Dawn light had begun leaking over the garden, a bird hopped on the lawn. He fed slices into the toaster, made a pile of toast and jam, poured her a glass of milk. She watched him, expressionless. Outside in the dawn, the dreamy rain fell.

She said, 'Is my mother dead?'

'I don't know. Would you like us to try to find out?'

'If you save lives, does God owe you?'

'There is no God.'

'Barbara says there is.'

'Grandma Barbara has many delusions.'

She didn't laugh but persisted, 'Do you believe in ghosts?'

'There are no ghosts.'

'You're allowed to cut people with a knife. You could kill them if you wanted to.'

'Scalpel. Not knife. Anyone could kill someone with a knife. When I use my tools it's to fix people, make them better.'

Elke drew a face in the crumbs on the table. 'What if dead people can see us? If they want to come back, they're crying to come back, but they're stuck in the other place forever.'

He put his hand on her arm. 'No. No, it can't be like that.'

Now he crossed the Harbour Bridge and drove out of the city. Beyond Albany he hit a long patch of roadworks and drove through slaloms of orange plastic cones, directed by men in reflective vests. They were resurfacing the motorway and the road was white with dust. He passed the road crew and speeded up, his windscreen speckled with the pale grit swirling across the road, and when he turned on the wipers the glass was immediately smeared and grey. He slowed, peered. The wipers made a rough scrape-scrape on the glass; disliking the sound he pulled over and used a piece of cloth to wipe off the dirt.

He'd stopped on the edge of a hillside, looking down on a sweep of beautiful, undulating land dotted with sheep. The sheep's bleating drifted up the hill, the wind sighed in a stand of pine trees, below him a hawk turned and turned above the paddocks. To the north beyond the headland the sea reflected the afternoon sun in dazzling points of light.

This weariness . . . He wiped dirt off his hands and thought about his last conversation with Da Silva. If she didn't give up and if he were charged in relation to Weeks's death, he could be struck off the medical register. If they took away his practice he might as well kill himself.

He imagined Mereana browsing through the newspaper. Scanning the Death Notices, leaning forward . . . Simon Lampton! Dead!

He saw Mereana's face. Her green eyes. Chipped nail polish, slim legs, a scar on her hand. Nothing shocks her. She has a sarcastic laugh, is quick to anger, is kind. She is twenty-eight, clever, poor, has lost everything, even her child, and when he visits her he feels as though he's crossed into a different world, stepped outside time, and he loves her.

Weeks was dead, it was an accident, he would have done more harm than good calling an ambulance. *Repeat this. Keep it in your head.*

But now he'd lied to the police the consequences of discovery could be much worse, and perhaps he'd made an appalling miscalculation, imagining such a crime could remain unsolved. Still, he could hope. The police weren't superhuman . . .

Suppose he rang Marie Da Silva now and told her everything, explained why he hadn't come clean. He imagined the relief as he unburdened himself, appealed to her: Ms Da Silva, what would you have done? I had no choice; I did no harm; I sought only to minimise damage to my family and friends. (Not to mention to the government.) But think about it: he would be supplying her with a motive for harming Weeks. And *had* he wanted to harm him? He could hardly remember now, the whole terrible day was a blur. No, he had only wanted the trouble to go away. Yet he could imagine what his blonde tormentor, aggressive little Marie, would say to that: 'You wanted the trouble to go away. So you came up behind him and pushed . . .'

Da Silva, with her rare eyes. Like Claire, that mix of youthful aggression and vulnerability. When Claire was on the warpath you could deflect her with a show of coldness. She would fix those big clear eyes on you, look suddenly lost. She always thought she was 'just being rational'; it took her by surprise, hurt her, when she made people angry.

He was still standing on the side of the road. A truck roared by, the blast of its slipstream shaking the car. The sheep sent up their mournful cries. It was fanciful to compare Da Silva to Claire, to imagine he could outwit or bully a trained detective. He got in the car and drove.

Confession

No one knew where Ford was. Karen said he'd been playing tennis with Garth and now he'd gone walking over the dunes, but the beach was empty as far as Simon could see except for a couple with a dog and some kids hurling themselves, screaming, off the top of a bank of sand. He went out to the road and asked Ray, who was sitting in the gate house with his feet up doing the *Herald* crossword. Ford hadn't been past. On his way to the Little House he met Tuleimoka, who shook her head, no.

He said, 'Thanks. Oh, Tulei? I was just wondering . . . Jung Ha?'

'She is leaving.'

'Why?'

Tulei raised both hands and adjusted the comb in her shining black hair. Her expression was hard, closed. 'Don't know. Between her and Missus.'

He went to the edge of the main lawn and saw Ford had walked south, out to the point, where there was a seat under a crooked pine tree and waves breaking on the rocks below. When he got there Ford was stubbing out a cigarette on the edge of the wooden seat.

'You're smoking again.'

'Only two a day since Emily left. There's no one to nag me.'

Simon sat down. 'I'll nag you. Even two a day's bad for your heart. You know that, don't you.'

They watched the gannets diving, hitting the water like missiles.

'You need someone to nag you. There must be lots of women would love to have you, have some kids with you.'

Ford said, 'I did have Emily's kid while we were together.'

'I know, you said she was obnoxious. But you'd love your own.'

'No, she wasn't obnoxious. It was difficult, that's all.'

Ford lit another cigarette and glanced at Simon. He said, 'The day before Emily left, the council had redone the pavement outside the house, made verges and planted grass seed. There were long strips of dirt scattered with the seed. Caro walked on ours, left her footprints all over the soil. I was annoyed, I said don't be such a destructive little shit, now the grass won't grow, you've squashed the seed. Emily and I had a row because I'd told Caro off and she decided it was the last straw, she was off. A couple of mornings after they'd gone I came out of the house, and in the dirt were Caro's footprints. No other grass had grown, but where she'd stepped, the shoots had come up exactly in the shape of her shoe. These little green footprints made of grass.'

A gannet plummeted into the sea.

'That summed up parenthood for me,' Ford said.

'Well, I suppose. You're often wrong, and it's always your fault.'

Ford chewed the edge of his thumbnail. 'If you walk on the seed, pack it down, it must make it grow faster. Anyway, for days, until the rest of the verge grew, I walked past her little grass footprints.'

'I'm sorry, Ford.'

Ford shot the half-smoked cigarette into the dunes, rubbed his eyes. 'Ah, don't be sorry. She was pretty obnoxious. And Emily wasn't May.'

'No loss then.'

'No. Smoke?'

'Very funny. No thanks. Ford, I need your help.'

'That sounds serious.'

'It is. Ford, I've done . . . a terrible thing.'

The sun was melting and sinking, the sky was strung with wispy ropes of fine red cloud. Ford had his head in his hands. Beside him Simon sat and stared hopelessly at the sea, silver and flat like mercury; it looked chemical, congealed. He put his hand on Ford's shoulder, but Ford shook him off. 'Shut up,' he said. And a bit later, 'Christ.'

'Ford?'

'I'm thinking. How could you? What were you . . . ?'

'I told you, it was an accident. I didn't do it. It just *happened*.'

Ford straightened up, 'This woman. The South Auckland woman he was asking about, you've never heard from her again?'

'No.'

'And the police have phone records and they've questioned you more than once, and they barged into a work seminar. And they said Weeks had your name written down in his house, along with the name of the woman. Have the police looked for the woman?'

'I don't know.'

'And after the, the *incident*, you drove away through the suburbs, avoided commercial areas, drove home and then went to work. And you hadn't been in to work first, only got as far as the street outside work. Why did you go home after you'd been to Weeks's?'

'I put Karen's car back and took my own to work.'

'You were driving *Karen's* car?'

'Mine was making a noise and smell, overheating. We'd left Karen's at the house while we were at Rotokauri, so I called in to see Claire before work and I took it.'

Ford stared.

'It was just chance I took her car.'

'Just chance.'

'Yes.'

'So as far as work's concerned, you turned up that morning at work, on time, in your own car.'

'Yes.'

'And then, after work, you drove back to Rotokauri in your own car, the one with the funny noise and smell.'

'Yes. I made it back and then took it to the Rotokauri Garage.'

'And no one saw you at Weeks's.'

'I assume not, or I would have heard.'

'But they can track your whereabouts through your cell phone. They'll have a record of you going up Weeks's street.'

'No, I turned the phone off. Oh, and then I left it in my office mailbox in the street, before I went to Weeks's.'

Ford looked at him. 'You turned off your phone and left it behind at your office.'

'It kept ringing, my secretary was hassling me. I wanted a clear head.'

'You took your wife's car. You left your cell phone behind. You removed evidence from the scene. You lied to the police.'

'Yes, but none of it was calculated. It just happened.'

'Not calculated. Or planned?'

'Honestly, Ford.'

A long silence.

'Did you want to harm the guy? Did you mean to?'

'No. He threatened me, he gave me a fright, but I didn't want to hurt him. I've never hurt anyone in my life. You know that.'

Ford scratched his stubble. 'It just *happened*. It's an interesting defence.'

'I swear the only reason I didn't tell anyone is because of how it would look. The damage was done . . . had happened. It was an accident. Think of the harm I'd do to the Hallwrights, to Karen, all of us, if I told.'

Tapping an unlit cigarette on his arm, Ford looked uneasily at

Simon, put the cigarette back in the packet, rubbed his hair into a tangled mess. Silence. He walked away across the top of the dunes, kicking the marram grass.

Finally he came back. 'I don't know what's happened to you.'

'Ford . . .'

'This is bad. I can't believe it. You're with these corrupt people. And now . . .'

'For once, spare me your fucking moralising. These "corrupt people", as you call them, have got nothing to do with it. I'm trying to protect them.'

Ford stood over him. 'You want to be with the Hallwrights because they make you feel respectable, like you've made it. You've never got over Aaron. Even now he's dead.'

'Don't talk to me about that violent prick.'

'Aaron never killed anyone.'

Their eyes locked. Simon stood up.

Ford planted himself square, big arms folded. 'You going to attack me now? Going to kill me?'

Simon wanted to smash him. 'Aaron has nothing to do with it.'

'Aaron wouldn't have had anything to do with Hallwright.'

A sound escaped from Simon, almost a laugh, incredulous. 'Aaron was a drunk and a loser. Who *cares* what he would have done?'

'But he was clever. He was ruined, bad; sure, you could say he was a disgusting bastard, but he wouldn't have associated with Hallwright. He had political standards.'

'Oh that's hilarious. You're going to hold *Aaron* over me. As an ethical standard.'

Ford pointed at him. 'You're better than these people. The only reason you cling to them is low self-esteem.'

'Low self-esteem!' Simon bent over, squeezing his aching knee. 'I associate with the Prime Minister because I've got low self-esteem. That's rich.'

Weak laughter made him shake. He lowered himself down on the seat. A stab of hot pain went through his kneecap and he bent over, bumping his face against Ford's leg. He grabbed Ford's thigh and pressed his forehead against it, rode the pain.

He let go. Ford sat down beside him. Silence, then the click of a lighter, Ford blowing out a long cloud of smoke.

Simon watched a group of seagulls pecking at something on the sand. 'What am I going to do?'

Ford said distantly, 'I keep going over it. You say it just "happened". But you've managed to get away with it without leaving much evidence. Could you have meant to do it subconsciously? Would it be possible to commit a crime without consciously intending to?'

Simon groaned. 'Don't get abstract. I need your help.'

Ford picked a bit of tobacco off his lip, his voice deliberate. 'You always looked down on Aaron, despised him. Distanced yourself. Both you and Karen've accused me of taking after him.'

'We haven't.'

'But is there a bit of Aaron in you after all?'

They looked at each other, and the tiny gleam of malice in Ford's eyes made Simon hollow. Would Ford turn on him, now he had the power?

'The bad seed,' Ford said.

Had he made Ford hate him?

The pain in his knee was so bad it seemed to have its own sound, a blare in rhythm with his heartbeat. He waited, hung on, instinct telling him to hope; if you endured his baiting, Ford would come round. Having punished you, he'd show his real face.

Aaron said, 'Not so respectable now, Dr Lampton.'

Eyes, nose, jaw, even the shape of the teeth, he saw his father's face, and when he looked down he saw his father's big, strong hand holding the cigarette, lifting it to the thin, derisive mouth, drawing in smoke and letting it curl.

He jumped up, his face blazing, Ford got up, pushed him, the knee felled him and he sank down on the seat. Ford got his arm in a hurting grip, stared into his face, then shoved him roughly sideways and walked away.

Simon looked at the birds skimming over the sea in the last of the light. Could he have formed a subconscious intention to hurt Weeks? An evil spirit within, the spirit of Aaron: there was horror in the idea and he rejected it; it wasn't possible to shape events subconsciously. And yet so many of his problems had been brought about by impulses he didn't understand. He didn't know why he'd sought out Mereana; he didn't know why he'd loved her and then hated her. All he could do was try to control the mess he'd made.

The cold thought came to him: it had been a mistake to confess. Ford had gained an enormous power; he despised Hallwright, and he was right that Simon and Karen had sometimes called him a chip off the old block. How could he resist giving them their comeuppance? He could potentially damage the National government too, and he would find *that* a deliciously amusing prospect.

Seeing his brother coming back along the dune Simon steeled himself to the anticipation of grief. Losing his family, friends, practice. His whole life.

Ford stood over him. 'The question is whether you can ride it out. Whether the police will draw a blank and leave you alone. My guess is no.'

'No?' Simon could hear the pleading in his voice, relief too that Ford's tone had changed. *Little brother.*

Ford paced. 'There's too much to interest them. They're harassing you, interrupting you at work, probably trying to make you worried. I can't really see how you can get away with it. There's always evidence somewhere. Forensics.'

Simon broke in, 'But there are lots of unsolved crimes. Look at *Crimewatch*. The police are on TV every week asking for evidence.'

Ford looked grimly amused. '*Crimewatch*. You've been watching it, have you? Boning up?'

'I could lose everything. My whole life.'

'Like Weeks lost his.'

'It was an accident. He came after me, hounded me, threatened everything I've built up, everything I've worked for, and it was all for his stupid meaningless *art*. He talked about his *art*, the fucking vampire, as if he wasn't playing games with real people's lives.'

'Art. No wonder you had to kill him.'

Simon counted to ten,

'No matter what you say, I reject your bullshit about subconscious actions. I did not mean to hurt him.'

'Is there anything you've left out?'

'No. The woman detective did say they'll need to talk to me again.'

'Did she. We need to prevent it.'

'How?'

Ford went on pacing. The sky behind him was marbled with red, the dunes were a black line.

Simon looked up, remembering. 'The detective might have implied Weeks rang other people. I'm not sure. Weeks asked me about Roza. He asked if she'd had a wild youth, mentioned drugs. He said someone had told him a story about her. A woman.'

Ford walked away again, came back. 'Two choices. You sit and wait for the police to come to you. Perhaps they won't and it'll all go away. But the more often they talk to you, the greater the risk you'll be implicated. The alternative to waiting for them is, you ask for help.'

'A lawyer. Know any good ones?'

'Not a lawyer. Better than that. Talk to your best friend. And *his* oldest, most slavishly loyal friend.'

'To David. And Ed Miles.'

'Who is . . .'

'The Minister of Police. I can't do that. Confess?'

Ford thought about another cigarette, checked himself, put it back in the packet, clicked his lighter. 'Not a confession, not if you do it right.'

'I can't see how it can help. I might as well ring up the police. Miles *is* the police.'

'Make it worth his while.'

'He can't control police operations.'

'I bet he can, if it matters enough to him and his beloved leader.'

'It'd be illegal, also probably impossible. There must be checks against political interference.'

'Well, yes.'

'And why would he?'

Ford sat down next to him. 'You said yourself you've done something terrible. You've also said, and you're right, that if it comes out it's going to affect all of them, because you're part of the group and you've done it while you're staying with them. So why wouldn't they do anything to make it go away?'

'I can't tell them.' At the thought of it, an ancient, familiar sensation burned in him. Shame.

Ford stretched and rubbed his chin, scraping the rough, day-old stubble. 'Maybe they'd just throw you to the lions and hope they can ride it out, but I bet they'd rather not.'

'But I can't.' He couldn't face the idea. 'They . . .'

'They won't like you any more? All your rich and powerful friends. Poor Simon. You made it and then you blew it.' Ford's tone wasn't mocking now; worse, it was sad. Or *was* it mocking? An empty, falling sensation: was Ford leading him to disaster out of some evil impulse of his own? A 'subconscious' one, even, now that Simon's position was threatened? Simon heard Aaron's bad laugh, saw his teasing eyes. He used to think there was something of the *slave* in Aaron; part of that was, if you were on form he'd leave you alone, be deferential even, but if he sensed you were weak he'd start circling, ready to attack.

Ford put his hand on Simon's shoulder. 'One way to do it—'

Simon stood up, nearly went down again, the knee letting out a horrible click. 'I'll deal with it myself.'

'What?'

'I shouldn't have bothered you. It's my problem; you don't need to be involved.'

Ford looked at him, searching. He put out his hand.

The clicking knee struck Simon's nerves, anger flared in him. 'I'd better get back. I need to pop some more pills, this fucking knee.'

'Listen, Simon.'

'No.'

'I understand. You don't want to lose . . . *all this*.' Ford waved a hand back at the big house, lit up now, yellow windows against the dark sky.

'You don't care if I lose it. You think it's immoral, worthless.'

'But I don't think *you're* immoral and worthless.'

'You self-righteous prick. You'd like to see me in a cell, chanting some Buddhist mantra, learning the error of my materialistic ways. You forget about the people relying on me, my wife and kids, my patients.'

'I don't want to see you in a cell.'

Simon hobbled, stumbling on a clump of marram grass. Ford got up and gripped his shoulders, steadying him. 'Look at you, staggering around. You've got to get that leg looked at again.'

'Fuck off.'

'No, I'm not fucking off. I will help you. I want to help you if I can.'

'How can I trust you?'

'You can. Now listen, I've got some ideas.' He pulled Simon down on the seat.

When they set off towards the house it was dark on the dunes. Ford led the way and Simon followed, placing his feet in Ford's footprints. He had one hand out, ready to catch the back of Ford's shirt if the knee gave way and he fell.

Falling

Johnnie had run out of the house early, and joined them at breakfast. Now he was perched on David's knee and inspecting Simon closely. Simon inspected him back. Unnerving child. He needed to grow into his eyes, which were too big for his face. Having spent all his time around adults the boy had a watchful quality; Karen said it made her squirm. She often made negative comments about Johnnie; it was a way of criticising Roza.

Tuleimoka sat on a park bench on the other side of the lawn plaiting her hair, while Chad or Troy staggered back and forth carrying boxes from one outhouse to another and Ray and Shaun conferred on the path that led to the beach. The light flashed off their mirror shades. A breeze crossed the dunes, flattening the silver marram and rustling the dry bushes, swarming over the lawn and billowing under Tulei's skirt. It flew up and she grappled with the material, her glossy black hair tumbling free. Shaun put his head back and laughed, clapping a hand on Ray's shoulder. A boat droned out into the bay, smacking over the waves.

One of David's phones was beeping and vibrating on the table, another started to ring. He bumped the boy off his knee and gestured across the lawn at the nanny, who stood up and began to cross the grass, holding her skirt carefully bunched in one hand.

David ended one call, the phone rang again, he talked for ten minutes, walking back and forth between the bright flower beds. Simon shaded his eyes against the glare. The sun had burned through the humid, misty cloud; the light was already strong even though it was still early in the morning. At the beach the waves were breaking in long, even rolls, the shorebreak was big and churning and foamy, so pure white it hurt to look. A grey heron flew low overhead, its slow wings sighing, *creak creak*.

Roza, Karen and Sharon Cahane emerged, heading for the tennis court followed by Garth, who was lugging a bulky sports bag and wearing cuboid yellow shoes. Distant screech of Sharon's laugh. She stopped, one elegant foot up, balancing with a hand on Garth's shoulder while she adjusted her shoe, Roza waited and Karen, looking tiny next to the other two, stood at a slight distance. Simon waved but she was frowning off at the dunes. She looked vulnerable standing alone; he would have liked to join her and put his arm around her, to talk about mundane things.

'Let's walk,' David said. 'Let's limp together, you and I.'

They took their usual route through the dunes, followed by Shaun and Ray and preceded by two other men who had been inspecting the beach and were now standing by the long wooden boat ramp, kicking their feet in the sand, watching.

David asked about the knee, Simon told him: it was his anterior cruciate ligament; he'd be seeing the orthopaedic surgeon next week.

'I nearly had my leg amputated, you know that?' David said. 'When I came off my bike, the car actually came to rest on it. Passersby lifted it off. I got to hospital and they were going to take the leg off it was so mangled, and then the shift changed, some new surgeon breezed in and said no, let's have a go piecing it back together. It was a bit of a punt, and a marathon effort they told me.'

'You were lucky.'

'Very. And now I'm full of nuts and bolts.'

Simon waited, then said, 'I need to talk to you.'

'Yes?'

'Something unusual's happened the last week or so.'

A phone went off. David checked the screen, let it ring out. 'Unusual how?'

Simon paused, squinting at the glittering sea. 'I've been visited by the police.'

'Police. Here?'

'In the city, they've come to my rooms when I'm working.' Simon looked around. There were a few people at the water's edge, some early swimmers, Ray and Shaun and the other men keeping pace but not close enough to hear.

'What did they want?'

'While I've been staying here a man called Arthur Weeks rang me. He was some kind of journalist. He got hold of my cell number, I'm assuming from my secretary, and rang me, fishing. He wanted to know about Rotokauri, about all of us. Gossip in other words. Once I realised he wasn't a patient I hung up. He tried again, I told him to go away. Remember those magazines kept ringing Karen all hours of the day, wanting to know about Elke and Roza. I thought, more of that.'

'Right.'

'Now, apparently, he's died.'

David glanced behind: Ray picking up a shell and skimming it into the sea, Shaun talking on his phone.

'Died.'

Simon made himself talk slowly, casually. 'He's had some kind of fall and died, and the police came to me because they found he'd rung me. They had phone records. I thought nothing of it, just a routine inquiry. But they came back, once when I was at a medical conference, of all places. I don't know why they thought it was so urgent. I felt slightly as if they were harassing me.'

Silence.

Simon went on, 'They didn't tell me anything, just asked why this Weeks would have rung me. I told them he was obviously fishing for information, gossip.'

'Sure. That seems pretty straightforward.'

'But there was more. They said they'd discovered he was writing a screenplay about a Prime Minister, a National Party one, they'd found it in his flat. I said that explained exactly why he'd rung me. He must have wanted material.'

David let out a sound, dismissive, possibly amused. 'A screenplay.'

'Anyway, it's not important, only I thought I should mention it because it's the police, and I thought you'd want to know. And also because they asked one odd question that concerned me: they asked whether I thought anyone would want to harm Weeks because of what he was writing. I asked what they meant by that . . . I got a bit, I don't know, indignant; it seemed a cheeky thing to ask. The man's certainly been snooping around, but that's hardly something you'd care about.'

David's phone went, he looked at the screen, answered it. 'Colin. Ten minutes.'

He took Simon's arm, signalled to Ray and Shaun, they all turned and started walking back towards the house. 'So what are they thinking, this Weeks person was ferreting around, wanting to write about me, so I had him thrown off a cliff? That's a nice story.'

Simon waited.

'How long's this been going on? Why didn't you mention it to me?'

'I'm sorry. I'm telling you now. I assumed it was nothing at first, just a minor, routine police inquiry.'

'You should have told me straight away.'

'Sorry.'

'Does anyone else here, anyone at Rotokauri know about this Weeks? He talk to anyone else? Or have you?'

Simon looked at him, expressionless. 'No one. Far as I know.'

'And what's in his screenplay about a prime minister?'

'They didn't tell me. They just said they're reading it.' Simon added, 'Apparently it's about a tall, fair-haired, left-handed National Prime Minister who walks with a limp.'

David snorted. 'Well, in that case it had to be me who killed him. Obviously. Although couldn't I just have sued him?'

Simon tried to smile.

'Or does he make this blond, left-handed leader out to be a great man? In which case they might say I was paying him.'

'This Weeks was some sort of arts person, probably made the PM out to be a prick, but who cares. It hardly matters.'

David took a Blackberry out of his pocket, checked it. 'I'll talk to Miles.'

'Right.'

'You said he fell? Did they actually say the death was suspicious?'

'All they said was he fell and died, I don't know where or how. It could have been an accident. I assumed they thought it might be suspicious because they're asking questions.'

'So they didn't give much away.'

'No. But they asked that one odd question, would anyone want to harm him?'

'I'll mention it to Ed. In the meantime don't tell anyone about this, not Karen, not your socialist brother, and definitely not Cahane. This is the kind of non-issue journalists love to turn into an issue.'

'Of course.'

'I don't want Cahane getting wind of anything unusual. He's an opportunist and he's virtually clairvoyant, so don't even think about it while he's here. It's about time he left, by the way. I've given him enough hints. He can't tear himself away from Roza, can't blame him there.'

David sighed. 'Arthur Weeks. Have I heard that name somewhere? "The weak shall inherit the earth."'

'The meek.'

'Eh?'

'The meek shall inherit — Oh, nothing. It doesn't matter.'

'Whatever, this is the kind of little detail Graeme Ellison specialised in. Anything where delicacy was required. He would have had a quiet word with this one and that one, finding out. Knew everyone, finger in every pie, old Graeme. He kept Ed Miles in line too.'

'Oh?'

'Ed's a zealot. Every now and then he needs a leash. Roza calls him the Disciple. Or the Handmaiden. She's very cruel about poor Ed, but he's a good soldier.'

'The best, I'm sure.'

'Ed and I go back to the beginning, before the Ellisons. The Ellisons gave us money and advice and contacts but Ed's a fixer. I tell Roza, leave Ed alone. He's a believer. And a brilliant operator. We wouldn't have the high popularity without Ed, he's always known exactly how to frame our policies, pitch them to the punters. If you're popular you can sell people anything, even policies they don't like.'

Simon looked away. Was David using the royal we? The chrome blue sky, seagulls riding over the glassy swells, the hazy outline of a distant island in the gulf. He said, 'Great to have people you can rely on.' His mouth was dry and he heard the strain in his voice but David was distracted, fiddling with his iPhone, and didn't seem to notice. He sent a message, touched Simon's arm. 'Don't quote me on any of that.'

'Of course not.'

'I can talk to you in the way I could talk to Graeme. I value that.'

'Good.'

'Petty politics. You and Roza are above it. Take it as a compliment.'

He palmed an Arcoxia and two painkillers, poured water, rattled ice out of the dispenser in the Little House fridge and knocked back the pills, the cold making his scalp shrink. The pain was still playing a tune in time with his heart. He dressed, suit and tie, black socks and shoes, and as soon as he put it all on he was sweating. He passed the tennis lesson, Garth standing behind Sharon Cahane and showing her how to angle her forehand smash while Roza waited, languid, elegant, faintly bored, standing on one leg, a foot lightly resting on her calf. Across the court Karen rose up on her tiptoes and nodded and listened, her face flushed, blonde hair sticking to her plump cheeks. He called out and they waved him off; he limped to the car, paused, went back, hooked his fingers in the wire. He called to Karen, 'Want to come?'

'Oof. Sorry! What's wrong with me today?'

She stooped for the ball, annoyed. 'What, Simon? I'm trying to focus.'

'We could drive in together, you could check on Claire, we could have lunch.'

'Claire? She won't want me interrupting. She loves having the house to herself.'

'You could do some shopping.'

He wanted her next to him in the car chatting, a string of details about the children, the house, a new holiday destination, an idea for renovating the kitchen; he wanted to reach over while he was driving and squeeze her arm lightly, a touch, just a touch.

Garth was poised, racquet extended, ball held in position, about to serve. Roza bounced her palm against the taut strings; Sharon waited then put her racquet between her knees and retied her ponytail. They all looked at Karen.

'Honestly, Simon. We're playing a game here.'

'OK. See you.'

Garth unleashed his serve; Karen lunged and hit the ball with the frame of her racquet, sending it smacking into the wire next to Simon. He ducked.

She didn't look at him, went for the ball, frowning.

Marcus and an unidentified suntanned girl strolled past, sharing an iPod, one earpiece each. Saves having to talk to each other, Simon thought. No awkward silences. The boy gave him a slightly defiant smirk. He heard, 'That's my dad . . . Yeah, I *know*.'

At the exit one of the silent muscle crew behind the glass, Jon or Shaun, made his fingers into a pistol and saluted. Ray opened the gate, an insolent little smile on his chiselled face. Simon stared straight ahead, gripping the wheel. This was crime: you couldn't go past a policeman without your heart speeding up. He rubbed his thigh, trying to redirect the nerves that spread fire from his knee to his heart to his head, a highway of pain, the pills taking their time to kick in. He pictured a remote beach, no sound except the sea, blazing enamel sky, his knee burrowed into the hot sand and Karen next to him, pressed against his side. Her lovely head on his arm, her breath on his cheek, talking to him: furniture, foreign travel, credit card bills, school reports, car maintenance, problems with the help, her words, familiar, loved, ordinary, safe, would rise and fall, blur and lull.

He overtook a truck, drove faster, sped on, as if he could outrun the pain.

The hospital doors opened and a young couple came out: a woman holding a toddler by the hand and a man lugging an infant seat, the newborn baby's wrinkled head just visible in its cocoon of wrapping. The young father reached down to arrange the covers, his expression so reverent and solemn, so burdened with love that something came loose in Simon and he actually reached for his phone; it would take one call, they would come for him, they would show him to a room and he would tell them what he had done, killed a defenceless young man, left him dead on the concrete; he saw the sprawled limbs, the curled fingers, the shoeless foot in its boyish sock.

A shiver of glass, the doors opened again. 'Simon! There you are. The situation's changed since I rang. And it's not one situation now, it's two!'

And then he was walking fast along the corridor and entering the hot room, the notes pushed into his hands, a woman writhing and moaning on the bed and a man fidgeting and sweating. You could feel the aggression coming off the man, the animal anxiety; he wanted action, he wanted an emergency response *stat*, and looking at the notes Simon saw he had a point.

'OK, we'll need to perform a caesarean. Just a couple of minutes, we'll have the anaesthetist.'

The man's shoulders slumped. Relief. Then he was furious. 'That woman,' he pointed at the midwife. 'We've been here for hours. She's done nothing.'

'Let's discuss that later. We've got a baby to deliver.'

'She's a fucking idiot.'

A nurse soothed the man into a chair; the midwife started telling Simon why she wasn't an idiot, he signalled to her to leave it. Examining the woman, he bumped his head against the side of her knee; she apologised politely then went into a contraction. Suppressing a shriek of pain she kneed him hard in the nose. Her eyes were closed, her face was screwed up, her teeth bared. He was blinking away tears, turning to speak to the nurse when the woman grabbed wildly and caught hold of his arm, gouging her nails into his skin. He stood and waited until the contraction had passed and she relaxed and breathed out, sobbing under her breath. She let go and he looked at the red marks on his arm as blood welled up and ran in a thin stream down his wrist.

'Whoops,' the nurse said, reaching in and pressing a sterile pad on his skin.

The man's voice rose, he was going for the midwife again, the midwife wasn't taking it well and the nurse went to help.

Opening her eyes, the patient saw him holding the reddening pad. 'Oh God, did I do that?'

'It's fine.' He dabbed at the blood, chucked the pad in the bin.

'I'm so sorry.'

'Don't worry. It's nothing.' He put his hand on her shoulder, held it there. 'You're going to be fine.'

In theatre he put his hand on her arm again, steadying her as if he was doing it for her benefit alone, and when he'd got the baby out and put the flailing, slippery creature onto her chest he caught sight of the plaster covering the welts where she'd gripped his arm, and he would have liked to lie down beside her, to stretch out his aching limbs and hold her, press himself close to life.

He sat at a desk typing notes. Outside in the corridor the argument with the midwife had started up again, the father of the new baby threatening to make a complaint. Simon had his doubts about that midwife himself, he'd met her before and found her aggressively anti-doctor. She was all about natural birth, even if that meant a near-death experience for mother and child. Only when she'd messed it up and there was foetal distress and all kinds of disaster for the mother would she make the panicked call for the expert. His mind wandering, he fingered the plaster on his forearm. A man's voice repeated, 'Who's in charge here? Who's in fucking charge?'

A nurse put her head around the door and he sidestepped the argument, now grown louder and involving a security guard, and followed her down the hall to a room in which the female members of a large family had assembled to witness the grand event; he had to angle his way around the aunties and grannies and cousins to get to the labouring patient, and at every fresh development the group burst into prayers and singing. Someone had brought a guitar, and the relatives snacked incessantly, keeping up their strength between songs.

The birth was straightforward despite earlier anticipated complications, they didn't have to send the audience out into the hall, and the baby emerged to claps, cheers, whoops and high-fives, Simon and the midwife and the attendant paediatrician working in an atmosphere of festive chaos, communicating without words, occasionally smiling in spite of themselves at the antics of the aunties. The baby was a handsome brown giant, nearly eleven pounds, as smooth and peaceful as a Buddha. The paediatrician took a phone call in the middle of his examination and Simon held the child briefly, looking down at the glossy dark eyes. The baby was awake and calm and unknowing, unaware of its power. The strong little hands clawed the air, Simon bent his head closer, wrinkled fingers brushed his face. The midwife bustled in to take the bundle. Looking up he saw the mother watching him.

'Beautiful baby,' he said, embarrassed, and turned away.

He changed and left the building, swigging lukewarm coffee from a takeaway cup. Heat struck up from the asphalt, bright light glanced off the parked cars. His steering wheel was hot to touch, the car seat cooking his legs, burning pleasantly through to his sore knee. He drove out through the dead, sunstruck suburbs, past the park where the grass had turned brown and the hedges looked sparse and dry.

His waiting room was full of women and Clarice was in one of her moods. She swept about, refusing to make eye contact, sunk in a grand gloom. In the chilled air of his office he shivered, something walking over his grave.

Two patients in, he looked down at his notes, pen poised, delivered his next polite question: 'Have you tried having sex yet?'

Red marks bloomed on the patient's neck, shot into her cheeks. 'No. Well, not actual sex . . . I mean . . . it's complicated.'

There was a silence, she laughed at the wrongness of 'it's complicated', the image of not-actual sex hanging in the air. He pressed on, used to this. They often laughed; a minority were extraordinarily frank. At the public hospital recently a heavily tattooed woman with a ring pierced through her lip had snapped at him, 'Sex? No. Not unless you count blowjobs.'

A few were blunt and candid but many clammed up; a lot of information could be conveyed with a look, a blush or a laugh, with words left unsaid. He thought of Ms Da Silva and her silent companion. How much had he told them without actually speaking? Had he blushed, hesitated, turned pale, left out telling parts of sentences? Police were trained to notice. But perhaps many of the people they dealt with were simpler, more unguarded. No, it was folly to assume so.

The patient was squirming. Embarrassed by her blush she'd gone redder still. (A vicious circle he encountered often.) He could have said, If you knew what I'm thinking you wouldn't blush. (You might turn pale.) If only I could touch you, lay my cold hand on your fiery cheek. You see, my whole life is falling away and when I reach out there's nothing . . .

He laid down his pen, slapped his thighs. 'Well. You've healed up beautifully. Any problems give me a call, but I don't expect you'll need to for a long time.'

She thanked him, dropped her handbag, bumped into him as he saw her out the door. When she asked about the bill Clarice's icy disdain threw her into further confusion; eventually, puce-faced, she floundered out as Simon was calling the next patient.

Clarice, now on the phone, said no, loudly, six times. No explanation, no pleasantries, just no. He wondered what was being asked by the poor supplicant on the other end. And whether he could persuade Clarice to start taking antidepressants.

'I'm afraid not,' Clarice said, and slammed down the phone.

His next patient plucked the skin around her hollow middle and whispered, 'I've put on so much weight.' She had baby-fine hair through which he could see her white scalp, down on her cheeks, red veins on pale eyelids. Her shoulders were sprinkled with dandruff and loose hairs.

He checked the admission notes. Forty-two kilos, and she was not short.

'You're underweight.'

She looked coy, simpered, picked fluff off her jacket, her expression lit with smiling paranoia: she wasn't fooled. He was part of the regime, the conspiracy to make her fat. Mad, he thought. Anorexia actually makes you mad. The thinner you get the crazier you become. Another vicious circle. What if he leaned back in his chair, steepled his fingers and said, 'Listen, fatso. Listen, you unfuckable lardarse.' Would that be enough to finish her off? It came to him how sane the last patient had been, with her strong body and her fiery blushes, her mortified laughter. This one was what his mother-in-law would quaintly call 'away with the fairies'. It was usually the parents that started it, wasn't it, forcing girls to finish meals, making food the currency of control. She had an inward look and a faint, bitter smile as he explained he was recommending she see a specialist psychologist, glad there was no immediate need to examine her; she looked so fragile, as if you'd leave bruises all over her, and she was emotionally volatile, the kind of person who generates endless complications. Get it wrong and she'd be screaming, and the state she was in now you'd always get it wrong.

As though about to cry, she squeezed her eyes shut. He looked at the space between her neck and her shirt collar, at her fine, vulnerable bones; he caught a sense of the pity he was trying to keep at bay as he slapped the cardboard file shut, handed her a note, stood up and ushered her to the door.

'See my secretary.'

His hand looked like a massive paw shaking hers. Her fingers were cold. She stood at the reception desk facing Clarice, who glared over the rims of her reading glasses. Thin, hunched shoulders, child-sized limbs;

she looked so lost. He remembered breaking up the DVD of Arthur Weeks's film about a young woman with green eyes.

The sound it made, like the cracking of tiny bones.

In the mall he found books for Karen and Claire and magazines for Elke who didn't like reading, and then spent twenty minutes being shown expensive tennis racquets in a sports shop. He wasn't quite sure what he was doing. Told it would be better if Karen and Marcus tried the racquets themselves, he bought a T-shirt for Marcus and headed for the car park. He drove to the house, calling out to Claire as he unlocked the door but already sensing she wasn't home. The hall was full of afternoon sunlight, dust revolving in the air.

He looked around, snooped a bit. The kitchen was tidy, even the food in the fridge was neatly arranged, her sensible veges and soups and low-fat dairy stacked in tidy piles, labels all up the right way. Unlike the eternally skinny and graceful Elke who lived on lollies and junk food, Claire dieted and jogged and survived half the time on carrots but with little effect; she was always cursing her figure, had spent her life at war with her own body. She felt she was too tall, her legs and bum were too fat; she was always hiding parts of herself under loose clothing. It was no use his telling her she had beautiful eyes and a terrific mind and a strong body she should be happy with, he could only hope she would work that out.

He sensed that Karen's dislike of Claire was partly aesthetic: her daughter wasn't pretty or chic enough. Claire's look of Ford was enough to put Karen off; she had Ford's brains and stubbornness and big, clear blue-grey eyes, and she shared her uncle's lack of sartorial sense. Karen swore by retail therapy, but shopping was Claire's idea of hell. Simon had heard Karen pointedly praising Elke's outfits in front of Claire. Divide and rule. If Karen had been confident she wouldn't have resorted to it, but she had to put Claire in her place. It was a pity. Karen went off like a banshee if he got in on the act; she insisted their elder daughter was impossible, she made herself unlovable and the friction was all her fault.

Claire would be out for a run. He went upstairs and looked in her room. The bed was made, the desk covered in paper held down with coffee cups and textbooks. He left the book he'd bought on her pillow, a note inside the cover. How to tell her he loved her? He settled for cheery and short, xxx at the end.

Hoping she might pound up the path in her running gear he sat on the garden wall and listened to his phone messages, the hot bricks burning the back of his legs. He called, but her cell phone went to voicemail.

They would be all right, Elke and Claire, and Marcus too. They were pretty much grown up, they had a conscientious mother and a family trust full of money, and all three knew their father loved them. It was a private compulsion of his, making sure they knew he loved them. He remembered the loneliness of childhood.

Time was an arrow and this was the point of it, he was adding up the score. He didn't think he could get away with his half-truths to David. He needed to make sure his affairs were in order, as much as a person's affairs could be said to be in order when he was about to lose everything and go to jail.

Karen, the children, his patients. Was this where he would leave them? It was time to start driving but he went on waiting for Claire, sweating in his suit, the afternoon sun sending down a relentless glare. What would he find when he got to Rotokauri? A little reception: Ray, Shaun, Jon, Ed Miles smiling thinly in the background? And perhaps Ms Da Silva herself, jinking a pair of handcuffs . . .

What do you care about? He thought about Ford's nagging, his insistence that 'apolitical isn't good enough'. Ford had wound up his last censorious harangue with, 'Admit it, Simon. Under your friend's government the gap between rich and poor has got so wide it's a scandal.'

It now occurred to Simon that every time Ford told him the gap between rich and poor had got wider, something in him thought: good. He'd left his poor past, made it to the right side of the gap, and if there was a distance between himself and the past, so much the better. David must feel like this too. This was why his most consistent message was that he stood for 'aspiration'. He was aiming at people like himself and Simon. The ones who'd succeeded through their own efforts were the ones who cared most about keeping the gap wide. Simon's own lack of politics was really politics of a basic kind: I am one of those who want poverty to exist so we can affirm our own sense of well-being.

He recognised the force of the feeling, saw it was morally wrong, and also saw that Ford didn't understand it. Like Claire, Ford assumed that if you made people aware of inequality they would naturally want to remedy it. It hadn't occurred to him that the 'haves' would reject the idea of levelling society, even if you could show them a way to make everyone better off. For all Ford's talk of people being animals he hadn't grasped this aspect of the animal kingdom; for all his and Claire's intellectual toughness there was an innocence about them. They believed in the goodness of people.

'Greed is good' had the unspoken corollary: poverty is good. So long as it was someone else's.

Simon gently flexed his knee. He thought: don't mention these musings to Claire.

At Rotokauri, drinks were under way under the pohutukawa. Sharon Cahane had her foot up on a stool, her ankle wrapped in a bandage.

The Cock leaned back in his chair. 'My wife will use any excuse to be waited on.'

Sharon rattled her empty glass suggestively at Trent, who advanced with a jug in which pieces of fruit bobbed in a thick, clear liquid. He bent and poured, she wafted a napkin over her suntanned décolletage and said to the Cock, 'Your sympathy is touching.'

'My wife swathes herself in bandages at the slightest mishap. Some call it a cry for help . . .'

Sharon's laugh caused Trent to start. The jug wobbled.

'In my wife's case I merely call it strategy.'

The women leaned together, tapping pretty nails on their glasses.

'A cry for help.'

'He's off again.'

'He's got that look on his face.'

'If only he'd wear a sunhat. Colin darling, you look boiled.'

David and the Cock, summoned by a staffer, went off for a conference call.

Ed Miles suddenly stood up, shaking his sleeve, a pink stain spreading on the material. 'Christ, Juliet. Can't you be careful?'

Sharon said, languid, 'Ooh Ed, your beautiful shirt. Is that a new one?'

Juliet's cheeks were scarlet. 'Sorry.' She grabbed a napkin and tried to mop his sleeve; he snatched his arm away. 'You've done enough damage, thanks.'

There was an awkward silence.

Roza said, 'I don't think people should talk to other people like that in my presence.'

Ed smiled with difficulty at Roza. Red spots appeared on his cheeks.

She said, 'If they do, I think they should apologise. What do you think, Sharon?'

'Oh definitely,' Sharon drawled, fanning her chest, her eyes on Trent. Juliet looked down, her face rigid.

A little flare of rage burned in Ed's eyes. He shrugged, smiled again at Roza and said, 'So sorry. I'll just nip off and change.' He threw a napkin on the table and left.

'Hmm,' Sharon said. 'Touchy!'

Juliet took a breath, fluttered her hands. 'Oh, what can you do with them?'

Roza pressed her lips together, gave her a look of polite enquiry. '*Do*? With who? Whom?'

'Men are hopeless, you know.' Juliet smiled weakly and waved her hand, tipping over Karen's glass, which was fortunately empty. 'I'd better just go and . . .' She didn't finish, pointed across the garden and rushed off.

'Off to fuss around him,' Sharon said. 'Off to grovel.'

'Men are hopeless,' Roza repeated slowly. 'Do you know, I *hate* that one. Men are hopeless. So when men do nasty things — cheat, lie, beat us, make us wear our burqa — we don't complain. We say cosily, "men are hopeless". It's the flipside of "all men are beasts" and it's just as meaningless. It's worse because it's slavish.'

'Touched a nerve, have we?'

Roza smiled, 'Oh shut up, Sharon.'

'My husband's definitely hopeless.'

Karen joined in their laugh, giving Simon a look. 'Yeah,' she said.

Silence. Roza and Sharon glanced at her and then at each other, amused lift of eyebrows. Karen blushed.

'Not wanting to gossip . . .' Sharon said.

They laughed, since this was her usual opener to gossip.

'Not wanting to gossip, but Janine told me she and Peter Gibson are going to counselling.'

'Oh, *her*.'

'Roza, you're such a snob. Just because she wears leopard-skin miniskirts.'

'Whole matching leopard-skin outfits. And drives that massive sort of tank. And her husband with his gold chain.'

'And his dental implants. Those sparklingly whitened gnashers.'

'But they're extraordinarily rich,' Karen said.

Another pause. Roza and Sharon looked at her.

'Yes, they are,' Sharon said, as though encouraging a child. She turned back to Roza. 'They're going to counselling because he had an affair with some little twenty-year-old.'

'Ugh.'

'Is that all you can say? Peter and Janine are very dear friends.'

Roza laughed, 'Oh, rubbish.'

'Well, of course, Colin only puts up with Gnashers for his own mysterious business reasons. Anyway, Janine's panic-stricken old Toothy-Pegs is going to leave her.'

Roza signalled to Trent for a refill of diet Coke, held up her glass, thanked him nicely. She said, 'Gnashers won't leave her.'

'No?'

'No, he loves her. They're perfect for each other. She should just keep calm and carry on.'

'Well, that's sage advice,' Sharon said, brushing some invisible thing from her neckline.

Roza looked intently at her glass. 'I'm not convinced by the idea of counselling.'

'Why not?'

'I don't know.'

'You and David would never need it. You're a dream couple.'

'It's not that. But what if a marriage is like a work of art? A completely unique work created by two individuals. How can an outsider intervene?'

'That seems a bit complicated. What do you think, Simon?' Sharon leaned towards him, rattling the ice in her glass.

He was realising the folly of mixing painkillers with Trent's strong fruit punch. Tilting his glass at Roza he said, '*She's* a work of art.'

'Ah, such a gentleman. And how was your day at work?'

But he'd caught sight of Ed Miles heading back across the lawn, and didn't reply.

Politics

'Coming,' Roza said. 'I'm just talking to Johnnie.'

The Green Lady walked on the lonely shore with the Ort Cloud, the Dead White Cat, the Red Herring and Tiny Ancient Yellow Cousin So-on. Soon and Starfish followed.

"A rolling stone gathers no moss," the Red Herring observed, and Tiny Ancient Yellow Cousin So-on added, "My enemy's enemy is my friend." The horizon was a haze of red against the black sea, and the Bachelor's bed could be seen driving over the treetops, the feathers of the Cassowaries spiky in silhouette, the Bachelor lounging on the cushions, evening cocktail in hand.

"Look!" said the Green Lady. At the far end of the beach in the dusk, a figure was walking towards them.

It was Soonica, and she was alone.

Johnnie was handed over to Tulei, who backed out of the room with a disapproving look. Roza said under her breath, 'Bless you, Tulei.'

In the dining room Roza told Karen she would have to move to the far end of the table because Ed enjoyed her company so much and she was sure they could squash in, Trent having brought an extra chair.

There was an atmosphere of low-level tension among the help, even an outbreak of bickering, with Trent flouncing campily out of the room and Troy banging the door. The first course was cold and the second arrived in uneven batches, after which Simon heard David say to Roza, who was remonstrating with Shane or Chad, 'You fire Jung Ha out of the blue, you get chaos in the kitchen.'

Simon gave up pushing his cold meal around the plate. He leaned close to Roza. 'The gap between rich and poor. Ford says it's getting wider.'

Roza dabbed her mouth with a napkin. 'I know what your brother thinks.'

'What about you?'

She looked vague. 'When I was growing up, my father was the fourth-richest man in the country.'

'Your money got David started.'

She glanced around. 'Don't say that to him.'

'I wouldn't. David always says you're not interested in politics.'

'I'm not.'

'Ford says apolitical's not good enough. It's not intellectually good enough.'

She smiled and said, 'Your brother's so fierce', in the indulgent tone all the women used for Ford, as if he were a noble savage: so sexily primitive and unspoiled. Which was a tremendous irony, Simon thought sourly, given that Ford regarded the women of Rotokauri as frivolous and anti-intellectual, and condemned their refusal to discuss anything serious.

Even Karen had started echoing the lenient tone. What a chameleon she was. Irritated, he'd reminded her, 'But you hate Ford.'

'He's lonely, the poor man. Don't be nasty about your own brother.'

'What? I *love* my brother. You're the one who said he shouldn't even come here.'

'Oh, don't be mean-spirited, Simon.'

Now he whispered to Roza, 'Is the gap between rich and poor too wide? I've just had a big tax cut and I earn a million a year. I didn't need it. The poor got a tiny tax cut and a rise in GST. So the gap is . . .'

The look she was giving him was hard, faintly amused, slight curl of the lip.

'Darling Simon. Don't try to be Ford. It doesn't suit you.'

Simon walked slowly along the path under the trees. Light spilled across the lawn and voices and music came from the open French windows of the big house, where David had shown no sign of wanting to go to bed. Figures moved behind the wire in the artificial green light of the tennis court. He heard Elke laugh. 'Fuck *off* Marcus,' she said. Beyond the dunes the sea was calm, with a sheen of moonlight. Someone called his name, he turned.

Ed Miles took off his glasses, polished them on a handkerchief and put them on, a studied move. Simon gave what he hoped was a look of mild inquiry. 'It's a beautiful evening.'

Miles looked down and smiled. 'Oh yes.'

Simon said, too sharply, 'Well, I'm off to bed . . . ?'

'David wants a word.'

'Now?'

'He's in the main office.'

Miles walked beside him. Were the three of them going to talk together? Should he ask Miles whether he'd found anything out? The adrenalin had started to run around his body, hard and sharp, as strong as pain, but his hands were steady. It was like this in the operating theatre; even on the rare occasions when things had gone wrong and some urgent reversal was required, his hands did not shake.

They crossed the deck, passed Ray and entered through the glass door, Miles following Simon.

David was leaning on his desk, his arms folded. Simon looked at Miles in the reflection of the glass, saw him nod at David and walk out, closing the door.

'Just wanted to give you an update,' David said.

'Sure.'

'Ed's been looking into the question of the young man.' David went to the glass and looked out at the sea beyond the dunes. There was a light moving in the distant sand hills. The tree at the point was like the black outline of a man, arms outstretched. 'Ed can't interfere in operational police matters.'

'No.'

'But he can enquire. He tells me there's potential here for inconvenience. It's the kind of thing that could be picked up by the media.'

'Potential for inconvenience . . .' Simon almost felt like laughing.

'A lot of inconvenience.'

Simon looked down at his hands. 'You think they might invent some nonsense around the fact he was writing about a prime minister? One who looked like you, the limp and so on?'

'I really don't know, but if there's material on which to base nonsense, they'll use it. Ed will do what he can, and just between you and me, he can do a lot more than we'd ever admit to. Do you know what I mean?'

'I think so.'

'We have to preserve appearances; the separation of the powers must be maintained.'

'I understand.'

'But I want you to know Ed's on the case, and Ed's the best person to have on your side. One of his special talents is calming things down.'

'Calming things down. Sounds good.' Simon was about to say 'thanks' but stopped himself. Instead he said, 'That must be a relief for you. You won't want hacks making up ridiculous stories about you and a dead stalker.'

He glanced up. David was looking oddly at him. He went on, 'You don't need that kind of distraction, with all you want to achieve. And what if Cahane got hold of it? The guy's so ambitious he's about to explode.'

David made an amused sound. He came close. 'You look tired. Go to bed. I'll see you for breakfast.'

'I will. Thanks for filling me in.'

'There's one other thing. I've been talking to Roza.'

Simon felt his hands twitch. He flexed his fingers. 'Oh yes?'

'I think it would be good if Elke came to us when we go back to Auckland.'

'Came to you. You mean to live?'

'If anything inconvenient were to come out of this, Simon . . .'

Simon said blandly, 'But it won't. You said it yourself, it's a non-issue.'

'We hope it is. Nevertheless . . .'

'I don't understand.'

'Roza thinks Elke's at a bit of a crossroads. She's worried about her psyche.'

Simon raised his eyebrows. 'Her psyche? The girl's hard as nails.' He added hurriedly, 'I mean that in a good way. She's totally positive. Bouncy. Rock solid.'

'Her mother doesn't think so.'

'Karen does.'

David lowered his voice, 'Right. But don't you think her real mother would have the surest feeling? I agree with Roza. Elke shouldn't be exposed to anything potentially upsetting.'

'Nothing upsetting is going to happen.'

David's tone was mild, soothing, 'But we don't know that. At the moment Ed's described the situation as inconvenient. That means it has the potential to go pear-shaped. We don't know that it will, but best to be prepared, eh?'

Simon was silent. David put his hand on his arm, squeezed. 'I can say this to you too, just between us, because we're friends. I worry about Roza's state of mind too. I need her. And I need her to be happy.'

They looked at each other.

'You're tired. Go to bed, have a rest, and in the morning you can tell Karen what we've discussed.'

'Yes, sure,' Simon said.

'One more thing: Elke's nearly grown up. She can choose for herself where she lives. So you'll have to encourage her to make the right choice.'

Simon wished him goodnight. When he approached the door, Ed Miles opened it from the other side.

He limped out to the point and sat on the wooden seat. It didn't make sense: the Weeks problem had the potential to cause the Hallwrights as much unpleasantness as it did the Lamptons, so Elke would be no less protected if she was living with them . . . But how strange that he kept forgetting! He was the one who'd killed Weeks, who could be charged and tried, even jailed. Or at least shamed, struck off and ruined. David didn't know that; he had no idea that Weeks and Simon had met. Or had he? How thoroughly had the Police Minister delved into the evidence? It was another terrible aspect of crime, the not knowing.

No matter how much David knew, he had made it plain Simon was compromised, and would be obliged to do as he was told. And if Elke didn't want to live with the Hallwrights, he would have to persuade her.

Something rustled through the dune grass, pattering this way and that over the rocks and shells. A cold feeling. 'Nothing's fair,' Ford liked to say. 'It's just another day in the jungle. If you're weak, watch out.'

David had made the kind of decision he made all the time; he would help Simon, he would deploy Miles, and in return he would have Elke, because Roza wanted it. If Simon didn't comply, he'd be on his own. He remembered what Claire had said to Karen: 'The Hallwrights couldn't care less about you. You know who they care about? Each other.' He remembered the darkness he'd perceived in Aaron, something competitive and watchful that was worse than lack of love.

Just for a moment, alone on the cold dune, he allowed himself to let go. His face pressed into his sleeve, emotion shaking him. He'd begun an affair with Mereana because he loved Roza so deeply he'd lost his way. His troubles were caused by love. The wry thought came to him: at least it means I'm not that bastard Aaron Harris.

He listened to the waves breaking over the shells. A shooting star crossed the sky, making a white scratch in the blackness. There was no light pollution out here; he watched a satellite travelling through the glittering chaos of the Milky Way. These nights when the stars were so bright it seemed strange that they should be fixed and still, the only movement the satellites nosing between them. He had a sense of the vastness and indifference of the cold void above and all around him the dunes were alive with sounds, the scuttling of small creatures, shifting of sand, the wind hissing in dry seed pods and rustling in the marram. After a long time he limped back on the path through the dunes, crept into the warm silence of the Little House and opened the second bedroom door.

Elke was asleep with the window open, the blind blowing in the breeze and the moonlight shining in. The bedclothes were rumpled, one of her feet was uncovered; she sighed, turned, sprawled, lay still.

Dawn came, and with it the tuis. Was any other creature such a relentless critic? They started before 4 a.m., even before the sun had come up; they were madness, fever, insomnia, yearning, and they let him have it when he was low. The self-righteous bastards. How did they always know how he felt?

Now, the usual dialogue took place in the Lampton bed.

'What's wrong? Stop fidgeting.'

'It's the tuis. I hate them.'

'Don't be silly. It's just birdsong.'

'Song? You call that song? That dirge? That *criticism*?'

He lay awake, trying to keep still. He needed to talk to Ford but couldn't face the prospect of telling his brother what David had asked. Pictures surfaced in his mind: Roza's expression as she talked to Elke, Roza smiling at Karen, David watching Roza. Overcome with weariness, he felt he'd never sleep again.

At six he got up and walked down to the beach, waded in and swam along the shore, kicking with his good leg. When he got back he showered, making enough noise to wake the others, and sat down to wait on the deck.

Karen roused Elke, who was booked for a tennis lesson. They wandered out onto the deck in their tiny Lycra dresses, both drinking coffee, Karen with yesterday's paper. Elke had a little infection on the side of her mouth and a piece of food stuck on her front tooth, her beautiful eyes were puffy with sleep and her hair was wild, with yesterday's hair tie tangled in it. The sight of her made a pressure swell in Simon's chest.

'By the way . . .' he said.

Karen frowned over the paper. 'Seven down.'

Elke leaned on her shoulder. 'Disinterested.'

'Doesn't fit.'

'Uninterested?'

'No.'

'I hate crosswords,' Elke said. She flopped down on a deck chair and put her feet up on the veranda rail. She threw a crust onto the grass, the birds swooped down and started to hop and squabble. 'Look at the beautiful tuis.'

'Fuckers. Don't encourage them,' Simon said, his mind on automatic. Karen clicked her tongue disapprovingly. Elke laughed.

He said, 'By the way, I talked to David last night.'

'Hello, lovely tuis. Dad hates you but I think you're beautiful.' Elke ran in and fetched the bread, broke up some slices and threw a spray of crumbs. Three sparrows landed, followed by two aggressive mynah birds.

Simon fixed his eyes on Elke's back as she leaned over the rail. 'David and Roza are keen for you to go and stay with them when we get back to Auckland.' He didn't look at Karen. 'I think it's a good idea.'

Karen put the paper down. 'What? Simon, we've been through this.'

Elke's face had gone blank, she opened her eyes wide. 'Oh.'

'It's lovely that they're so keen to have you,' Simon said.

'She doesn't want to,' Karen said. 'She wants to stay with us. Where she belongs.'

Simon got up and walked to the rail. He looked down at his hands; they were steady. 'I don't know why you're so insistent about it, Karen. It seems like a good idea to me. She's going to travel with them, go to America. And Johnnie loves her, and their house is closer to the university than ours, so it's nice and convenient.'

Silence. The birds hopped and pecked. He looked at Karen, then quickly away. There wasn't only anger in her expression, but confusion, dismay.

'I think we should be flexible,' he said.

Elke said, 'So you want me to.'

'I . . .' His throat closed over, he swallowed. 'I think it's a nice idea. Spend some time with your mother.'

Karen made a sound. He didn't look.

Elke shrugged. 'Whatever,' she said. 'No problem, Dad. Anyway,

I'm going to tennis.' She threw the rest of the crumbs onto the lawn, ran down the steps and away up the path.

Karen went to the edge of the deck, turned to Simon. 'How could you say that?'

'Listen—'

'No.'

'We have to let her go.'

'She doesn't *want* to go. She thinks you're throwing her out, that you've rejected her.'

'We should let her be with Roza. That was the deal when we got her.'

'*No it wasn't*. Roza was nowhere around. She was completely abandoned. She's my daughter.'

'She's Roza's too.'

'No.'

'Karen. If you want to have anything more to do with the Hallwrights, you should let Elke live with them. If you don't, they'll cut us off.'

'Then *let* them cut us off. Let's have nothing more to do with them.'

Simon spread out his hands. 'You'd give up the friendship? Give up . . . all this?'

'All this? You value all this over Elke? Over *our daughter*?'

'We don't have to give her up; we'll still see her if we stay friends with the Hallwrights. If we don't, we risk losing her *and* them.'

'No.'

'Just think about it. Don't do anything silly. Stay away from Roza today and try to put it in perspective.'

She stared. 'I don't think I know you at all.'

He hardened his tone. 'This isn't some . . . Victorian melodrama. Just promise me you'll think about it. And don't go near Roza or David until you have.'

She didn't say anything.

He said, 'Do you really want to give it all up? Rotokauri? Everything we've shared with them? What are we losing really, if she swaps houses? It's a minor readjustment. The closer we stay to them, the closer we'll be to Elke. And vice versa.'

She started to say something, he cut her off. 'Don't do or say anything that will make us all worse off.'

The birds had lined up on the veranda rail, fluffing out their feathers. Karen gave him a numb stare. He put his arms around her. 'I'm trying to work out what's best.'

She said, 'Perhaps you take after your father after all.'

He waited then said, 'Sit down, darling. Just sit down for a minute.'

She allowed him to push her into a deck chair. He took her hand. 'Elke's eighteen. She'll be wanting novelty, experience, travel, all that. The next thing she'll do is find a flat with one of her five thousand closest friends. On the other hand, if she moves in with the Hallwrights, we'll keep her close. All we have to do is maintain our friendship with them. And you don't really want to give them up, do you? There's a lot to look forward to. That ball you and Roza are working on, the fundraising thing with Trish Ellison. The other thing, for the children's hospital. All that work'll go to waste if you cut Roza off, the effort'll be for nothing. Roza can't do it, she's so disorganised, she barely pays attention — I know she swans about getting her nails done and leaves you lot to do the work, darling, everyone notices that. She needs you and Trish and Sharon and Juliet to carry out your plans. People are depending on you. You've got to think about that.'

She lifted her chin, stared off into the distance. 'That's all true . . .'

'Come on then. Let's go and have breakfast.' He squeezed her hand.

She pulled away. 'You're talking about our daughter leaving us.'

'She'll do that anyway.'

'Claire hasn't.'

'No, but she will. Kids grow up and leave. What you have to do is stay in touch.'

They crossed to the main lawn, where Saturday breakfast was being served under the pohutukawa. Ed Miles was dressed in khaki and shoes without socks. He seemed to be trying to get at something stuck between his teeth, his tongue working around his pale gums. Without joining in the conversation he glanced continually from one person to the next.

The Cock, wearing mirror sunglasses, was peeling an apple with a knife, his long, thin fingers working spiderishly, the twist of peel dangling and jerking above his plate. David laughed at something he'd just read in the newspaper, nudged the Cock and put his big blunt finger on the article. His guffaw was crude, blokey, too loud; his face looked rough with sunburn and faintly thuggish. The Cock gave a thin smile. The sun shone through a gap in the branches, playing a white lozenge of light on the Cock's big bald forehead. Simon suddenly felt he was looking at people he'd never seen before. There was something grotesque, venal, ugly about them.

David laughed again, a harsh sound. 'All right, Simon?'

'Morning.'

Roza and Sharon were eating fruit salad with long spoons and Juliet peered out at them from under a floppy hat.

Sharon inspected her reflection in the back of her spoon. 'Juliet says there's a spike in UV today. Treble the risk of melanoma.'

'Hi guys,' Karen said.

There was a silence. The spoons clinked on the glass bowls. Sharon and Roza glanced at each other.

Karen sat down, hesitant.

Simon gave Roza a cold look. She returned it with her usual coy and wicked smile but there was something behind the smile, a carelessness.

'Coffee's preventative,' Juliet said to Simon. 'I read it. Stops you getting skin cancer.'

'I'd better have one then.' He looked at Trent, who appeared to be sending a text. 'Trent?'

The young man put the phone in his pocket.

'The only trouble is, coffee makes me so jumpy,' Juliet said. She tugged on her hat brim, looking unhappy.

'Don't forget me, Trent,' Sharon said, touching her cup with her spoon, a light ping. Trent poured the coffee with a sly flourish. The Cock watched them.

A magpie burst out of the bushes, sudden flurry in the air, squawking.

'Hello, and how's your wife?' the Cock said to Trent.

Sharon turned to him. 'Eh? Who are you talking to?'

The Cock smiled around the company. 'It's astonishing what my wife doesn't know. It's what you say, my dear, when you see a single magpie. It's bad luck to see a single one, good luck to see two. When you see one, in order to ward off bad luck you say: hello, and how's your wife?'

The sarcastic ping of nails on glasses.

'What a mine of information he is.'

'He's a walking encyclopaedia.'

'It's so useful, having him come out with things like that.'

Roza said sweetly, 'And what are you planning to do today, Karen?'

Karen's smile faded. 'I thought we were . . . tennis?'

'Change of plan. Sorry, didn't we say? Juliet and I are having a session with Garth.'

'Oh.'

Ed said, 'You must be getting fit, Karen, playing all that tennis. Great for the figure.'

Karen twisted in her seat. It was painful to watch. Simon was keeping his anxiety at bay but a little flare of anger started up in him, threatening his control. All this was his fault; Karen's suffering was his fault.

'We're going to miss you after this holiday, Colin,' Roza said, patting the Cock's sleeve.

'But we won't be far away,' the Cock said, still eyeing Trent, who was busying himself with cutlery. 'David and I will be back at work. Tackling the big problems. *Unemployment*, for example. The tragedy of *job loss*.'

Trent glanced at the Cock, quickly looked away.

Sharon selected a grape, pincered it between finger and thumb. 'Please don't talk about the economy while I'm eating.'

The Cock held up his hand. 'You're right. It wouldn't do to strain my wife's brain so early in the morning.'

Sharon cackled.

'We wouldn't want her to black out.'

Roza picked up a banana. 'Would you like one of these?' she asked the Cock. He gave her a sideways, amused look, took it from her and weighed it in his hand. The effect was suggestive. David watched with a neutral expression.

Juliet fidgeted, clasping her freckly hands together. 'You know what? It's going to be a great year.'

'It is going to be an excellent year,' the Cock said to Juliet, who blushed. 'Your husband's going to reduce the crime rate. Aren't you, Miles.'

'I already have. If you'll just build me some new prisons.'

'To me, it's one of the most important things,' Juliet said in a hushed voice. 'Getting criminals off the streets. The violence . . . They give them bail and then they go out and just . . . kill people.'

'Oh please,' Sharon said. 'We said no politics at the table. Pass me that banana, darling. You look simian, clutching it in your paw like that.'

'Simian. The year *is* beginning well. My wife has learned a new word.'

Ed Miles said, 'We're going to get even tougher on crime.'

'Great,' Karen said. 'No excuses. Lock them up and throw away the key.'

Ed said, 'I'm sure your husband agrees, Karen.'

They all looked at Simon.

Silence.

'Violent criminals, Lampton. Lock them up and throw away the key?' Ed Miles said.

'Oh, absolutely,' Simon said.

They walked over the dunes, down onto the beach. The heat made mirages, patches of blackness hovering over the sand, like holes torn in the mesh of the sky. The tide was high, the sea was vigorous, great walls of pure white foam rolling towards them over the shells, sighing back into the surge. Seagulls rode on the easterly, crying their sad cries.

Karen stumped over the sand, the wind whipping her hair around her face. 'You see the way they're treating me. The way Roza's behaving now she's got her way.'

Simon shifted the heavy bag onto his other shoulder. His knee burned. 'She'll change when the Cahanes leave. Sharon's a bad influence.'

'It's nothing to do with Sharon. Roza's freezing me out because she knows she's getting Elke.'

'No, it won't be like that.'

She rounded on him. 'For once, why don't you tell the truth? If Roza freezes me off I'll never see Elke, she'll poison her against me. You've obviously never cared about Elke, you're made of ice.'

'Keep your nerve,' Simon said. A wave surged up, cool water flooded around his ankles. The gulls screamed. 'Stay friendly with the Hallwrights, maintain contact with Elke.'

'I say we persuade Elke to come with us now. Just leave. Cut them off.'

'You can't do that. It would be wrong. Roza is her mother. And anyway . . .' He hesitated.

'What?'

He said, expressionless, 'Even if you fall out with Roza, David and I are close.'

'You care more about that than about Elke.'

'That's not true.'

'You never wanted her. You didn't want to adopt, remember? You thought it would be too much trouble.'

His mouth twitched. 'Well. I was right.' Little Elke. *She was the ruin of me.*

'Are you actually smiling? You cold bastard.'

Little Elke Lampton. Oh, Karen, you will never know. How much I loved her then and still do now, how I searched for her in others, how that led me to the woman who doesn't resemble Elke when she's still yet mimics her exactly when she walks and smiles, how I lost my will to succeed and loved a young woman until my will returned and I hated her, how a young man came to call me to account and I was filled with rage and drove him . . .

Ahead was a sandy lump on the beach, the seagulls whirling around it. When they got closer they saw it was a dead seal. There was a red hole in the place that used to be its eye and one flipper was raised, as if in a last appeal to the void.

They walked past it in silence. The seagulls bombed and pecked and screamed. He looked at the merciless birds worrying the dead thing, swooping up with shreds of meat dangling from their beaks. The waves broke closer as the tide advanced, the water reaching the heavy corpse, running in foamy streams around it, hissing away again over the shells.

'This is all there is.' He pointed. The wind blew the stink of decay at them.

'What do you mean?'

He said, 'This is all there is unless there's love.'

'I think you've gone mad, Simon.'

'It's my fault. Elke, Roza. All of it is my fault. I love you.'

She sat down on a dune, clasping her arms around her knees. He sat beside her. They looked at the sea where a rip had formed, the current washing out across the line of breakers, creating a channel between the waves. There was an object floating on the rip, rising high on the swells, disappearing in the troughs. Foam flew up, whirled in the air, broke into droplets.

'I don't know what you care about, Simon. What do you care about, really?'

'You. I care about you. It's been a difficult year. I've had a terrible fear of losing all of you.'

'You've been depressed,' she said.

Depressed. *Beside myself.*

'Yes I've been depressed, but I've realised something. The only thing I care about is you. Our family.'

'How ironic then, that you want to send our daughter away. To live with a woman who'll make sure I never see her.'

Simon watched the object borne away on the churning rip; it was far out at sea now, just a speck.

'It's true,' he said. 'I've done wrong. But how can I make it right?'

Power Junkie

They were grouped in the drive, waiting for the car. The Cahanes' luggage had been piled up by Chad and Shane, Sharon was giving orders and the Cock was pacing and talking on his phone. Ed Miles frowned, whispered savagely in Juliet's ear; she ducked her head and looked stricken.

Roza went on, 'So respectable Helen Schlegel has an affair with Mr Bast. She runs away to hide the scandalous pregnancy, but her sister and Mr Wilcox catch up with her and find out. And when Mr Bast comes looking for her, Mr Wilcox's son hits him with the flat side of a sword. Poor little Bast clutches at a bookcase and it falls on him, and his weak heart gives out.'

'Right,' Karen said.

'They made a film of it. Mr Bast walks from the city into the country to look for Helen. He walks through fields of bluebells, all night, to go to her. It made me cry.'

'How romantic,' Karen said.

'Mr Bast's lower class but special. He loves music. Early on he tells the Schlegels about walking all night, from the middle of the city clear into the country. They think it's a terribly novel idea.'

Simon looked at his watch.

'The twist in the story is that respectable Mr Wilcox has also been having it off with the lower orders. He's actually had an affair with Mr Bast's disreputable wife, ten years before, in Cyprus, when she was only a teenager. And left her in the lurch.'

'It all sounds very complicated,' Karen said.

Roza said, 'Oh, it's not really. I'm sure you could grasp the plot, Karen. If you concentrated. It's not much different from real life. Only the funny thing is, when it was published, people said the plot wasn't plausible, because it involved these liaisons between the classes. Well, they could believe Wilcox would have it off with Mrs Bast when she was a little slapper in Cyprus, but they absolutely couldn't go for the idea that Helen Schlegel would start bonking Mr Bast. It was unthinkable.'

'Here's the car,' Simon said.

The driver brought the heavy BMW to a stop next to the pile of bags.

'But these things do happen. Don't they, Simon?'

He faced her. 'I don't think we've ever had quite the same level of class distinction here.'

'You're looking very chirpy, darling,' David said, arriving with Ray and Jon.

'I am in rather a good mood. It's such a beautiful day. I've been telling them about *Howard's End*.'

'Oh yes. Is that the movie I can't stand with the old bat and the house and Anthony Hopkins acting like there's an umbrella up his arse?'

'That's the one.'

'Such a philistine, your husband,' the Cock said.

'Isn't he. *Howard's End* was actually a novel before it was a film, by the way.'

'No doubt,' David said.

Roza snorted.

'My wife, meanwhile, packs so many bags that we need a bus. Fortunately she's expert at driving the Sherpas.'

Sharon came breezing around the car. 'Are you coming?'

'You mean you're actually ready? I thought you'd need another hour.'

There was a long farewell. Sharon kept thinking of another thing to say to Roza and the Cock was inclined to hang around, kissing Roza three times and vowing to get hold of a copy of *Howard's End*.

'I don't think my wife has ever read a novel. She prefers the *Woman's Weekly*.'

'I'm like David,' Sharon said, looking at herself in a small mirror. 'I don't have the time.' She painted some gloss on her lips. Mwah.

'I know. You're too busy saving the world, darling. And getting your hair done.'

'Stop droning on about *books*. You know you'll go berserk if there's traffic.'

Ray and Jon stood ready to open the gate, the driver drummed his fingers on the steering wheel; across the lawn Shane or Chad, wearing a wide-brimmed hat, skimmed the surface of the swimming pool with a long-handled net. Trent packed the last bag into the car and stood back, his eyes on the ground. He hadn't once looked in Sharon's direction.

Ford emerged from the side gate as the Cahanes drove past. He raised his fingers in what could have been a wave and then slung his towel over his shoulder and hurried off between the hedges. He would be keeping away deliberately, in a mood of fastidious high-mindedness, not wanting to shake Colin Cahane's hand.

And then the car passed through the gate and droned off along the coast road, and there was a desultory silence before the group broke up and trailed back across the lawn in twos and threes. Simon saw Ford already in the dunes, heading for the beach.

On the path to the house Elke appeared, dressed in tiny denim shorts, a halter top and high-heeled sandals.

'There you are,' Roza said, kissing her cheek. 'Ready?'

Elke nodded, her eyes sliding away from Karen. David came forward and the three of them stood in an awkward embrace, David, Roza and Elke. The Lamptons were forced to stop and wait.

'Kodak moment,' Karen said.

'She looks a bit like a model, doesn't she?' David said, and Roza made a play of inspecting the girl with pleasure.

Simon put a restraining hand on Karen's arm. *For God's sake, Roza. Since when were you such a ham?* But the look Roza gave Karen now wasn't sentimental, it was implacable and cold. Simon saw what she was thinking, what she had always been thinking: that Karen had stolen her child. All the time the Lamptons had spent caring for Elke didn't mean anything to Roza except insult and theft; their very presence was a reminder that she'd been an unfit mother. Now Roza was fit and Karen would be punished. In matters of love the mind is not rational, nor is it fair. Roza would have no mercy for Karen. There would be no mercy.

And Elke wouldn't look at them. If she felt rejected by Simon's suggestion she should leave them, Roza would reinforce that. Karen was right; the connection would be lost.

'I'm going to pack,' Karen said.

The Hallwrights stepped aside. Roza smiled. 'Get Trent to give you a hand.'

Simon watched his wife cross the lawn looking small and dumpy, her shoulders hunched. She raised the heel of her hand to her face, perhaps wiping away a tear. Roza drew herself up, her eyes actually seeming to shine. Her triumph was indecent; he was angry and then with wearying suddenness his imagination turned. What if, when I was young and desperate and ill, someone had taken possession of my child . . .

Roza said, 'Here comes the Bible-banger. Let's rescue Johnnie and get going.'

Did Roza hate him too? He didn't think so. But what about those strange, charged remarks she'd made, when she'd seemed to suggest she might turn against him as well?

'Where are you going?' he asked.

'Into town. We're taking Johnnie to a movie. Then some disgusting burger joint.'

Tulei and the little boy were wandering across the grass hand in hand, Tulei carrying a bunch of lavender and Johnnie wearing a woven flax headband with feathers stuck in it.

'I'm a Niuean chief,' he said.

Tulei picked him up; he hugged her, pressing his cheek against hers. She peeled him off and handed him to Roza. 'Here's your chief.'

Johnnie said, 'Can Tulei come to the movies?'

'We're going to give Tulei some time off.'

'I want her to come!'

'Don't forget to wash your hands,' Tulei told him.

'God, how many times. A bit of dirt's good for him.'

'Tulei likes movies. She told me. She likes *Star Wars*.'

'Does she now. Right. Let's get going.'

'Pecause you've been digging in the dirt and playing with feathers and there are germs . . .'

'Oh, for God's sake. I'll dust him with insecticide. Will that make you happy, Tulei?'

'I'm sorry Missus?'

Roza ushered Elke and Johnnie ahead of her, rolling her eyes at David. 'Bye, darling. We'll take Ray. And Jon can drive.'

'Can I hold Ray's gun?'

'No!'

They went off across the lawn.

David said, 'Tulei. Got any, you know?' He mimed smoking.

'Oh, sure. How many you want?'

'Give me three. Four. You got four?'

'I give you whole packet. Five left.'

'Have you got more for yourself?'

'Sure, in my room.'

David winked and put a twenty dollar note in her hand; she tucked it in her pocket and went off towards the house.

'You going to the pool?' David waved a cigarette and Shaun, who'd been lounging against a tree, snapped to attention and brought a lighter. David lit up and blew out a stream of grey smoke. 'Roza's happy today,' he said.

'Karen's not.' It was sharper than Simon had intended. He added, 'She's just sorry the holiday's over.'

David consulted his giant designer watch. The chunky strap like chainmail, the series of implausible dials, as though for deep-sea diving. It looked suddenly absurd.

'Shaun? Where's Dean? He's late.'

The young man nodded, flipped open his phone.

Two rosellas flashed between the trees. Simon asked politely, 'How's it going with the arse?'

'Roza says she can't understand why anyone would want a bigger arse.'

'Maybe just firmer.'

'Firmer. Stronger. No, prouder. That's it. I want a proud arse.'

'Of course, you know Dean's . . .'

'Gay. Yes. I've noticed that.'

'So his interest in your arse is . . .'

'A gay interest. You're impugning Dean's professionalism. He has a degree. In . . .'

'Arses?' Simon's face was stiff with feigned heartiness.

'He tells me his approach is *holistic*.' Bored and impatient, David walked over and punched Shaun on the arm. 'Well?'

'He's on his way.'

Simon shaded his eyes, scanned the dunes. 'I think I'll go to the beach.'

But David had turned away and was waving to Dean, who was dragging an enormous sports bag along the path. He thrust his cigarette at Shaun. 'Get rid of this. Pretend it's yours.' He took out a little aerosol and sprayed it in his mouth. 'How's that?'

Shaun said, 'Peppermint and smoke.' David laughed.

Simon headed onto the hot sand hills, looking for Ford. The beach was crowded in every direction; squinting along the hot stretch he couldn't see Ford. Heat waves rippled over the sand, obscuring his view. There was a crowd of surfers out near the point, waiting for the best of the swells, and a lone swimmer chasing the waves, lifting both arms out of the water in a powerful butterfly stroke. Ford liked to bodysurf, although he'd condemned the waves at Rotokauri as pathetically small by his standards. He liked to go to west coast black-sand beaches like Piha and Karekare, and get hammered by real surf.

Simon's phone went off. In the bright glare he shaded the screen with his hand, couldn't see who was calling. He answered.

'Dr Lampton. Marie Da Silva.'

Silence. He looked at the surfers riding over a big, smooth swell.

'How are you, Dr Lampton?'

'Good.'

'Detective O'Kelly and I would like to see you again.'

'Great.'

'Glad you approve,' she said.

Simon sat down on the dune. *Aren't you sounding jaunty. Little rare-eyed Marie.*

'Where are you now, Dr Lampton?'

He wondered if she could hear the waves. The seagulls. A quad bike droning by. It would be a mistake to sound uncooperative. Or would it? If only he knew how to do this.

'Why do you ask?'

'Because my colleague and I would love to see you.'

Love . . . He didn't like the satirical tone. It was way too cheerful.

He waited, then said, 'Can't we just talk on the phone?'

'I don't like the phone. I prefer face to face.'

'I may come into the city tomorrow. I'm not sure. Can I get back to you?'

'OK, shall we come and see you there?'

'Where?'

'At Rotokauri.'

'Look, I've got to go to the hospital tomorrow. I'll be at my rooms briefly, at midday. How's that?'

'Super.'

He closed his phone. Super. Was she sounding so bouncy because she'd uncovered something new?

A group of gulls had landed nearby and were edging towards him on their red feet. He looked at their round eyes with tiny black pupils, their white heads turning, as if they were conferring together. There was a tight feeling in his stomach. Miles was supposed to be fixing this. Ford had said it: the more often he was bailed up by little Marie, the greater the danger he would give something away. This must be way beyond routine inquiry now. They just wouldn't leave him alone.

The possibilities: perhaps Miles wasn't able to 'calm things down'. A minister couldn't officially interfere in the workings of a police investigation. Or maybe Miles, or even David, had decided there was some advantage in letting the investigation run. Ford might have been wrong reckoning they'd do anything to make the police go away. Who knew how David had decided to play it; he was, after all, the most cunning person Simon knew. Had he seen an opportunity to get rid of the Lamptons, now he had Elke taken care of? Or was that fanciful? And how much control did David really have over Miles? That devious, manipulative prick could have ideas of his own.

He shouldn't have listened to Ford, couldn't even be sure his brother's offer of help was genuine. Ford was so awkward and eccentric, so (come to think of it) *bereaved*; there was no reason why he'd know how to deal with a delicate situation. He cursed Ford's confident self-righteousness, his fucking opinions. Big brother, always marching around telling people what do. Why had he listened, why did he always listen? Fuck Ford, fuck him.

But the next moment he was scrambling up the dune, looking for Ford out at the point. The surfers were paddling for a wave, competing for space, and there was the swimmer, his arms chopping the surface, taking his place among them. He rode the wave with his head out of the water, arms outstretched as if he was flying. The wave carried him in so far that when he finally stood up he was only thigh-deep in the churning shorebreak, hitching up his baggy togs. Simon shouted, jumping back when the breakers hissed up the sand, but Ford was already looking out for the next set of swells. He launched himself and swam away, leaving Simon yelling his name at the seagulls. Sudden chill as the wave caught him and filled his shoes.

He gave up. Walking away into the sand hills he thought about Mereana: she'd been sentenced to jail and they'd taken her baby away, and when she'd got out she'd successfully fought to reclaim the child but it had contracted meningitis and died. Ed Miles talked about being tough on crime and Juliet wanted to bring back the death penalty because, she said, life imprisonment was not enough. Simon had kept out of those discussions, hadn't even thought about them, but he could have told her now: imprisonment is enough. Look at Mereana, what she lost. (Losing a child because you've messed everything up: Roza, you know all about that.) And if I'm imprisoned, dear Juliet, you might as well kill me, because I will lose everything I value and love. Including thousands of female patients, both public and private, who benefit from my expertise, not to mention the babies over whose difficult births I preside. And I don't see how I will get those things back: family, friendships, practice, patients.

Karen liked to talk tough on crime too. What a laugh. Simon in jail. *Where's your lovely husband these days, Karen? We never see him at the golf club.*

Bitter laughter shivered through him, but how easy it was to forget. He was railing against fate, full of self-pity and self-justification, and yet what about Weeks? Had he deserved to die? No one deserves it. It happens. It just happened.

But just as Ford had said, on the way to Weeks's flat he'd left his phone behind, told no one where he was going. Had he, in some part of his mind, intended harm? A phrase surfaced in his mind, something Ed Miles had repeated to him: *We tell people: you make life happen.*

He sat down at the base of a steep dune. The wind had worn the sand into shelves, patterns swirling through the layers. Closing his eyes he saw Weeks's young face, the dark, eager eyes, the sly turn of the mouth, like a boy provoking his father: *Actually, I've written a screenplay about a National Party Prime Minister.* The marram shivered in the breeze, the dune sheltered him from the direct sun, there was nothing but light and silence beyond his body and he drifted and slept—

May came out of the dazzling glare, her hair wet, her arms full of hibiscus flowers. Behind her the sea was calm, as though her presence had stopped the wind; looking at her he was neither sleeping nor waking, he couldn't move, he tried to say her name but she spoke:

'Did you know there's a giant black hole at the centre of our galaxy? In three billion years' time we're going to collide with the next-door galaxy, Andromeda.'

His head and his eyes were full of light.

She said, 'So where is the pain?'

He thought about it. The answer surprised him, made him slightly embarrassed, he struggled to bring out the words. 'The pain? The pain is *everywhere*.'

'Fix it,' she said.

'I don't know how.'

Her expression was harsh, 'Then you will never find your way back in.'

He looked where she was pointing and saw the most splendid, beautiful mansion, a paradise.

She turned to face the horizon and he saw a black cone of cloud with points of light in it, sweeping towards the beach. The black thing was made of dragonflies. She was absorbed in it and flew away.

He woke. There was a rainstorm out at sea, hanging like chainmail. Cloud shadows dark on the water, metal curtains of distant rain.

Roza would be at the pool at six in the evening, to do her lengths. This was decreed in the fitness programme written for her by Garth, and she was sticking to it religiously. The regime was having an effect; Simon had never seen her so radiant, so toned and svelte.

By six, Johnnie would be talking movies with Tulei and Elke gone dreaming off to take stock of the pile of shopping bags unloaded from the car by the bustling Troy and Chad: clothes, shoes, trinkets, toys; and Roza would have squeezed into her most sporty and businesslike bathing suit, and rolled her towel into a sausage under her arm, and snapped her goggles on top of her head like a second pair of eyes, and be making her way, humming under her breath, along the path between the hedges, her flip-flops slapping on the hot concrete. Behind her, possibly, would creep the pallid figure of Ed Miles, who liked to perv at her while she was swimming (from a deck chair, peering over the top of the *National Business Review*) and also possibly Ford, who was hopelessly in love with her, and who seemed to materialise whenever Simon had a chance to talk to her alone.

Simon wondered about this while he waited for her: why a man like Ford would love Roza, whom he would label (because she was apolitical) 'frivolous' and 'not intellectually good enough'. He would love her despite (or, ironically, because of?) these flaws, would be overwhelmed by the sheer force, power, whatever you wanted to call it, of her sex appeal. Her charisma. Her imperious, unreasonable femininity. Her musical laughter at the expense of hapless men. And her high heels and her beautiful legs and brown breasts, and all the reasons why Simon loved her and had ever since he'd met her. But Ford had knocked Simon off his pedestal. He knew now, little brother knew: he would never have enough of the thing Roza wanted. He had seen the way things stood. In the company of the two brothers Roza's gaze slid from Simon to Ford, in the same way that men's eyes passed over plain Claire and stopped abruptly at Elke, with a pulse of animal interest.

He waited, in a trance of calculation. No matter what he'd done, consciously or otherwise, he couldn't sit back and let Weeks destroy him. If he was stuck in a crime story — increasingly a horror story — he would try to shape the plot. It was the Hallwright government's mantra: *Don't wait for life to happen to you. Make life happen!*

Here she came, unlocking the gate and letting it clang behind her. Not wearing flip-flops but elaborate sandals with high wedge heels. And not in her sporty swimsuit but the outrageous white-and-gold bikini that left very little to the . . .

Was she expecting someone? Was she got up like that for Ford?

Simon coughed. *Roza, I'm shocked. Disappointed in you. Dressed like a common . . . And who for? Whom?*

'Hi,' he said in a cracked voice. It sounded like the strangled noise the bastard tuis made at 4 a.m.

'Simon, hi!'

She spread out her towel and sat down on a sunbed. She was wearing mirror shades, silver holes in her face.

He wanted to say, *I loved you. But you . . .*

'Roza, we need to talk.'

'Mmm?' She barely moved her head. 'Are you annoyed about Mr Bast and Mr Wilcox and the slapper in Cyprus? Sorry. I can't help teasing you.' She reached out a hand. 'It's only because I love you.' Her warm fingers touched his arm.

He said softly, 'It's all right.'

'Poor Simon.' She looked over the top of her shades. 'You looked so tense today. I felt guilty.'

'I confide in you and you take the mickey,' he said, hoarse.

'Bad of me.'

He touched her hand. 'It doesn't matter. I've had something *much more* important on my mind.' He needed to hurry; they would have company any minute. 'Listen. I've had this worry. I've got to tell you. A man rang me on my cell phone recently. He was a journalist, wanting gossip about all of us. I got rid of him, but he rang back. I got rid of him again . . .'

'Yes?'

'Well, I've been visited by the police. They told me the journalist who rang me has died.'

'Died. What of?'

'He was young and he had a fall. They are investigating the death, and they found he'd rung me. They looked at his phone records.'

He studied her face. Her eyes were hidden behind the opaque silver shades.

'You with me so far?'

'Yes,' she said.

'I told them all I knew, that he'd rung me and that I'd got rid of him. When they were asking me about it they told me he'd been writing a screenplay about a National Party prime minister. A blond, left-handed prime minister who walks with a limp, would you believe.'

'A screenplay.'

'Yes. And they asked whether anyone would have wanted to harm the guy because of what he was writing. I said that was a ridiculous idea, which it is.'

She frowned. 'Is this something we should mention to David?'

Had David really not spoken to her about it? He couldn't tell.

'I have told David. He's going to get Ed Miles to look into it.'

She grimaced. 'Ed.'

'But there was something I didn't tell David and Ed.' He waited, then went on. 'I didn't tell them that Weeks — that's the dead man's name — asked me about you.'

'About me?'

'He asked me whether you'd had what he called a wild youth.'

She drew her mouth down on one side, tough, amused. 'I suppose you could call it that.'

'He mentioned something about you having a "relapse". Drugs, he said. He told me he'd met a woman called Tamara. She had a surname that started with Gold, Goldsmith or Goldwater. He said this woman had given him information about you that was negative, not flattering, concerning drugs. He also mentioned your housekeeper, Lin Jung Ha.'

Roza didn't move.

He went on, 'I noticed you'd fired Jung Ha — and I wondered . . . I'm sorry Roza, I don't mean to alarm you or interfere in your business, but when you fired Jung Ha I wondered whether Weeks had rung you too. There was something the police said: they asked if I knew how Weeks had got hold of cell phone numbers and they seemed to be talking about more than one number. And when you fired Jung Ha I thought, that's a coincidence, since Weeks mentioned her. I thought, has Roza been worrying about the same thing I have?'

'I don't believe this.'

He waited.

'You're suggesting I fired Jung Ha because she spied on me? Revealed some dirt to this man? About a "relapse", you call it?'

'I thought the police might be suggesting . . .'

She pointed her finger. 'I fired Jung Ha because she's been incredibly surly for a year.'

'Oh. That's fine. It's just the way it looks. I mean, it's a coincidence you firing her, so you can see why I wondered whether Weeks had rung you.'

'I don't like the sound of this, Simon.'

He could have laughed. *You* don't like the sound of it. 'Sorry. But the man's dead, and the police are being very tiresomely conscientious about their investigation. I thought you'd want to know, because, well, to be honest, I was thinking of Johnnie.'

'Johnnie!'

'I know — we all know — what a good mother you are. How Johnnie adores you, how close you and he are. I wouldn't want anyone casting a doubt on that.'

Now she laughed, not nicely. 'Casting a doubt. What on earth do you mean, Simon?'

'All this is delicate. But we're friends, so we can be frank. I care about you deeply; anything that hurts you, well, I couldn't stand it. With this talk of drugs and relapses, I wouldn't want anyone to raise the idea that they should worry about Johnnie, just when you've just got it all sorted with Elke.'

She clutched her towel. 'Worry about Johnnie? What rubbish. What "relapse"? I *did not* take drugs when I was pregnant with Johnnie.'

They looked at each other.

'I did not. Johnnie's perfect. They can't say that. And neither can Tamara Goldwater.'

Silence.

'Roza I've upset you. I'm sorry.'

'My children . . .'

'Yes.'

'My children are the most important thing in my life.'

'I know. That's why I don't want anything bad to happen. We need David to make this go away.'

She squeezed the towel against her chest. 'I'll talk to David. Not Miles.'

Simon pretended to consider. 'Miles makes me nervous. In something like this, when you're talking about the children, delicate personal matters, do you trust him?'

'No. But David can control him.'

'So long as you're sure. This Weeks person was a snoop and a stalker. He shouldn't be allowed to cause you damage . . .'

'David won't let him. I'll make sure of it.'

'. . . no matter what he found out about you.'

The gate creaked: it was Juliet Miles. She waved and disappeared into the pool house.

Roza stood up. 'I must find David.'

Simon got up and said in a low voice, 'One other thing. Karen and I would like to have Elke at our place for a bit longer. Claire's still at home, and she's going to give Elke some tuition. Up to you, of course. I was going to suggest it earlier, but I've been preoccupied about the police and what this fellow said about you. I don't know who else he might have told, or what he was talking about with this Tamara person, and I don't know what period he was talking about with this "relapse", whether it was supposed to be when Johnnie was a baby or when you were pregnant with him. I don't know what he put in his screenplay, whether it's got anything about drugs in it. You'd have to ask . . . *the police.*'

She looked at him, her teeth slightly bared, and he felt her taking in every implication of what he was saying. For a second he thought she might hit him. She raised her hand and he controlled the impulse to flinch, but she only drew her sunglasses down, and he looked into her eyes.

'You want, you'd like Elke to . . .'

He waved his hand noncommittally. 'Just a thought. Talk about the Weeks problem with David and see what you think. The main thing is that Johnnie and Elke should feel secure.'

She came close, eyes searching his face. 'Simon . . .' He smelled her perfume, felt the hairs lifting on his scalp. She smiled, her eyes were ice.

'Simon, you surprise me. I didn't think you had it in you.'

Understanding

The final morning, Karen was in a bossy flurry of packing, toting armfuls of clothes, elbowing him out of the way, reaching under the bed and coming out with dusty items held between finger and thumb. Sensing work to be done, Elke and Marcus had made themselves scarce, leaving their usual fantastic mess. Karen loaded Simon up with bundles and ordered him out to the car and he trudged obediently back and forth, surprised at the amount of luggage.

He was in a state of tension bordering on madness. The previous day he had driven into town to his clinic, called in at the hospital, returned to his rooms in the afternoon — and Ms Da Silva hadn't shown up. He'd even lingered in his rooms after five o'clock, and she hadn't appeared. There was no sign of her or her silent colleague O'Kelly. And nor had she called.

Barely able to contain his restlessness, he decided on a last swim. He invited Karen along, guessing she would decline: still too many things to do. She tucked her hair up into a baseball cap and went on with her organising.

Ford was hitching a ride back to town with them, but Simon wanted to get him alone. He found him out the back of the Little House, emptying sand out of a sports bag.

'Last swim? Come on.'

He waited impatiently for Ford to change.

'Let's go the long way,' he suggested, grabbing Ford's arm, heading out towards the point. When they were out of earshot he said, 'She hasn't called or been to see me. The policewoman.'

Ford said, 'That's good, that's a good sign.'

'But the signs weren't good, before. The police rang me again, they wanted to re-interview me. I realised I'd have to do something more. So I spoke to Roza.'

'To Roza!'

'I had to do something.'

He described the exchange at the pool. Ford listened. 'You didn't want to talk about it with me first?'

'I kept looking for you; you were nowhere to be found. The police had rung me again, they wanted to see me. Ed Miles hadn't fended them off. You said it yourself, the more often the police talk to me, the more trouble I'm likely to be in. I knew what they were going to be asking next: Where were you on the day of?'

'You've got that covered. You were here then you were at work.'

But Simon's mind now went back to the conversation at the pool. He saw Roza's expression, hard, opaque, her chin raised, her eyes coolly appraising him. *Simon, I didn't think you had it in you.* He squared his shoulders.

Ford looked worried, as if he couldn't take it in. 'You think she'll be desperate to get David to do anything to bury the whole thing?'

'If there's any hint she's mentioned, David will act. He'll do anything to protect her.'

'God.' Ford rubbed his chin anxiously.

Simon said, 'The police haven't come back. They haven't called.'

'And you told her you want to keep Elke with you.'

'There can be no half measures with Roza.' Simon set off towards the point. He said over his shoulder, 'Believe me, I know. It's the only way to play it with her. She's a junkie for power. That woman will only pay attention if you go nuclear.'

Ford walked in silence. Eventually he said, 'Simon, if you've managed to get out of this, will you leave these people behind?'

'These people?'

'The Hallwrights. The Cahanes. Miles. They're . . . moral imbeciles.'

'And I'm not?'

'You don't have to be.'

Simon stopped and looked at Ford steadily. 'I'm not finished, Ford. *I'm not finished.*'

They headed out towards the point, Simon lurching ahead on his painful knee, Ford following in his tracks, close behind.

When Simon came to find Roza to tell her they were ready to go, a ceremony was taking place on the parched grass under the pohutukawa. Johnnie held out the glass jar and solemnly unscrewed the lid.

'Go free, spider,' Roza said. 'The prison door is open.'

There was a silence.

'He's not going,' Johnnie said.

Roza laughed. 'Give him a shake. That's right. There he goes. Whoops. Stretching his little legs.'

Another silence.

Johnnie said, 'If you were an animal, what would you be?'

Roza spread out her fingers, made the shape of wings. 'I would be a dragonfly,' she said. 'And you would be my nymph.'

Johnnie reached down towards the spider, now groggily unfolding its legs in the grass.

'Make Soon talk.'

Soon and Starfish looked out the window and saw that the Bachelor had landed in the clearing. They went outside.

He told them, "The Green Lady and Soonica met secretly on the beach at dawn."

Starfish asked, "What were they talking about?"

The Bachelor laughed, a strange little chuckle that made Starfish feel almost frightened. "I believe they were coming to an understanding," he said.

The Bachelor leaned down to Soon. "They talked, then they embraced. And before they parted, Soon, the Green Lady said one word to your sister. Do you know what it was?"

"What?" Soon asked.

"She said your name."

Soon

'Let me take one more photo. Please, Johnnie darling.'

'No.'

'No? Monstrous child! Mummy will be "heartbroken".'

The boy narrowed his eyes. 'Make Soon talk.'

'Only if you do as you're told.'

'Only if you make him talk.'

Roza said in a hushed, soupy voice, 'Mummy's eyes filled with tears when Johnnie forced her to beat him.'

'Make Soon talk!'

The mother and the boy with their intense eyes, their identical smiles, moved slowly along the path, absorbed in the rhythm of their exchange. Simon thought: I have never seen two creatures more strangely attuned.

Roza ran her hand over the boy's hair, inspected him with pleasure. 'At least you've had a shower. Tulei will be pleased; you were starting to get dreadlocks. Did you put the money in your safe? I can't believe you've stung me for another five bucks.'

The new housekeeper, Friend, emerged with a school bag and lunch box and Roza took the bag, adjusting it on Johnnie's shoulder.

'Thanks, Friend. Hello, Simon.'

He greeted them from his seat by the Hallwrights' pool. They were back in the Auckland house and he'd been summoned by David. 'Come over for breakfast,' he'd said on the phone. 'Something to tell you.' Across the suburb the city buildings were ranged against the washed, cloudless blue of the early February sky.

Friend said, 'First day school. Doesn't he look handsome in new uniform!'

Johnnie stood looking tiny in shirt, tie and blazer. His hair was plastered down, his face unusually clean. His expression was neutral.

Roza straightened his collar. 'Mm, it's a bizarre rig-out really, isn't it. Why the blazer? He'll die of heat. And as for the weird cap . . . And a crimson *tie*, for God's sake.'

Friend was disapproving. 'King's Prep. Is wonderful school. Very well respected.'

Roza grinned at Johnnie. 'Fabulous get-up, darling.'

Johnnie laughed.

'King's is a school for the cream of Auckland: rich and thick,' Roza said to Friend. 'I think that was a joke of Samuel Beckett's.' She glanced at Simon.

Friend looked high-minded; she was used to Roza carrying on this way, as if she and someone else present, usually the little boy, were sharing a private joke. Friend was known to agree with Tulei: Missus was far too lax with the horribly intelligent child. Nothing was censored in front of him; in fact, Roza was even more likely to share her anarchic cracks, her habit of swearing and her shockingly inappropriate vocabulary with the boy than she was with adults.

'First day at school. Good luck!' Simon said. He looked at Johnnie's sturdy little legs, his feet in poignant new sandals. A tuft of the boy's hair had escaped the plastering and was standing straight up, and there were freckles on his suntanned nose. He was a small, touching figure and then you looked into his eyes and saw how alert, how powerfully noticing . . .

He sat and waited. A helicopter buzzed along the skyline. The Hallwrights' gardener, Conscience, ran his clippers over the topiary, smoothing hedges into cones, squares, balls. Patterns of light turned rangily in the pool like paper stars, folding and refolding. Friend went away, reappeared and placed a cup of coffee in front of him.

Mother and son took a turn around the garden. They passed Simon's table.

Johnnie said, 'Tulei says a story has to have a moral.'

Roza spread out her hands. 'Does she now. She would. The moral is: there is no moral. No moral, no God, only forces.'

Simon and Roza looked at each other over the boy's head. Simon said, 'Only forces. So are there any forces for good?'

She pretended to think. 'Hmm. I don't know, Simon. Are there any of those in the world?'

'How about love. And politics.'

But Roza only gave him one of her unreadable smiles.

He waited half an hour, until David came out of the house talking to his new personal assistant. According to David, Roza had got rid of the previous assistant, Delwyn, and the one before that, Dianne, before settling on a sturdy young woman with bad skin and no sense of humour: Debbie. Now David said, 'Action that, er, Del, Di . . . Debbie. Let me talk to Simon.'

Friend bustled out with more coffee. David sent a couple of quick emails, took two calls, then put the phone on the table and faced Simon. 'Let's have some breakfast.'

When Friend had taken his instructions and gone to the kitchen he said, 'Right. I've got the full story from Ed Miles. Weeks was out of his mind.'

'You mean . . . intoxicated?'

'I mean drugged. On prescription medicine. He was an insomniac, hounded his GP about it, apparently. There's a list of sleeping pills, strong ones. There were levels of the stuff in his blood: Ed tells me he's seen a report recording the levels as high. They think he woke after taking medication in the night, headed for his car and stumbled against the fence. It was a wire fence, quite low, and it collapsed under him. He fell head first down the retaining wall, died instantly of neck and skull fractures. He wasn't able to break his own fall because he was too impaired.'

Simon waited then said, 'I was worried by that ridiculous question the police asked me: would anyone want to harm him because of what he was writing. I'm glad it's so clearly an accident. They can't make any trouble out of it for you. No lurid stories: Hack Nosing Around PM. Was He Pushed?'

He hesitated, then added, 'God knows what rubbish he put in his screenplay. He seemed to be desperate for salacious gossip.'

'Indeed.'

'It's called *The Night Book*.'

'How do you know?'

'The cop told me.'

'Ed's taking care of it. No one will be interested. Weeks wasn't writing for any commission. No reputation for writing movie screenplays, not a great deal of track record. Well, the man was practically a drug addict by the sound of it.'

'I wonder what's in it. The screenplay.'

'Who cares?'

Simon looked at him, expressionless. David would surely get hold of the screenplay. But Ed Miles would look at it first. *Let's hope David can keep Ed under control.*

Ray had brought the car to the front of the house. They walked across the gravel. David paused, his hand on the car door. 'How's Elke?'

'She's fine. Looking forward to the American trip.'

'Roza's happy at the moment, too.'

'I'm glad.'

'The Weeks thing will be referred to the coroner.'

'Good to know it's not a problem.'

They shook on it.

Those weeks in early February: they kept calling them the hottest on record. The streets retained the heat of the day and the nights were stifling, the city breathing hot air back at itself. Two o'clock in the morning, unable to sleep in the upstairs bedroom under the roof, Simon went down for a glass of water, walked around the quiet house, eventually stretched himself on the sofa in the cooler air of his study. He could feel the loved presences in the sleeping house: Karen, Claire, Elke, Marcus, his family safe and near. Closing his eyes, he dozed.

He was looking down from a tall, narrow upstairs window like an arrow slit. A black shape, a dog, crossed the lawn; the shadows rearranged themselves like holes in the fabric of the air, blacker than black. There was the round eye of a bird, cruel, shiny, opaque, and a voice, May's, whispered close to his ear, *'Somewhere, someone knows.'* He saw a haze of bright colour, something red writhing up out of it. He started, struggling to wake himself. There was an insistent electronic sound.

His cell phone was beeping and vibrating on his desk, about to shake itself onto the floor. He picked it up, lay back on the sofa. It would be a woman in labour or a gynaecological emergency; he would have to go in to the public hospital. He answered, resigned, eyes closed, 'Simon Lampton.'

'Simon. It's me.'

'Hello. Who's speaking?'

'Mereana.'

He sat up.

'It's Mereana. Sorry, I know it's the middle of the night there.'

He said her name. The voice came to him through the phone static. 'Simon, I'm coming back to New Zealand. A job offer . . . out of the blue . . .'

The room was very dark. He had a sense of falling.

She said, 'I have a son. I think it's time you met him. Soon.'

A son.

'Simon? Simon?'

The hottest February ever, records falling, who knows where it will end. Is it climate change, will the planet last for the children and their children? But there's no time to consider the planet or the children, or the terrors of the hot dark hours, no time to wonder what the future holds, *soon*. After the hottest night, for Simon Lampton the stunned and reeling morning: an urgent call, the speeding drive to the hospital, a corridor, voices, feet squeaking on the floor, he enters the bright room and they're coming at him with forms and printouts and notes: patient brought in by Westpac rescue helicopter, a protracted labour, placenta may be knitted to old caesarean scar, blood set aside for transfusion, and the pregnant woman's moaning on the bed and a man's wringing his hands, there's a toddler screaming in the corridor, a door slams, the sound is abruptly cut off, above his head a neon light ticks and whirrs, he looks down at the woman, a moment of stillness. *Increase your tolerance to uncertainty.*

He carries out an examination. Yes, life is on its way, it will not wait; life will kill her if he doesn't get a move on . . .

Putting his hand on the woman's arm, he holds it there for a moment, as if it's her alone he's keeping steady. The air trembles and reels, and then holds firm.

'I'm here,' he says. 'My name's Simon Lampton. Everything's going to be fine.'